THE CANDLESTONE

DRAGONS IN OUR MIDST

The Candlestone
Copyright © 2004 by Bryan Davis
This edition published in the UK in 2009 by Candle Books
(a publishing imprint of Lion Hudson plc),
Wilkinson House, Jordan Hill Road, Oxford OX2 8DR
Tel: +44 (0)1865 302750 Fax: +44 (0)1865 302757
Email: candle@lionhudson.com
www.lionhudson.com

Published in the USA by Living Ink Books,
an imprint of AMG Publishers
6815 Shallowford Road
Chattanooga, Tennessee 37421

Distributed in the UK by Marston Book Services Ltd,
PO Box 269, Abingdon, Oxon OX14 4YN

The Candlestone is the second of four books in the youth fantasy fiction series,
Dragons in Our Midst.

All Scripture quotations, unless otherwise noted, are taken from the
NEW AMERICAN STANDARD BIBLE, copyright © 1960, 1962,
1963, 1968, 1971, 1972, 1973, 1975, 1977 by the Lockman Foundation.
Used by permission. All rights reserved.

ISBN 978-185985-782-3

This book has been printed on paper independently certified as having been
produced from sustainable forests.

Printed in Malta
First printing 2009
10 9 8 7 6 5 4 3 2 1 0

To the keepers of the light

When we set flame to a candle, we bring light to the world.
When we build stone upon stone, we erect the temple of God.
But when candle and stone are removed from the foundation,
The light is captured, imprisoned, destroyed.
How great is the darkness!

Let us never forget our first love,
And our light will spread across the world.

Recap of Volume One: *Raising Dragons*

Hello readers! My name is Bonnie Silver, and I'd like to tell you what has happened so far in the story. Back in the sixth century, most dragons were evil, so dragon slayers tried to kill them. Merlin, of King Arthur fame, used a miracle to transform the good dragons into humans to protect them. Still carrying dragon genetics, a few of them married into the human race and produced children, including Billy Bannister and me. Billy is able to breathe fire, and I have dragon wings! Unfortunately, I have to wear a backpack all the time to keep them hidden.

A few months ago, a slayer killed my mother, so I hid in the foster care system. Transferring from home to home, without a friend in the world, I was so glad to meet Billy at school. We had something in common; we were "different". But trouble brewed when our principal, Dr Whittier, became suspicious of my past. He tried to look in my backpack, but Billy used his hot breath to rescue me.

Dr Whittier is really a slayer named Devin, a descendant of an Arthurian knight by the same name. During our escape from him, he stowed away in our airplane and forced it to crash. Everyone except Billy's father got out safely, but instead of dying, he transformed back into a dragon!

We battled Devin in a mountain wilderness. Devin sliced Billy's scalp to the skull, but Billy's friend Walter and our teacher, Professor Hamilton, arrived just in time to save Billy's life. Later, when Devin was about to slay Billy's father, I used an amazing sword that somehow made Devin disappear. Only a pile of armour and this strange gem called a candlestone remained.

What's weird about the candlestone is that it seems to drain power from Billy and me. When we're around it, we get weak and sick. After I zapped Devin, I threw it into the woods as far as I could. I hope I never see it again.

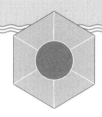

CONTENTS

CONTENTS

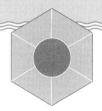

ACKNOWLEDGMENTS

To my faithful wife, thank you for being an enduring light in my life.

To my seven torches in the wilderness, may this book inspire you to carry your lights in every sphere of influence you reach. You were called to be lights in dark places, and for as long as I live, I pledge to lead the way, following the Light of the World to the ends of the earth and beyond.

To my friends at AMG – Dan Penwell, Warren Baker, Rick Steele, Dale Anderson, Trevor Overcash, and all the staff – thank you for keeping the light burning.

To my editors – Jeannie Taylor, Barbara Martin, Sharon Neal, and especially Becky Miller – thank you for helping me polish all those smudges to make this book shine.

MERLIN'S PROPHECY

When hybrid meets the fallen seed
The virgin seedling flies
An orphaned waif shall call to me
When blossom meets the skies

The child of doubt will find his rest
And meet his virgin bride
A dragon shorn will live again
Rejecting Eden's pride

A slayer comes and with his host
He fights the last of thee
But faith alone shall win the war
The test of those set free

A king shall rise of Arthur's mould
The prophet's book in hand
He takes the sword from mountain stone
To rescue captive bands

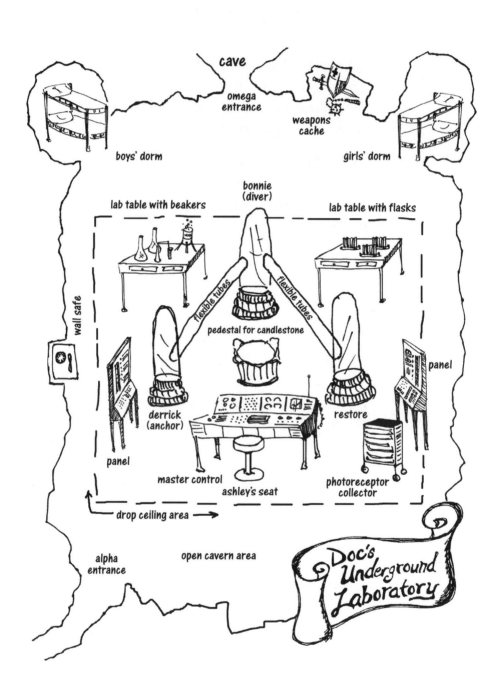

cave

omega
entrance

weapons
cache

boys' dorm

girls' dorm

bonnie
(diver)

lab table with beakers

lab table with flasks

Flexible tubes

Flexible tubes

wall safe

pedestal for candlestone

panel

derrick
(anchor)

restore

panel

master control

ashley's seat

photoreceptor
collector

drop ceiling area

alpha
entrance

open cavern area

Doc's
Underground
Laboratory

1

THE ART OF WAR

With sword and stone, the holy knight,
Darkness as his bane,
Will gather warriors in the light
Cast in heaven's flame

Out of the blackness a growling voice rumbled, "She will come." The rough words reverberated, bouncing off shrouded walls that echoed dying replies.

A solitary man listened in the dark room, lit only by flickers of soft light coming from his hand, a dozen fireflies in a jar. They danced with hopeless wings in stale air, waiting for death to arrive, their distress signals only serving to guide the scientist as he paced the stone floor. "And what makes you so sure she'll come?" his voice replied, tiny and squeaking by comparison. "She won't trust me. Why should she?"

The rumbling voice responded. "You don't understand her; you never did. She listens to a call that rises beyond your senses. . . . she has faith." The growl changed to a deep sigh. "But, alas! What would you know about faith?"

"More than you think." The scientist held up the jar and watched the dimming flashes. "I do know this; it was by her faith that you're in this predicament. I hear she was quite handy with that sword."

The growl deepened, its bass tones making the ground tremble. "If you really think she knew I would end up in this prison, then you're a bigger fool than I thought." After a few seconds, the echoes died away again, and the voice became soft and melancholy, like the lowest notes of a mournful cello. "You have no worries. She will come. She is driven by forces you cannot possibly understand."

The last flicker of light blinked out. The scientist picked up the jar and opened the lid. With a quick shake he dumped the dead fireflies onto the floor. "Very well." His voice stretched out into a foreboding snarl. "We shall see."

Swish! The gleaming sword swiped by Billy's face, its razor point slashing the air and its deadly edge humming a threatening tune in his ear. He jumped back, his cheeks turning red hot. *What an idiot I am! Another mistake like that and this fight will be over in a hurry!* He planted his feet on the tile floor and raised his sword, careful to keep it from stabbing the low ceiling. Eyeing his opponent warily, he slowly counted to ten. *Gotta keep my cool. I'm never going to win if my brain's fried. Besides, this sword weighs a ton. No use wasting energy.* Drops of sweat pooled on his brow and streamed down, stinging his eyes and blurring the light from the ceiling fan's globe. The fan's whirling blades blew a cooling breeze through his hair, a welcome relief in the spacious but stuffy rec room.

His opponent charged, his sword raised to strike. Billy dodged, swiping at the attacking weapon from the side as it passed, and the clank of metal on metal rattled his brain. His opponent twirled and set his feet, bending his knees to brace himself. With his sword held out in defence, he waited.

Billy puffed a loud, weary sigh as he readied his sword for an attack of his own. Heavy, sweat-drenched clothes clung to his body, and the weight of the hefty blade dragged his tired arms downward. He dared not let it fall.

His opponent, a tall, lanky man of considerable years, was quick and agile at the start of the battle but now slower and deliberate. He had spunk, though, a real kick-start in his old engine, and that last charge proved his stellar swordsmanship.

Billy lifted his sword, pointing it at his mentor and remembering what he had taught. *"A knight opposes his enemy face to face. A stab in the back is the way of the coward; a pre-emptive strike of death is a strike of fear. If you must fight, attack your enemy head on. That is the way of valour."* Billy took a deep breath and charged, pulling his sword back. His opponent met the blow, and the swords clashed once again. This time Billy pushed downward, then back up in full circle, wrenching his opponent's sword from his grasp and flinging it away. He dashed to where the ringing blade fell and stamped both feet on its polished steel. He lifted his own sword, and with a pretend scowl, dared his opponent to approach.

"Way to go, Billy!" a young male voice shouted.

A female voice joined in. "Yay, Billy! You were awesome!"

A surge of heat prickled Billy's face, and he drew in a deep, satisfying breath while nodding toward his friends, Walter Foley

3

and Bonnie Silver. Walter slapped Billy on the back and helped him remove his helmet. "I told you you'd win if you used my helmet. Hambone licked it for good luck."

Billy accepted a towel from Bonnie and wiped his forehead, pushing his short wet hair to the side. Bonnie pressed her thumbs behind the front straps of her ever-present backpack, as locks of her straight blonde-streaked hair caressed her navy polo shirt. Her blue eyes sparkled, greeting Billy with silent messages of congratulations.

Billy smiled. His training was paying off. He felt stronger than ever, certainly not like he did on the mountain, the last time he wielded a sword in a real fight. He had nearly lost his life battling Sir Devin, the dragon slayer. Next time, if there were to be a next time, he would be ready.

A hearty voice boomed from nearby. "Well done, William!" The heavy British accent made its owner easy to identify, his teacher, his mentor, his friend, and now, his conquered opponent, Professor Hamilton. The professor approached with deliberate, stiff steps and his tall form cast a shadow across Billy's face. "William? You seem rather pensive. Are you all right?"

Billy wanted to say, "I'm fine," but his muscles ached, a good, satisfying ache.

He lifted his wet shirt, peeling it away from his shoulder. "I'm sore, but I'll be all right. I was just thinking about the fight on the mountain." He laid the sword on the floor and pulled off his protective gloves. "Do you think I'm ready? I mean, we've still never fought all out. And we're not really using the same equipment those guys had, you know, the authentic battle armour and stuff."

"No, we're not." The professor picked up his vanquished sword and slid it into a scabbard on his back. "We battled 'all out', as you say, with foam swords early in your training. Just now we did restrain our thrusts with our metal replicas, but it was still a strenuous workout. Yet, until we can combine the weight of authentic swords and armour with the passion of unrestrained zeal, we'll not be sure you're ready." He unfastened the scabbard and tossed it onto a nearby sofa. "You see, I have no true armoured helmets, and my fencing guards are inadequate for mortal combat, so I'm afraid it's not safe to attempt an unrestrained match."

Billy ran his thumb along the edge of his blade, leaving a shallow slice in his skin. "Is it 'safe' if we don't prepare for real?"

The professor slid off his headgear, a modified Washington Redskins helmet, his white matted hair pulling up with it, creating a frenzy of wet strings. "Your point is well taken, William, but we would have to find a better sparring partner for you. Your potential opponent will not likely be a creaking old man such as myself." He ran his hand through his tangled hair and examined the logo on his helmet. "And I'll have to find suitable armour. The authentic helmets I've seen don't have an American Indian on the side."

Walter took Billy's sword from his hand. "This sword is so cool!" He rubbed the etchings on the blade. "This looks like a picture of two dragons fighting, but what do the other marks mean?"

The professor stroked the blade with his index finger. "There's quite a story behind these runes." He gave a tired sigh and gestured with his head toward the hallway. "Walter, I trust that your father won't mind if we build a fire and sit in the den while I tell the story. Although our swordplay generated considerable body heat, we will cool off quickly. But first, I must visit the water clo—I mean, the restroom, and clean up a bit."

Billy tugged at his plastered shirt again. "And I have to change these sweaty clothes."

Walter ran ahead. "I'll start the fire!"

Bonnie joined Walter in the den. He was already holding a lit match next to a rolled up newspaper stuffed under a pile of logs in the fireplace. The end of the paper flared, but the flame soon died away.

Bonnie adjusted the left strap on her backpack and peeked over Walter's shoulder. She had been wondering what Walter had seen on the mountain after he kept the dragon slayer from following her that day back in November. Now was her chance to probe her friend for the truth. Had he discovered her dragon wings? She gently cleared her throat. "I was just thinking, Walter. When I was watching Billy fight just now, it reminded me of when you hit Devin with the tree limb."

Walter tore a second match from a matchbook. "Yeah? It wasn't much. It's not so brave to bash someone's head when he's not looking." He struck the match and set the end of the paper on fire again.

Bonnie watched the struggling flame and shifted her weight to her heels. "I . . . I was wondering, though, about how you showed up in the field to help us, right when we ran into the search party. Did you follow us down the slope?"

Walter struck a third match and held it against the newspaper, waiting for it to catch. He shrugged his shoulders. "I saw your tracks in the snow. It wasn't hard."

Bonnie crouched next to the hearth. "What I mean is, did you see us on the way down? Or did you just follow the tracks?"

"Ouch!" Walter shook his hand and sucked his scorched finger. "I was super pumped after whacking Devin, so everything's sort of jumbled in my memory. I don't remember all the details." He stood up, still sucking his finger. "What difference does it make?"

Bonnie straightened her body and folded her hands behind her. "When you met us at the bottom of the trail, did you see . . . anything peculiar? I mean, it seems like you're Johnny-on-the-spot all the time, so—"

"So you're wondering if I 'spotted' anything?" Walter dried his finger on his jeans and flashed a grin. "Maybe I'm like an angel. Maybe God puts me in the right place at the right time."

Bonnie smiled back, reading Walter's playful tone. "You think so?"

"Why not?" He pointed toward his back. "Except I don't have any wings. That would be cool." He stuffed the empty matchbook into his pocket and rushed toward the doorway. "I think Dad just bought some starter logs. I'll go get them and another matchbook." He almost slammed into Billy as he dashed from the room, deftly spinning around his friend. "Back in a minute. Gotta get something to start the fire."

Billy, now wearing a fresh long-sleeved shirt and his favourite cargo trousers, pushed his moistened hair back. He spied the blackened matches at the front of the fireplace and then winked at Bonnie while nodding toward the door. Crouching at the hearth, he leaned toward the stubborn logs and waited for Bonnie to block the room's entrance. She stepped into the doorway, using her body as a shield to hide Billy's deepest secret, the dragon trait handed down to him by his father. Walter was a great friend, but Billy didn't want to let him know about his dragon heritage. Not yet.

Billy took in a deep breath and blew a stream of fire at the pile of oak, spreading it evenly across the wood. Within seconds, the logs ignited, shooting flames and smoke into the flue above.

"Knock, knock."

Bonnie spun around. "Walter!"

"Mind if I come in?"

Billy jerked himself up to his feet, and Bonnie jumped away from the door. Walter sauntered in carrying a bag of paraffin kindling and set it next to the hearth. He nodded toward the blazing logs and smiled. "Nice job. You got better matches than I do?"

Bonnie put her hand over her mouth, apparently holding back a snicker, and Billy folded his arms across his chest. "I guess you could say that."

The professor entered, his face washed and his white hair plastered and parted down the middle. He carried the sword at his side and sat in an easy chair next to the fire. His face beamed. "William, I must reiterate my pride in your effort. You were outstanding with the sword."

"Yeah," Walter agreed. "You rocked!"

Billy bowed his head, his face burning. "Thanks."

The professor's eyes narrowed at Walter. "Rocked?"

"Yeah . . . rocked. You know; he was awesome. He really kicked . . . uh . . . gluteus maximus."

"Is that similar to being the cat's pyjamas?" the professor asked.

"The cat's pyjamas?" Walter repeated. "What's that?"

"It's an American idiom. It refers to someone who is well liked because of his accomplishments. I see, however, that it has passed out of common usage." The professor gestured for his three students to gather around. "Shall we discuss the sword?" He placed the blade on his lap and pointed at the etched writing.

"Some of these lines are inscriptions in an ancient dialect," he explained. He rubbed his finger along one face of the blade. "This one says, roughly speaking, 'May the Lady's purity never depart from the one found worthy to draw the sword.'"

"The lady?" Bonnie asked. "Who's the lady?"

"The Lady of the Lake. The legends say that she gave Excalibur to King Arthur."

Bonnie rubbed her finger along the raised pattern on the wooden hilt. "A lady gave it to him? Can a lady be strong enough to battle with a sword like this?"

"I think a sturdy woman could wield it," the professor replied, handing it to her. "Give it a try."

Bonnie grasped the hilt with both hands and held the blade up, her feet spread apart as if bracing for an attack. She waved the sword through a series of pretend manoeuvres, and the professor's eyes followed the blade's swings and parries. "You seem to have no trouble carrying it," he noted.

Bonnie returned the sword to the professor's lap. "I guess it's not as heavy as I thought it would be."

The professor slid the sword back into its scabbard. "It's probably not as heavy as the real Excalibur, but its mass is substantial."

"It seemed heavy to me," Billy said.

"As it should, William; you worked with it for nearly an hour today, non-stop. But I perceive that Miss Silver is considerably stronger than her frame would suggest."

Bonnie's face flushed. "I'm sorry, Billy. I didn't mean to say—"

Billy waved his hand. "It's all right. I know what you meant."

Walter picked up the scabbard and examined its ornate designs, an embossed angelic creature with knights on each side bending a knee in respect. "Do you think those Arthur stories are true, Professor?"

A dreamy expression floated across Professor Hamilton's face, the dancing fire reflecting in his eyes. "Arthur is the stuff of legends, the search for the Holy Grail, the splendour of Camelot. It's hard to decipher truth within the myriad tales." His scholarly air returned as he took the scabbard from Walter. "It seems that each new storyteller tried to outdo the previous one, not really caring whether or not his tale was true. Legends are, after all, not meant to be historical fact. For example, I certainly doubt the existence of a goddess in a lake, but I have no doubts that Arthur once wielded the great and mysterious Excalibur."

He caressed the scabbard again, his finger pausing on one of the worshipful knights. "This is a replica handed down through many generations; its shape and details are based on legends and descriptions in journals. Many tried to copy Excalibur's image, but no one could reproduce its power."

Bonnie's eyebrows arched up. "It had power?"

The professor placed his fingers around the hilt and drew the blade out a few inches. "Power incomprehensible. Whosoever held the sword in battle could not be defeated, as long as the wielder was pure of heart. And the offensive powers in the hands of the holy were a terrible sight to behold."

Bonnie put her hands behind her back and shifted her weight toward her toes. "Does the real Excalibur still exist?"

The professor glanced from Billy to Walter to Bonnie, as if searching for something in each set of eyes. "I have no doubt about it, Miss Silver. I have hunted for it throughout the world, following many rumours and obscure tales. Finding it would make my life complete. You could say that it's something of a Holy Grail for me."

"What about the sword that guy took from Whittier's office?" Walter asked. "Didn't it have some kind of marks on it?"

Billy bit his lip to keep from laughing. He remembered Walter's story of his adventure with Professor Hamilton when they searched for clues in the principal's office. One of the slayer's cronies had come in and picked up a sword from its hiding place while Walter and the professor watched in secret. When Walter told the story again just a few days ago, he acted out every event, using a baseball bat for the sword and coaxing Hambone to play the part of the professor.

The professor slid the sword into the scabbard. "Your memory is accurate, Walter. That sword had many similar characteristics, but I couldn't be sure of its identity. I would like to pursue that lead at the appropriate time." His eyes fell on Billy and Bonnie, and his gaze lingered, making Billy feel uneasy. The professor went on. "And I suspect that there are some people I know who might be able to enlighten me concerning its whereabouts."

Billy twisted his shoe on the carpet like he was squishing a cockroach. How could the professor guess what was going on? He wasn't there when Bonnie battled the slayer in the mountain forest, and no one told him that Bonnie dropped the sword while flying away from the battle scene.

"In any case," the professor continued, "my sword is adequate for young William's training. While this replica is valuable, its symbolism is paramount for his development. His skill in swordplay will become necessary before long. And there is no concern for the replica's safety; it is practically indestructible."

Billy stepped away from the dying fire. Its flames had toasted his backside, and his hair had dried. "When are you going to explain all that to me – I mean, the stuff I'm training for?"

"In due time, William. I'm just putting the pieces together myself." The professor rose to his feet and strolled around the room, holding the sword casually across his shoulder. "Since you were expected to be out of commission for quite a while, I sent our mystery book to a friend of mine, an expert in antiquities. He has completed his analysis and will return the book in time for class on Monday. I assume that when we decipher it we will learn a great deal."

Billy folded his arms across his chest and rubbed his aching biceps. Thinking about that book and how it had come into their hands made him feel sore all over. During his ordeal on the mountain with the powerful dragon slayer, Billy sat against

11

the trunk of a tree, his hands and feet bound. The slayer opened a book and claimed that reading from it would summon a dragon, whom the slayer wished to kill. The poem sounded sort of like English, but Billy couldn't understand it. The words seemed archaic and symbolic; they just didn't make any sense. Clefspeare, Billy's father in dragon form, showed up before the poem ended, so it was unclear whether the words actually summoned him or he had sensed his son was in danger and flew to his rescue.

Since Billy was severely wounded in the fierce battle that followed, his memories of the details were fuzzy, but he recalled the professor's amazing crossbow expertise that saved his life that day. How could this wrinkled old guy be so daring, so agile? He could handle a crossbow and a battle sword with great strength and endurance, yet excel even more in his intellectual pursuits. This affable professor was becoming more and more of a puzzle.

The professor stopped his pacing and gazed at the fireplace, sighing before turning to face his students again. "William, I hope you and Miss Silver will carefully consider telling me what you know." He fingered the designs on the replica's scabbard. "I have discerned that you're confused and frightened, and I understand completely. I believe I would be, too. Both of you were severely wounded, yet you have mended at a miraculous rate. These are among the many perplexing mysteries to be solved." He straightened his whole body, his head held high. "I hope you will decide that you can trust me with your secrets. To be quite frank, I think I have earned your trust." A smile appeared on his wrinkled face, though a hint of sadness crept into his eyes. "Good night, students." He turned and stepped quickly out of the room. Seconds later, the front door clicked open, then closed with a muffled clap.

Billy flopped into the easy chair and slapped his hands on the chair's arms. Bonnie sank onto the sofa with a sigh, her brow knitting into three deep furrows. Walter sat on the far side of the sofa, his feet propped up on the coffee table, one shoe on top of the other. He picked at his fingernails, then retied his shoes, his eyes wandering toward Billy and Bonnie every few seconds. He finally jumped up. "I'd better make sure Hambone's warm." With a graceful bound, he dashed from the room.

Billy put his hand to his ear. "Bonnie, was Hambone whining?"

She smiled and shook her head. "Not a whine or a woof."

A sparkling gleam shone in Bonnie's eyes, though only the fading light from outside and a few dying embers in the fireplace illuminated the room. Billy sighed. "Either Walter has mind-to-mind connection with that dog or he knows more than we think."

"Uh-huh, I think he knows something."

"You do? Why?"

"Just some things he said to me today. And you know the professor's going to put all the pieces together before long."

"Yep. He'll figure it out sooner or later." Billy walked over to the small den window, and his thoughts travelled to the distant horizon, hills stretching into tree-covered mountains. He pictured the leaf-strewn battle scene and the dark, breezy cave. Bonnie joined him, and together they gazed at the deepening winter – thick grey clouds, cold, leafy breezes bending naked trees, tiny snowflakes threatening to bring millions of their friends later that night.

Bonnie's phantom reflection appeared in the window, smiling and peaceful. Billy kept his eye on the transparent image and pushed his hands into his pockets. "I think I'd better talk to Dad. I've only seen him once since I got hurt, and I was still pretty bad off then. I didn't ask him about a bunch of stuff that doesn't make any sense."

She leaned against the windowsill, bending forward to make room for her backpack. "A bunch of stuff? Like what?"

13

"Like, what's the deal with the sword you used on the mountain? And what happened to the slayer and that crazy candlestone? Stuff like that. And if I'm going to tell the professor everything, Dad should give his permission. Don't you think? I mean, I know the professor's going to ask lots of questions, so I'd better have a few more answers ready." Billy placed his hand on his stomach, and, with his lips forming a circle, he created a perfect ring of smoke and pushed it into the air. "Besides," he added as the ring expanded, "I've been practicing fire breathing, and I want to show Dad how I'm doing."

Bonnie put her hand through the ring, scattering the remaining smoke. "You're going to ask your mum to fly with you back to the mountain?"

"Uh-huh. Tomorrow if we can. We have a primitive airstrip up there now, so it's easy to get in and out."

She placed both palms on the windowsill and pushed herself up. "Then can I go with you?"

"That would be great, but isn't tomorrow the big day, you know, the thirty-day deadline?"

Bonnie put her hands on her hips. "How could I forget? Mr Foley wants to finish the adoption paperwork as soon as possible. The judge said he would sign it for us even though tomorrow's Sunday."

"Mr Foley? Aren't you going to start calling him 'Dad'? That's what Walter calls him, except when he's acting crazy and calls him 'Pop'."

She ran her fingers through her hair and then hitched up her backpack, her eyes toward the floor. "Not yet. That's going to be hard to get used to. I called my real father 'Daddy' for so long . . . until he betrayed me."

Tears welled in Bonnie's eyes, and her pain drilled a hole in Billy's heart. How could anyone, especially a father, give an awesome girl like Bonnie over to a dragon slayer? And now she was on the verge of being adopted by Walter's parents, two really cool adults who still had no clue about her dragon heritage. Still, everything might work out great. If her real father didn't make contact in time, the judge would declare abandonment and let the adoption go through. The tension must have been terrible for Bonnie, like waiting for William Tell to shoot an arrow at the apple on her head.

Billy cocked his head and playfully tapped on the window. "I know what you mean. I'm going to a cave in the mountains tomorrow, and I'll be calling a huge dragon 'Dad'!" He placed his hand on Bonnie's shoulder and pointed, as though he were showing her something in the distance. "Can you see it? I'll be going, 'Dad! Dad!' and then I'll hear a roar, and a huge rush of flame will come flying out of the cave. And then I'll go, 'Dad! There you are!'"

Billy and Bonnie laughed together, and Billy noticed his hand resting on her shoulder, his fingers crossing the strap of her backpack. When their eyes met, her smiling countenance melted into a sincere, searching gaze. Billy pulled his hand away and cleared his throat. "Anyway, since it's your big day, I think you'd better stick around here. I should be back the same day or early the next."

They sat down on the sofa, and Bonnie placed her hands in her lap, nervously rubbing her thumbs together. "But what if we do hear from my real father? I don't know what I'd do without you here to talk to, I mean, if he wants me back and stops the adoption."

Billy glanced out the window toward the mailbox at the street. "There's no mail tomorrow, so the only way he could contact you would be by phone, right?"

"I guess so. Why?"

15

Billy kept his eyes on the street while rubbing his chin. "I don't know. Maybe you should come with me then. Maybe it doesn't make much difference whether you're here or not. I mean, even if your father called, Mr Foley would be the one to talk to him." He turned back to Bonnie and sighed. "But I'm not even sure if Mum'll have time to go or what the weather's supposed to be like tomorrow. Since they finally started rebuilding our house, she's always busy with that, too."

"When will she be back?"

He glanced at a clock on the wall, an old cuckoo with dangling, weighted cones. "It'll be a while. She spent all day training a new pilot to carry skydivers, so she has to catch up on paperwork. She was pretty worried about the training. Dad used to do that kind of stuff."

Bonnie stood and stepped toward the window again. Billy joined her and pushed the window up, letting in a cold, fresh breeze. Walter was playing "fetch" with Hambone in the leaf-covered grass. The old hound wore a thick doggy sweater, so he probably didn't mind a little romp on this blustery January day. The dog's owner, Arlo Hatfield, a hunter who lived in the mountains, never dressed his tracking hounds in anything so spiffy. Hambone yipped and raced through the leaves, grabbing a ragged ball and rushing it back to Walter.

Billy leaned out the window. "Hey, Walter! Give the old dog a break!"

Walter and Hambone stopped. The hound sat on his haunches with his long tongue hanging out. "He's posing for you," Walter shouted back. "He knows you're doing a portrait of him."

Bonnie shivered and rubbed her hands over her arms. "You're doing a portrait?"

Billy slid the window closed. "Yeah. You want to see it?"

"Sure!"

Billy led Bonnie to a small utility room that Walter's father had converted into a serviceable art studio. He stepped over to the far corner where he kept his easel, dodging several rolled up posters and an empty frame. Gandalf, Billy's cat, lay curled up on the stool under the heating vent, so Billy remained standing. He lifted the cover of the sketchpad and flipped several pages over to find his drawing.

Bonnie let out a chuckle. "That's Hambone, all right. Those big sad eyes and long ears are perfect!"

"Thanks. You think Mr Hatfield will like it?"

"He has to. It's beautiful! With all those shades of grey it looks almost like a black and white photo. It's so real!"

Billy reached into the deep, side pocket of his cargo trousers where he always kept paper and something to draw with. He pulled out a pencil and signed the bottom of the portrait, including his trademark – two letter B's, the first one reversed, sitting back to back with the second. "Well, it's the least I could do. He didn't have to lend me his favourite dog."

"Are you going to give him the drawing when you visit your dad?"

"If I can. Mr Hatfield doesn't have a phone, so I can't call him to see if he's home."

Walter ambled in, holding a pretend phone and talking in a high-pitched hillbilly twang. "Hallow? Do yew have a number fer Arlo Hatfield? The city? Nowheresville. You know, rait over dere next ta Boondocks? Yeah, I got a drawin' fer him. He caint read, so I drawed a pitcher fer him."

Billy roared with laughter. Bonnie held her fingers over her lips and turned crimson. Following her lead, Billy tried to stifle his own laugh, letting out a snort through his puffed out cheeks.

Walter continued, exaggerating the accent even more. "Naw, he don't have no phone. Why in tarnation wood I want to go and tawk to that critter on the phone? Yew caint send no pickshures over the phone. What kine of fool do yew take me fer?"

Billy snatched the pretend phone from Walter's hand and held it to his ear. "I'm sorry, ma'am. He's a bit loony. We're sending him back to the electric shock room now."

Bonnie folded her hands in front of her and feigned a snobbish air, her eyes closed and her nose raised. Her lips trembled between a frown and a smile. "Well, while you two, ahem, gentlemen decide who's the more loony, I shall be in my room writing my English essay. I suggest that you do the same. Evening is at hand, and it is due on Monday." She started walking out, maintaining her stern librarian frown, but she burst out laughing and hurried down the hall.

18

Bonnie flipped on her desk lamp. With Billy's mother out late, the Foley household had opted for an à la carte dinner. Bonnie had brought in a sandwich and salad from the kitchen and placed them on her desk blotter along with a tall glass of water. Although it was time to relax, she kept her wings hidden in her backpack, choosing to endure the discomfort rather than risk someone popping in on her while she perched on her chair like a freakish bat.

After kicking off her shoes and socks and changing into a comfortable set of sweat clothes, she sat at the desk and chose a felt-tipped pen from her collection of markers in the middle drawer, pausing a moment to read the calendar hanging on the wall directly in front of her. She leaned forward and carefully drew a dark "X" on today's date, the second Saturday in January. The box for Sunday was already filled, a happy face surrounded by pink and yellow flower stickers. At the bottom of the box a caption read, "Adoption Day!"

Bonnie deposited the felt pen in the drawer and pulled out a three-ring binder, a fat notebook stuffed with paper. The first hundred or so pages were filled with flowing script – her journals, a number of writing assignments, and a sizable collection of stories and poetry. Although Billy and Walter shared a computer for their written work, Bonnie preferred the feel of setting pen to paper and letting her words pour out from mind to hand. Her script revealed her moods – the weightiness of the day exposed in dark, heavy strokes, or happiness riding the page on sweeping loops and roller-coaster m's. The blank pages summoned her eloquence more than any word processor ever could. And clacking on keys just wasn't the same. Computers produced too many distracting beeps and pop-up windows to get any thoughtful work done. No, this way was much better, the soothing slide of her lovely silver Papermate on the crisp, white sheet.

Tonight, as she wrote her essay entitled, "Counting the Cost," her uneven script meandered, frequently slipping below the rule line. Dark ink blotches told of her weariness, and her supper remained barely touched. Through bleary eyes she stared out the window at the thickening fog. The clear, breezy evening had given way, and a cooling blanket of rich mountain air had seeped into the valley in thick soupy layers. The short days of winter had brought once again an early sunset, and mist shrouded the last remnant of twilight. Darkness had fallen, and even the porch lights were swallowed by the engulfing gloom.

With her eyelids drooping like heavy curtains, she jerked her head up. Her eyes flashed open at the sound of a call, her name whispered in a long, dying echo. It was soft, yet urgent, as though a loving hand had rung the dinner bell to signal suppertime while she was playing in a field far away, or the wind had picked up the call and carried the syllables to her ears, lengthened and distorted, but still distinct and familiar – Mama's voice.

Bonnie looked around. No one else was in the room.

She had heard that same voice several times over the last few weeks and had assumed her mind was playing tricks on her. She missed her mother so badly that part of her brain thought she was still around, in the next room making the bed, or in the kitchen cooking dinner, or in the rocking chair ready to read her a story. Although the voice sounded sort of like her mother's, it wasn't exactly the same – somehow it carried the chill of a haunted house.

With no hope of staying awake at her desk, Bonnie got up and slid her window open. The breezeless air outside allowed the mist to seep into her room in wet creeping fingers, caressing her face with damp coolness and sending shivers across her arms. A faint trace of wood smoke tinged the air, a sure sign that the mountains had lent their freshness to the valley.

What a great way to shake off her sleepiness! Although darkness had fallen, it was a little early to go for a fly. She usually waited until late at night when everyone was asleep, but the fog would surely keep her hidden. She climbed out the window and onto the roof, a trick she had perfected over the last few weeks. Since her second-floor bedroom was the only one that faced the rear of the house, it was perfectly placed for her covert escape.

Bonnie took a deep breath of the wet, cool air, and, glancing all around to verify her privacy, she unzipped her backpack, letting it dangle until her nimble wings pushed it off. Once freed, her dragon wings unfurled and spread out behind her body, the span extending more than twice her body's length.

Her roof escapes were times for solitude, unhurried respites for introspection and prayer. She sat just above the eaves, pulling her knees up and admiring her surroundings. She loved how the upper branches of the trees drank from the grey, hovering mist.

She marvelled at how birds flitted so differently in a night fog, with rapid wing beats and without chirp or song.

As darkness wrapped her body, she threaded memorized verses through her mind, allowing them to come out in whispered song. She especially enjoyed singing a passage from a psalm of David, having set it to a tune herself during one of her many rooftop visits.

> *Whither shall I go from thy spirit? Or whither shall I flee from thy presence?*
> *If I ascend up into heaven, thou art there: If I make my bed in hell, behold, thou art there.*
> *If I take the wings of the morning, and dwell in the uttermost parts of the sea;*
> *Even there shall thy hand lead me, and thy right hand shall hold me.*
> *If I say, Surely the darkness shall cover me; even the night shall be light about me.*
> *Yea, the darkness hideth not from thee; but the night shineth as the day:*
> *The darkness and the light are both alike to thee.*

With a long, satisfied sigh, Bonnie rose to her feet and climbed to the apex of the roof. Her flying experience told her that fog layers are often shallow. She hoped to be able to cruise above them, finding light in the moon and stars. With a mighty flap and jump, she was off! Propelling herself nearly straight upward, she catapulted into the mist, her hair and face dampening as she flew. She pushed onward, beating her wings against the cool air and watching, but the wet vapour persisted, thinner as she flew upward, but still too murky to be safe.

Not wanting to get too high and fearing she wouldn't be able to find her way home, she levelled off and began flying in

21

a small circle, peering downward for any hint of light. She felt she was swimming rather than flying, streams of water soaking her hair and dripping into her eyes.

Bonnie had no doubt that she was higher than the trees; her only concern was how to land. After a few more seconds, she spotted a light down below. It was small, but bright enough to pierce the fog. She let her wings extend fully and glided toward the steady beam. As she approached, she thought she recognized the glow as a neighbour's halogen yard lamp. She would have to act quickly, land on the run, stuff her wings into her sweatshirt, and sprint about one block home. She folded in her wings and went into freefall, planning to unfurl them again just in time to parachute to a soft landing.

When she came within fifty feet of the light, it moved! It wasn't a yard lamp at all; it was the glow of a car's headlights! What should she do? It was too late to abort her landing. She was falling too rapidly.

Bonnie spread out her wings and pulled against the air, flexing her mighty canopy in the dark grey mist. She drew one wing in slightly and swerved, zipping just in front of the moving car's windshield and angling toward the kerb. The car brakes squealed. With her legs already running, Bonnie's bare feet hit the ground, but she toppled forward, rolling into the roadside grass. Before she could get up, she heard the car door slam, and footsteps pounded on the road. She was stunned, feeling stark naked with her wings exposed and no hope of hiding them in time. Should she run? Should she wait, hoping the fog would mask her presence?

Then, from the dark shadows of a hundred nightmares, a tall spectre strolled out of the soupy mist. Bonnie's eyes shot open, and she gulped.

"Daddy!"

CHAPTER 2

COUNTING THE COST

Bonnie jumped up to run, but her father caught her wrist and pulled her back, grabbing her other arm to hold her in place. His hands felt like iron clamps, and the pain of his clenching fingers stiffened her body.

"Settle down," he said. His voice was forceful but not coarse. "I'm not going to hurt you."

"Right," Bonnie grunted. "Tell that to my mother." She drew back her foot and kicked him in the shin as hard as she could, stinging her bare toes. He let out an angry yelp and shoved her backward, making her fall heavily on her bottom. With a flap of her wings, she was up again, leaping into the sky. Her father grabbed her ankle and jerked her to the ground, this time throwing her onto her back and pressing her hands against the cold grass.

Bonnie knew she was beaten. Her father had always been athletic, with strong, toned muscles and an agile body, and now he seemed more powerful than ever. With her unusual genetics she was stronger than a lot of grown men, but she was no match for him, and with her wings crumpled between her back and the ground, she had no hope of escape. Trying to breathe under his crushing weight, she gasped. "If you don't let me go, I'll scream!"

He slapped his hand over her mouth. "I don't want to hurt you. Just listen to me!" She shook her head violently, let out a muffled scream, and then tried to bite his hand. She read hot anger in his grey eyes. Sweat beaded along his brow, making his short red fringe stick to his forehead. He pushed against her cheeks with his fingers, squeezing them against her teeth. He made a shushing noise, his face so close she could smell his coffee breath. "If you'll just be quiet and listen, I'll let you up. Don't be stubborn. There's a lot you don't know, and I have news about your mother."

Bonnie's arms fell limp, her eyes wide open, the stinging pain jolting her into compliance. Her father slowly released the pressure on her face and smiled. "I thought that would cool your jets. Are you going to be quiet and listen?"

Bonnie nodded and tried to calm down, but she couldn't stop her gasping breaths.

"Good." He stood up and helped her to her feet.

She brushed herself off and then glared at him, trying her best to show distrust and anger at his rough treatment.

"Your mother hid your tracks well," he began. "I was still trying to find you in the foster system when the ad showed up."

Bonnie took a deep breath and folded her arms in front of her chest, trying to hold back her tears, but she couldn't keep her voice from shaking. "Mr Foley and I thought an ad was the best way. We hoped you wouldn't see it. The state said we had to make an effort to notify you."

He let out an agreeable laugh. "Your plan almost worked. I didn't see the ad, at least for a while. Someone told me I should be checking the papers for an abandonment summons, so I went back and found it, about two weeks ago now."

"Two weeks? Why didn't you call?"

"I had to prepare. I had a lot to prepare. And I wanted to show up in person and surprise you."

"Yeah, right," she said, squinting and putting her hands on her hips. "I'll bet you did." She wanted to stay on the defensive, to be tough and uncooperative, but his comment about her mother burned in her mind. She just had to ask, but she crossed her arms again and looked away, feigning disinterest. "So what's the news about my mother?" She glanced back to catch her father's expression.

He stared at his feet. For the first time he seemed hesitant, unsure of what to say. He lifted his gaze, and his expression turned soft, his brow rising and his eyes wandering. "I assume you think she's dead."

Bonnie's heart skipped. She could hardly breathe. She almost choked on her response. "Of . . . of course, she's dead. I saw her die."

His penetrating eyes and her exposed wings made her feel like a naked lab rat. He had always had that effect on her, staring at her as though his gaze could pierce her soul.

"You're not a doctor, Bonnie. You only thought she was dead. When I found her, she was near death. Her vitals were almost imperceptible. But she was alive. Badly wounded, to be sure, but alive. And she's alive now."

Bonnie's chest heaved. Now she knew she would cry. "I don't believe you!" She trembled, her face contorting and her voice cracking. "If she were alive she would have found me. She knew how."

25

"I'm sure she would have, but she's been in a coma. We have pretty high hopes, though. You know how strong she is, and being an anthrozil, she has more strength than normal humans."

Bonnie frowned and narrowed her eyes. "Anthrozil?" She had heard that name once before from Devin, but she didn't want her father to know she recognized it. Her suspicions now rang true. Maybe he really was in league with the slayer. "What's an anthrozil?"

"It's a name I came up with for what you are. The DNA seems to indicate that somehow you're fully human and fully dragon. You have the complete code for both species. 'Anthro' is a common prefix for man, and I got 'zil' from 'Godzilla', the movie dinosaur. Anyway, your mother still has some of the toughness of the dragon species in her, so she managed to survive."

Bonnie's defences began melting. She wanted to believe her mother was alive. She wanted to go back to a normal home with a real dad who wouldn't treat her like a science experiment. But it just couldn't be. She couldn't trust this man, this awful monster she had learned to despise. For months and months she had blamed him for her mother's death. Wasn't he the one who had used them like guinea pigs? Hadn't he led the murderers to their home? Couldn't this be another trick to bring her back into his lab and possibly into the clutches of the dragon slayers?

He held out his hand. "Your mother calls for you, even from her coma. Maybe if you answer, it will help her wake up."

Bonnie's hands trembled. There *was* a voice! She had heard it so many times! Her legs grew weak. She felt tears, hot and wet, joining the cold misty dew on her cheeks. "I . . . I don't know what to think." She sniffed back a sob. "I don't know what to believe."

Her father nodded and sighed. "I understand. I know you don't trust me, and I don't blame you. I was suspicious of that Devin character when he started asking questions about your mother, but I never told him about you."

Bonnie wiped her tears with her knuckles. "How long did you know Devin?"

"For quite a while. He was interested in DNA research and proved to be very knowledgeable, so I let him team up with me. Since dragon DNA is remarkably similar to human DNA, the research was complicated. I thought our combined expertise would help me pursue my goals, so I told him about my anthrozil theory. When he first learned that I was using dragon blood, he demanded to know where I was getting it. I refused to tell, of course, but when his demands became increasingly violent, I let some information slip and he found your mother." He lowered his head and shifted his weight uneasily. "I'm just glad my mistake wasn't fatal."

He extended his hand again, his fingers trembling. "Come back with me," he said, tears forming in his eyes. "Maybe together we can right this wrong. I couldn't do it by myself. Maybe you can call her back from the dead."

Bonnie stared at his hand, the hand she had feared for so long. Now it reached for her to take it in hers, to be led away from a life she loved and into the unknown. How could she trust him? Maybe it was all a lie, a trap to bring her back to his awful lab, to be jabbed again with needles, to have her blood drawn time after time after time. But how could she not go? If there was any way his story could be true, that her mother really was still alive and she could possibly help her, she just had to do it. Wasn't it worth the risk?

She lifted her arm and began to stretch out her hand. The rough tussle had forced her sleeve up toward her shoulder,

staining her arm with grass and dirt. As she raised her bare forearm into the glow of a nearby streetlight, she saw tiny white
scars, the remnants of dozens of needle marks.

He reached out farther to take her hand, but she drew it
away, stepping backward in the same motion.

"No," she said softly.

"But—"

Bonnie stepped back again and her voice strengthened. "No!
No, I can't!" She turned and shot into the air, her wings explod-
ing into flight.

His voice shouted behind her, muffled and distorted in the
fog. "I'll come back in the morning. Think about it. You may
be your mother's only hope."

Bonnie found the roof and landed softly near her backpack. She hustled to put it on, breathing heavily and sobbing.
When she pulled the last strap tight, she climbed back in the
window and wiped her face with the dinner napkin. She stifled her crying and looked around the room, wondering what
to do next.

What could she do? Who could help her now? This was her
legal father wanting to take her home. She wasn't sixteen yet;
she had no right to declare emancipation.

Haunting memories of emotional tortures streamed back in
flashing visions and vivid detail – the look in her mother's eyes
and the deep gash in her abdomen, a replay of her last words
gurgling in blood, and the weeks of lonely journeys from home
to home in search of someone who would take in a scared
orphan who was hiding a terrible secret.

"Don't let . . . let them find you," her mother had said as
she lay dying. "There's another dragon . . . I'm sending you to
find him. Don't come back here unless I call for you." With a

last burst of strength, she cried, "Now run, dear child! You know where to go!" She sighed a last breath and made no other sound. And Bonnie ran, ignoring the tears, the horrible pain, never looking back, never stopping. In the last few weeks, with the Foleys opening up their home to her, she felt like she had finally stopped running, but the pursuing demons had now caught up, and they cast their dark shadows on her very door.

Bonnie repeated the words to herself. *"Don't come back here unless I call for you."* And now her mother had called, or at least that's what her father said. And she had heard her call, that voice crying deep within her soul that she thought was just her brain cracking up. Now she felt the phantom sound as an irresistible pull, a loving voice begging her to believe. But why should she believe? Her father had lied so many times before, pretending to be a loving husband and father while fostering an alliance with a demon. Why should she believe him now? *But what if it's true this time? I have to help her! What choice do I have? I can't just abandon her.*

The thought of hiding brought feelings of darkness, the same loneliness she had suffered in the foster homes, and it made her feel ashamed and cowardly, like she would be turning her back on her mother in her time of desperate need. The decision was too awful to make, and who could possibly be wise enough to help her? Nobody on earth could ever understand all her feelings.

A poster on the wall caught her eye, the same poster that had helped her so many times in the past, a drawing of an angelic girl praying on her knees by her bed. The little girl's eyes were focused upward, and the caption said, "Trust in the Lord with all thine heart; and lean not unto thine own understanding. In all thy ways acknowledge him, and he shall direct thy

29

paths." Bonnie had grown accustomed to that pose herself, but this time she would pour her heart out like never before. She had no choice; she had no understanding of her own to lean on.

Falling on her knees, she folded her hands on her bed, allowing herself to weep out loud. With her backpack securely hiding her wings, she had no fear of someone walking in unexpectedly. She just cried out to God, her words cascading from her mind and her feelings pouring out in heart-rending sobs.

My cup of wisdom is poured out, my Father, empty and dry. My heart aches. My very bones feel crushed by this burden, a shadow falling on my soul like Sheol's dark loneliness.

Her prayer went on and on, her eloquence natural and free flowing, the product of her dragon-influenced mind and maturity. As she prayed she felt the warmth of relief, the soothing blanket of God's love wrapping around her chilled soul. She had already been through worse struggles. She could get through this, too. Although her aches were being assuaged with a spiritual balm, she cried on, the release bringing cleansing satisfaction, the joy of being held in her heavenly father's arms.

30

With his easel turned away from the studio door, Billy sat on a stool, his pencil fine-tuning a facial detail on his sketch paper. Every once in a while, he glanced up at the closed door, wary of a surprise visitor. Although he had a dragon's ability to sense approaching danger, he still felt slightly paranoid. This was his secret project, one that poured out a mystery in his heart. He sighed and shook his head, pressing an eraser on a lower part of the portrait and rubbing out a line. *I can't remember exactly what the blade looked like.*

He pushed the stool back, and, blowing his heated breath on his cold hands, he surveyed the entire picture. Bonnie stood in a flowing white robe, her wings fully expanded. With her arms out-stretched, she held a glowing sword, but not in battle position. The blade rested in her palms as though she were presenting it to whoever was studying the portrait. With her eyes blazing blue, she seemed to beg that it be taken and used by her valiant knight.

What was it about Bonnie that was so different? Was it power that blossomed in her spirit? Was it peace? Yes, she prac-tically gushed with peace. Even with all the problems she faced, she seemed to walk in a garden of serenity. Billy longed to walk the same path, to find peace even as he struggled over the loss of his father. At least if his father were truly dead, he could cher-ish fond memories. Instead, his father's shadow lurked in the shape of a winged monster, and its haunting presence never let him rest. Every time he thought about his dad, he could feel the boiling cauldron in his belly, a deep-seated anger that sometimes took control of his mind. He felt abandoned, alone. If there was a God, why did He take his dad away?

31

A gentle knock sounded at the door. Billy flipped the page to his drawing of Hambone. "Come in."

Walter's nose appeared first, protruding through the open-ing. The hinges creaked in the otherwise quiet house as Walter's whole face appeared.

Billy put his pencil on the page, but he didn't make a mark. "Whassup, Walter? Is it my turn on the computer?"

Walter gestured with his finger. "No. Just follow me."

Billy tiptoed behind Walter down the hall. They reached Bonnie's bedroom door, and Walter whispered, "Listen."

Billy pressed his ear against the door. Within a few seconds he heard the distinctive sounds of mournful sobs.

"Did you go in and talk to her?" Billy asked. "Do you know what's up?"

Walter shook his head. "You know the rules about her bedroom. No trespassing for us y-chromosome types."

A new voice entered the hallway. "Is something wrong?"

Billy swivelled his head and kept his voice low. "Mum. You're home."

"I just got back." She set a plate of food on the hall table – a thick sandwich, several raw baby carrots, and an apple. "Is Bonnie okay?"

"She's crying. Is it all right if I check on her?"

His mother's brow furrowed, and she took a step closer. "Sure."

Billy tapped on the door with one knuckle. "Bonnie? You okay?"

There was no answer.

Billy turned the knob and pushed the door slightly, allowing his mouth to penetrate the opening. "Bonnie? . . . Um . . . It's Billy. Walter and my mum are with me." He waited and listened.

A faint reply floated into the hall. "It's okay. You can come in."

Billy opened the door and stepped in. Bonnie was kneeling with her hands on the bed. Her crying had subsided, but she didn't look up. To Billy, the sight was wondrous. In her praying posture, Bonnie was an angel, beautiful in form and radiant in appearance. He imagined her hidden wings spread out to shield her body, protecting her from whatever tortured her mind. Billy didn't know much about praying. He had done it a few times, but he wasn't sure if it really ever worked. When Bonnie did it, she seemed to glow, even through her bitter tears.

With his mother and Walter following, Billy edged toward Bonnie's bed and stood at her side. His mother knelt and gently rubbed her neck. "Bonnie," she said tenderly. "What's wrong?"

Bonnie lifted her head, her wet eyes red with grief. "I . . . I was outside, and he was there."

"Who was there?" Billy asked.

"My father."

"Your real father?!"

She nodded and started crying again. "He . . . he wants me to go back to Missoula with him."

"To Missoula! But what about—" Billy wanted to kick the bed, but he just tapped it with his toe. He glanced at Walter, wondering how far he could question Bonnie without giving away their secrets.

Walter put his hands in his pockets and stepped toward the hall. "I'm going to get a cold, wet cloth for her."

Billy's mum tugged Walter's sleeve. "Bring a dry towel, too."

Walter nodded and hustled out of the room.

Billy whispered. "He's going to make you go?"

Bonnie stood up and turned slowly to sit on the bed, her head bowed. "I don't think so," she continued. "At least, he didn't say that. But I think I need to go with him."

Billy pushed his fingers into his hair and grabbed a handful. "Need to go with him!? Why?"

She looked up, and her voice cracked. "He says my mother's not dead."

Billy's mum sat next to Bonnie. "Not dead? I thought you saw her die."

"I thought she was dead when I left her, but my father says I was wrong. She's in a coma, and he says she calls for me."

Billy let out a huff. "And the sound of your voice might snap her out of it, I suppose?"

"Yes. How did you know?"

"Sounds like an old movie I saw."

"And did it work?"

"Well . . . yeah." Billy walked to the other side of the room and came back, holding his palms up. "But this isn't some corny old movie; it's real life. And how can you trust him, anyway? Didn't he rat on you and your mum to a dragon slayer?" Billy closed his eyes while he paced. Something wasn't making sense, and he couldn't put his finger on it. There were so many weird things happening lately he couldn't put it all together.

Bonnie's eyes followed Billy around the room. "That's exactly what I asked myself. That's what I've been asking God. How can I trust a man like him?"

He stopped in front of Bonnie's poster of a praying girl. "Well, asking God and all that is great, but maybe you should ask your father for proof."

"Proof? Like what?"

He waved his hand toward the poster. "Like a picture, a picture of your mum in the hospital bed. Or we could call the hospital and ask about her condition. If she's there, they'll tell us. But if she's really dead, there'll be a death certificate somewhere. I'm sure Walter's dad can dig that up."

Billy's mother rose and stood next to Billy. "He's right, Bonnie. I'm sure we can get to the bottom of this."

Bonnie's eyes sparkled with new life. "Can you believe it? When he held out his hand to me, I almost took it. I almost left with him then and there."

Billy's face burned, a surge of compassion coursing through his body. His muscles flexed as if ready to go to battle, and he tried to think of some way to communicate his feelings to Bonnie, some way to strengthen her, too. "You can believe this," he said, extending his hand toward her, "you can always trust me. This hand will never lead you astray."

Bonnie took his hand and pulled herself to her feet. Her fingers caressed his ring, the ring that held the rubellite stone his father had given him, and her matching ring clicked against his. "I will never forget those words," she said softly. "I do trust you."

At that moment Walter walked back into the room, a white facecloth in one hand and a towel in the other. Bonnie took them gladly and washed her tear-streaked cheeks. She took a deep breath, and her face regained its usual glow. "We'd better get some rest," she said. "We have a lot of detective work to do tomorrow."

Mr Foley strolled into the dining room carrying a cup of coffee and a yellow legal pad. Walter and his mum sat on one side of the table, and Billy's mother sat between Billy and Bonnie on the other side. They were still dressed in church clothes, having arrived home to a scant brunch that Mr Foley had prepared while they were gone. The leftovers lay scattered around the table – half of a cold piece of toast on a serving plate, shallow pools of milk at the bottoms of cereal bowls, and orange pulp clinging to the rims of several glasses.

Mr Foley took a seat at the head of the table, grabbed a pen from his ear, and scratched a note on his pad. "Okay, I made a bunch of calls. There *is* an Irene Conner listed in the hospital database in Missoula, and she is in a coma." He sipped his coffee and drummed his fingers on the table. "I pulled all the strings I had, but we couldn't come up with a death certificate. That's not conclusive, though. I couldn't raise much activity so early on a Sunday morning."

He looked at Bonnie, his face turning dark and sad. "In any case, Bonnie, your father showed up. We can't declare abandonment. He'll have to relinquish his rights voluntarily."

35

Billy grabbed his spoon and tossed it into his bowl. "Fat chance of that."

"That only means we can't legally adopt you," Mr Foley added, "at least not yet. It doesn't mean you have to go with him. We can fight for child endangerment, but that would be hard to prove, since all he did was draw blood. It's fair to assume he was qualified to do it, and we have no idea what he was doing with your blood."

Bonnie kept her gaze fixed on the table, and she nodded with tight lips and a firm chin. "Don't I have to take the chance?" She looked up, tears glistening in her eyes. "If there's any chance at all, don't I have to take it?" She extended her arm, pointing westward, her voice trembling. "Didn't Billy risk his life for me up there on that mountain when the only proof he had was a lock of hair? Shouldn't I do the same for my own mother?" She sniffed and covered her face, her tears flowing in earnest.

Billy stood up, his face burning. "What I did is history. And I was wrong; you weren't there on that mountain. That doesn't mean I wouldn't do it again. I would! But Devin fooled us, and he has so many cronies, he could be fooling us again. Should we just waltz right into another one of his traps without checking it out first? I say we demand a video, or at least a picture of Bonnie's mum in the hospital." He sat down again and put his chin on his fists.

Billy's mother draped her arm over Bonnie's shoulders. "That shouldn't be hard to arrange. Surely someone can email us a digital photo."

"Right," Walter agreed. "I'm with Billy. I wouldn't trust this guy as far as my mother could throw him."

Mrs Foley's forehead wrinkled. "As far as I could throw him? Why me?"

"I've seen you throw," Walter replied, shrugging his shoulders. "Sorry, Mum, but you throw like a sick duck."

"A sick duck?"

"Yeah. Remember when you threw the baseball and it hit the window?"

"Yes. So?"

"Well, you barely quacked it."

A shower of boos and balled-up napkins rained on Walter, but the doorbell interrupted the jeers. Bonnie jerked her head toward Billy. Her eyes gave away her fear.

Mr Foley rose from his seat and answered the door in the foyer. His voice drifted back to the dining room. "Yes, Dr Conner. I'm Carl Foley. Come in. We've been expecting you."

"Thank you, Mr Foley. Call me Matt. Bonnie told you I'm a doctor?"

"Yes, a research professor in pharmacy at the University of Montana, newly appointed dean, if I'm not mistaken. I must admit that I have checked up on you."

The two joined the others at the table. Dr Conner tugged on his shirt cuff, then dug his hand into his pocket. "That's perfectly understandable."

"Yes," Mr Foley went on, "and Bonnie told me she talked with you briefly last night when she was out for a walk."

Dr Conner glanced at Bonnie and smiled. "A walk?"

Bonnie turned crimson and shifted her backpack higher.

Billy edged between Bonnie and her father. "Mr Foley, didn't she say she just went out for some fresh air?"

"Right," Mr Foley replied. "What's the confusion?"

Dr Conner pulled on his cuffs again and straightened his watch. "None at all. It's just that she was kind of zipping along when I saw her. I wouldn't have called it walking."

37

Mr Foley tapped his thick fingers on the table and cleared his throat. "Dr Conner, Bonnie and I have discussed this, and considering the circumstances, I think you would agree that some sort of positive proof of your claims is reasonable. After all, technically you are not the legal custodian. She's in the foster system now."

The doctor's lips pursed, and his tone hardened. "You're requiring proof to allow me to take my own daughter home? Don't give me that nonsense about the foster system. She was made a ward of the state without my consent and without a court order."

Billy had to admit that Dr Conner had a good point. Their demands of proof seemed pretty silly now.

Mr Foley squared his shoulders. "If you want a legal fight, Dr Conner, I assure you I can deliver one. If, however, you can prove that Bonnie's mother is still alive, I'll have no legal grounds for keeping her here."

Dr Conner cleared his throat and resumed a congenial air. "Considering the circumstances, I can agree to that. Have you called the hospital?"

"Yes," Mr Foley replied, "the operator reported that your wife is listed in their computer as a patient, but we were wondering if someone at the hospital could send us a photo of her."

Dr Conner lowered his head a moment and then raised a finger in the air. "No need to bother anyone for that. I have a picture on my laptop. I'll go and get it." Without waiting for a response he hurried outside.

Billy fingered the handle on his spoon and flipped it out of the bowl. He mentally followed Dr Conner's progress to the car and back. Did Bonnie's dad really have a photo of her mum? Could it be a fake? If he could produce a photo, how would they be able to tell a real one from a phoney? After several more seconds of uneasy silence, Billy spoke up. "It has to be a recent photo. We don't want anything from months ago."

"Right," Mr Foley agreed, drumming his fingers again. "It has to—"

Dr Conner re-entered, unzipping a leather case. "I took one yesterday morning before I left for the airport. I thought Bonnie might want to see a picture of her mother." He placed the computer on the table, and the screen flashed on, taking a few seconds to boot up. The doctor tapped the keyboard, and a photo replaced the screen's desktop, an image of a woman covered by blankets up to the chin of her calm, pale face. A feeding tube protruded from her nose, and various medical supplies and equipment surrounded her bed. A photo of Bonnie sat on a table next to a vase of wildflowers.

Bonnie drew closer to the screen. She covered her mouth with one hand, and two suppressed sobs pushed through her nose and lips. "It's her," she cried, her voice tortured but still under control. "It's my mother!"

Mr Foley blinked twice and tapped the base of the laptop. "May I use the computer for a moment, Doctor?"

Dr Conner turned the screen his way. "Be my guest."

Mr Foley pecked a few keys. He let out a low "Hmmm" and then rotated the computer back toward Dr Conner. "The file is time-stamped yesterday morning."

Dr Conner nodded. "I understand your mistrust." He pulled a disk from the laptop case and inserted it in the drive. "I'm making a copy for you. You can check it all you want. You'll see that it's authentic. My wife is very sick, and all I want to do is help her and get my daughter back." He popped the disk out and handed it to Mr Foley.

39

Billy clenched his fists. He wanted to argue, but his supply of reasons was hurtling off a cliff like a bunch of lemmings.

Dr Conner rose from his seat, packed up his laptop, and threw the strap over his shoulder. "Bonnie, I know you don't trust me yet, but when you see your mother, I'm sure you'll feel better about everything."

Bonnie's wet, red eyes darted all around. Billy could only swallow hard, trying to push down the swelling knot growing inside.

As if reading the fervent distrust in the room, Dr Conner added, "My flight is a private charter, but I don't have permission to invite anyone. Otherwise you would be welcome to join us." He placed a business card on the table. "This is my address. Please come and see us anytime. Just give me a call." He then extended his hand to his daughter. "Bonnie, we shouldn't delay. We have to drive to the Charleston airport. Remember, your mother is calling you. Will you come?"

Bonnie glanced toward Billy, but he had no idea what to say. His mind was shouting, "Danger! Don't go!" but he couldn't tell if it was his dragon "danger signals" working or his tremendous distrust of this man who would take away his friend.

Bonnie turned back to her father and nodded. "I'll go."

She took his hand and the two walked toward the door. She looked back, and Billy read a message of courage in her face. Tears streamed, but her countenance remained stoic, her chin firm once again. It said, "No goodbyes. I'll be back." Then she silently mouthed words that Billy read easily – "Trust me."

Dr Conner shifted the laptop case and buttoned his sport jacket. "I'll purchase her immediate needs and send for her belongings. Thank you for taking such good care of her."

When the door shut, Billy jumped up from his seat and ran to the front window in the living room. Dr Conner and Bonnie slid into the car, and Bonnie lifted the visor on the passenger side. Before the motor started, she held up her fist, clearly displaying her rubellite ring. A few seconds later the car disappeared around a corner.

Billy plodded back to the dining room. Seeing every eye set firmly on him, his tangled emotions swirled in a dizzying array of hate, love, anger, and compassion. He balled up his fists, his rage growing to overwhelm all other feelings. He just had to let it out, somehow blow off steam without blasting fire. He started with a whisper. "I can't believe this!" His voice then grew with every word, spelling out his anger in face-contorting passion. "I just let a monster take her back to her nightmares! She told me how scared she was of him, and I didn't do anything about it!"

His mother and Walter joined him. She rubbed his back, and Walter smacked his fist into his hand. "We'll get that creep," he said, his face aglow in crimson. "My dad will figure out what he's really up to."

Mr Foley gripped Billy's shoulder and squeezed it hard. "We may have quite a battle on our hands, so we have to keep our heads on straight. It won't help for you to lose your temper." He pulled the diskette from his pocket and turned toward Walter. "Call the professor. I'll need help examining the photo."

"Got it!" Walter hurried for the phone.

Billy took a deep breath and let it out slowly. "Could you ask him to bring the sword again, Walter? I want to take a picture of it."

"And get some more practice, maybe?" Walter asked as he punched in the phone number. "If he brings the other sword, I can spar with you."

Billy's mum massaged his neck, pressing her strong fingers into his taut muscles. "That's a good idea. It'll do you good to

41

practice and get your aggressions out. After listening to that fraud, I'd like to get a few hacks in myself."

"Practice didn't help us keep Bonnie here, Mum. I mean, I've been training like crazy, you know, to battle like a knight when the time comes. But now this guy just waltzes in the door and waltzes right back out, taking Bonnie to who knows where, and we just let them go." He leaned over and whispered, careful to keep his sizzling breath away from her ear. "I was so mad, I could've turned him into a giant French fry right in front of everyone."

"I know what you mean," she whispered back. "And I'd have supplied a gallon of ketchup. But I don't want you getting put away for murder."

"No way. Who'd ever believe it? We could've just called it a case of spontaneous combustion."

42

Billy leaned over Mr Foley's shoulder and blinked at the image before him. The hospital photo filled the computer screen, a large flat panel display sitting prominently on Mr Foley's mahogany desk. Something was wrong, but Billy couldn't quite put his finger on it.

Walter burst into the office. "The great guru of graphical gawking has arrived!" he announced as Professor Hamilton followed him inside.

Billy shoved Walter's chest. "How long did it take to dream that one up?"

Walter grinned and shoved him back. "About two seconds. It beats 'the cat's pyjamas has arrived', doesn't it?"

"Just barely."

Professor Hamilton handed each boy a sword. "Shall we get our aggressions out in a profitable manner, gentlemen?"

Billy grabbed the Excalibur replica and opened the double French doors that led to the rec room. As soon as Walter was ready, Billy lunged forward and their swords clanked together. He positioned himself near the office entrance, hoping to watch Mr Foley and battle Walter at the same time.

Mr Foley extended a photo of Bonnie's mum to the professor. "I emailed the hospital image to a friend of mine, Fred Hollings. He's a real techno-geek who's trying to start a computer company in the industrial park. He might be able to tell if this pic's authentic or not, but he's out of town right now."

The professor studied the image on the computer screen for several minutes, zooming in on numerous details and rubbing his chin thoughtfully. He alternated between the photo display and the Internet browser, poring over dozens of web pages. Billy's mother and Mrs Foley entered the rec room, whispering to each other while they watched their sons practice. Finally, Professor Hamilton cleared his throat. Billy stopped his sword in mid-swing, letting it drop to his side, and everyone crowded into the office.

"It is my opinion," the professor said slowly, "that the image is indeed a genuine digital photograph of Miss Silver's mother. The facial features in the image are too close a match to the other photo to be counterfeit. Such a fake would be extraordinarily difficult to manufacture."

Billy hiked the sword up to his shoulder. "So Bonnie's mum really is in a hospital in Missoula? Dr Conner was telling the truth?"

"Oh, no. I didn't say that at all. I'm quite sure he was lying."

"Lying?" Mr Foley repeated. "What do you mean?"

"He told the truth about this being a photo of his wife." The professor pointed at the computer screen. "He lied about the time. This photo was taken at least four months ago."

43

THE DRAGON'S LAIR

Billy let his sword dangle from his fingertips until it finally dropped to the floor. "Four months ago, Professor? How do you know?"

"Yeah," Walter added. "That wouldn't be long after Bonnie came to West Virginia."

"The flowers in the vase give away the season," the professor said calmly, pointing at the screen again. "They are glacier lilies, which usually bloom from March through July, perhaps as late as August, but certainly not in January. It's not likely that a local florist cultivates such wildflowers in the dead of winter, so I deduced the date by logic."

Billy's mum tapped her head with her finger. "You just happened to know so much about glacier lilies, Professor?"

The professor waved his hand in friendly dismissal. "Oh, no. I have only recently learned about your West Virginia varieties, and I'm not at all familiar with those from Montana. I am, however, quite proficient at horticulture in general. The British wildflowers are exquisite, and I enjoyed them immensely in my home fields. I merely noticed the lovely flowers in the photo and searched the Internet for a match. With my current knowledge, finding the species was not difficult." The professor pushed the eject button and handed the diskette to Mr Foley. "It's a simple matter to alter the date and time stamp on a computer file. Dr Conner took an older file and renewed it on his computer, apparently with this kind of deception in mind."

Billy smacked his fist into his palm. "So he *is* a liar! I knew it!"

"Yes, William. And I would think a man who would deceive us would not have Miss Silver's best interests in mind."

Billy's mum picked up his sword and extended the hilt toward him. "Billy, let's get packed and make a flight plan. We're going to Montana!"

Billy grabbed the sword and pumped his fist. "Now you're talkin'!"

"How many passengers can you fit?" Walter asked. "I'll squeeze into a suitcase if I have to."

Billy pushed Walter's arm. "As if I'd leave you behind."

Walter raised his eyebrows and his cheeks sagged like a young basset's. "Can I go, Dad?"

Mr Foley whispered to his wife, then tapped the professor on the back. "I'd feel better, Prof, if you'd go along. They might need you to help figure out what's going on."

Professor Hamilton stood between the two boys and pretended to bump their heads together. "Of course. With all of my students in Montana, I would have no one to teach here."

Billy's mother laid her hand on Mrs Foley's shoulder. "We have room for everyone."

"I'll go wherever my husband goes," she replied, giving his hand a squeeze.

Mr Foley stroked his wife's hand lovingly. "I have a trial tomorrow, but I can make calls from here and do a little more detective work. If the trial ends before you get back, we'll hop a flight to Missoula. I don't expect it to last more than a day, but you never know."

Billy's mum discussed the flight arrangements with the Foleys and shared her strategy for packing. While he listened, Billy noticed the professor's gaze resting on him, and he stared back at his steely grey eyes, as if caught in a gravitational pull. The professor seemed to be searching for a light in a dark cave or for the correct turn in a dizzying maze. Was he looking for an answer to a question? Maybe he was trying to reveal one of Billy's carefully guarded secrets.

The others in the room buzzed quietly about several issues, leaving Billy relatively alone with Professor Hamilton. The professor broke their silence and whispered, "Will you trust me?"

Billy pulled away from the professor's mesmerizing gaze. He drooped his head and kept his eyes on his old tennis shoes. The right one pressed its toe into the floor. "I . . . I do trust you," he finally said, looking up again, "but some of the secrets aren't mine to reveal."

"Yes, of course," he said, nodding. "I assumed Miss Silver plays a major role."

"Not just her. She'd trust me to tell you if I thought it was right." Billy's ears perked up when he heard his mother mention making their first stop in the mountains, a short jaunt west of town, to "visit a friend and get advice." The thought of seeing his father again made Billy feel warm, and maybe a little bit scared. The sight of the massive dragon was enough to scare anyone.

Billy managed a weak smile. "I'll tell you what. I can explain a few things as soon as we take off, but we're going to stop and ask someone's advice up on the mountain where we battled Devin. If he says it's okay, then I'll tell you everything." He extended his hand. "Is that a deal?"

Professor Hamilton shook his hand firmly. "I will gladly make that deal, William." His head tilted and his brow wrinkled. "Who is your friend? I heard the story of the hunter. Are you going to ask his advice?"

Billy laughed. "You mean Arlo Hatfield? No, but I'd like to see him again. I drew a picture of Hambone for him."

Billy's mother extended a bag of cheese puffs toward him. "Then bring it along. I'm sure we can arrange to have it delivered." She offered the bag to the professor. "So, when can you be ready?"

The professor smiled and waved his hand at the bag. "I shall return in less than an hour, Madam." He pulled his watch from his pocket and wound it. "And, William, I have the mystery book once again. Its properties are quite astounding. I suspect that we will be informing each other about many things before this day ends."

With Billy in the co-pilot's seat and his mother flying the plane, the professor and Walter leaned forward in their two-seat passenger bench. The sound of the buzzing props nearly drowned Billy's voice. "I can't tell you everything yet, but basically, Bonnie's the one who took care of the slayer. She used his sword, and from her description, it looked a lot like your replica of Excalibur. Anyway, she said a really bright beam of light surged out of it, almost like a light sabre from *Star Wars,* and when she pointed it at the slayer, he vanished in a flash of sparks that kind of swirled around and disappeared, like water going down a drain."

"Just like flushing a toilet, huh?" Walter swirled his finger in tightening circles as he lowered it toward the cabin floor.

Billy slapped at Walter's arm. "No, genius, not like a toilet. Anyway, that strange stone I told you about, the candlestone, was there on the ground. We think that had something to do with it. What do you think, Professor?"

The professor pulled a pair of old-fashioned spectacles from his shirt pocket and slipped them on. "I'm certain the candlestone is involved, William."

"Really? How?"

The teacher opened a satchel he had at his side. "Now is a good time to show you the book." He withdrew a leather-bound volume. The cover was about the size of an eight-by-ten photo, with raised runic characters that looked like a bunch of lines and dashes – nothing like the lettering in the ancient King Arthur lore the professor had used at school. The book's two covers pressed together a modest collection of parchment, making the volume about the thickness of a notebook computer. The professor opened the delicate binding to the first page and held it on his lap. "There is mention of the candlestone in this book, and it's a clue to what the verse means."

"The verse?"

"Yes, there are verses, strange and cryptic. The initial three pages are intelligible. The first one claims the author was Merlin."

Walter shifted to get a look. "Merlin! That's so cool! What did he write?"

"I suspect that it's a journal of sorts, somewhat like a modern diary, but, as you might expect from Merlin, it contains a great deal of mystery."

49

Billy leaned around his seat to get a better view of the strange diary. The ragged yellowed parchment held strange looking characters, none of which he recognized as English letters.

"The first page," the professor went on, running his finger under the odd lettering as he translated, "merely states,

The Musings of Merlin
A Servant of Our Lord, the Christ
A Collection of Prophecy, Poetry, and Pedantry

"The next page adds our dash of mystery. It says, roughly speaking,

As you read, reflect. Though blank to the evil eye, the page will be painted in the vision of the wise, and in the language of his time shall my words come hither. Do not despise prophetic utterances, for they expose and condemn an oath falsely divined. Beware, however, lest you reveal a page before its predecessor is complete. It is the patient soul who finds the desire of his heart.

"And page three contains poetry of an ancient sort in an old variety of English. It starts with a title, 'To Call a Friend, If a Dragon's Friend You Be', and an explanatory note, 'Those who call must beware. One who summons lightning from heaven to strike his foes may find his enemies picking through his own charred bones.'

"The actual body of the poem follows." He drew a folded sheet of paper from his shirt pocket and spread it out over the book. "I took the liberty of writing down a translation, and I added a simple rhyme and metre pattern that the author seemed to design for this poem."

Come thou bane of devil's mount
Secure thy fortune in thy breast
Diamonds, pearls, and emeralds count
And rubied crowns upon thy crest

Fly to me O ancient sage
Who gathers light to draw his breath
Proving why the heathen rage
Against thy life, to seek thy death

Darkness hates thy light-filled soul
'Tis truth it shrouds with evil thought
Take thy place, thy dragon's role
From wisdom's lake O give me draught

Shall I use yon candlestone
Absorbing light to steal thy fire
If I shouldst lie beneath its trone
Excalibur builds my funeral pyre

God, my lord, do send my plea
To dragons' ears both far and nigh
Send me help I ask on knee
Transluminate me lest I die

51

Walter leaned back and propped his head against the window. "Wow! Now that's a cool poem!" After a few seconds his face puckered up, and he lifted his head again. "What does it mean?"

"I'm still working on it, Walter. Clearly it's a summons, a prayer to call a dragon, and with the properties of Excalibur and this candlestone becoming clearer, the meaning of the poem is taking shape. I have not decided, however, what 'trans-luminate' means."

"What's on the next page, Professor?" Billy asked.

"Remarkably enough, the remaining pages, I'd say fifty or so, are completely blank. It seems we have many pieces missing in our puzzle. And that brings me to my most burning question, William. You haven't told me what became of the sword or the stone."

"Oh, yeah. Well, Bonnie couldn't lug the sword all the way back down the hill—"

"I suppose not," the professor interrupted, "especially with her knee making her unable to walk."

"Yeah, right. Her knee. And she threw the candlestone into the woods."

"If she threw it, then it wasn't too heavy to carry, I would guess."

"Well, uh, no, that is—"

The professor folded his spectacles and slid them back in his pocket. "I understand, William. Clarity is elusive when you are honour bound to hide the details. I assume you will tell me more once you have permission from your friend, correct?"

"I want to tell you, Professor, but I really have to wait."

"Of course you do. It's clear that the story has many holes that beg for filling. I have deduced that the sword and the candlestone are the keys to the entire mystery, though I do not yet see the purpose of the stone. The sword, however, must be the true Excalibur. It had the power to transform matter into light energy when wielded by one who has a heart made pure by God and—" The professor halted, his mouth dropping open.

"What's up, Professor?" Billy asked.

The professor smacked his forehead with his palm. "Transluminate! Of course!" He retrieved his spectacles and tapped his finger on the page. "*Trans* means change, and *luminate* refers to light. The poem uses the word *transluminate* to describe Excalibur's method of transforming matter into light. I should have thought of that immediately."

Walter let out a snort. "It's okay, Prof. What did it take you? A whole minute?"

The professor laughed and laid his palms on top of the diary. "You are kind, Walter to . . . how do you say it? Cut me some slack? In any case, it seems that the mystery is beginning to coalesce, and the clues point to Excalibur. If you could show me the approximate place of its disposal, William, I should like to search for it while you visit your friend."

"I can only guess and point out the area from the sky. It's probably within walking distance of where we're going to land though."

"Very well. While you are consulting your friend, I shall have a look around."

After landing on a crude airstrip atop a grassy mountain, Billy and his mother secured Merlin II and joined their two passengers standing by the wing tip. Professor Hamilton studied his handheld GPS while Walter peered over his shoulder. A chilly alpine breeze blew against their heavy jackets, and Billy and his mother began bundling up. The north-westerly winds bent the brown, snow-speckled grass, signalling a renewal of winter's icy spell.

"I anticipate," the professor said, pointing down the eastern slope, "that our search should begin about one and one-third kilometres in that direction." He tucked the GPS under his arm and stretched a taupe beret over his wild hair. "Does that sound correct, William?"

"I think so." Billy fastened the next to last button on his lined Washington Redskins jacket. The bottom button was missing, lost in his backyard after he tackled his father during a Thanksgiving Day football romp. He pulled a baseball cap out of his jacket pocket and pressed it over his head. "Bonnie could tell you better than I could. I'm just not sure."

"Very well. It should take about fifteen minutes to get to our starting point, and we'll search for about thirty minutes. Then we'll meet you back here in, shall we say, one hour?"

Billy waited for his mum's okay. While listening to the conversation, she had squatted in her navy blue corduroys and red windbreaker to retie the laces of her hiking boots. At last, she nodded. Billy raised his index finger. "One hour sounds good."

"At least one of us will be here," his mother added. "The other might stay with our friend."

"The mystery dude?" Walter asked. "Will we get to meet him?"

Billy's mum smiled at Walter. "If you do, don't call him 'the mystery dude'."

The professor checked his GPS coordinates and pressed a button with his thumb. His black leather jacket wrinkled, and blowing tufts of thick white hair protruded from his cap. "Shall we go now, Walter? We must step lively."

Walter and the professor marched down the hillside, the professor relaying coordinate data in his British dialect. His voice faded as their forms shrank in the distance.

When they had travelled out of earshot, Billy turned to his mum. "I guess we'd better get going." He picked up a cardboard tube that held his drawing of Hambone. "Dad already knows we're here."

"You can sense that?"

Billy stepped toward a slope that descended at a right angle to the one the professor had chosen. "Sort of. He probably heard Merlin's prop anyway." They left the grassy area and entered a sparse forest. As they walked onward, the growth thickened. Leafless branches above made stick-figure shadows on the carpet of brown, crackling leaves. Bright sunshine poured through, enough to take the edge off the dry chill and to sharpen the earthy landscape.

"I guess we don't have to worry about any ambushes around here," Billy said. "There's no place to hide, and with all the crunching leaves you could hear someone coming from a mile away."

His mother stepped up to a stone and vaulted over. "No slayers lurking, that's for sure." She patted a side pocket on her windbreaker. "But if one does show up, he'll find out you're not the only one packing heat."

As they plunged deeper into the forest, the towering trees gathered into dense columns of massive, wooden sentinels. The two hikers manoeuvred through the twisting maze, shuffling through a familiar path and talking in soft whispers, giving each other reminders of where to turn as they approached rocks and trees they had marked on their previous visit. After winding their way through the heaviest wall of trees they had yet encountered, the oaken soldiers gave way, opening into a tiny glade surrounded by a wall of stone on one side and a fence of winter-stripped oaks on the other.

Billy pointed upward. "With that canopy over us, it looks sort of like the ceiling of a church. I didn't notice that last time."

A halo of thick branches stretched above to create an ornate ceiling of knobby fingers overarching the flat, leaf-strewn ground. The sanctuary's rock boundary towered almost to the tops of the trees and bent over to create an arch. Where the arch met the trees, the sun was squelched, and the shadows painted a black curtain on the mossy stone wall, the shadowy entrance to the cave.

Billy and his mother walked straight toward the granite blockade, passing through the dark curtain as though its shadow had reached out and swallowed them up.

"It's not as cold in here," Billy said, his voice resonating in the damp recesses of the yawning tunnel.

His mother pulled a flashlight from her belt clip and flicked it on. The stream of light shot out into the depths of the cave, and swirls of mist dashed through the beam in currents of newly awakened air.

"I hear him," Billy said. "He's here."

"I do, too."

A glow from somewhere in the midst of the cave brightened as they ventured farther in. A deep rumbling grew in their ears, like the churning of ocean breakers. They turned a corner and beheld the sight they had journeyed to find. Shrouded in a dome of sparkling light sat a massive winged dragon.

CHAPTER 4

EXCALIBUR

Walter stopped beside the professor. "Is this the spot?"

Professor Hamilton eyed the GPS. "I believe so, Walter. It matches the coordinates I calculated, but it's all based on a guess I made while in the air."

Walter kicked at a pile of dead leaves and surveyed the bare trees that stood like sleeping wooden skeletons on the gentle incline. "Okay. What now?"

The professor marched across the slope, his head turning from one side to the other. He sniffed the brisk air as though a scent might give him a clue. "We'll just have a look around."

"If the sword is here, won't it be covered by leaves?" Walter picked up a rotting maple leaf and tossed it into the wind.

"Good point. Be sure to shuffle your boots as you walk."

The two searchers dragged their feet across acres of uneven terrain, kicking up dozens of small logs, stubbing their toes on hidden rocks, and wetting their shoes in concealed snowmelt puddles. In spite of their logical, criss-cross search pattern through the layers of countless leaves, they knew they could be shuffling right past their quarry, perhaps missing the sword by mere inches.

After about twenty minutes the professor pulled his pocket watch from his trousers. "We're running short on time, Walter. We'll start heading back. Perhaps we can return with a metal detector on another day." He pointed up a rocky slope. "We'll hike over that rise and cover an area we haven't seen yet. It's a roundabout way of getting back to the plane, but we should make it on time."

"Suits me, Prof." Walter followed his teacher over the protruding crags, struggling at times to scale the larger boulders that the professor chose to climb rather than go around. His teacher's agility amazed him as the older man scrambled along with his lanky arms and legs.

The professor stopped near the top of the hill and placed his hand over his eyes to block out the glittering sun. Suddenly, his body stiffened. "Walter, did you see that?"

Walter shielded his eyes and stared in the same direction. "See what?"

"That glimmer." He pointed downslope toward a group of protruding rocks that interrupted the treescape about a hundred or so yards away. "Over there!"

Walter caught a glimpse of a bright reflection, like the sun's rays bouncing off a car mirror. "Yep. Got it marked."

The professor marched straight toward the rocks, and Walter bolted down the hill to lead the way. Just before reaching the boulders, the two stopped and stared. A gleaming sword quivered in the wind, its blade wedged deep within a large stone.

The professor gasped. "Excalibur!"

Bonnie blew on the car window's glass and wiped it clean with her sleeve. The view of her old home brought a stream of poetic memories. The mountains that bordered Missoula were always tall and majestic, but this time of year they had settled into their long winter's nap, undressing their trees in the usual way, shaking off leafy garments in the early autumn winds, waiting to be covered in frosty white raiment. There was little snow on the bare limbs today, though a thick blanket dressed the base of the trunks, like silver skirts on pencil-thin supermodels. The road from the airport to the university was clear and dry, but dark clouds loomed in the mountains. A sporadic ensemble of flakes danced across the hood as the Ford Explorer roared onto the campus road.

The hill that towered over the University of Montana carried a huge, block letter *M* prominently emblazoned in the frosted grass near the top. On warm, sunny days dozens of students and faculty members climbed the hill, negotiating the steep inclines on a path that switched back and forth across the hillside's broad face. Today, with snow threatening, the trails remained empty except for a dusting of frozen white and a lone bird flitting around the gigantic letter.

Throughout the trip, Bonnie answered only the most necessary questions. Since the private chartered flight had required no security check, her wings remained safely tucked away in her backpack, so she didn't have to dream up any ways to dodge a search. She and her father were the only passengers in

59

the small jet, and the lack of conversation made the flight seem interminable.

Now, after parking near the Skaggs Building, which housed the Department of Pharmaceutical Sciences, Bonnie knew she would have to break her silence. She had hoped to go straight to the hospital, but for some reason her father had to stop by his office.

"I have to pick up something here," he said as he got out of the Explorer. "And there's someone I want you to meet. She'll be travelling with us."

Bonnie pulled her coat on over her backpack and climbed out, her curiosity piqued by her father's boyish smile. She followed him toward his office across a snow-patched, grassy field on a narrow footpath, worn to the dirt over the years by hundreds of tromping feet.

They rounded the corner of the building, past two enormous white panels that looked like oversized garage doors, but Bonnie didn't see any way they could open. The boxy structure loomed over her, its bricks showing off patterns of red, black, and grey, a vivid contrast to the tiny flecks of white falling from the darkening sky. Square, borderless windows hid the interior with dark, reflective glass, making it look like a secret headquarters for a government agency or a prison for dangerous spies. With gloomy grey clouds silently hovering, the building seemed morose and lonely, not the exciting institution of higher learning she knew it to be.

After taking an elevator to the third floor, they crossed the carpeted hall to the entrance of an office suite numbered 340, not the same workplace Bonnie remembered. Her dad's smaller, cramped office used to be on another floor. This suite held the office of the dean, and a nameplate carried her father's name.

"When did you get the promotion?" she asked.

Her father turned the knob and pushed the door open. "A few months ago. The president likes my work."

A young female greeted them from behind the waist-high receptionist's desk. "Good afternoon, Dr Conner." With a big smile she extended her hand over the desk. "And you must be Bonnie. I'm Ashley Stalworth. Pleased to meet you. Your father's told me all about you."

Bonnie took her hand and shook it firmly, trying to return her genuine smile. "Hi, Ashley." Bonnie tried to read the girl. She looked too young to be a college student, maybe seventeen at the most.

"Ashley is supposed to be a junior in high school," Bonnie's father explained, "but the school's science department couldn't challenge her, so they sent her here. She's a true genius, and she's helping me with my research."

Ashley put her hands behind her back and blushed, and Bonnie caught her glancing at the lump under her coat, her hidden backpack. *He told Ashley all about me? I hope not everything!*

Bonnie's father picked up a briefcase from the floor in front of the desk. "Do you have everything packed?"

Ashley held up a large wooden case with squared corners. "The latest results are in your briefcase, and the samples are in here."

"Then let's hit the road."

Bonnie's mind raced with questions. What was the research? How had her father become so familiar with a high school girl? But the most important question burst through her thoughts and came out verbally. "Aren't we going to the hospital to see my mother?"

Her father hurried out the door. "No. I'll explain on the way."

61

Ashley locked the office door, using a set of keys that hung from her belt loop. Bonnie's father had already punched the elevator call button and now stood inside the waiting car. Ashley stepped hurriedly away, lugging the suitcase and holding out her free hand, gesturing for Bonnie to join her.

For some reason, Bonnie wanted to grasp this friendly girl's hand, a little sister kind of feeling she had never had before, but she declined with a brief nod and a smile. There were too many weird things going on, too many unanswered questions to allow herself such familiarity.

Ashley didn't seem to mind Bonnie's refusal. She just marched into the elevator, and Bonnie followed. The slow car lowered the silent trio back to the first floor, and they clopped along the shiny terrazzo floor toward the exit doors. Once outside, Ashley dutifully strode behind her professor across the field to the parking lot.

Bonnie stayed close, eyeing every detail through the thickening snow flurries. Ashley wore designer jeans, modestly cut, fairly loose fitting and riding high on her slender waist. With her coat slung over her shoulder, her long-sleeved blouse was exposed, feminine but not fancy, tucked in and accentuating her fit body. She was obviously athletic, with toned muscles tightening the sleeve on the arm that lugged the heavy case. The stiffening breeze threw its weight against their bodies, blowing Ashley's shoulder-length brown hair around her face.

Bonnie shivered. *She must have logs burning in her belly. I'm freezing with a coat on!*

When they arrived at the Explorer, Ashley set her case down and opened the front passenger door for Bonnie.

Bonnie tapped her knuckles on the back window. "Why don't we sit together?"

Ashley smiled. "Great! We have a long drive ahead of us. Maybe we can get to know each other."

Bonnie pulled off her coat and slid into the back. By the time she was seated, her father had already started the motor. "A long drive?" she repeated. "What's going on?"

Her father backed the SUV out of the parking space. "We're not going to the hospital. We're going to a lab that I built up near Flathead Lake, a couple of hours away. Because of your mother's deteriorating condition, the doctors gave up hope. I was advised to authorize the removal of her feeding tube in order to let her die. I couldn't do that, of course. There's hardly any death more cruel than starvation. So, I had your mother moved to my lab quite some time ago, and I've been taking care of her myself."

"Some time ago? But what about the picture? I thought you took that yesterday."

"Actually, I took it a few weeks after you left Montana. I faked the date to get you to come home. If I had explained everything, I would have had to reveal some secrets I wasn't ready to reveal."

Bonnie scowled, a feeling of dread creeping along her skin like a thousand hairy bugs. "You mean, you lied?"

Her father stared straight ahead, waiting for a traffic light to change. He paused, as if trying to think of a good answer. Bonnie could hardly stand the delay. For a moment she watched her father's furrowed brow in the rear-view mirror, but the sight of what looked like another lie brewing made her feel nauseated. She turned her head to watch the worsening weather. Large, wet flakes fell all around, sticking easily to the grass, but melting as they tumbled to the warmer road surface. When the light changed, her dad cleared his throat. "A lie is

63

sometimes necessary to save a life, Bonnie. And that's what I'm trying to do, save your mother's life. When we get to the lab, I'll explain everything, and I think you will be very pleased at what you see."

Bonnie dug her fingers into the armrest. *Why did he lie? Sure, lying to save a life is one thing, but lying to your own daughter to send her back to her nightmares is another!* She rubbed her hand up and down her sleeve. The thought of a laboratory gave her the shivers – needles puncturing her skin over and over again, each one drawing yet another tube of blood. Her arm itched and her head pounded, but she would face a ten-foot-long needle and give a whole gallon of blood if it meant helping her mother.

Now that she was back in Montana, the strange haunting call grew louder. It had to be her mother calling; it had to be. And now she was probably only a couple of hours away from seeing her again, face to face.

Professor, it looks like it's stuck right in the stone!"

"Indeed, it is, Walter." The professor walked all around the head-high boulder, rubbing his gloved fingers along its granite-like faces. "Extraordinary! It sliced the rock like it was a rotting mushroom, and there's not a hint of rust on the blade even after weeks of exposure!"

"And the markings look like the ones on your replica. It's Excalibur, all right!" Walter climbed up on the boulder and, straightening up his athletic body, grabbed the hilt. "Hey, Professor! Want to see if I'm the rightful king of England?"

"Pull all you wish, Walter. The legends speak of a sword in a stone, though most say it was not Excalibur. I expect, however, that we're seeing history repeat itself, and Excalibur may show us the rightful heir."

At first Walter tugged lightly on the sword, then with all his might. When it didn't budge, he gave up, gasping for breath. "I guess . . . I guess I don't qualify."

The professor waved his hand for Walter to come down. "I have no doubt that you have strength, Walter, but an heir to the throne you are not."

"Then the sword's stuck there? How are we going to get it out?"

"I have a theory, but—" A ringing cell phone interrupted his explanation. The professor reached for the phone on his hip. "Charles Hamilton speaking. . . . Yes, Carl. I'm with your son on a mountain. We're still in West Virginia. . . . No, of course not. You may call me anytime. . . . Yes, that is important news. I'm not sure what it means for our journey, but we will soon find out. I will try to call you tonight to let you know our progress. If you discover anything further, please let us know right away." He pressed a button on the phone and held it at his side.

"What's up, Prof?"

The professor returned the phone to his belt, his hands moving slowly as he snapped it in place. "Your father got through to his sources. They found a death certificate for Miss Silver's mother."

"Wow! So Bonnie's mother really is dead!"

"I'm afraid so, Walter. Although it pains me to say it, we must leave the sword behind for now. We should hurry back to the airplane to meet the others. I think this news corroborates my earlier fears; Miss Silver is in serious trouble."

The dragon peered at his visitors, his red-centred eyes wide open and gleaming. As Billy and his mother crept closer, the massive beast rose to his feet and stretched, scattering the dome of light into thousands of sparkling glitters rolling across the floor, fizzling and fading away. For a moment, darkness filled the cave, but a flash of streaming fire hurtled from the dragon and splashed onto one of the walls, the flames igniting the rag-covered top of a torch that hung in a metal stand. The old-fashioned lantern held none of the beauty of the dragon's natural illumination, but it brightened the cave.

The dragon had been resting in his regeneracy dome, a term Billy's father had recently explained to him as though he were quoting from a textbook. "Encircled and undergirded by various gems and polished stones, a dragon radiates light from his luminescent scales. As the light bounces off the smooth facets of his bed, the rays dance with excitement, gaining more power during the light's ionic agitation. While the dragon sleeps, he absorbs the recharged radiance, and the give-and-take respiration creates a dome of light around his body, giving him the sustenance that all dragons need, photo-energy that surges through his body like blood through a human's."

With this vital refreshment, the dragon now appeared vigorous and well rested. His two enormous outstretched wings flapped, shifting him toward them, and his regal face seemed to smile.

Billy's mother inched forward. "Jared, it's so good to see you again." She reached out and clumsily touched his closest flank.

"Marilyn, dearest one," the dragon replied, "I am enraptured to see you again. But, please, call me Clefspeare, for I am no longer a man. Jared, your husband, has died."

Billy's mum lowered her eyes and sniffed, and she covered her mouth with her fist. Billy stepped forward, shuffling his boots in the loose dirt. "Uh, Dad."

The dragon swung his neck around and drew his head near, his hot breath flowing across Billy's hair. "I will allow you to call me 'Dad'," Clefspeare replied, "though I prefer my dragon name. You need to reckon with the fact that your true father is gone. Jared's son lives on, though Jared is no more."

Tears welled in Billy's eyes. He clenched his teeth and balled his hand into a fist. His mission was too important; he had to keep his composure. "We have some important news, and we need your advice."

"I will help if I can."

Billy told Bonnie's story in as much detail as he thought necessary. He also explained the presence of the professor and Walter on the mountain and their desire to know what was going on.

"So . . . Dad. What do you think we should do? Should we let the professor and Walter in on everything?"

Clefspeare heaved a deep sigh. Sparks flew from his nostrils, settling on the cave floor and dying out on the cold ground. "It was wise and noble of you to ask my permission," he finally replied. "While you are away retrieving your friends, I shall consider what I will and what I will not tell. You may bring them to me, but do not prepare them. I know Walter, but I have never met your professor. How a person reacts to a shocking discovery helps me evaluate his character."

Billy didn't understand what Clefspeare meant, but he was willing to do whatever it took to get the ball rolling. "C'mon Mum! Let's go get them!"

"No," the dragon said, his gentle but firm command echoing throughout the cave. He cast his gaze on Billy's mother. "Let your son fetch his friends. We need this time to talk." She nodded, her head still down.

Billy didn't have time to worry about her; she was in good hands . . . *Or wings, I guess.* Clutching the flashlight, he hustled out of the cave and retraced his steps to the plane. He knew he might be early, so he waited patiently, bouncing on his toes to

67

keep warm, not caring that the cold breeze bit his tightening cheeks. After a few minutes the professor and Walter made their way up the slope, huffing as they strode up the steep incline.

"It's okay," Billy called. "My friend said you can come and talk to him."

The professor halted and let out a few puffs. "Very good." He took in another breath and seemed back to normal. "I also have two news items for you. We found the sword, and it is Excalibur."

"That's awesome! Where is it?"

Walter posed as though he were trying to pull the sword out again. "It's stuck in a rock. Caught like a twenty dollar bill in a politician's hand."

"And you can't get it out?"

Walter shook his head. "Not a chance, unless you know someone who's kin to a king."

Billy squinted at his friend. "Kin to a king? What're you talking about?"

"We shall address that issue later," the professor said. "The other news item is more pressing. Walter's father called. It seems that Miss Silver's mother really is dead. They were able to find a certificate of demise just a short time ago."

A boiling sensation festered in Billy's stomach, and icy chills spread across his skin. His teeth chattered as he stalked down the slope. "Come on," he called with a wave of his hand. "Let's get this show on the road!"

Walter followed Billy, but the professor paused. "Shall I retrieve Merlin's diary from the airplane? Will your friend know anything about it?"

"He might," Billy called back. "It's worth a try."

Professor Hamilton climbed the slope back to the airplane and returned with the book tucked under his arm, and the three marched down the slope. After covering this route so recently, Billy was able to hustle across the leafy terrain without any delays.

When they arrived at the cave, Billy pointed out the shadowy entrance. "It's right here where the stone turns dark."

"A cave?!" Walter exclaimed. "Who's your friend? Fred Flintstone?"

"This is not the time for jesting, Walter," the professor chided. "I believe we are just beginning to probe a series of mind-bending mysteries, and I can feel the excitement of adventure racing through my bones. Let us conduct ourselves as men now and not as boys. I perceive that we shall need all of our cunning and strength." He pulled off his beret and held it in both hands. "Lead on, William."

With the professor and Walter close behind, Billy entered the tunnel, a cold shiver running up his back. This wasn't a game; it was life and death. A bad decision could keep them from finding Bonnie before it was too late.

They rounded the corner. The moment of truth had arrived. The great secret would be out – his dragon nature revealed. How would the professor take it? Would Walter understand?

Billy's legs shook as he entered the inner chamber. The light of the torch illuminated his fellow travellers' faces, the dancing flame reflecting in their narrowing pupils. The professor's mouth gaped, but Walter stood calmly, a huge smile growing on his face.

The dragon's pointed ears perked up and rotated in all directions as though they were satellite dishes searching for a distant signal. He bowed low, a formal, stately bow of submission. After clearing his throat to speak, Clefspeare trembled as though shaken by awestruck wonder.

"Master Merlin. You have returned at last!"

69

CHAPTER 5

THROUGH THE VEIL

The drive to Flathead Lake cut through a long, mountain-bordered valley. Dark clouds hovered over the peaks to the right, while bursts of dancing flurries pelted the windshield. The gorgeous scenery and friendly conversation with Ashley drew Bonnie into a pleasant state of distraction. Her worries about her mother faded to a mere nagging feeling in the back of her mind. "So what do your parents think about your research projects?" Bonnie asked. "Do they mind you being gone a lot?"

Ashley hesitated, and her shoulders sank with her lowering voice. "My parents died when I was a toddler."

A lump grew in Bonnie's throat. "Oh . . . I'm so sorry." She reached out her hand, and Ashley took it, intertwining her fingers with Bonnie's and placing it on her lap. Bonnie was a bit startled by Ashley's affection, but it felt good, the melancholy touch of a sad friend. Bonnie swallowed the lump and caressed Ashley's hand with her thumb. "Do you mind telling me how it happened?"

Ashley tightened her chin and shook her head while staring at the friendly clasp of hands in her lap. "I'd tell you if I knew." She turned to Bonnie, and her smile slowly re-emerged. "You see, my grandfather adopted me. He's the only father I can remember. I even call him 'Daddy'. He's a widower, so all we have is each other." She returned her gaze to her lap and sighed. "I must have asked him a hundred times what happened, but he kept telling me it was too awful to talk about. I looked through old newspapers at the library, but I couldn't find anything about accidents or fires, or anyone who knew the story, so I finally decided to try to forget about it."

Bonnie felt her own stories welling up, the loss of her mother and how she suspected her father of contributing to her death. She whispered, "Do you remember your parents at all?"

Ashley freed her hand and pushed back her hair. "Sometimes I think I remember them, images now and then, but it's not much, so I can't say I miss them." Ashley's smile made a complete comeback, and a refreshed glow shone in her eyes. "Daddy's been the best father any girl could ask for. He's gentle and sweet, and he loves to sit and talk about anything that's on my mind, except, of course, my parents."

Bonnie smiled with Ashley but still kept her voice low. "He sounds wonderful! Do you have to spend much time away from him when you do your research?"

"No. He's the main reason I'm involved in the project. When I started, he was getting old and feeble, so I made sure he stayed where I could be with him if he needed me. We both live in the lab complex now, so I get to see him every night."

Bonnie drew her fingers up to her chin and raised her voice. "He lives in the lab? Whoa! This lab is a motel, too? When are you going to tell me what's going on there?"

Ashley gave her a coy smile and leaned back in her seat. "You'll find out soon."

Ashley's refusal to explain brought Bonnie's nagging thoughts to the forefront again. Not knowing what was going on or where they were heading was driving her crazy! She sighed and settled back in her seat, letting the awesome landscape consume her thoughts. To her left Flathead Lake stretched out for miles and miles, a magnificent blue expanse of silky smooth water, a tree-lined mirror for the heavens. She vaguely remembered riding on a boat there once when she was little, but after her wings started growing, she didn't get to go again, to the lake or to very many other public places.

To her right, a series of dirt and gravel driveways led to precarious heights in the foothills and mountains, each one a mystery. Who lived at the ends of those paths? Were they lonely way up there where the snow-filled clouds shrouded their homes? Did they store up months of supplies and hibernate for the winter, ready to emerge when the sunny days of spring melted their fortresses of ice?

Images of hiking in snow-covered forests seeped into Bonnie's mind, her short legs scampering over deep drifts and a strong hand holding her up from one side. That was a long time ago . . . back when she looked normal.

With haunting memories and mysteries all around, Bonnie felt trapped, riding in a vehicle driven by a man who might really be a monster. Her stomach churned like a bubbling vat of curdled milk. She was so far from home, even the Montana home she used to know. And now—

"I . . . I think I'm getting sick," she announced.

Her father tightened his grip on the steering wheel and slowed down. "Do we have to pull over now, or can you last till we get there? It's less than thirty minutes."

Bonnie pointed at a store up ahead, a Conoco station with a homemade sign on the front – BARBARA'S MARKET. "Can we stop there? I think I'd better run to the bathroom."

"Okay. I'll go ahead and gas up while we're here. Do you need any money for anything?"

"No." Bonnie patted her jeans pocket. "I still have what you gave me at the airport."

With the snow falling in thicker streams, Ashley and Bonnie hurried toward the shop, not bothering to pull on their coats for the short jaunt. The fresh breeze and quick march had already relieved Bonnie's nausea, and her brain kicked into gear. All these delays in seeing her mother weren't making any sense. She had to let someone know where she was and how to find her.

After she brushed the lingering flakes from her shoulders, Bonnie surveyed the colourful assortment of convenience grocery items, tourist souvenirs, and grab-and-go fast foods, her eyes darting around as she stepped toward the restroom in the back of the store. She spied a carousel of postcards on her right, pausing to quickly scan the bank of cards nearest her.

Ashley grasped the card rack with one hand. "I thought you were sick."

"Uh, I am. I mean . . . I was." Bonnie pushed her thumbs behind her backpack straps and hitched it higher. "I'm feeling better. I guess I just needed to move around. I think if I wash my face I'll be fine."

"Okay. I'm getting a drink. Want anything?"

Bonnie shook her head. "I'm fine. Thanks." When Ashley turned around, Bonnie grabbed a postcard and stuffed it into her back pocket before heading to the restroom. Once inside, she splashed cold water on her face and dried off with a paper towel. She then pulled the postcard from her pocket and a pen from her backpack. One side of the card had a photo of Flathead Lake, and the other side carried the name of the store imprinted near the bottom. It was perfect. She sat down, wrote a note, and addressed the card.

With the postcard still in hand, she slowly opened the restroom door, but it flew open on its own, and a friendly faced elderly lady stood in front of her. Bonnie jumped back, holding her hand over her heart and pressing the postcard against her shirt.

"I'm sorry, dear," the lady said. "I didn't mean to frighten you."

Bonnie took a deep breath to quiet her pounding heart. "Oh . . . that's okay. I thought you were someone else."

The lady stepped into the restroom and gestured toward the card in Bonnie's hand. "Careful. You don't want to bend that pretty card." She turned on the water and picked up a bar of soap. "Is it for friends back home?"

"Uh . . . yes. It's for close friends. I'm visiting from West Virginia."

The lady gave her a knowing nod, her short grey hair bobbing around her perky eyes. "We get lots of folks from the East. Not as many this time of year, but we do get them."

"We? Do you live around here?"

"For sixty-five years," she replied with a proud smile. "I run this store."

Bonnie fished in her left front pocket and withdrew a wrinkled five dollar bill. "Please, ma'am, I'm in a big hurry." She smoothed out the bill and extended it toward the lady, trying to keep her hand from shaking. "Will this cover the cost of the card and postage, and would you mail it for me? I need it to get there as soon as possible."

The lady looked at her hand for a moment and then caught it in her own, closing Bonnie's fingers around her money. She leaned over and whispered. "Is everything all right? Are you in trouble?"

The lady's fingers felt warm, and Bonnie let her hand relax in her tender grip. "I'm okay. I'm with my father, but I haven't seen him in a long time. I'm just . . . kind of nervous."

The lady nodded slowly. "Oh. . . . Nervous. . . . I see."

Bonnie drew back and handed the card to her. She then presented the five dollar bill again, this time without shaking.

The lady laughed and waved her hand. "Oh, don't worry about it. I'll be glad to mail it for you." She eyed Bonnie carefully once more. "I'll send it the fastest way possible."

"That's awesome! I can't thank you enough!"

"Just tell your friends back home to come out for a visit."

Bonnie headed for the exit and turned back. "That card might just do the trick."

Professor Hamilton straightened up, his body as stiff as a flagpole and his eyes glued to the amazing, giant creature bowing before him. The professor had said he expected strange events, but seeing a real dragon, and a prostrate one, no less, obviously caught him off guard. He clasped his hands together and cleared his throat. "Merlin? Why do you call me Merlin?"

The dragon peered through his partially closed eyes. "Master, I have not seen your face in over a thousand years, but your image was etched into my mind as surely as the commandments were chiselled into tablets of stone by the finger of God. I remain your humble servant, Clefspeare."

"Clearly this is a case of mistaken identity, Mr Clefspeare. My name is Charles Hamilton. I am a homeschool teacher, former professor at Oxford University, and specialist in Arthurian history and legends. Although I am very familiar with the history and myths surrounding Merlin, I assure you that I am not he."

Clefspeare rose to his former sitting position and stretched out his neck. "Remarkable!" the dragon kept repeating as he moved his head to take in the teacher's image from various angles. "Then it has happened! It must have happened!"

The professor kept his body stiff, but he moved his eyes to follow the dragon's glowing face as it glided all around. "Sir, having a dragon such as yourself examining me with such fervour is quite unnerving. I shall be glad to answer whatever questions you wish to ask, but I must request that you proceed before I leap right out of my shoes."

Billy grinned and slapped his hand over his mouth. "Yeah, Dad," he said, speaking between his fingers. "What's up?" He glanced over at Walter, and his friend's composure surprised him. He was smiling, almost laughing, like he was enjoying a funny movie.

Professor Hamilton turned his head toward Billy, squinted, and mouthed, "Dad?"

"Yes," Clefspeare said. "I am Billy's father, in a manner of speaking. Forgive me for my emotional outburst. I was a human for over a dozen centuries, and seeing your face brought a flood of fond memories from days long ago. Though you did not know this before today, you are the image of Merlin, the great prophet, and, not only that, you carry his journal. The leather cover bears his scent to this day. But we will discuss your resemblance and how you came by the book in a moment. We have urgent business in Montana."

The professor set the book gently on the ground and pulled a copy of the hospital photo from his coat's inner pocket. "Yes, the matter of Bonnie Silver." He displayed the photo for Clefspeare. "I assume that William has apprised you of all that he knows, but there have been new developments. Walter's father has discovered a death certificate for Bonnie's mother, so her father's pretext was false. This makes his character that much more doubtful, even sinister, I would say."

Clefspeare gazed at the photo for several seconds before responding. "You have spoken well; these developments are distressing. In order for me to help you, however, it is imperative that you understand my history. Being a man of sound intellect and training, I assume you want to know everything about how a dragon could be Billy's father."

"Yes, and any extraneous details that might help me combine your knowledge with my own to solve other puzzles we have unearthed."

"Such as?"

The professor returned the photo to its place and retrieved Merlin's diary from the ground. "Such as this book. Its mystery is great. I have pondered its meagre contents for hours, yet I have solved very little. We have also found Excalibur, but we don't yet have it in our possession. It's imbedded in a stone quite nearby, and I'm afraid King Arthur is no longer available to extract it."

"I will help you understand the book soon enough," Clefspeare replied. "Perhaps when I tell my story, you will figure it out for yourself as well as the mystery of Excalibur's power. I advise all of you to have a seat. It is a long tale, and although Bonnie's fate depends on swift action, I assure you that understanding this story will help you in rescuing her."

The dragon waited for his audience to sit comfortably, and he raised his head high. First, with a puff of dense smoke, he blew out the torch, and blackness descended on the cave. Then, with a soothing, hypnotic tone, he spoke in a quiet voice, and the words reverberated in gentle echoes. "Do not be distracted by thoughts of the day or your cares for loved ones. Cast your eyes deep into the darkness and see the images of antiquity. Let your thoughts walk through the winding cave; let your minds wander into the past.

"I am Clefspeare, your guide into forgotten days, the age of knights and kings. Follow my light and see the ghosts of the past come to life before your eyes." The dragon blew a ferocious stream of white-hot flame against the cave wall, filling the entire cavern with intense heat and light. Then, in a second, the blaze disappeared. Yet the wall held a glowing imprint of the flame's violent massage. Fiery characters emerged, first a man wearing a crown and then a man and a woman in front of him, each on bended knee. They seemed to move, animated somehow by the crackling, pulsating cinders. As his listeners watched in awestruck silence, Clefspeare gave the characters voice.

"Clefspeare, I dub you Jared, son of Arthur." The king tapped the bowing man's shoulder lightly with a gleaming sword. "By this decree, I name you my son, though truly you are closer than any of my natural offspring." He turned and tapped the lady's shoulder, touching her long flowing blonde hair that draped her sparkling white gown. "And you, dear Hartanna, I dub Irene, for your very presence brings peace to my soul. You are now my daughter, a treasured princess, who I hope will always find peace within the walls of my palace."

King Arthur lifted Excalibur from Irene's shoulder and then handed the blade to an old man who stood uneasily at his right side. The sword maintained its faint white glow, strong enough to illuminate the wrinkled hands of the older man, yet it seemed no more than the brightest candle among the dozens that lined the inner court of the king's palace. When the older man slid the sword into its sheath, the ornate scabbard swallowed the glow, allowing the candlelight to spread throughout the room.

The two men stood on a raised platform, not as high as a stage, but high enough to display the honour and authority of anyone who would sit on the throne at its centre. Arthur lifted a scroll that had rested on a table at his side. "For your protection, I have entered your names as Reginald Bannister and Tabitha Silver in the official records as my adopted son and daughter. Hide your identities well, for if your enemies discover them, you will be chased by bloodthirsty hounds for centuries to come. I suggest choosing different surnames for yourselves for the time being, though you may return to Bannister and Silver to protect your inheritance when a safer time comes."

Jared lifted his eyes toward the king and slowly stood up. "Sire, I humbly accept your gracious bestowal of your good name. May I always bring the name of Arthur honour and a good heritage."

Irene stood at Jared's side. "I, too, am honoured, Your Majesty." She rubbed her hand across her bare forearm. Her skin seemed to radiate silvery white. "Having shorn my scales, and with them the dignity of a dragoness, I feel clothed once again with the integrity, nobility, and heritage that your deeds have inspired. May I wear this livery well."

King Arthur's solemn face broke into a proud, fatherly smile. "Well spoken, my friends. I trust that I will be able to live up to my duty and keep you safe in your new skin. Have the other dragons taken the necessary steps to secure their safety?"

Jared glanced at Irene and then back at the king. "The ladies have taken new names and blended into life in the nearby villages, as you instructed. We do not know, however, what has become of Irene's brother, Valcor."

The king's brow lifted. "The other male dragon?"

"Yes. With Gartrand's death, he and I are the only remaining males. He disappeared soon after our transformation."

Arthur stroked his short, greying beard. "Hmmm. Perhaps his secrecy is for the best."

Irene nodded. "That is what we thought. Devin will never be able to learn his whereabouts from us, even through torture."

"Very true. And speaking of Devin, now that our ceremony is complete, we must make haste." He turned to the man at his side. "Merlin, is there any new word?"

The older man raised a long staff and set its end on the platform floor. He placed Excalibur on his chair and cleared his throat. "No, Sire. My counsel stands. Devin's traitorous band could attack at any moment. I have arranged for your knights to secretly assemble at Blood Hollow, so I suggest that you leave through your escape route at once to convene with them. Gawain will meet you at the tunnel exit and escort you to the other knights."

Arthur strapped on his armour and weapons, then took his sword from Merlin's seat.

Merlin grabbed Arthur's wrist. "But you must leave Excalibur."

Arthur pulled away from the prophet's grip. He lifted Excalibur, extending his arms to display the sheathed sword in his palms. "Go into battle without the sword?" He strapped the scabbard to the belt around his waist. "I should say not!"

Merlin held out his hands. "I have more need of it. Devin's tiny army is counting on surprise to win. When you arrive, your forces will crush him like a shoe on a cockroach. Should you come late, Excalibur is my only hope for survival."

Arthur placed his hand on Excalibur's hilt and hesitated, while outside the door the distant sound of clanking steps shattered the evening's quiet meeting.

"There is no more time," Merlin urged, his hands shaking. "Trust me! Leave Excalibur and fly to Blood Hollow. Gawain will have a sword for you."

Arthur unfastened the sword from his belt, scabbard and all, and handed it to Merlin. He then scrambled to a door at the corner of a nearby wall and shut it behind him. The secret door disappeared from sight when its edge met the perfectly matched wall.

Jared hurriedly put his arms through the sleeves of a purple robe, not Arthur's formal council robe, but one that the king often wore during evening meetings. "Should I put on the crown?"

Merlin helped him straighten out the sleeves. "No. Your hair is a close enough match, so the robe should be sufficient. Just keep your back to the door. I expect Devin to enter at any moment." He turned to Irene. "You may face the door, kneeling before our 'king'. Can you make yourself cry?"

Irene shook her head. "Not without provocation. I have not yet learned all the ways of women."

"Then try to look sad, as though entreating the king for someone's life."

Within seconds a servant came to the inner doorway of the court. "Sir Devin to see His Majesty."

Merlin nodded to Jared, who spun around toward the back of the room. Irene dropped to her knees and extended her folded hands toward him, twisting her face in counterfeit pain. Merlin stepped to the entryway to intercept the quickly marching Devin. "His Majesty has a guest, Sir Devin. May I give him a message for you?"

82

Devin looked over Merlin's shoulder at Irene and squinted for a few seconds. "Is the lady ill? She seems to be having intestinal distress."

"Not sickness; her entreaty is a private matter. We will be in prayer for her for the next half hour, and then I shall escort His Majesty to his chamber if he wishes to go."

Merlin noted a hint of a smile in Devin's otherwise stoic expression. Devin bowed and spoke in his most formal and reverent voice. "Please give His Majesty my blessings, and I will spend the entire half hour on my knees as well." Devin gave Merlin a polite nod. "Good evening to you, Master Merlin." The knight left the court with the same quick march that brought him in.

When the door closed Jared turned around. "Do you think it worked?"

"I think so. A man who is not trustworthy rarely trusts anyone, yet, I believe that our ruse has convinced him that King Arthur is in this room."

Irene stood and approached Merlin. "Then how soon will he attack?"

"He believes he has a half hour, so I would guess we have only half again of that before he strikes." Merlin bent down and knelt on the platform, and Jared and Irene joined him. "We should pray, as I told Devin we would, but not for the lady's entreaty, rather for the king's quick return with his men."

After a few moments of silence, Merlin stood and pulled Excalibur from its sheath. The sword blazed, and Jared jumped to his feet, his heart pounding at the sight of its brilliant, unearthly glow. Irene's eyes widened to take in the beauty. It shone much more brightly than when its gentle flat side dubbed them Arthur's adopted heirs. Now it looked ready to sever the heads of a thousand hardened soldiers.

Merlin waved the blade slowly, and a blinding beam of light shot from its tip and burned a hole through the ceiling. "It will cut boulders and oaks for any warrior that wields it," he said, "but its greatest power is reserved for the hands of the holy."

Merlin tilted his head upward as though talking to someone suspended in the air. "I am now certain that the king will not arrive in time. I will have to use Excalibur to extinguish the enemy, and in the process, I will conduct my greatest experiment."

"Experiment?" Jared asked.

Merlin cast his gaze on Jared and Irene. "Excalibur does not merely cut," he continued, "it transforms. It changes matter into light energy; it transluminates. If I wield it to kill, its radiance will shatter a man's bones into shards of flashing luminescence, and his remains will be absorbed into a candle's breath or crushed by the ignorance of a dark shadow. And his soul? If it is not somehow trapped on the earth, it will be sent straight to the judgment seat of God."

Jared stared, enraptured by the old man's explanation, while Irene stood equally transfixed, frozen in fear on the cold stone floor.

"Jared, you and Irene must enter the tunnel door for safety. When Excalibur's power fills the room, all who remain will be transluminated, perhaps even you, though you now wear the king's name. Since I bear the sword, I think I will not die, but since I am not of Arthur's lineage, I am still vulnerable. I believe I will be changed."

"Changed?" Irene asked. "Changed into what?"

"As with the rest, my body will likely become light energy, though I think I will survive. Whether I will live on in spirit or not, I cannot say. Perhaps I will come back in another form, as another person, restored to physical matter."

"Reincarnation?" Jared asked. "As the heretics teach? May heaven forbid!"

"Not at all like reincarnation, Jared, but I am impressed. You have learned your theology well in such a short time, though you may need to learn to express it with a bit more grace. I'm hoping my adventure will be as Jesus taught when speaking of John the Baptist, 'et si vultis recipere ipse est Helias qui venturus est'."

"I . . . I do not understand."

"Neither did his disciples, even when it was spoken in their own tongue, for they did not have ears to hear. You, on the other hand, have not yet learned Latin. It means, 'And if you care to accept it, he himself is Elijah, who was to come.'" Merlin picked up an old book that rested next to his chair and showed Jared and Irene the back of the title page. "Can you read this?"

They looked over Merlin's shoulder. "Yes," Jared said, "The words are quite clear."

Irene nodded her agreement. "I do not understand the riddle I see, but I am able to read the text."

Merlin turned the page. "And now?"

Jared smiled at Merlin. "Is this some kind of jest, Master? The page is blank."

Merlin put one hand over Jared's eyes. "It is as though a veil is covering your eyes." He then lifted his hand and waved it over the page. "And now, Jared, son of Arthur, can you read it?"

Jared stared at the book's crisp, clean page, and this time dark script appeared, beautiful handwriting, phrases cut into poetic lines. For some reason, however, he could not bring them completely into focus. "I see the writing, but it seems to float, as though I am seeing it through a thick dark glass. I cannot read it."

"Before this day is over," Merlin said, "the words on this page will become clear." He placed the book into Jared's hands and picked up Excalibur. "This is my perpetual diary. Guard it with your life. In some ways it is more dangerous than the great sword, but only a wise man will glean from its counsel. To understand its wisdom requires the brightest of lights and the greatest of the abiding gifts."

They heard the sudden clanking of soldiers' weapons and marching footsteps. Merlin pushed Jared and Irene toward the corner door. "Go! Go!"

They hurried to obey. Jared knew he had no place in this matter. Having become a human only a few weeks before, he understood neither his standing nor his responsibility in the domain of men. Holding the treasured diary in his arms and seeing Irene to a safe place in the low hallway, he shut the door almost completely. He left a crack, just enough to watch the action, but not enough, he hoped, to allow Excalibur's lethal radiance into the secret chamber.

Two armed men broke down the door and stretched loaded bowstrings back to their ears. Merlin stood tall, holding the great sword in both hands, its point straight up. The men stopped, mesmerized by the brilliant glow, while six others poured through the door, each halting as they beheld the sword.

Jared searched through the faces but couldn't locate Devin. Would he come later to try to assume the throne? *The slimy worm! Letting his lackeys take the brunt while he prances on daisies out in the garden!*

When a band of twelve or so had arrived, Merlin waved the sword in a great circle. The treacherous soldiers seemed rooted to the stone floor, their legs trembling like saplings in a storm's fury. A single beam from Excalibur's tip multiplied into hundreds, flashing in all directions until they joined together into a massive tidal wave of light.

The luminescent surge washed through the court, and particles of sparkling light buzzed through the traitors like starving locusts. Their bodies melted away, and only swirls of twinkling effervescence remained, shields and armour clattering to the floor to mark where men had once stood.

Just before Excalibur's beam flashed into his corner, Jared slammed the door shut. He could almost feel the rush of light crash against his escape hatch. He hoped its probing fingers would find no cracks, nowhere to seep through to grab another victim.

Jared pressed his hands against his body – his solid, intact body. Irene sat against the opposite wall, holding her arms around her knees. A single, wall-mounted lantern reflected in her wide eyes. Jared pressed his ear against the thick door but could hear nothing.

He waited, nervous and uncertain. The light had flashed around the room as if driven by wrath – possessing an intellect, a mind of fury. Never before had he felt such terror. As a dragon he had feared nothing, but now, without scales or lethal breath, he was helpless, trained only in the rudiments of combat.

Still carrying the book, he slowly pushed the door open, mentally shushing its barely audible squeaks. With one eye he peeked into the courtroom, trying to adjust to its candlelight. Gradually, the shadows dispelled. The room was barren; only dark lumps of armour lay scattered over the white stone floor, like black toadstools polluting a pristine field.

Jared gestured toward the wall lantern and whispered to Irene. "You had better put out that light so you will stay hidden."

Irene nodded and stood to blow out the flame.

"Will you be frightened?"

"I was a dragon," she replied, a sad smile gracing her lips. "I am accustomed to dark places."

Jared stepped out into the metallic debris. He walked to the throne's platform and placed the diary on Merlin's chair. Littered beside the throne lay the remains of the first traitor, a swirl of sparks rising like glittering smoke. Jared picked up a shield and an empty mail shirt. *The undergarments are gone but the armour remains! What does it all mean?*

Jared stiffened. Rapid footsteps carried from the hall into the room, growing louder by the second. He looked back to see Irene peeking out of their hiding place, and he signalled wildly for her to get back and close the door. She ducked back inside, leaving the door partially open.

Jared rushed to a curtain behind the throne and twisted the silky fabric around his body. Through the veil he could see Devin march into the room. His shoes clacked and echoed in the strangely quiet chamber and then stopped dead still.

The armoured knight stalked from the doorway to the centre of the chamber, picking up mail shirts and letting them clatter back to the floor. He pivoted toward the throne, staring as if he could see Jared wrapped in the purple fabric. With a lunge, he leaped onto the platform and then stood still with his hands on his hips. Jared's heart thumped so hard he could feel it pulsing in his throat. Should he fight? Should he run?

Devin suddenly leaned over. When he stood again, he held a sword in his hand – Excalibur. Its residual glow shone brightly, piercing through the veil. Devin, the lone remaining traitor, the self-styled knight, tightened his grip around the hilt, and the sword's light vanished.

I'm such a coward! Jared steamed. *If I were still a dragon, I'd—*

Devin sheathed the sword and turned away. Jared heard the evil knight's steps and the cackling of his maniacal laugh as he left the room. "Palin! Bring the stone!" he yelled, his voice fading in the distance.

Chills covered Jared's skin, goose bumps that chided him, each one calling him a milksop for hiding like a thumb-sucking toddler behind his mother's skirt. A boiling factory of rage and embarrassment sent pulses of blood toward his eyes, turning his face hot. When he was a dragon he would have sent a tsunami of white-hot fire roaring out of his mouth and nostrils to personally escort "Sir" Devin into a dragon's version of hell. *Welcome to my inferno you sniveling caitiff!* Yet, Jared had become the sniveller, and cold sweat replaced the fiery blasts. *Do all humans feel this way? Why do I feel so small and sick?*

Jared snatched a mail shirt from the ground and threw it angrily across the room, his gaze following it as it slid to a stop in front of Merlin's chair, his empty chair.

The book!

He scrambled over the armour and frantically searched around the chair, the throne, and then back to the chair. The book was gone!

Jared fumed. It must have been Devin! He was the only person in the room, the only one who could have stolen Merlin's diary!

I am the worst of invertebrates! I let the man I called a worm steal two of the greatest treasures in all the world!

Jared grabbed a sword from the floor and screamed, "Devin, you son of a leprous jackal! You recreant thief, plucking treasures from dead men's bones! Come back here and fight like a man!"

Jared's eyes shot wide open when Devin appeared at the door, his shoulders squared and his jaw firmly set around a vicious smile. A gleaming gem swayed in front of his chest, dangling at the end of a gold necklace and absorbing swirls of sparkling light. It seemed to carry his malevolence as it drew in light as easily as the evil knight drew breath.

For a moment, Jared wanted to run. He had learned some swordplay, but he had little hope of matching blades with a knight, even a self-proclaimed one! His mind battled his body, and he cursed his petrifying fear.

If I run from this serpent, I will be the worst of infidels! It is time to be a man! He held his ground, raising his sword in a defensive posture. Devin laughed derisively and set the diary on the floor. He lifted the gleaming Excalibur with both hands, marched to meet Jared, and knocked his sword away with one swing of his forearms.

"No time to kill you properly," Devin said. "The king's army is closing in on the castle, so I came back here to search for an escape." He looked past Jared toward the secret door, still ajar. "I cannot allow you to tell the king of my where-abouts, so I shall have to dispose of you without giving you a fair fight."

Devin raised the sword again. Jared leaped forward, tack-ling the evil knight and wrestling him to the floor. As they fell, Jared felt Excalibur's sting, the edge of the blade catching his neck and slicing deeply. Jared rolled on the floor in agony, blood spurting like a scarlet geyser.

Devin grabbed the diary and hustled for the escape door, closing it securely behind him while Jared lay writhing and pressing his palm against the haemorrhaging artery. The last thing Jared remembered was a dozen gauntleted hands lifting him, and then everything went black.

"Jared survived," Clefspeare continued as the cinders on the wall faded to black, "but he was not the same man. He vowed never to hide from danger again nor fear any weapons of this earth." Clefspeare relit the torch with a fiery snort, and everyone in his audience rubbed their eyes to adjust to the light. "He learned the ways of men and lived as one for over a thousand years, only to be returned to the draconic state you see before you now. Irene watched the cowardly Devin rush right past her, and she ran to help her adopted brother, carrying him to the physician with the help of the king's knights who arrived only moments later. She, like Jared, married a normal human over a thousand years later, and she gave birth to a daughter, whom they christened—"

"Bonnie," the professor finished.

"Yes. Bonnie. And she, like my son, has dragon traits. Billy has fiery breath with protective scales in his mouth, while Bonnie has dragon wings and can fly."

"Wings hidden in her backpack," the professor said in wonder. "Who could have guessed?" He stared at Billy, as though seeing him for the first time in his life. "Are there any others? Any other dragon children?"

"That is a mystery. In order to maintain secrecy, the remaining dragons rarely communicated with one another. I knew that Irene had a daughter, and I had heard rumours of other children. The slayers have been obsessed with finding any that might exist, and they know such children might not always be easy to identify. There are characteristics of dragons that are not unique to our species. Humans have a portion of them, so these may be magnified when one parent is also a dragon. We are great storytellers, so their gift could be profound eloquence. You might also see unusual strength or deep wisdom. It's hard to say what these unions might create."

Walter jumped to his feet. "C'mon!" he said, pulling Billy up and slapping him on the back. "Show us some fire breathing!"

"Walter, be polite," the professor warned. "Young William may find such a display embarrassing. After all, his talent is not exactly commonplace."

Billy scratched the cave floor with the toe of one shoe. "No . . . it's all right. I'll show you guys." Actually, the professor was half right. Billy did feel some embarrassment, but at the same time he felt relief, and he wanted to show off for his dad anyway.

He turned toward an empty part of the cave and stepped into the shadows. After taking a deep breath, he opened his mouth in a wide circle. With his chest muscles taut, he began exhaling slowly. A narrow stream of yellow flowed out. It grew rapidly, brightening until it became a blazing river of flames, stretching out over a dozen feet before vaporizing into a column of grey smoke. Billy pushed the fiery jet for ten seconds, his face turning beet red, before he finally closed his mouth and slapped his hand across his chest. "Whew!" A ring of smoke passed through his lips and wafted into the darkness.

"Cool as ice!" Walter shouted.

"Bravo!" the professor added, clapping. "William, that was amazing!"

Clefspeare sighed, letting a few sparks fly into the cave's flowing air columns. "Yes, Billy, you have developed your gift quite well." The dragon pushed on his haunches and dragged his body closer to the professor. "Now I believe you know all of the basic facts, Professor Hamilton, and Billy can fill you in on the details, but there are mysteries remaining to be solved."

Professor Hamilton rubbed the front of Merlin's diary and opened it to the blank page. "Now we have two of the mysterious treasures restored to us, and it's clear that the slayers never discovered how to make these pages reveal their secrets."

Clefspeare's scaly brow furrowed. "Yet they have used Excalibur in a way I do not yet understand. It gave this son of Devin youthfulness and vigour, though he could not use it to transluminate his victims."

"Then we must make sure they don't get it back," the professor said. "I thought perhaps your son might be able to draw the sword out of the stone."

Billy's heart jumped. "Me?"

The professor placed a hand on Billy's shoulder. "I had suspected that William is in the royal lineage, and your story bears that out. It was an adoption, to be sure, but it was legal and fully binding."

Clefspeare growled, his eyes shining like a ruby laser. "You are right; the sword must be kept out of evil hands." His eyes then slowly dimmed, and his voice mellowed. "I believe the evil rock Master Merlin called the candlestone could be housing Devin's light energy, his mortal essence, within its prism walls. After I recovered my strength, I searched for the cursed thing for days, but I could not find it. I can only guess that his dark henchman returned to collect his remains. If Palin and Dr Conner are in the slayer's service, they may have formed an alliance to restore their master. How they would use Bonnie is a mystery, but they are already using her love to deceive her. There is no greater motivation than love . . . and no greater evil than treachery."

Clefspeare lowered his head to Billy's eye level. "Your professor may be right about the sword and the stone. Remember Merlin's prophecy.

A king shall rise of Arthur's mould
The prophet's book in hand
He takes the sword from mountain stone
To rescue captive bands

93

"Try to pull it out," the dragon continued, "but if you cannot, you may use Merlin's prayer to call me. I will help you if I can."

Billy couldn't believe what he was hearing. *Royal lineage? Pull out a sword? Who were they trying to kid?* He dragged his toe across the dirt again. "I . . . I'll do my best. Anything for Bonnie."

Professor Hamilton gasped. With the diary lying open in his hands, he stared at the pages, his mouth agape.

Walter rushed to his side. "I can read it! It's even got normal words, not that old English stuff or funny looking letters."

"Yes," the professor agreed, breathless and excited. "I see it now! The veil is lifted. I know we're in a hurry, but I must read this to everyone immediately."

CHAPTER 6

THE CHAMBER OF LIGHT

Heavy snow pelted the windshield as Bonnie's father drove deeper and deeper into a dense mountain forest. The Explorer bumped along on a narrow, snow-covered hiking path and swerved around sharp, slippery bends. Nail-biting drop-offs fell away on one side and steep slopes rose on the other. The tyres slipped through the deepening snow, all four wheels churning to avoid a sideways slide over a precipice.

Bonnie kept one hand in her lap, the other fastened to the armrest as she watched the deteriorating conditions through the frosting window. She was accustomed to heights, but her wings would be of no help should the SUV plunge into one of the gorges. Though she tried to hide her nervousness, she gripped the armrest more tightly with every swerve.

Ashley's eyes stayed focused on the tree-lined path ahead rather than on the rocky cliffs below. Her folded hands seemed relaxed, her thumbs merely caressing each other through the jolting bounces. Bonnie closed her eyes. *Ashley must have travelled this path dozens of times. My father's probably driven through snow like this before.*

Bonnie bit her lip. For some reason Ashley's familiarity with her father's new life annoyed her. Was it jealousy that her father had found a replacement daughter of sorts? Or was it distrust that her new friend could be allied with this man whom her bad memories had painted as a demon over the past several months?

The Explorer slowed to a crawl at the crest of a hill in a more open part of the forest. It then turned left onto a side path, a narrow clearing pockmarked with icy potholes. Each divot surrendered its snowy covering as the SUV bucked and bounced through them and finally stopped. Bonnie tried to find a house or a cabin as she peeked through the window's crystals but saw only a scattering of poorly dressed trees standing around in the snow.

Her father got out, opened the left rear door for Ashley, and motioned for Bonnie to slide over and get out on the same side. Bonnie glanced to her right to see if anything barred the door on her side, but there was nothing there.

Bonnie slipped on her oversized coat and stepped out into the wintry Montana storm. Cold wind blasted her face, and her shoes sank in the snow. While she laboured to pull her feet from the wet drift, her father retrieved the cases from the cargo space, handed the larger one to Ashley, and marched farther up the crude driveway. Ashley extended her free hand toward Bonnie and pulled her out to more solid ground. Snow seeped into Bonnie's socks, weighing down her feet. She hoped their hike wouldn't be a long one.

With snow pelting their heads and wind blowing icy flakes into miniature white tornadoes, they trudged to a head-high mound of rocks pressed into the steep upslope of the mountainside. A wooden door, no more than five feet high, had been crudely wedged into the rocks, and lumpy mortar filled the gaps between the frame and stone.

The makeshift door was so small, Bonnie thought it might open into a woodshed or a tool storage shack. Her glance fell on a large letter *A* carved in the door at waist level exposing fresh wood grain not yet weathered by Montana's cruel winter.

Bonnie rubbed her gloved hand on the marred wood. "What's the *A* for?"

Ashley set down her load and stretched a rubber coil that held a key chain to her belt loop. "It's a capital alpha," she explained, "a Greek letter. We had another entrance that we called Omega, but it's closed now." Using a long silver key, she unlocked the door and pushed it open on its creaking hinges. "Are you ready for a big surprise? It won't be long now."

Ashley's genuine smile promised a good surprise, so Bonnie kept her hopes up. Maybe her mother really was around some-where. Maybe this entrance led to the lab Ashley talked about, even though it looked more like the opening to an ancient mountain-top outhouse.

Her father bent over, pushed his head through the doorway, and plucked a flashlight that dangled from a hook on the inside wall. He flicked it on and ducked through the entrance. "Follow me," he said before disappearing inside.

Bonnie peered in. All she could see in the wide flashlight beam was a downward stairway leading into darkness.

Ashley picked up her case and motioned with her head for Bonnie to follow. They both bent over to pass under the door's upper frame, moving out of the bitter cold and into quiet still-ness. "Should I close the door?" Bonnie asked softly. Even her quiet voice sounded like a trumpet in the narrow stairwell.

"Yes," Ashley whispered.

Bonnie pushed the door until she heard the latch click in place. The waving flashlight beam bobbed down the corridor, her father's breaths passing through it in rhythmic puffs of white. Their footsteps clopped and echoed, making their furtive march sound like a small army stomping down the stairs.

"Stay close," Ashley warned, raising her voice. "It's pretty far, and it gets steep in places, but it levels out in a few minutes."

Bonnie didn't count the number of stair steps exactly, but she guessed it was getting close to two hundred, with each wooden plank becoming shorter and narrower than the one before. As Ashley had said, the descent eventually levelled out, the stairwell smoothing into a narrow tunnel they had to negotiate single file. Loud drips echoed from somewhere up ahead as if big water drops plunged into static pools, and they played a rhythmic harmony to their crunching steps. The floor felt like crumbling asphalt, but at least it was dry.

They marched on in silence. The darkness of the corridor seemed to seep into Bonnie's mind. How difficult would it be to climb back to the surface when they returned . . . if they returned? A feeling of dread crawled across her body, like roaches skittering across a dirty kitchen floor. Something was wrong, desperately wrong.

Professor Hamilton cleared his throat and squinted at the page, speaking slowly as he read.

The veil once pierced is split for good
By truth's sharp sword it's torn
Take care that all can bear it well
That all may be reborn

Without the sword the war is lost
Excalibur's edge must fight
Yet not with foes of shield and sword
But those who veil the light

Bring here the sword of Camelot
To read of wisdom's page
Without its words, instruction blurs

He stopped and pulled the book close to his face. Billy dared not breathe.

"What's up, Prof?" Walter blurted out. "What's the next line?"

The professor reached for the corner of the page. "Perhaps the next page will tell—"

"No!" Billy shouted, jumping toward his teacher. "Don't turn the page! Remember the warning!"

The professor stopped and put his hand on his chest. "Yes, William." He took a deep breath. "Of course. This page must be completed first."

Billy looked over the professor's shoulder, the shadow of his head bobbing on the page as he studied the mysterious script. "It sounds like we have to get Excalibur if we're going to read the rest of it."

Billy's mother clenched her hand into a fist. "Then let's get moving! There's no telling what Bonnie might be going through while we just stand around here." She grabbed Billy's upper arm. "Let's yank that sword and head west! I know a pharmacy professor who's in for a big surprise when we show up there. We'll give him some medicine he'll never forget!"

Billy pumped his fist and grinned. "Mum, I love it when you're ready to bash a few heads together!"

"Yeah, Mrs B!" Walter agreed. "Let's go kick some gluteus maximus!"

Ashley turned a knob and pushed open a door. Bonnie followed, stepping out of the cool corridor and into a balmy cavern. She felt the gentle caress of warm air seeping in from unseen vents. The room was dark except for a bright crack of light streaming from under a door to her left and her father's flashlight beam meandering up the wall.

"Hit the lights, Ashley."

Ashley's hand appeared in the beam, reaching for a series of switches on the wall. Then, in concert with four clicks, rows of ceiling lights flashed to life, incandescent flood lamps and banks of fluorescent panels illuminating an enormous underground chamber.

Bonnie's eyes took a few seconds to adjust. A circular laboratory about a hundred feet in diameter had been erected in the centre of the cavern and elevated on a low platform. A thousand tangled cables snaked underneath like thick, black spaghetti.

The lab was a technological maze, a dizzying collection of instrument panels and glass enclosures. Everything was oriented around a point at the centre where a flat marble pedestal stood, a sort of stunted ionic column about four feet high and maybe a foot in diameter.

Three instrument panels formed an arc around an inner circle, each one spaced evenly apart and about twenty feet from the centre. The panels were a techno-geek's dream come true – at least a dozen rows of dials, sliding bars, diodes, and who-knows-whatsits covering the black acrylic front.

Three tall glass cylinders, like life-sized china doll display cases, stood between the panels and the centre pedestal. The panel nearest the door, covered with twice as many buttons and meters as the other two, faced the cylinder on the opposite side.

A drop ceiling, a matrix of suspended tiles and fluorescent lights set in plastic frames, floated over the raised lab area – a hovering bank of spotlights in the midst of a canopy of darkness.

Ashley gazed at the magnificent laboratory and then at Bonnie, her eyebrows raised. Bonnie wanted to make Ashley happy, so she tried to think of something nice to say, but she hadn't come here to be impressed by a technological assemblage of gadgets from the Bat Cave. She couldn't begin to appreciate what it was all for. For all she knew it could be a garage sale in comic book land. She wanted to find her mother, and all this gawking at gadgetry wasn't getting her anywhere.

Bonnie took a step forward and nodded. "This is . . . amazing. Um . . . What is it?"

Ashley pulled off her coat and hung it on a wall hook. "It's our lab. It's the most advanced mechanical photosynthetic lab in the world."

"Photosynthetic? You mean like what plants do to make food?"

"Very close. Plants change light energy into food. We're trying to create physical matter from light energy in a very different way."

Bonnie glanced to the side to check on her father. He was at a table by the wall unloading and examining the cases they had brought. She took another step toward the platform. "How does photosynthesis have anything to do with pharmacy? I didn't know my father was into stuff like this."

"He's not, or at least he wasn't. That's why he needs me." Ashley scooted toward the array of instruments and gestured for Bonnie to follow. "This research combines physics with chemistry, and it will take a while to explain, but it's the most exciting project I could ever imagine. We've come a long, long way in a very short time."

Ashley seated herself at the master control panel. "This panel," she said, flipping on a switch, "controls that photo tube right in front of me." A low hum sounded from the seven-foot-high cylinder on the opposite side of the circle, and a bright light flashed on from its smoothly curved cap, making it look like a futuristic transporter tube. The bass drone reverberated throughout the cavern, and gentle vibrations radiated from the floor and into Bonnie's legs.

Ashley pointed to a slider bar on the panel. "If I were to move this up, the beam inside the dome would activate, becoming more and more agitated the higher I slid it."

Bonnie's pulse quickened as the quivering floor sent a buzzing sensation into her teeth, and tiny beads of sweat popped up on her forehead. She took off her outer coat and laid it neatly on a chair. "What does the beam do?"

Ashley flicked off the cylinder's light, and the tremors faded along with the drone. She walked back to Bonnie and spoke softly, almost in a whisper. "It mimics Excalibur's beam, the light energy you used to transluminate Devin."

Bonnie bit her bottom lip until it hurt. *Excalibur's beam? Transluminate Devin?* How could Ashley know about Excalibur and Devin? And what did she mean by transluminate?

Ashley clutched one of Bonnie's forearms and drew her close. "I know about you," she whispered. Then with a quick look at Bonnie's back, she added, "And your wings."

Bonnie let out a low gasp and stepped back, but Ashley held on. "Shhhh! Don't worry. Your father knows that I know about you, but I've learned a lot more than he thinks I know."

Ashley put a hand on Bonnie's pack. "Shall I help you take this off so you can get more comfortable? I really want to see your wings, and, besides, everyone here knows about them."

Bonnie shifted her weight from one foot to the other, and her ears turned warm. Ever since she was little, her wings had been a secret, even an embarrassment, worse than an ugly zit or a bad haircut. But Ashley seemed gentle and sincere, so when she reached over and loosened the straps on the backpack, Bonnie didn't pull away.

"You said, 'everyone'," Bonnie noted as Ashley slid a strap down her shoulder. "Is there anyone else here besides you and your grandfather and my father?"

Ashley's hands stopped moving, but her voice didn't flinch. "Actually . . . yes. But I'd better let Dr Conner tell you about them."

"Them? More than one?"

Ashley pulled the backpack away, letting it fall to the floor, and Bonnie unfurled her wings, stretching them straight back and then out.

Ashley's eyes widened until they looked ready to pop out. "Wow! I knew they had to be big to carry your body weight, but . . . Wow!"

Bonnie's whole face grew hot. Ashley's gawking made her feel more freakish than ever. She bowed her head, hoping her face wouldn't give away her thoughts.

Ashley cleared her throat, and her jaw and chin relaxed. She leaned over and whispered, "I think I know how you feel. It's not as obvious in me, but I'm different, too."

She spread her arms out toward the centre of the lab. "Look around, Bonnie. I designed all this, and I helped build it. My brain is a freak; it works so fast, it's like a supercomputer on nuclear steroids. The kids at school think I can even read their minds. I can analyse and deduce so well, I'm usually saying what they're thinking as soon as they realize they're thinking it themselves. That's no way to make friends. Do you think any of the girls want to be around me, believing I can read their minds? No way! And the guys? Forget it! When I come around, I've seen them put their hands over their ears."

She mimicked her description, raising her own hands to cover her ears. "What are they thinking? That their thoughts leak out? Of course it's ridiculous, but it doesn't change anything." Ashley caressed the outer rib of Bonnie's left wing, and her voice dropped again, catching in her throat. "I . . . I've heard them call me . . . mutant . . . and alien. . . . I know how it feels. And sometimes . . . it makes me wonder. Maybe they're right. . . . Maybe I am a mutant."

Dr Conner joined the girls, one hand in his pocket, the other carrying a spiral notebook. "I see you two are becoming acquainted."

Bonnie read the familiar expression on his face, a smiling glow that had fooled her for years. With her wings exposed, everything seemed out in the open – vivid, clarified, transparent. Now she saw in his smile the pearly whites of a polished hypocrite, a charlatan scientist. His act was wearing thin. It was time for him to deliver. She crossed her arms over her chest and tapped her foot on the floor. "Can I see my mother now?"

"Very soon," he replied. "I promise."

"Is she here?"

"Yes. I'll explain in a moment." He handed the notebook to Ashley. "The samples are excellent. I think the photoreceptors are working. I see no reason why we can't begin in the morning, but let's set up a communication session for tonight."

Ashley's smile stretched across her face. "Great! I'm going to check on Daddy first. I'll be back." She grasped Bonnie's wrist and gave it a squeeze before jogging toward a far corner of the lab.

Bonnie's father picked up the backpack from the chair, lifting and lowering it a couple of times. "Is something in here?"

"Just my journal. I can't fit much else when my wings are in there."

He laid the pack on the chair with her coat and buried both hands in his pockets. "I've heard about your dangerous adventures, and you've been very brave. I'm asking you to be brave once again, because only you can rescue your mother. That's why I brought you here."

It was a practiced speech, like many she had heard through the years. Her father's eyes gave away a hint of insecurity, like he was covering hidden fears, conveying urgency and dread. But his speech, and so many other things, weren't adding up. What did he really know about her adventures?

Scenes from her battle with Devin flashed through her mind, the slayer's gleaming sword heavy in her trembling hands and his hateful eyes glowing with vengeance. The memories pumped adrenalin through her body, and her heart beat like the wings of a hummingbird. She fought against the overwhelming thoughts and her father's powerful sway over her, but she couldn't keep her lips from trembling. She gulped, barely able to speak. "What do I have to do?"

The professor pointed as he hurried through a path of thick leaves and scattered stones. "It's just over this rise."

Walter and Billy jogged after him, and Billy's mother tracked close behind. When they came to a clearing, the professor stopped and pointed again as he tried to catch his breath. "There . . . there it is."

Billy and Walter halted next to the professor, and they gazed at the awesome sight. The sword stood upright, as straight as a boot camp cadet waiting for a drill sergeant to bark out a command.

Billy's mother caught up. "What are we waiting for? Let's do it!"

She ran ahead to the foot of the stone, and the others hustled to join her. "C'mon, son," she said, making a cup with her interlocking fingers. "I'll give you a boost."

Billy shook his head, stripped off his gloves, and handed them to his mother. "Thanks, Mum, but I can make it." He leaped to the first ledge and grappled the top of the stone. Two seconds later he stood next to the sword, ready to grasp its hilt, but he paused and leaned down. "The prophecy says I have to hold the diary."

The professor stretched his lanky body and handed up the diary. Billy stood again, holding the book in his left hand. With his right, he grasped Excalibur's hilt, pausing a second and taking a deep breath.

Billy tensed his muscles, and as he tightened his grip, heat radiated from the sword. Steam rose from the crack in the rock, and the sword moved easily, like a spoon in thick pudding. Billy pulled it out effortlessly, his eyes wide and his mouth open. He stared at the blade, the newly exposed portion glowing hot. His right arm trembled under the sword's weight, but he managed to raise the blade high above his head.

Walter pumped his fists. "Yes!"

Billy's mother gave Walter a high-five, and the professor copied their actions, clumsily giving high-fives to each of them.

Walter clambered up the stone and gave Billy a manly embrace. He slapped him on the back and relieved him of the book. With two catlike leaps, Walter was back on the ground handing the diary to the professor.

"Bring Excalibur down, William," the professor said as he opened the book. "We must make haste."

Walter rubbed his eyes and peered at the ragged parchment. "I can't see any new lines, Prof."

Billy joined them, gripping Excalibur with both hands. The professor eyed the book closely. "William, hold it nearer. I can see something."

As though summoned by the sword itself, new words slowly appeared on the page, matching the calligraphic script of the lines above. The tantalizing letters grew clear and bold.

The professor gestured for the others to stand back, and he cleared his throat. "I shall begin reading with the first line of the previously unfinished quatrain."

> Bring here the sword of Camelot
> To read of wisdom's page
> Without its words, instruction blurs
> For all who hear the sage
>
> The candlestone conceals a trap
> Where Satan's minions dwell
> In darkness she will seek her joy
> And find the gates of hell
>
> A sword, a knight, a fiery son,
> Transluminated heir
> Shall enter into darkest realm
> To battle in its lair
>
> Beware, O knight, of easy prey
> Who stand with back yet turned
> For cowards strike a blinded foe
> And die for what they've burned

107

The professor paused. He brought the book closer as though he were trying to read microscopic print. "That's all I can see. The metric beat and rhyme scheme are complete, and the script nearly fills the page. Perhaps that's all there is."

Billy held the sword close to the book again. "Then we should be allowed to check the next page. Let's see if something shows up."

The professor lifted the top corner. "Very well." Everyone drew nearer to look as he turned the page.

"It's blank," Walter said. "Blank as my brain during a maths test and empty as my stomach is now."

The professor closed the book and tucked it under his arm. "Obviously the book has nothing more to reveal at this time. Let's hurry back to the plane and decipher this new conundrum." He placed a hand on his stomach. "Perhaps we'll be able to think more clearly once we have taken a meal."

Billy's mother smacked her son's gloves into his palms. "Then let's get airborne! There isn't anything left to do here. Jared—I mean, Clefspeare said he'd deliver Billy's drawing to Arlo's porch, and we have the sword."

Billy pulled his gloves over his hands and heaved the weighty sword up on his shoulder, holding the hilt with both hands in front. As he trudged through the forest, the final stanza of the poem smouldered in his mind. "Prof, the last part of that poem, the part about cowards striking a blinded foe. What do you make of it?"

The professor kept his stride, his white hair bouncing under his beret. "I thought you might find its lesson familiar, William. I've said something similar many times. A knight opposes his enemy face to face. A stab in the back is the way of the coward. If you must fight, attack your enemy head-on. That is the way of valour."

"I remember. But what if he wants to kill you? Shouldn't you take him out before he takes you out?"

"Yeah," Walter agreed. "What's wrong with a surprise attack on the bad guys? They deserve it, don't they?"

The professor halted and faced his students. "If God commands a surprise attack, then so be it; he has done that before. But a brave warrior assumes that his Lord will protect him as he charges with confidence into battle. He will even call out to his enemy to stand face to face." The professor's furrows deepened, and his skin seemed to turn grey. "Considering the words of this prophecy, we can assume that God has ordained that we carry out no surprise attacks. Do you understand?"

Walter nodded. "Sure, Prof. I get it."

Billy kept his eyes focused on his mother who was standing by a large oak tree up ahead, waiting for them to catch up. "Yeah, I think so."

The three continued down a dirt path, quick-marching through the forest. The professor's warning blistered Billy's mind. *No surprise attacks.* He twisted his neck to eye Excalibur's blade. He held in his hands the ultimate weapon, one that could vanquish the dragon slayers and rescue Bonnie. He understood the poem well enough to know that Bonnie was in trouble – something about Satan's minions and the gates of hell. But what could he do? He had practised long and hard, and he felt the urge to zoom to Montana and do a little transluminating on Devin's cronies, or at least whack their ugly heads off. Was he brave enough to do it face to face?

The feel of his fingers wrapping around the sword's hilt brought courage, but something was wrong. The blade's surface held all the strange etchings he had expected, and it was as heavy as a bundle of crowbars, but it lacked lustre; in fact, it was dull. *Shouldn't it be glowing? That's what all the stories said, and it shot out a beam when Bonnie held it. Sure, I pulled it right out of the stone. That was cool. But why isn't it working now?*

He tried slipping off his gloves again and holding it with his bare hands, but that didn't change anything. Had anyone else noticed? Billy wished he had a scabbard so he could sheathe the sword and hide its apparent impotence. As he hiked onward, the sword's weight pressed on his shoulder, pinching his skin even through his jacket. If the sword was such a burden when carried like this, how could he possibly wield it in battle? He couldn't make it glow; he could barely even hold it up! He boosted the blade higher on his shoulder and kept moving, listening to the leaves crunching under their hurried steps. He couldn't help but feel they were all rushing headlong toward a whirlpool, and he didn't even have a paddle.

Bonnie sat on one of the swivel chairs. Her father stooped and placed a gentle hand on her knee. "This is all very difficult to explain," he said softly, "so I want you to pay close attention."

He licked his lips and blinked before clearing his throat to continue. "You may not have guessed what happened to Devin. Excalibur transformed him into light energy, and the candlestone absorbed his fractured particles into itself. Devin's cohort, Palin, saw your battle from a distance but couldn't get there in time to help. After you threw away the stone, he knew he couldn't battle both you and a dragon without it. Even though you flew away, Clefspeare was recovering, so Palin waited for him to leave. He searched for hours but never found Excalibur. He wondered later if you flew away with it, but I told him it was much too heavy. You'd never be able to fly with that much weight.

"Anyway, he found the stone and he brought it to me, thinking I could help him resurrect Devin and reconstitute him. He knew Devin and I had worked together, studying dragons and their ability to use light energy to extend their lives. I was the only person who might be able to help.

"You see, back then we had Excalibur in our possession and learned quite a bit about how it works. When Devin took off on one of his rabid dragon hunts, I insisted on keeping the sword with me, because our analysis of its power wasn't finished, but I promised to send it to him if he needed it. Later, he convinced me that he could capture a dragon for our research if he only had his sword, so that's how it came back into his hands. Apparently it's lost forever."

Bonnie didn't know exactly where the sword was, but she had a good idea of the area where she dropped it. Since she didn't trust her father, she decided it was best to keep quiet, at least for now.

He gestured for her to stay put and stepped toward the wall. With a flick of his wrist, he spun a dial a couple of times and opened the door to a safe. He pulled out a lockbox, sliding the small metal case with great care, and brought it to Bonnie. He opened the lid a crack, and Bonnie stood up and peeked inside.

The candlestone! Even with this minute exposure, it seemed that a darkening cloud enshrouded the box, the loss of light starting at the edge of the lid. Bonnie felt a small dose of the same queasiness she experienced on the mountain when the slayer first showed her the stone, the bane of every living dragon.

Her father snapped the box shut. "Palin's claim that the stone had captured Devin intrigued me, so I told Palin I would look into it, but, of course, I had no intention of bringing that monster Devin back to physical form. I wanted to create a test

111

to see if he was somehow really within those crystal walls. That's where Ashley came in. In our efforts to mimic a dragon's ability to capture light energy, she had already helped me build miniature synthetic photoreceptors that could attach to human tissue, so, with her knowledge of physics and physiology, I thought she could come up with a way to figure out what's going on in there."

Bonnie's father motioned toward Ashley's equipment. "When you see how all of this works, you'll be amazed."

Bonnie pointed at the box. "So is he in there? Inside the candlestone?"

"Yes, and he's fully alive."

"So what does that have to do with Mama and me?"

He stepped back toward the safe. "When Palin brought the candlestone to me, your mother's health was rapidly deteriorating. I was desperately trying to bring my photoreceptor research far enough along to help her, but there wasn't enough time." He slapped the safe's door shut and spun the dial. "I decided to take a drastic step. I transformed your mother into light energy and allowed the candlestone to absorb her, keeping her safe for the time being, hoping that some day I could restore her when my research provided a way to keep her from dying."

Bonnie's throat caught, and she swallowed hard. "And now you've found a way?"

He nodded. "Indeed I have."

The words shot through her brain like machine-gun fire. It was just too much to take in. *My mother's in a wall safe? That's impossible!* Yet this lab and all its equipment lay before her, all the futuristic machines that made a *Star Trek* studio look like a toddler's collection of Lego models. And there was the candlestone, definitely the same gem that sucked the slayer into its grasp like a light-slurping straw. Her father couldn't possibly have gone through all this trouble just to trick her. "What do I have to do? How will you bring Mama back? How did you transform her in the first place?"

Her father pointed toward a dark corner. "Ashley's coming back. I'll have her explain everything else to you. She'll take you to the girls' dorm so you can get ready."

"The girls' dorm?" Bonnie surveyed the vast chamber. "Are there other girls here?"

"Yes, there are a few others. Ashley will introduce you and answer any questions you have."

Ashley walked slowly up to them, her head drooping. "Something's wrong with Daddy." She lifted her eyes, tension outlined in tight lines on her forehead. "He says he's fatigued and dizzy. He looked kind of green, so I put him to bed."

"Probably just a virus." Bonnie's father gave her a gentle push toward Ashley. "Why don't you introduce Bonnie to the girls, and I'll go check on him."

Ashley nodded, her brow still furrowed. She smiled at Bonnie, but her lips quivered. "Did he tell you where your mother is?"

"Yes, but it sounds too crazy to be true."

Ashley guided her toward a door at the opposite side of the chamber. "Crazy is right, but we'll get it all sorted out for you. For now, let's get you measured and settled in, and you can meet your dorm mates. They're quite an unusual crew, but you're pretty unusual yourself, so prepare for some gawking."

113

CHAPTER 7

SPEAKING TO THE DEAD

With no firefly light to guide him this time, Dr Conner inched his way through the blackness, his right arm extended as he groped for the inner gate. Finding the iron bars, he ran his fingers across several of them in search of the latch. After fumbling with his keys, he pecked at the metal door with one, missing the keyhole a few times before finally unlocking the deadbolt.

The air felt wetter than usual. A musty odour filled the cavern, and the damp, oily bars slipped in his hands as he pushed the gate to the left. The metal frame squealed through its top and bottom runners, echoing in tiny chaotic squeaks, like a swarm of bats awakened to go on their nightly rounds.

He paused, listening. Unnatural breathing, laboured and intimidating, drifted through the darkness. Within seconds, a gruff voice replaced the low rasps.

"Is she here?"

Dr Conner trembled and cleared his throat, trying not to sound mousy. "Bonnie has come. As you predicted." He walked through the gate and into a cave, his shoes tapping on the stone floor.

The deep voice spoke again. "And is she going to do it?"

"We're preparing her." Dr Conner stepped farther into the cave and stared into the black void. "But she doesn't know yet what's involved. If she's unwilling, I'll have to take drastic steps."

A loud, rumbling sigh filtered through the darkness. "She is willing. She will give you no trouble."

Dr Conner edged closer. "What if I told her that she may not survive?"

"I don't think she would give it a second thought. Apparently you have not yet understood what drives her."

Dr Conner squeezed his keys in his fist, feeling them bite into his skin. "Yeah, yeah, I've heard it before. 'I don't know what love is, so I'll never understand Bonnie.'" He felt a pebble under his shoe and kicked it away, listening to its tumbling clicks die out in the depths of the cave. "Well, it might be very interesting to put her to the test. Self-preservation instincts are stronger than love. That's why I have my doubts."

"No!" the voice roared. "That's why you're a fool." The final word bounced off the walls – "fool, fool, fool" – denouncing Dr Conner like a wraith from a haunting nightmare. The voice paused until the last echo faded, then continued slowly. "Irene's daughter understands love. Her mother's life is more important to her than her own, though she has no idea that Irene is no more. Perhaps by watching her, you will learn what motivates your enemies."

"I didn't come here to be lectured." Dr Conner released his grip on his keys and let them dangle from his finger. "My firefly colony is dead, so you'll get nothing but candles until summer comes. Remember, you're still alive because I find you useful, so you should show me a little more respect. You know my real reason for bringing Bonnie here, and it wasn't to rescue you."

The voice growled. "Perhaps not, you simplistic fool. But don't be surprised if your plans fail. Love may turn on you and set all of your captives free."

Dr Conner let out a huff, pivoted on his heel, and inched away, his arm extended. His fingers sifted through his keys until they clasped a diode light attached to the ring, and he pushed its button, sending a thin beam toward the exit. Finding the open gate, he followed the light, but it bent and scattered, as if trying to reverse its course. He released the button, killing the beam, and hustled to the exit. With the squealing of metal on metal and a final clank, he slid the gate closed and firmly set the lock.

117

The purring sound of a propeller filled the plane's cabin, a whispered lullaby in Billy's ears, but there was no time to sleep; too many puzzles remained unsolved. He turned in his co-pilot's chair to huddle with Walter and Professor Hamilton. The professor, seated behind Billy with Merlin's diary propped open on his lap, kept a bent finger on one line of text while Walter looked on from the other side of the aisle.

The failing daylight illuminated the text, and they stared at the mysterious words, reading them aloud between bites of cold meat sandwiches and crackers.

"It's gotta be Bonnie," Billy said. "She's looking for her mum, and she's going to find trouble instead."

The professor nodded. "Agreed, William. And it appears that the candlestone is involved in the deception. 'The candlestone conceals a trap where Satan's minions dwell.' What do you make of that?"

Billy shook his head and put his foot against the side of his mum's pilot seat. "Well, if Dad was right, and Devin is inside the candlestone, then he could be Satan's minion. And remember, Dad said Devin walked in with it around his neck after his knights got blitzed by Excalibur, so maybe there are more bad guys in there."

The professor raised his index finger. "Therefore, the plural *minions*."

"Right. But I can't see how they could hurt Bonnie from in there."

Billy's mother grabbed his foot and dropped it to the cabin floor. "Well, we know the candlestone makes you and Bonnie feel weak. I guess it could be used as a weapon."

Walter lifted a cracker to his mouth. "How could a little crystal hold someone inside? It doesn't make any sense."

The professor opened his sandwich and inspected the meat inside. "Walter, there are many realities in life that don't make sense to our limited understanding; they seem warped, out of line with what we know. As truth is revealed, however, what was once absurd is able to untwist as our minds grasp what we witness. This poem, for example, seems to describe what someone has seen with his own eyes, so we shouldn't take his witness lightly. But you are right, in one sense; we should not simply accept what seems absurd without corroboration." He took a bite of his sandwich, waiting to swallow before he continued. "Let's follow this logically from the beginning, step-by-step. William, do you remember how you described what happened to the slayer after Excalibur transluminated him?"

118

"Well, Bonnie said there was a flash of sparks, and they swirled around, like water going down a drain." Billy made a circular motion with his forefinger to illustrate.

The professor tilted his head upward. "Yes, yes, a drain. That is the word you used, and it reminds me of something." He flipped to the previous page in the book. "Here it is, in the prayer to summon a dragon."

Shall I use yon candlestone
Absorbing light to steal thy fire
If I shouldst lie beneath its trone
Excalibur builds my funeral pyre

"Apparently," the professor went on, "the one who wrote this prayer considers the candlestone as a dangerous weapon of last resort. 'Shall I use it?' he asks himself. We know the candlestone absorbs light, and we know Excalibur changes a person into light. So, when he says, 'Excalibur builds my funeral pyre', he could mean that he's risking getting caught in the absorption if the sword is used in combination with the stone."

Walter swallowed his last bit of cracker and wiped his lips on his sleeve. "I don't get it, Prof. What do you mean?"

The professor rubbed his chin for a moment and then raised a finger. "Let's put it this way. Using Excalibur and the candlestone in combination is like battling someone in a space ship and you punch a hole in a wall to create a vacuum. Your enemies are instantly killed, but you manage to put on a space suit just in time. You're alive but trapped forever to float in space, never able to return home."

"But you'd run out of air," Walter said with a sly grin. "You'd die before long."

"Yes, Walter. I realize that. The illustration does break down, yet the parallels are there."

"Yeah, Walter," Billy chided. "Give him a break. He just means that the candlestone could be a safe place if you're changed into light by Excalibur. Punching a hole is like using Excalibur, and the space suit is like the candlestone."

"Exactly, William! Look at the poem again. The poet chose an interesting word, 'trone'. There are a number of meanings for the word, but the one that sparked my memory of this passage is William's use of the word, 'drain.' A trone is a drain. The poet may be taking literary licence, but perhaps he sees light as draining into the candlestone, and Devin at this moment is lying under it. This poem, therefore, is an eyewitness account of an event similar to what Mr Clefspeare theorized. Devin is literally a victim of a luminescent whirlpool."

Walter's eyes sparkled. "Wow! That's like a nightmare I used to have. When I was little, I dreamed about getting sucked down the bathtub drain." He brushed cracker crumbs from his hands and leaned back in his seat. "But what's that got to do with Bonnie?"

Billy's heart raced like a thoroughbred. He had an idea that seemed too awful to be true, but he had to bounce it off the others to see if it made any sense. He tried to keep his voice calm. "I think I know," he said softly. He half-closed his eyes and laid his head back on his seat.

Walter tapped Billy on the side of his head with his knuckles. "Then let's have it, Sherlock. What's the deal?"

Billy's mother chimed in. "What is it, Billy?"

"Yes, William. We are all in great anticipation."

Billy chewed on his lower lip. Why had he spoken up? The others expected an answer, and he felt their eyes boring holes through his skull. He had no choice. "They're going to send Bonnie into the candlestone to get Devin out."

Walter reached over and felt Billy's brow. "No fever." He closed Billy's eyes with his fingers, but Billy slapped his arm away. "Billy must be hallucinating if he thinks Bonnie's going to try to rescue the slayer."

The professor laughed at Walter's antics. "You're correct, Walter. Such an act would be counter to her character, but on the other hand, William's theory has merit. Remember, Bonnie doesn't know that her mother is really dead, so we can't be sure how an unscrupulous man could manipulate her with lies. Perhaps she might be persuaded by deceit to enter the stone, or even by force or threats."

"Maybe." Walter chewed another cracker thoughtfully. "But we have Excalibur. How can Bonnie change into light energy without it? And even if she does, how can she bring anyone out of that thing? Won't she and Devin still be sparks of light if they do come out? I think it would just suck them right back in again."

"Very perceptive questions, Walter. There are still missing pieces to this puzzle."

Billy sat up. "But will we be too late? How long till we get there?"

His mother pointed at a folded map and ran her finger along a highlighted route. "We'll have to stop for fuel, but we're not carrying any cargo. I think we can make it in about eight more hours, depending on the weather."

Billy looked at his watch. "What's the time zone in Missoula?"

She studied the map again. "I think it's mountain time."

121

The professor closed the diary and pulled a gold chain from his pocket. An old-fashioned watch dangled at the end. "Yes, Marilyn. The Pacific zone begins at the western border of Montana." He flipped open the cover and checked the time. "So our watches are two hours ahead of those in the Treasure State."

Walter reached for the chain, and the professor let him take the watch. "The Treasure State, Prof?" He rubbed the faded lettering on the front cover, then handed it back.

"Yes, the nickname refers to the importance of mining there, Walter."

Billy set his watch back two hours. "Then we'll get there at about midnight, Treasure State time, and we'll start some digging of our own."

"Midnight sounds about right," his mother said. "You and I can take turns napping and flying, and Walter and the professor can try to sleep. Maybe we can find a motel and get a few more hours before Dr Conner's office opens in the morning."

Billy put his hands behind his head and leaned back. "Sounds like a plan. We'll be his first appointment, if he's there."

Billy's mum pointed to the console where she kept Dr Conner's business card. "It's at the university, but we don't know if he has office hours or classes in the morning."

"Don't worry. We'll find him." Billy put his hand several inches in front of his mouth and blew gently on his fingers. "I think it's time I had a heated discussion with him."

"Hey," Walter said, his face perking up. "Speaking of heated, think we can get a pepperoni pizza when we stop for gas?" He pointed at Billy with his thumb. "With old lava breath here, we can keep it hot the rest of the way to Montana."

"Sure. Some hot food would be great. What do you think, Professor?"

"Yes, I enjoy pizza. But could we get one with mushrooms? If I were to eat pepperoni, I don't think you would enjoy my company in this enclosed cabin."

Ashley unlocked a door on the far side of the chamber, and Bonnie followed her into a narrow, linoleum-floored hallway, drawing in her wings to keep their outer edges from scraping against the rough plaster walls.

Three equally spaced, wooden doors lined both sides of the long, well-lit corridor. A small cardboard sign hung on each, but Bonnie couldn't make out what the colourful lettering said. The dull white walls and floor were clean but unadorned with decorations of any kind, and a faint scent of ammonia hung in the air. Bonnie scanned the corridor for the source of the odour and spotted a mop and bucket in a corner at the end.

Ashley locked the door behind her. "I'm going to call the other girls to come and meet you now." In a sing-song voice she shouted, "Come on out! Bonnie's here!"

Several loud thumps sounded from within the rooms, and two doors flew open on opposite sides of the hall, revealing four running girls of different shapes and sizes. With big smiles and wide eyes, they all stopped about five feet away from Bonnie, staring at her with gaping mouths. The tallest girl, a green-eyed redhead, edged forward, and the others followed, their expressions alternating between fear and delight. The redhead cautiously reached for one of Bonnie's wings, but when they moved to open more fully, she jerked her hand back.

"It's okay," Bonnie said softly. "You can touch it."

The girl, about twelve years old, smiled and caressed the golden brown wing with her fingers. Her hands were pasty white, matching her pale face and neck, a stark alabaster background for her myriad freckles. The other girls joined her, giggling and whispering oohs and aahs.

"What are your names?" Bonnie asked.

The redhead spoke up. "I'm Karen." With a finger she tapped the tallest of the other girls on her blonde head. "This is Stacey. She's eleven." Karen moved her hand to a shorter dark-skinned girl. "This is Rebecca, but we call her Beck. She's nine." Karen then pointed to a petite Asian girl. "And Monique is four, but we always call her Pebbles."

"Pebbles?" Bonnie repeated.

Karen grinned and cracked her chewing gum. "Yeah. When Doc found her, she was so hungry she was trying to eat pebbles."

"Doc?" Bonnie asked. "Who's Doc?"

"Your father," Ashley said.

Bonnie raised her head and slowly nodded. "Oh . . . okay." Devin had mentioned a "Doc" back in West Virginia, proving the partnership her father admitted having with the slayer, but she still didn't know how close their ties were. Maybe her dad didn't really trust Devin and was simply picking his brain for research, just like he had said. Bonnie wanted to get on with it – to find the truth . . . and her mother. But with the girls continuing to caress her wings in silent awe, she felt stuck. She took a deep breath and caught Karen's eye. "And do you have a nickname?"

Stacey piped up. "We call her Red."

Karen bopped Stacey playfully on the head with her fist. "My name's Karen, you silly goose!"

Bonnie stifled a laugh. "And how old are you, Karen?"

"Thirteen," she replied, shrugging her shoulders. "But I can't prove it."

"No birth certificate," Ashley explained. "You see, your father took these girls in. They were either street kids, abandoned children, or runaways – nobody wanted them." She placed a hand on Karen's shoulder. "Karen's mother left her out in a snowstorm when she was just a toddler, and she's been in the foster system ever since. Six months ago she ran away from an abusive home and wound up wandering the university campus looking for a job. A lady at Human Resources called your father to tell him about her, so he took her in.

"Dr Conner found Stacey in an alley with a man who . . . well, let's just say he didn't have her best interests in mind. I'll bet that guy won't be bothering any little girls again after Doc got through with him. Anyway, Stacey refused to tell Doc where she came from, so he just kept her.

"Beck came over the border from Baja California, and both her parents died in the desert. A California family hid her for a while and then sent her to some friends here in Montana. That family dumped Beck into the foster system, and your father heard about her. They were going to ship her back to Mexico. Doc has a friend in the foster system who let him keep her, until they, as he put it, 'can look into the matter.'"

Ashley patted Monique on the head. "And little Pebbles is a long story. We think she's Korean, and it looks like she was smuggled into a port on the Washington coast, probably for a black market adoption. Anyway, your father was surf fishing with a friend, and she was wandering on the beach trying to find something to eat. There was no one else around. The poor little girl was trying to bite into pieces of drift wood and pebbles."

Bonnie gazed into Monique's wide brown eyes. "Wow! That's amazing! How does he just 'find' these girls? That seems too weird."

"Pebbles was first," Ashley explained. "After taking her in, he actually started looking for orphans. Once a month he went into bad parts of town at night looking for runaways. And he asks his friends to call him if someone needs a home. He feels he can help them, and at the same time they can help him with his research."

Bonnie took Monique's hand and held it close to her side. "Well, it's awesome that they have a home now, but how can they help him?"

Ashley waved her arm toward the dorm rooms. "Go on back now. You'll get to talk to Bonnie more in a little while."

Ashley's abrupt dismissal of the girls seemed awkward. Bonnie caught a glimpse of Karen's arm as she drew her caressing hand away. *Are those needle marks?* A sense of dread came back stronger than ever. Karen paused at the doorway to her room, stared at Bonnie for a second, and then ducked inside.

Ashley unlocked the first door on the left. "This is your room. The other girls live two to a room so they don't get lonely. I'll be staying here with you, if that's all right."

Bonnie cleared her throat to quell any trembling in her voice. "Sure. I guess so." She read the homemade cardboard sign on the door. It said, "Alberta Einstein."

Ashley ushered her toward the open door. "You look tired. Why don't you rest up? The bathroom is the last door down the hall on the left, and there's a shower there, too." She put her hands on her hips. "Does the room look okay? Check it out."

Bonnie poked her head into the dorm room. Two beds on opposite walls displayed their dressy attire – colourful, quilted bedspreads and lacy dust ruffles. Soft, light blue carpet covered the floor, matching the hint of azure in the off-white walls.

One side of the room seemed "lived in". A poster of Albert Einstein hung on one wall, and a drawing of the cavern laboratory had been taped next to it. The most prominent feature, however, was a strange painting, the portrait of an old man – old, that is, from the neck up. His face was worn and haggard, but his body exuded youthful muscles, bulging through a track athlete's uniform. He was planting his feet at the start of a race, ready to sprint from the block. A caption read, "Daddy's Dream: A Sagacious Mind in a Robust Body," and the painting was signed by Ashley.

Bonnie opened the closet on her side of the room. A burst of colours greeted her eyes, a dazzling assortment of beautiful dresses and stylish slacks hung from the clothes rod, and boots, shoes, and sweaters lay in cubbyholes beneath. Bonnie couldn't believe it. "Are these for me?"

"Uh-huh. I had to guess your size from an old photo. I hope they fit."

Bonnie pulled out a dress and held it up. She draped one of the long turquoise sleeves down her arm and smiled. "It looks perfect."

"Then I guessed right; I won't have to measure you. I'll help you alter them for your wings later. I couldn't guess where to make the slits in the back." Ashley stood in the doorway and pushed her hand through her hair. "For now, you should get some rest. I'm going to set up a communication session for tonight, and you'll want to be wide awake for that."

Bonnie put the dress back in the closet. "Communication session? With who?"

"I'll explain exactly how it works when we do it, but I've built a way to communicate with the life forces inside the candlestone. It may be hard to believe, but within a few hours you'll be talking with your mother."

127

CHAPTER 8

VOICES IN THE DARK

Dr Conner spun the dial on the wall safe and then steadily guided it through its combination stops. After he reached the final number and turned the handle, he heard an unexpected click. He spun around to see Ashley stepping out of the dorm's hallway and locking the door behind her.

Dr Conner slid the candlestone's protective box from the case and gingerly walked it to the marble pedestal at the centre of the chamber, setting it gently in place.

Ashley strode to his side and lifted the lid a crack. She peered at the candlestone for a moment before closing the box again. "How's Daddy doing?"

"I'm sure it's just a virus. I gave him something to help him rest, so he's sleeping."

Dr Conner walked the few steps back to the main control panel, sat down at its swivel chair, and flipped a switch. A device that looked like a futuristic ray gun rose slowly from the floor near the pedestal, stopping when the gun's barrel reached the level of the candlestone's box. "Is Bonnie asleep?"

Ashley joined him. "If she's not, she will be soon. She looked real tired, so I told her to get some rest." She pointed to a line on a flat panel monitor. "If you're going to shoot it now, you'll have to set the distortion allowance to about seventy-five."

Dr Conner turned one of the dozens of knobs while watching the monitor. "And what did she say about the girls?"

Ashley scratched her head through her tangled hair and leaned over to read a stream of data that began flashing on the screen. "Not much. They were excited to see her, and she was friendly, even when they crowded around and wanted to touch her wings."

Dr Conner rotated a dial, clicking it from zero to eight. A thin beam shot out from the gun, painting a tiny crimson circle on one side of the candlestone's leaden box. "It would be better if she doesn't talk to them privately. Do you understand?"

Ashley sighed and nodded. "Yes. I understand."

Dr Conner's eyes darted over the controls. "Which voiceprint is in memory right now?"

Ashley pointed to a switch. "Devin's. His is channel A. Bonnie's mum is channel B."

"He's communicating on alpha frequency, right?"

Ashley pushed her hair back with one hand and tapped a digital display with the other. "Uh-huh. That's where he's supposed to be. But I noticed lately that he's not always there, like he might be experimenting with other frequencies."

Dr Conner jerked his head around and glared at Ashley. "Nonsense! You must have been misreading it."

Ashley let her hair fall haphazardly and blew it out of her way with an angry huff. "Misreading it? Me? You're the one who didn't know which frequency to use just now."

Dr Conner turned his attention back to the controls and adjusted a dial. "I was just double-checking. And you should tell me when you notice something unusual in the stone, especially frequency drift. I don't want you speculating. You know what happens when your head gets in the clouds."

Ashley stepped back from the panel and put her hands on her hips. "In the clouds? What are you talking about?"

Dr Conner stood and pushed one hand in his pocket, slowly letting out a sigh. "I'm sorry. I shouldn't have said that. I should know better." He laughed and added, "Before you came here I didn't know squat about physics. How did you say it that day you got so mad at me?"

Ashley squeezed her lips together. "I said, 'You don't know a tachyon beam from a tackle box.'"

"That's right. Back then I was just a research panhandler begging for a government grant! Yesterday I turned down two geezers who practically threw their money at me."

Ashley met Dr Conner's gaze. "Well, using dragon blood was your vision."

Dr Conner pulled Ashley's hand into a handshake. "Then we're a good team, and I'll try not to forget it." He fished in his pocket for his keys and extended the key chain toward her. "As my teammate, would you please go up to the Explorer and get my spiral notebook? I left it on the front passenger's seat."

Ashley grinned, and her eyes sparkled. "Sure, Doc." She waltzed toward the Alpha exit door. "But I have my own set of keys, remember?"

"And would you hit the lights on your way out – switch them from manual to panel control?"

Ashley swiped at the light switches and closed the door behind her. Darkness flooded the chamber, and her steps faded in the corridor.

131

The scarlet laser beam knifed through the blackness, and a faint glow from the control panel diodes cast a ghostly light. Dr Conner followed the beam to the pedestal. He knew Ashley would be gone for a while. Although the hike through the tunnel was easy, the hundreds of upward steps that followed would slow even the best athlete.

He opened the box and took out the candlestone, setting the gem on the flat marble surface directly in the laser's path. The candlestone absorbed the red beam like a thirsty sponge; its surface glowed pink, then stark red as the light poured through every crystalline particle. After a few seconds, it became engorged with ruby light and spurted bright cherry sparks, like blood pumping from a pulsating heart.

The stone's exit facet leaned against a nickel-sized grid attached to the end of a curved glass pipe that protruded from the top of the pedestal. The drops of discharged light collected in the grid and sped through an optic tube that ran across the tile and into a floor-standing computer near the control panel.

Dr Conner returned to his seat at the controls and raised a black shield at the back of the panel, deflecting the glowing lights away from the candlestone. With the flip of a switch, large floor speakers on each side of his body began spewing static. As he adjusted a series of slider bars, the various sounds harmonized, coming together like altos and sopranos in a haunting electrostatic opera. With another click of a switch, the sound changed abruptly, and a deep, throaty voice replaced the operatic buzz.

"—delays are annoying me. Can you hear me now?"

Dr Conner snatched a microphone from the top of the control panel. "Yes, yes. I hear you. Can you hear me?" As the doctor spoke, each word etched a fluctuating pattern of red on the candlestone's surface.

"Yes, Doctor. It's about time you provided an update."

Dr Conner wiped beads of sweat from his forehead. "Of course. That's why I'm contacting you now." He swallowed hard before continuing. "Bonnie's here. She's anxious to see her mother, but I don't think she suspects anything. I plan to set up contact at nine tonight. Are you still able to mark time?"

"Yes. What time is it now?"

Dr Conner pressed a button on his watch, lighting up its analogue face. "Exactly two minutes after six in the evening."

"I've got it. Are your daughter's friends going to be any trouble?"

"Palin called. Our colleague in West Virginia says that they're on their way – the Bannister boy, his mother, another male teenager, and an old man. If they go to the address on the card, my greeting party will take care of them."

"The man is likely a teacher I know, Charles Hamilton. He is brilliant and cunning, but he is, as you say, an old man. Bannister, on the other hand, may be more trouble than you've bargained for. His breath can kill you with one puff."

"I've heard," Dr Conner replied, trying not to sound agitated. "But don't worry. Palin will be there."

"Good. He'll know what to do. We've battled dragons with more fire than that mongrel could ever blow."

Dr Conner pushed a hand into his pocket and felt for his keys. "Are you planning to kill him?"

"What I decide should be of no consequence to you, Doctor. Remember our deal. I'll spare the girl and leave her with you, but I get the boy, no questions asked. Understood?"

Dr Conner gulped as quietly as he could. "Understood. But I'm keeping the DNA markings encoded, just to make sure you keep your end of the deal."

"I understand completely. There's no honour among liars, is there Doctor? But you have nothing to worry about. Your daughter cannot fulfil the prophecy without the boy, so I can leave her in your protective custody."

Silence descended over the dark lab, and the red light ceased its flickering dance on the wall of the candlestone. Dr Conner glanced at the Alpha exit door and then at the door leading to the girls' dorm.

The sparks exiting the candlestone flashed to life once more. "Tell Palin to kill the others and bring the mongrel to me."

Bonnie opened the door to her room and peered through the crack. No one was in the hall. She stepped out, careful to set her shoes quietly on the floor and tiptoe to Karen's room on the opposite side of the corridor. The label on her door said in multicoloured strokes of wide ink, "Red and Pebbles." Bonnie didn't want to risk knocking, so she cautiously turned the knob and pushed the door open just a bit. She whispered, "Can I come in?"

Bonnie heard rustling and a thump. The door flew open, and Karen's bright, welcoming eyes appeared. She grabbed Bonnie's hand and pulled her inside before she had time to contract her wings. They bumped painfully against the door frame as she entered.

Karen peeked out the door before closing it behind her and then bounced back into the room. "Sit down," she said, pointing to one of the beds. "Pebbles won't mind."

Bonnie perched on the edge of the bed and watched the sleeping Asian girl. "Evening nap?"

"Yep. She has nightmares, so she catches a catnap once in a while." Karen plopped on her own bed, bouncing lightly, as if in time with music only she could hear. "So why'd you come to see me?"

Bonnie caught Karen's gaze straying toward her wings, but she pretended not to notice. "I just wanted to get to know you better. You know, to get an idea of what's going on here. You don't get to see an underground laboratory complete with a girls' dorm very often."

Karen laughed and winked. "No. I guess this isn't the traditional American home, is it?"

Karen's joyful laugh made Bonnie feel warm inside. "No, not exactly traditional," she replied. "Do you get to go outside? Do you have school? What do you do all day?"

Karen shifted her gaze toward the ceiling. "We don't go outside much," she said, regaining eye contact with Bonnie, "at least not lately. There used to be an easier way out than that long tunnel and those awful stairs. It's a little door that leads to a cave and then another tunnel. They called it the Omega exit, but I never found out why. It comes out at about the same level we're at, sort of like in a valley. There's a real cool place to play there, a creek and a grassy field, but I never went out much after the wildflowers sprouted. I'm real allergic to bee stings." She let out a sigh. "Anyway, I suppose it's covered by snow this time of year, and Doc says there's a monster in the cave now, so we can't go through there anymore to get to the valley."

"A monster?" Bonnie tried not to sound too doubtful. "Do you believe him?"

Karen nodded her head, her eyes bulging. "I've heard it growl; we all have. I imagine it's too dark in there to see it, but it's there all right. I thought at first that it might be a grizzly bear, but it doesn't sound like any bear I've ever heard. It's more like a Mercedes diesel engine without a muffler."

135

Bonnie dragged her teeth across her bottom lip. A monster? Was it a ruse to keep them in line? With all the equipment her father had, it would be easy to fool the girls into thinking something weird was in that cave. "What do you do here all day if you can't go outside?"

Karen tapped a stack of books on her nightstand. "When Ashley's here, she teaches us for a couple of hours a day and gives us assignments, and sometimes Doc calls one of us out to the lab to help him."

Bonnie clenched her hands in her lap. Karen had given the perfect opening to the subject she most wanted to know about, but she didn't want to seem too eager. "Help him? What do you do?"

Karen hesitated, her lips trembling as her smile faded. "Well," she said, glancing toward Pebbles, who was squirming under her bed sheet, "I . . . I'm not sure what I can tell you."

Bonnie tiptoed over to Karen's bed and sat down. She took Karen's hand in hers. "You might as well tell me everything. I think we're in this together now."

Karen sniffed, and a tear trickled down her cheek. "Okay. I guess it's all right." She nodded toward the hall. "We – that is, Beck and Stacey and me – we're part of Doc's experiment. He's trying to figure out a way to get people to live longer."

"Oh? What does he do?"

Karen rubbed her right index finger along the needle marks on her left arm, starting at the crook and ending a few inches before her wrist. "Well, he used to take our blood and then . . . and then put it back in after he did something to it. He said he's trying to make our blood work better."

Bonnie caressed Karen's tiny scars with her fingers. "Used to take it? What does he do now?"

Karen settled down somewhat and her voice became less fragile. "It changed all of a sudden. I guess you've seen the lab out there. It was a lot different a few weeks ago. A couple of guys came in, and they worked with Ashley to build those glass things and all those instruments. That's about the same time they wouldn't let us use the tunnel anymore. Anyway, now we do some really weird and scary stuff."

Karen's eyes welled up, and she clutched Bonnie's hand tightly, rubbing her knuckles with her thumb. "It doesn't hurt or anything, but it's real scary. He doesn't explain what's going on, except a little at a time."

Bonnie placed her other hand on top of Karen's. "Go ahead and tell me. Maybe I can figure out what's going on."

Karen pursed her lips, and when she continued, her voice trembled again. "Well, I stand in one of those glass things, and Derrick – he's a seventeen-year-old over in the guys' dorm – he stands in another. Then Ashley turns on Derrick's glass, and he disappears, and all I can see is a bunch of jumping light where he used to be."

She took a deep breath and closed her eyes. "Then, I see the light from his glass thing coming toward mine through something like a transparent vacuum cleaner hose, and then Ashley turns my glass thing on. All of a sudden, I see everything differently, but it's not like seeing at all. I can't really describe it. You sort of feel it, but you understand everything around you just like you're seeing it, only even stronger. Anyway, Derrick's light reaches through the tube and grabs hold of me, and I can hear him say, 'Hang on!' Then I'm sucked through a chute, flying down real fast like a big dip on a roller coaster. And it gets real dark, darker than anywhere I've ever been, sort of like floating in the middle of the universe, with nothing to sit or walk

137

on. I feel like a ghost, but I can't see anything, except the last few times they did it, I could see flashes of light, like night lightning far away."

Karen opened her eyes and relaxed her grip on Bonnie's hand. "It only lasts a little while, at least I think it's only a little while, and then I get sucked right back, back into my glass thing. I can open my eyes, and everything's back to normal, except—" She stopped and covered her mouth, letting out an embarrassed laugh.

Bonnie laughed with her. "Except for what?"

"Well, the first time, when it was over, I ended up wearing just my underwear. But it was all right; I had on long johns, 'cause I get cold in that lab." She held up her left hand, displaying a thin gold ring. "And this ring was on the floor next to my clothes. So was an ankle bracelet I used to wear. Every time after that, though, they gave me a long white robe to put on, sort of like a church choir robe, and I didn't end up in my underwear anymore."

"And what happened to Derrick?"

Karen pulled her hand from Bonnie's lap and gave a wave of dismissal. "Oh, he was fine. I don't remember what happened to his clothes 'cause I was worried about my own."

"Do Beck and Stacey ever do anything?"

"Yes, they take my place sometimes, but it's usually me, 'cause I'm older, I guess. It's always Derrick in the other one, though."

Bonnie thought for a minute, trying to fit the pieces of the puzzle together. She put a finger to her lips and spoke slowly. "I saw three glass domes out there. Did they ever use the third one?"

Karen shook her head. "They never told us what it's for."

Bonnie took a deep breath and blew it out in short, thoughtful puffs. "I can't figure out what's going on, at least not yet, but I'm going to have a look around tonight. Do you want to come with me?"

Karen shook her head again. "Ashley always checks on us and locks the hall door when she goes to bed. She's almost like a jail warden. But she and Doc are good to us. We have good food and TV and computers and lots of nice clothes."

"Hmmm." Bonnie rubbed her chin as she looked around the room. Each girl had a computer system, and there was an assortment of dolls, board games, and stereo equipment either pushed against the walls or stored neatly on various shelves. Karen also had a collection of model cars on her side of the room, along with a short stack of automobile magazines.

"You like cars?" Bonnie asked.

Karen blushed and folded her hands in her lap. "Yeah. I like to read about them, and I have some videos. I want to be a mechanic someday, maybe even in a pit crew for NASCAR races."

Bonnie then noted an encyclopedia set, an antique music box, and a huge collection of computer games. She let out a low whistle. "All this stuff makes me wonder where they get the money to finance this operation."

"I asked that a long time ago. There's lots of old rich guys who want to live forever, so it's easy to get money."

"Don't they have to prove that what they're doing works?"

Karen's eyebrows raised, her eyes widening like glowing emeralds. "Oh, they have proof, all right. Ashley's grandfather lives in the boys' dorm, and he got healthier every day. He was in a coma for a while, but the last time I saw him he was walking around. His muscles were getting stronger all the time."

"*Were* getting stronger?"

"Well, he sort of levelled out, I guess. I don't think he's getting any worse, though."

Bonnie tapped her foot on the braided rug, then dug her toes into a groove. "I wonder if Ashley would let me see him. Maybe he would give me more information."

Karen shrugged her shoulders. "Who knows? Ashley's real nice, but she keeps a lot of secrets. She likes to say, 'Too much information can make your brain choke.'"

Bonnie laughed and got up from the bed. She used both hands to help Karen to her feet and wrapped her arms around her new friend. "Yes, Ashley is secretive, but I'll bet I can find the keys and get us out tonight. I think you and I had better figure out what's really going on around here." She pulled away and looked into Karen's bright eyes. "Are you with me?"

Karen's head drooped. She drew her hands into fists, making her knuckles crack. "I . . . I guess so."

Bonnie hugged her again, this time wrapping her up with her arms and wings. "Don't let your heart be troubled, Karen. Someone is watching, and He's on our side."

CHAPTER 9

THE TRANSLUMINARY TRIANGLE

Bonnie spent the remainder of the evening in her room with only a desk lamp illuminating the area near her bed. She rested on her pillow with her eyes closed, sometimes dozing, sometimes praying. Normally she would have taken the time to jot some of her thoughts down in her journal, but she knew the old notebook still lay where she left it, out on one of the lab chairs. She wanted it back. She had spent too many hours recording her amazing adventures, her lonely wanderings, and her heartfelt prayers to have them exposed to an unauthorized reader or accidentally thrown away.

One of her prayers had been that someday her writing might help someone, maybe even change someone's life. Her own story had been one of heart-rending loss changed into great gain – sorrowful valleys that had transformed into exhilarating heights of love and joy. Maybe other troubled souls could be encouraged in the valleys of their own lives.

Bonnie awoke from one of her short naps to find a dinner tray next to her bed. A huge sub sandwich perched on a stoneware plate next to a pile of rippled potato chips. The sandwich was stuffed with shaved turkey breast, a dark green lettuce leaf, and sliced black olives. Her stomach growled its approval. As she leaned over and squeezed the roll to fit her mouth, honey mustard oozed out the sides and dripped onto her plate. *Oooh! That's so good! How did Ashley know what I like on a sandwich?*

Next to her plate a ripe Anjou pear held down a folded note. Bonnie pulled it out and read the handwritten words. "I hope you enjoy your meal. We normally eat together in the kitchen, but I didn't want to wake you. I'll come by later this evening. By the way, I found your backpack and journal. I put them and your coat in your closet next to your shoes."

My journal! Maybe Ashley really can read minds!

Bonnie took another big bite just as the door swung open. "Wake up, Bonnie!" Ashley called as she walked in. Ashley's cheery tone made the room seem brighter even before she flicked on the ceiling light. "Oh, you are awake. How do you like your supper?"

Bonnie set the sandwich on the plate, chewing, then licking the drips of mustard. She laughed, her mouth half full. "It's perfect! Thank you!"

"Do you want to finish it, or can it wait? It's time to talk to your mother."

Bonnie pushed the tray to the side and grabbed her shoes from the floor, chewing and swallowing quickly. "Does she know I'm here? Will she be surprised?"

142

Ashley withdrew a pair of dark brown hiking boots from Bonnie's closet. "Here," she said, setting the boots at Bonnie's feet. "Your shoes still look wet."

"They are." Bonnie eyed the boots with a smile. She slipped off the shoe she had put on and pushed her foot into one of the boots. It fit perfectly.

Ashley watched Bonnie loop the laces through the hooks. "We told your mother you were coming, but we haven't contacted her since you got here." She rocked from her toes to her heels, carrying some kind of clothing over her left arm. "It's all set up, though. We're just waiting for you."

Bonnie leaped to her feet and headed for the door. "Let's go, then!"

The two stepped quickly through the hall and out into the lab, Ashley pausing only to relock the hall door. The ceiling lights in the chamber were dim, but Bonnie could see well enough to make her way toward the centre where the candlestone sat on the pedestal, glowing crimson in the laser's steady beam. She felt a wave of nausea as she approached, so she walked more slowly toward the control panel, trying to fight off the sickness.

"Bonnie, wait!" Ashley caught up and handed her a white robe. "Here. Put this over your clothes."

Bonnie took the robe and slid it over her head while Ashley adjusted her wings underneath the material. When everything was smoothed out, Ashley pulled the robe's hood up. "Good," Ashley said. "It's big enough to cover everything."

Bonnie untwisted the long sleeves that wrapped her arms. She remembered what Karen had said about wearing a robe but wondered if there was another reason for it. "Is this some kind of protection?"

"Yes. It prevents light absorption. I don't think it will be perfect, but it should keep you from getting too sick."

"You knew about that? But how?"

"It stands to reason." Ashley fussed with Bonnie's robe, smoothing out a bunched place on one side so the hem would reach the floor. "But don't worry about that now. It's showtime."

Ashley led the way toward the control panel where Bonnie's father sat peering at the various displays and lights all over the board. Bonnie kept close behind, using Ashley as sort of a shield, though not to protect herself from the candlestone. The robe seemed to be working, but she felt nervous about seeing her father again.

Static filled the area with an irritating hum that nearly drowned Bonnie's thoughts. Ashley cupped her hands around her mouth and shouted. "Bonnie's here. Are you going to talk first?"

Dr Conner kept his eyes fixed on the monitor as he picked up the microphone and spread the hood over the control panel. "Yes. I'll do the introductions." He turned a dial, and the lights dimmed further until they went completely out. He licked his lips before pressing a button on the mike's throat. The static went silent. He spoke slowly into the microphone while Bonnie stepped closer, staring at the flaming red candlestone as it greedily drank from the glowing scarlet laser beam, spilling and spitting it out in red sparks on the other side. "Irene? Irene, are you there?"

He released the button and adjusted a knob on the panel, trying to smooth out the returning static. "Beta frequency is not as stable," he said, turning to Ashley.

She reached to push a slider bar. "Try raising the distortion allowance. That's worked before. I think beta's a little off from what we guessed when we first calibrated the settings."

The rasping noise died away, and they waited. Bonnie felt streams of sweat pour down her back, but her hands were like ice.

The speakers crackled back to life, a female voice pouring forth in a sweet, melodic alto. "I'm here. Is Bonnie out there?"

Bonnie took a quick step forward. Mama's voice! There was no doubt about it! She shouted, "Here I am! I'm right here!"

Her father extended the microphone. "She can't hear you without this."

Bonnie hesitated. Her father's eerie, dark silhouette morphed in the dim red glow that covered him with a deep crimson shroud. He looked like a spectre of death handing her a bloody rose.

She reached to take the microphone, and when she saw her hand shaking, she grasped the throat with both hands. Pushing the talk button with her thumb, she lifted it slowly and spoke, her voice soft and trembling. "Mama? It's Bonnie." She released the button and waited a few seconds, nervously licking her quivering lips.

145

The voice boomed again from the speakers. "Bonnie, my darling! Is it really you?"

Bonnie's tears flowed, and her legs wobbled. She replied, both laughing and crying at the same time. "Yes . . . yes, Mama, it's me." She wiped hot wet streams from her cheeks, and her voice broke into a mournful lament. "Mama, I've missed you so much!"

A few more seconds passed before a soft, comforting voice replied. "I've missed you, too, sweetheart! But don't despair, we'll be back together soon."

"But how, Mama? How?" Bonnie looked at her father and then at Ashley, searching their eyes for an answer.

The voice from the speakers became softer, more urgent. "Bonnie, I need you to come in here, inside the candlestone. I'll attach my light energy to yours, and you can draw me out."

With cold fingers of fear creeping all over her body, Bonnie could barely speak, her voice cracking and choking. "I . . . I'll do anything to help you, but I don't know how to get in there."

The loudspeaker coughed and spat out a round of rough static, and the voice disintegrated into buzzing chaos. Bonnie could barely make out the words. "Don't worry, honey. They'll teach you—" The voice died. Dr Conner twisted dials on the panel, but his adjustments were to no avail.

The microphone trembled in Bonnie's hand. She laughed, though streams of tears spilled down her cheeks. Her mother's confusing words mixed with the eerie lights and frenzied static. Steadying her hands, she pushed the microphone button again. "Mama? Are you there?"

Ashley touched Bonnie's shoulder and turned on a small lamp attached to the control panel. "It takes a lot of energy for her to communicate," she explained. "She has to decipher our energy input and then create a light energy answer for our computer to decode."

She took the microphone and set it on the control panel. "The computer then uses her digitized voiceprint to make the output sound like her voice. It doesn't take long for her to get too tired to continue." She tenderly wiped a new tear from Bonnie's cheek. "Remember, she was already mortally wounded when your father transluminated her, and her life force is still weak. But don't worry. She'll be fine. And if you're willing, you can help us get her out in the morning."

Bonnie's father switched off the laser, and the gun descended toward the floor. "That's the big 'if' – if you're willing. It's dangerous. We've succeeded in sending people into the candlestone, but only for a couple of minutes, max. They're not able to stay long, because they don't have the same make-up as you do. They have no natural light receptors, so they go into the stone out of the proper phase. We believe that you can go in and attach yourself to your mother and pull her out."

Bonnie gazed at the tiny stone, imagining a miniature universe within its crystalline cage. "How can I do that? Once I'm in there, won't it trap me like it did Mama and the slayer?"

Ashley flipped a switch on the panel's side. The static died away, and silence filled the room. "We have what we call an energy anchor, a boy named Derrick that we've trained to attach himself to the person going into the candlestone. He has a perfect record in being able to hang on to our diver."

"Diver?"

Ashley motioned with her hand, making it look like a person diving into the water. "That's what we call whoever's going into the stone."

Bonnie nodded slowly. "Okay, but how do they get changed back to normal?"

Ashley turned up the ceiling lights and gestured for Bonnie to come to the centre of the room. While Dr Conner put the candlestone away, Ashley explained the system of glass cylinders. "This one," she said, pointing to the cylinder opposite the main panel, "we call the diver's dome." She rubbed a slender flexible hose joining that cylinder to one that sat to the left of the master board. "It's hooked to what we call the anchor dome by this special tube. Each dome transluminates the person inside, and the anchor stretches his light energy through this tube and attaches himself to the diver's energy."

Bonnie imagined a stream of light leaping from one cylinder to the other, passing through what looked like thirty feet of vacuum cleaner hose and popping out at the other cylinder. The second cylinder stood a third of the way around the perimeter of the circle, so someone would have to stretch out real far to get it done.

"As you can see," Ashley continued, pointing back to the first dome, "the diver's dome has an outlet hole and a plain glass tube that ends near the candlestone. When I open the tube, the candlestone draws the diver's light into itself while the anchor hangs on. The anchor remains here in the lab, because most of his energy is held in the special tube between the domes where he can attach to crystalline spurs that mimic the candlestone's absorption properties, except that they don't permanently entrap his energy."

Ashley held out her two fists and pumped them like she was pulling down on a chin-up bar. "These spurs act sort of like friction grips for photons, something that Derrick can hang onto, anchoring him in place. After a while, as the candlestone keeps pulling, the anchor's attachment point gets stretched out, and he begins to lose contact with the diver. That's when we shift everything into reverse."

Bonnie put her hand on the hose. It felt like dimpled glass, wrinkled and semi-transparent. "Reverse? You mean you bring the diver back?"

"Right. I created synthetic photoreceptors, just like the natural ones your mother has in her blood and you have in yours. They change light energy into matter. That's why dragons live so long; they're constantly regenerating. I figured out how it all works by analyzing Excalibur's beam. I was able to capture the beam's profile, even though we were only able to turn the beam on in short bursts. I discovered that Excalibur's effects can be reversed by slowing the newly created tachyons and reversing their space and time framework, in effect, making them anti-tachyons. As their hyperlight speed slows toward the mass–energy asymptote, the photoreceptors cause the energy to begin a reassimilation process, using light-encoded cell structure information, data that should still exist in your mother's energy matrix."

Bonnie tried to replay Ashley's explanation in her mind, but the technical terms flew right by. As soon as her brain grabbed one of the hundred-letter words, another zipped through. It was like trying to grab a handful of fog. "I have no clue what you're talking about," she said, "but I heard one word that bothers me."

"One word? What word was that?"

"You said, 'should', that her information 'should' still exist. How do you know it'll work?"

Ashley ran a single finger across the dome's glass surface. "It worked for Derrick and the girls." She pressed a button at the base, and the dome began rising. "We first transluminated rats and then larger animals before we considered using humans." She sat on the base and rested her chin in her hands. "The animals didn't go into the candlestone, though, until we started training Derrick to be an anchor. We lost a few animals until he learned how to hold on, but now he's a real pro. He held on to a chimp that we sent into the stone, and it was a complete success. The chimp came back with all of her faculties and memories in place. After several perfect trials, we decided to send in Karen. We really needed someone who could tell us what it was like inside before we could analyse what it would take to draw your mother out."

"And what happened?"

"It worked fine. Karen is perfectly normal with no after-effects, except for being a bit embarrassed."

This part of the story sounded familiar, and Bonnie had a good idea why. "Embarrassed? Why?"

"We didn't figure it out at first, because Derrick always wore cotton, but it seems that the translumination only affects certain organic substances. Karen was wearing something synthetic and came back dressed only in her cotton underwear." Ashley laughed but stopped abruptly when Bonnie didn't laugh with her. "Sorry; I guess it's not really funny."

Bonnie waved her hand. "It's okay. I wasn't thinking about that." She felt better when she heard corroboration of Karen's story. It meant that Ashley was really telling the truth. Maybe she wasn't hiding anything after all, but there was something that still bothered her. "I was wondering why it's dangerous. It sounds like everything's working great."

Ashley rose from the dome base and heaved a deep sigh. "There's one part of the procedure that's never been tried. Although Karen was able to perceive another entity in the candlestone, she was never able to make contact with it." Ashley reached for one of Bonnie's wings and held the outside edge in her hand. "We believe that with your dragon-like genetics, you would probably transluminate into a similar photo-dimension, a sort of light energy frequency that matches your mother's, and you'll be able to find her. But once you attach to her, we don't know if you'll be able to pull her out or if you'll be drawn completely in and cut off from the outside world. It just hasn't been tested."

Bonnie peeked at her father through the corner of her eye. He was studying meter readings on the panel and scribbling notes in a spiral journal. She drew in a deep breath. "Where will my mother show up when I bring her out?"

Ashley released Bonnie's wing and smiled. "*When* you bring her out? I like your attitude." She led Bonnie to the third glass cylinder. "This is the recovery tube. We sometimes call it the restoration dome. When Derrick pulls you out, you'll be attached to your mother in your dome. We told her that she's supposed to go through another crystalline pipeline on the opposite side of Derrick's, passing through a series of photo analysers that will read her encoded light structure. You see, her encoding may be shifted or out of phase because it's been so long since she was transluminated. She went inside in an agitated state, but after a while, her light energy settled down. It's sort of like a reflection in a pond that gets disturbed by throwing in a rock. Eventually, the water settles down, and you can see the image again. All the parts of the messed up image are the same as the clear image, except that they're scrambled. So, if slowing your mother's tachyons doesn't create an auto-assimilation, I'll have to use the computer to rephase her structure."

Bonnie pressed her palms on her temples. "You're making my brain explode."

Ashley pulled Bonnie's hands down and laughed. "It sounds worse than it is. I tested it with a rabbit by messing up her encoding and shifting her frequency phasing. Then, I passed her light through the analyser. No problem. She came out a perfectly healthy bunny." She tapped on the cylinder's glass with her knuckles. "In short, a few seconds after you show up in your dome, you'll see your mother in this restoration dome. We don't know for sure what kind of condition she'll be in, but we're convinced that since we can communicate with her, she will be out of the coma, maybe even perfectly well. It could be that you'll be in each other's arms less than a minute later."

Bonnie's heart thumped in her chest like a dozen excited bongo drums. Could it really be true? Could all of this really work? Would she finally see her mother, who she thought had died months ago?

"We're waiting for morning," Ashley continued, "so Derrick will be wide awake and strong. Anchoring is a gruelling job, and he gets exhausted after just a few minutes. But that's okay, because we don't want to go longer than a few minutes anyway. The light energy begins getting out of phase in about 250 seconds. We have to be sure to throw it into reverse before we hit that time mark."

Bonnie put her hands on her temples again and closed her eyes.

Ashley's tone softened. "Did I give you a headache?"

Bonnie smiled but kept her eyes closed. "No. I'm just praying." She peeked under one eyelid. Ashley's lips parted, and her eyes widened, as though with all of her great intelligence and learning, she beheld a sight she truly didn't understand but wanted to learn more about.

Bonnie finished her prayer, opened her eyes, and took Ashley's hand in hers. "I'll do it."

Ashley grinned from ear to ear and began talking in rapid-fire fashion as she led Bonnie back to the dorm. "That's awesome! You need to get plenty of rest, and we'll make sure the robe fits you better so it won't drag the floor of the dome. But don't worry; it won't really matter anyway. It all gets changed into light. And translumination doesn't hurt at all; at least that's what they tell us. Derrick's done it about twenty-five times, and Karen's done it about a dozen or so."

As they entered the hall, Bonnie started laughing.

Ashley stopped abruptly. "What's so funny?"

Bonnie pulled a wing to the front and held the edge in her hand. "You act like you think I might be scared."

Ashley's dark eyebrows arched downward. "Aren't you?"

Bonnie grinned and shook her head. "I'm excited, but I'm not scared. Not really."

Ashley fussed with her keys as she unlocked their dorm room. "You must have a lot more faith than I do. I don't think I'd be so calm."

"Why? You're the one who's been propping me up, telling me why it's all going to work."

Ashley pushed the door open but blocked Bonnie from entering. "It's not the technology." She looked down the hall and then lowered her voice to a whisper. "Have you forgotten? Devin's in the candlestone, too."

Bonnie's throat grew a lump the size of a golf ball. In all the joy and excitement of hearing her mother's voice, she really had forgotten about the dragon slayer. "But . . . but he's on a different phase or something, isn't he?"

Ashley motioned with her head for Bonnie to come inside, and she closed the door quietly. She sat on the bed under the Einstein poster and patted the space next to her. Bonnie joined her, her legs trembling as she sat down.

Ashley kept her tone low. "Devin has always communicated with us on the alpha frequency, and your mother's always been on the beta. I think you'll go in with your mother's phase, and he probably won't even know you're there. But there's one problem. Sometimes I search for him in his phase, and I can't find him. I think something's up. I don't trust him."

153

CHAPTER 10

LOVE LIFTS THE VEIL

Ashley had been asleep for more than an hour when Bonnie decided to make her move. The room was nearly dark, but enough light came from under the door to allow her to find her way around.

Bonnie slipped out of bed and tiptoed across the room toward the wall hook next to Ashley's dresser where her keys dangled. She held up her nightgown's skirt to keep its hem from sweeping the floor. Ashley had been so sweet earlier in the evening to help her cut and stitch holes for her wings in the silky soft material. While they worked, they had chatted about sewing and clothes, and giggled while they flipped through the pages of an old magazine and made fun of the badly outdated fashions.

Bonnie lifted the keys from the hook and tiptoed to the closet. She slipped her jeans from the hanger, slid a new pair of tennis shoes from the shelf, and gently turned the doorknob until the latch gave way. With a gentle tug, the door swung open a crack, but the rusty hinge squawked like a bad-tempered chicken. Bonnie spun her head toward Ashley's bed. *Whew! Still sleeping.*

Folding her wings in tightly, she squeezed through the gap and left the door unlatched. After pulling on her jeans under her gown, she crossed the hall to Karen's door and gave it a couple of little taps. Less than two seconds later it flew open, and Karen appeared.

"You ready?" Bonnie whispered.

"Ready." Karen showed no signs of sleepiness, her eyes shining brightly.

Bonnie bent down to slip her shoes over the socks she'd worn to bed. She tied the laces hurriedly and then headed for the hall exit, winding up the lower part of her gown and tucking it inside her jeans as she walked. She stopped at the door and searched through the keys while Karen looked on. "It was one of the brown ones," Bonnie muttered, "but there's a bunch of them."

Karen pointed at a key with a rounded end. "I think it's that one."

Bonnie tried Karen's choice, and the lock turned smoothly. She cracked the door and peeked out into the dark laboratory chamber. The lamp of the main control panel gleamed in the dark, but there was no sound, no movement. Bonnie opened the door fully and entered the chamber, waiting for Karen to follow before silently closing the door.

Bonnie hopped up to the lab platform and headed straight for the main control panel, hoping to find her father's spiral-bound notebook. *Yes! There it is!* She picked it up, placed it under the lamp, and studied the last few pages, hoping to find a record of what she had seen for herself.

A strange array of numbers and letters filled most of the entry – characters that were hard to read, made with dark hasty strokes scratched across the paper without regard for the lines. Each number had a code letter next to it, but the cryptic message seemed indecipherable. Bonnie flipped back to earlier pages, scanning them for words she could understand. Finally, near the front of the notebook, she found something, a narrative pencilled in more careful script. She read while Karen looked over her shoulder.

Seeing that dragon's blood is the only real agent that can actually regenerate tissue, it has become clear through many trials that our triangle will only be successful in reversing Excalibur's transluminating process if we supply the tachyon engine with the receptors from the blood itself. The receptors seem impossible to synthetically produce, at least for this application. The lab rats were expendable. We can't risk trying it on humans until we have successfully restored at least a rat, and, ideally, a higher order mammal upon which we can test memory restoration. Ashley believes that her synthetic receptors will eventually work. Time will tell if she is correct.

157

That was the end of the script. The next page contained just a series of numbers and labels, so Bonnie flipped the pages forward, looking for more text. After about a dozen pages of cryptic data, she found a series of block letters. They didn't make real words, but they were separated into word-like letter strings. It started, "QRL AFXN NXC" and continued with similarly jumbled chains.

Karen whispered, "Does that stuff make any sense to you?"

"Maybe. Something about this looks very familiar." Bonnie thought back to a time when she and her father traded coded messages, a game that allowed them to write to each other about her dragon characteristics without anyone else understanding, even if someone happened to read one of their notes. It had been more than a year since the last time she decrypted his code, and he might have come up with a new system, but she decided it was worth a try. She tore out a blank sheet from the back of the notebook and found a pen on the control board.

After a few minutes of work, she came up with a translation and whispered it to Karen. "Her idea has failed, but replacing the synthetic receptors with real ones in the presence of the candlestone has made the process work until now. I will have to let her know eventually, but as long as her grandfather improves, she won't ask questions, and our investors will be happy. I can't explain it to her yet. I also cannot tell her why the blood has been so readily available." Bonnie looked up from the page. "Does that mean anything to you?"

Karen scratched her thick mane of red hair. "Well, they've mentioned putting receptors in my blood to see if they would work. I got the idea that it didn't take for me, but I think it did take for Ashley's grandfather. At least it did until recently."

Bonnie closed the notebook and waved it toward Karen. "Well, I'm not sure how old this entry is, but it was something my dad obviously didn't want Ashley to read."

Karen raised her eyebrows and smiled. "So Ashley's not the only one who's keeping secrets, huh?"

Bonnie put her hand to her chin. "Apparently not." She surveyed the cavernous room, looking for something – a new object, maybe another notebook, anything that might spark a new idea. She noted the banks of darkened fluorescent lights, several rows inset in drop ceiling panels. She wondered how high the true ceiling might be, but even if she were to walk to the cavern's wall and look up, it would be too dark to tell with only a single desk lamp for light.

She scanned across the chamber to a door in the far corner and pointed toward it. "Is that the door to the monster's cave?"

Karen nodded. "Yep. That's the one."

Bonnie laid the notebook where she found it and prowled toward the cave, but Karen didn't budge.

Bonnie glanced over her shoulder. "What's wrong?"

"Nothing." Karen scrambled off the platform but slowed as she drew closer.

When Bonnie reached the door, she noticed a strange shadow on the exterior. She ran her hand over the surface and felt the outline of a horseshoe-shaped symbol scratched into the wood. "I guess that's an omega, right?"

Karen tiptoed up to the door and angled her head to get a look. "Yeah. That's what Ashley told me, an upper case omega."

Bonnie pulled out the set of keys and tried several in the lock, each one failing. With only a few left, she turned to Karen. "Have you ever seen Ashley open this door?"

Karen shook her head. "No. I've only seen Doc go through."

Bonnie tried the last of the keys. "Hmmm. The things that Ashley doesn't know are piling up." She put her ear to the door and listened.

"Hear anything?" Karen asked.

"Shhhh!"

Bonnie detected a faint murmur but couldn't quite make it out. "It sounds like sawing wood," she whispered, "and then it changes to more like a train rumbling, and then back to sawing again. It's like an old man snoring and wheezing."

"Sometimes it's louder," Karen added, "more like growling or even moaning. If it's not a monster, I don't want to guess what else it could be."

159

Bonnie stepped back from the door and frowned. "Monster, schmonster, Karen. He's just trying to scare you."

"Scare me? Why would he want to do that?"

"To keep you girls in line, maybe?"

Karen took a quick breath and squared her shoulders. "No way! We don't give him any trouble!"

Bonnie gestured toward the boys' dorm hall. "Derrick, then?"

"Not a chance. He's real quiet and shy."

"Does Ashley ever say anything about the growling?"

Karen looked down and slowly shook her head. "Not that I can remember. If it's fake, she just seems to play along."

Bonnie pressed her lips together and squeezed one eye nearly closed. "Hmmm." She then pushed on the door with her shoulder while turning the knob, but it didn't budge. The sound of her grunt was followed by the wail of a faint siren. She stepped back, nearly stumbling. "Is that an alarm?"

Karen's eyes darted around. "You must have tripped something. Sounds like it's coming from the boys' area."

A sudden bump and click sounded nearby. The door to the boys' dorm swung open. Bonnie led Karen into a dark corner and whispered in her ear. "Let's wait here. Don't make a sound."

"Is somebody out there?" a male voice called.

"It's your father," Karen whispered.

Bonnie gave her a quick "Shhh!" and crouched, pulling Karen down with her. She watched her father walk by as he headed toward the light switches, one hand in his bathrobe pocket and the other reaching for the wall. Just as the fluorescent panels flashed on, Bonnie grabbed Karen around the waist and held one hand over her mouth before leaping into the air. She flew around and above the drop ceiling toward the upper reaches of the cavern, lugging Karen like a sack of wiggling cats.

Finding a stable rafter, she perched there while her father checked behind panels and opened storage closets.

Bonnie felt Karen's deep gasps against her hand, the rushing air blowing in and out through her nose. Karen's feet seemed secure, and they supported her weight on the rafter. Bonnie whispered in her ear, "Don't worry. I've done stuff like this before." She slowly released her grasp.

Karen whispered coarsely, "That was so cool! Are you going to fly down, too?"

"Shhh!" Bonnie clutched a vertical beam with her right hand and Karen's waist with her left arm. She took slow, shallow breaths of the warm, stale air, barely making a sound. Beads of sweat trickled from her brow and cheeks. Nothing moved. The rocky ceiling trapped the heat and exhaust from the laboratory equipment, and no outside vents brought fresh air into the chamber.

It took a few minutes for her father to satisfy himself that all was in order. He tested the door that had tripped the alarm, finding it securely locked. With a shrug, he flicked off the lights and disappeared behind the boys' hallway door.

Bonnie whispered. "Let's wait another minute. I want to make sure he's not coming back." The seconds seemed like hours. Their perspiration dripped, falling like hot, salty raindrops to the nearly invisible floor below. When Bonnie felt the sweaty wetness on Karen's shirt, she decided it was time to move. She released the beam and clutched Karen with both arms. "Okay. Hold your breath."

She leaped from the rafter, throwing her wings into a full canopy, flapping once to catch and hold the motionless air. The girls dropped to the floor, Bonnie trying to hit the concrete surface running. Karen's feet tripped over themselves, and the two

161

girls landed in a crumpled heap, rolling and grunting as their momentum carried them forward.

Bonnie jumped up and helped Karen to her feet. "Are you okay?"

Karen nodded, rubbing a sore spot on her elbow.

With her head tilted to one side, Bonnie listened, ready to fly again if necessary, but it seemed that no one had heard their spill. All was quiet.

Bonnie took Karen's hand. "Let's get back to our rooms. I don't think we'll learn much more tonight." They crossed the cavern, passing through the main lab, and reentered the girls' hall. Bonnie relocked the door and whispered to Karen as she led her back to her room. "I've figured out a few things but not everything. I need to talk to Ashley in the morning, and then maybe it'll get clearer." Bonnie pushed open Karen's door and placed a gentle hand on her shoulder. "Try to get some sleep. I'll see you at breakfast."

Karen smiled, and the tracks of dusty sweat smearing her cheeks expanded. "Okay," she whispered, and she turned to go into her room. At the last second she spun back around and grabbed Bonnie's hand. Standing on tiptoes she kissed Bonnie tenderly on the cheek. As a tear formed in Karen's eye, she said softly, "Thanks . . . for everything." With that, she tiptoed in and closed the door.

Bonnie put two fingers on her cheek. *Thanks for what? What have I done for her?*

She pulled the skirt of her nightgown out and slipped her shoes and jeans off, wadding them into a bundle, and then it dawned on her. *She thinks I was sneaking around for her, trying to figure out what they were doing to her, maybe find a way for her to get out. And why not? She's trapped here like a human guinea pig in some bizarre experiment. She's living a nightmare right before my eyes. She's an imprisoned orphan in an underground cage.*

Bonnie knew what it felt like – loneliness, hopelessness, despair. All this time, Bonnie had been thinking about finding her mother and not much else. Sure, the girls were important, but that's not why she was skulking around for clues.

Bonnie's lips trembled as she pictured Karen's grimy face and sad, teary eyes. As the image morphed, tears crept into her own eyes, one already dripping down her cheek. She saw shackles on Karen's wrists and neck, and Ashley holding a leash, smiling while leading Karen to the diver's dome. Bonnie balled her hands into fists, her face heating up until she thought steam might spew out her ears. She threw open her door, and light from the hall poured into the room. Ashley sat up, bleary eyed and blinking at Bonnie. "What's going on?"

Bonnie stalked in, closing her wings to get through and then opening them again in the middle of the room. She flung the keys and the wad of clothes on her bed and planted her fists on her hips, not knowing where to begin.

Ashley stared at her. "Are you okay? Are you sleepwalking or something?"

Bonnie pointed toward the hallway, passion erupting in her voice. "They're human beings!" she cried. "Not stupid lab rats!"

Ashley jumped up and marched to the door, closing it with an authoritative click. "Shhh!" she warned while reaching for the light switch. "Do you want to wake the girls?"

Bonnie kept pointing, her arm now shaking. "As if you really cared about them. Can't you see you're using them? They're people! I noticed no one ever mentioning *you* volunteering to get transluminated!"

163

Ashley walked slowly toward her bed. Her voice stayed calm, sounding almost condescending as she raised her eyebrows and chin. "I have to run the equipment, Bonnie. It would be suicide for a diver if something went wrong and I wasn't available to fix it."

Still fuming, Bonnie grabbed Ashley's arms and turned them over to expose the undersides. "But it's okay to use other people for pincushions, I see, and keep your own skin from getting gouged over and over again."

Ashley shook Bonnie's hands loose and pulled her arms back. "It's the same deal, Bonnie. If something bad happened to me, who would continue the research? No one else knows how the photoreceptors work."

Bonnie folded her arms across her chest. "Are you sure they really do work?"

Ashley's brow furrowed, and her eyes seemed to darken. "Of course I'm sure. My grandfather is living proof."

Bonnie moved her hands back to her hips, and her wings shuddered like they were trying to throw off a chill. "So you're willing to take chances with these girls but not with yourself? I guess it's okay if something happens to them, because they're not as smart as you are. I guess they're expendable."

Ashley folded her arms across her chest. "Well, I wouldn't put it that way."

Bonnie drilled her stare into Ashley. "Then how would you put it?"

Ashley stepped toward Bonnie, gazing down at her from her two-inch height advantage. "These girls would either be dead or on their way to prostitution by now if they weren't here. They have food and clothes, and their sacrifice will benefit the entire world."

Bonnie held her ground. "Sacrifice?" she repeated, leaning forward and waving her arms. "You call being imprisoned and forced to be a lab rat a sacrifice? The Nazis experimented on the Jews in the name of science. Oh, those wonderful sacrificial Jews! Wasn't it nice how they gave their lives for the benefit of humankind? And how about aborted babies? Isn't it sweet of them to lend their bodies to scientists for stem cell research? Some day all of humanity will give thanks for their sacrifice!"

Bonnie scowled and turned her back on Ashley, folding her arms and huffing. "For being so smart, you sure are clueless, Ashley. My father's got the wool pulled over your eyes big time."

Ashley's voice lowered, and she sounded more like a wounded puppy than an intimidating debater. "What do you mean by that?"

Bonnie turned back around. Pain branded Ashley's expression, and Bonnie's rapid boil slowed to a simmer. She didn't want to hurt her new friend; she just wanted to make everything right – to free her mother and the girls. But she wasn't sure how much she should tell Ashley, at least not yet.

165

"Ashley, there's a lot going on here that doesn't make any sense." She picked up Ashley's keys from the bed and jingled them. "Tell me. Why don't you have a key to the Omega door?"

Ashley blinked at the key ring, as if trying to focus through sleepy eyes. "I haven't had a need for it. Your father has the only one."

"But you have keys to everything else, right?"

Ashley squinted and paused for a second. "Yeah, I guess so."

"Well, what could be in that cave that's such a secret?"

Ashley let out an impatient sigh. "It's a passage that used to lead outside, but after we brought all our equipment in here, part of it caved in during a minor earthquake. It's too dangerous to go through anymore; that's why we named it 'Omega', the last letter in the Greek alphabet. It's sort of like saying, 'If you try to go through there, you're finished.' So, to protect the girls, your father has a continuous audio stream running on a laptop computer. It plays random monster noises that he downloaded from the Internet. He just wants to keep the kids from ever trying to go in there."

Bonnie nodded slowly. "I figured it was something like that, but why doesn't he want you to go in there? Maybe he's hiding something else."

Ashley pushed her hand through her tangled hair. "I can't imagine what." She pointed to her keys in Bonnie's hand. "I guess he doesn't want any extra keys left around for people to get ahold of."

"Okay, okay," Bonnie said, laughing. "I'm busted. At least you're right about that." Her tone turned serious again, and she gestured toward the hall. "But what about these girls, and what about Derrick? Do you really think it's right to use human beings as guinea pigs against their will?"

Ashley shrugged her shoulders. "I guess I saw them as willing participants. They didn't kick or scream or anything. We give them whatever they want, within reason, of course, and they do what we ask."

"But that's just the point. You're treating them like animals – you feed them, keep them warm, and clean their cages. So now it's okay to ravage their bodies? Don't you see that they're real people, and they're scared? Just because nobody loves them, you think you can use them?" Bonnie glanced upward and whispered a silent prayer. *God give me the right words to say.* She took a deep breath before continuing. "Well, I know someone who loves them, and He doesn't look kindly on mistreating orphans."

Ashley's brow knitted three rows of angry wrinkles, and her lips tightened into two pale lines. "Is this turning into a 'God loves everyone' speech? Because if it is, I don't want to hear it. Daddy kept trying to tell me that, always singing 'Amazing Grace', but I asked him to quit a long time ago. If God were so amazing or so loving, Daddy wouldn't have suffered so much, and I wouldn't be such a Brainiac freak." She waved her arm toward the hall. "If God loved Pebbles, she wouldn't have been left to die on the beach, wandering in a dirty diaper and spitting sand from her bloody lips. And if God loved Stacey, she wouldn't have been accosted by a pervert in a dark alley who would have abused her and left her for the other street predators to finish off. These kids were worthless throwaways. Nobody really loved them, and they wouldn't have amounted to anything. But at least we're making them into something useful, something they can be proud of."

Bonnie put one hand on her friend's shoulder. Ashley tried to pull away, but Bonnie held firm. "Ashley, love isn't based on what someone can give or how much they can do. I mean, everyone loves the rich and famous, right? But it's all fake. People just want to hang around them because they've got money. True love is treating bums and outcasts like they have diamonds in their pockets, even when there's nothing there but moths and holes."

Bonnie paused and pointed toward Ashley's painting on the wall. "It sounds to me like your grandfather was pretty worthless not too long ago, at least in other people's eyes. But your painting proves you had different eyes. You had eyes of love that saw past his decaying body and into his heart. I'll bet you can do the same for girls like Karen and me." Bonnie pulled up her sleeve and exposed the soft underside of her arm.

Ashley stared at her smooth skin, and, slowly, with trembling fingers, caressed her white needle scars. Bonnie pressed her own hand down on Ashley's and met her eyes when she lifted her head. "Don't you think these girls deserve our love, too, Ashley?"

Ashley's eyes grew wet, and she lowered her gaze. She sniffed hard and sat on the bed, her head bobbing.

Bonnie sat next to her, putting one arm around her shoulders and leaning her cheek on Ashley's dishevelled hair.

Ashley wept openly, halting and sniffing while she tried to talk. "You're . . . you're right. Deep inside I knew it all along. But I kept telling myself that it would . . . that it would all be over soon. We'd finish up and get these girls into good homes somehow."

Ashley put both arms around Bonnie's neck, and they held each other for a few quiet minutes, Ashley's gentle crying the only sound breaking the silence. Bonnie felt Ashley's tears soaking through her nightgown, and the warm wetness reminded her of a song. She sang the chorus softly.

"I felt every teardrop when in darkness you cried, and I strove to remind you, that for those tears I died."

Then she whispered, "Love opens our eyes, Ashley. It always leads us to the truth, even if it takes a long time."

Ashley looked up. Thin red lines bordered her narrowing pupils. "Truth? Are you sure you want the truth? If you ever heard one of Stacey's stories, you might change your mind."

Bonnie grabbed the bedspread and pulled it tight across the surface. "Believe me, I understand. I saw my own mother lying in a pool of blood." She swallowed away the catch in her throat. "Sometimes the truth is ugly; sometimes it hurts, but love helps us overcome evil in all of its deceptions and brutality."

168

Ashley blinked at Bonnie, and a new tear trickled down her cheek. "Yeah, I forgot about what happened to your mother. I can't understand how you're not boiling with rage at your father after all you've been through."

"Well, I don't trust him." Bonnie sniffed and wiped away a new tear of her own. "But I still love him. . . . I mean . . . I chose to love him, even though it wasn't easy." She pressed her finger on the bedspread and drew a cross, staring at it a moment before looking at Ashley again. "Don't you see? Love is a decision we make, even toward people who don't deserve it. It's the only way we can hope to win the battle against Devin, Stacey's nightmares, or your own fears."

Ashley wiped her sleeve across her cheek and looked toward the hall again, sighing. "Well, speaking of truth and fears, I have to figure out what Doc's up to, because I'm not sure he's telling me everything. My grandfather's getting sicker, and Doc doesn't want to call a doctor." She turned back to Bonnie and grasped both of her hands. "But I do know one thing for sure."

Bonnie felt the warmth in Ashley's fingers and the strength of her grip. She had good information about what her father was up to, but could she completely trust Ashley and tell her what she knew? "One thing? What's that?"

"I know you want your mother back. We need to get her out of that candlestone, and I'm not going to let you down."

CHAPTER 11

OLD WINESKINS

After a few hours of sleep in a Missoula motel, Billy sat bolt upright in bed. He had been dreaming about lightning – scattered, streaking bolts through an ink-black sky. It was peaceful at first, like watching a distant storm through a bedroom window while waiting for sleep to carry him away. But as the dream continued, the storm approached, stalking him as he tried to escape through dark, borderless realms. White-hot bolts crashed all around, hemming him in and finally trapping him in a circular cage of fiery, pulsating bars of pure light. One of the bars grew appendages and plunged its super-charged fingers into his chest, numbing his abdomen and thrusting an electric shock through every nerve, from his toes to the top of his head.

Billy let out a slow breath and shook his head. Whew! That was some wake-up call!

He slid out of bed, stretched his arms, and let out a big, blood-pumping yawn. Smacking his dry lips, he glanced at Walter, wrapped in his blanket like a cocooned caterpillar who never heard spring's reveille. Billy's mother lay in the other bed, curled to one side and hugging the extra pillow. The professor slept on a rollaway cot next to the door, his pillow on the carpet and one bare foot sticking out from under his covers.

Billy rubbed his eyes and read the digits on the bedside clock. *Six-fifteen.* He stood up and scratched his head. *I hate waking everyone, but we'd better get moving. I guess I'll use the bathroom first and let them sleep for a few more minutes.*

Billy trudged toward the glow of their bathroom "nightlight," glancing at the professor's open suitcase on the floor nearby. The light streaming past the slightly ajar door cast its beam on the book that rested on top of his clothes – Merlin's diary.

The old book lay open to the first blank page, or at least what had been the first blank page. From his place in the shadows, Billy stared at the bright surface of the yellowed parchment. Something new was there. He leaped toward it and knelt by the suitcase, trying to read the elaborate script. "Mum! Professor! Walter!"

"What? What?" His mother lurched to a sitting position. Walter groaned, but the professor was already walking toward Billy, smoothing out his hair and tucking in his shirt – the same shirt he had worn yesterday. Getting on his knees, he reached around Billy to his suitcase and fished out his spectacles. He slipped them on while Billy's mother scrambled to their side.

Billy tried to slow his breathing while he read.

No one tears a piece from a new garment and puts it on an old garment; otherwise he will both tear the new, and the piece from the new will not match the old. And no one puts new wine into old wineskins; otherwise the new wine will burst the skins, and it will be spilled out, and the skins will be ruined. But new wine must be put into fresh wineskins. And no one, after drinking old wine wishes for new; for he says, "The old is good enough."

The professor sighed and stood up, slowly taking off his glasses. "Very interesting." He stepped over to the bathroom and opened the door wide, allowing the light to pour over them. "It's from the Bible," he announced. "A parable of Christ."

Billy's mother placed her hand on the page and ran her fingers across the lettering. "What does it mean?"

"I have my opinions. It's fascinating that the quote is from a modern translation that came about long after Merlin's day."

Walter's sleepy voice chimed in from across the motel room. "Yeah, Prof, but didn't the book say that we would be able to read it in our own language?"

"Yes, Walter, you are correct. It's a curious phenomenon, however, that an old prophet would find a way to write new prose in a book, fifteen hundred years after his day, and in a dialect to which he is unaccustomed. I suppose, though, if a floating hand is able to write cryptic warnings on a Babylonian palace wall, then most anything is possible."

Billy rubbed his sleepy eyes and faced his teacher. "Floating hand, Professor?"

"Yes. That story is also in the Bible." Professor Hamilton put on his spectacles again and leaned over to reread the script. "It's a good thing Merlin has become familiar with our tongue. If he had written it in Latin, I would have to dust off an old textbook or two to translate it."

Billy's mother pulled her hand away from the page and stood up. "So, what does it mean?"

"I am familiar with the traditional interpretations of the Scriptural passage, but I'm not sure how the text applies to our situation. Considering our hurry, I should like to ponder it while I prepare for our departure. I will share my thoughts during our drive to the university."

Billy's mother and the professor folded up the rollaway while Walter sat on the edge of his bed, stretching and yawning. Billy knew he should get up and get ready, but he couldn't tear himself away from the book. This was the first time it didn't communicate in cryptic poetry, yet this entry was every bit as mysterious. But was the page finished? It looked like there was plenty of room for more. Maybe this message continued on the next page.

The mystery of the unknown dragged Billy down, like a hundred-ton weight hanging from his neck. The next page, although never seen and without a voice, beckoned like the beautiful sirens of Homer's *Odyssey*. Part of Billy's brain absolutely demanded that he turn the page, while another part whispered, "No, Billy. Danger lies ahead." He remembered the warnings, penned in Merlin's own hand, but they were distant, quiet voices, not like the screaming banshees in his head that cried out for the next page. The very warning seemed part of the temptation. What would really happen if he violated its words? If he never tried it, he would never know. No one would. And wouldn't that be a tragedy, not gaining wisdom that begged to be learned?

Billy's fingers, stiff, yet trembling, lifted the page, even as the battle in his mind raged on. His hand worked as if separated from his mind's commands, moving where he begged it not to go.

He turned the page. He let out a long breath as though he had just fought a great battle, but when he read the newly revealed words, he knew he had lost.

"William!" Billy heard the professor's heavy footsteps. "William! The page wasn't full!"

Billy couldn't answer. He could barely breathe. It seemed that a clamp squeezed his throat shut, tightening and cutting off his air supply until his lungs burned, begging for relief. He finally gasped and drank in precious air, puffing until his head swirled in dizziness. But he couldn't take his eyes off the book. Every word he read pounded in his brain like a judge's gavel after a death sentence.

The professor's warm breath glanced off the back of Billy's neck. "William, I fear that this is very bad news. What you have revealed is a dire prophecy, indeed."

"Yeah," Billy replied, his voice low and weak. "I kind of guessed that."

Billy's mother and Walter drew nearer as the professor read aloud.

Of covenants broken, covenants lost
A promise made yet torn in two
Thou never learned salvation's cost
And now bring forth thy vengeance due

Cruel yokes and whips designed for slaves
No, not for heirs nor sons by birth
They tear the backs of stiff-necked knaves
Who think their power comes from earth

Yet hope remains, dispelling fears
A faithful heart, entrapped, alone
Who prays for thee unceasing tears
And casts appeals before his throne

The soul set free must face the beast
And break his chains to fears of earth
To free the faithful heart of love
And prove the seeds of royal birth

175

The professor picked up the diary, slapped the covers together, and with a quick thrust, tucked the book tightly under his arm. His face reddened, and his eyes narrowed. "I believe that I shall keep it by my side from now on." He closed his suitcase and carried it into the bathroom. "If you don't mind, I would like to go first. I am fast and tidy, and I would like to hasten outside to consider this matter alone." He shut the door, leaving the rest of them in darkness.

Walter bounded over his bed and flipped on the lights. Billy's mother reached for her son with both hands and pulled him to his feet, wrapping an arm around his shoulder as he straightened. He knew she was trying to give comfort, but it didn't help. Once again he had lost a battle, this time with his own mind. He pummelled himself inside, using insults he wouldn't throw at a dog. He felt weak, helpless, and trapped, like a beast in a cage, proud and deplorable at the same time, and most of all, selfish beyond belief.

When the professor came out, he gave Billy a sad smile and a pat on the back. He said nothing, yet Billy felt like his teacher had poured healing salve on a deep wound. The sting was diminishing, but a heavy, ponderous weight remained. After the professor bundled up and went outside, the other three hurried through quick showers and revolving door bathroom sharing before joining him.

Billy stepped into the cold, dark Montana morning, two suitcases in his gloved hands. With Walter following a few paces behind, he jogged across the parking lot, his teeth already chattering when he caught up with the professor. "Brrrr! It's gotta be about two degrees out here."

The professor opened the rear door of their rented Jeep and took a suitcase from Billy. "It's four degrees, William, on the Fahrenheit scale, of course."

Billy threw his suitcase into the back. "Four degrees? Professor, is there anything you don't know?"

The professor pointed toward a bank sign across the street. "I was merely taking note of the local media report. It has been dropping ever since I came out."

Billy watched the bank sign announce the temperature in shivering single digits. The numeral four flashed once, then changed to a three. "How about that! My guess was pretty close."

"We're not here to audition for the Weather Channel," Walter said. "Let's just get our freezing backsides moving and get something hot to eat."

Billy jogged back to the motel and carried Excalibur out in a long florist box they had found next to a dumpster at the rental car depot. His mother followed, hustling through the crackling cold air.

"Walter's hungry, Mum." Billy poked Walter's lean stomach. "As usual."

She pointed down the street at a set of bright neon lights. "We can grab something at that burger place."

The professor clasped his arms and bounced on his toes. "Just some hot tea for me, and I'll be fine."

After a quick and quiet breakfast of meat-filled biscuits and orange juice, they headed for the university. Billy's mum followed the signs pointing to the campus while the professor sat stoically in the passenger seat. Billy sat with Walter in the back and kept his eye on his teacher. The old professor's gaze was locked straight ahead, his left arm stiff against his side, binding Merlin's diary in place.

Billy wanted to get a conversation going, but he felt timid, low, and unworthy. He nudged Walter and whispered. "Ask the professor about what we read in the book this morning."

177

Walter nodded and leaned forward. "Hey, Prof! So what's with all that stuff about old garments and new wineskins?"

The professor angled his head toward the boys, his eyebrows turned downward. "I'm afraid I cannot tell you Walter, nor anyone, for that matter, at least for now."

Billy had hoped for news that would lift his spirits, make him feel clean again, but the professor's guarded words hit him like a truckload of sweaty gym socks. The diary held a secret, an old secret, the key to his longings. So far, he had lost every important battle he had fought, only to be rescued by someone with more wisdom or courage. He lacked something – something important he couldn't name but that he saw in Bonnie and the professor. This book, filled with ancient wisdom, had whispered cryptic messages into his soul, messages that would surely lead him to what he desired with all his heart, and the only man who seemed able to interpret it had decided to clam up.

Billy's mum stopped at a traffic light and sighed. "If it's just a Bible verse, Professor, why can't you tell us what you think?"

The professor laid the book on his lap and placed his palm on the cover. "While I was in the shower, it occurred to me that William's temptation was understandable. I had projected my own strength upon him, assuming he could exercise self-control according to my own inner constitution. Such an assumption, of course, is nonsense. William has much to learn, and I fear that most of it will come through trials and suffering, as it did for me in my younger years.

"In any case, when I was preparing to leave the water closet, I desired to read the new poem again, but I first turned to the Scripture on the page before, and the rest of that page had appeared."

He tucked the book under his arm again. "But I'm afraid that I am unable to tell you what it said. The text itself forbade me from even explaining it. It only gave me leave to inform you of my warning, my gag order, if you will. I'm afraid that I am now the only one who may read the book, at least until it gives me leave to share it with others."

Billy's shoulders drooped and his throat tightened again, but he managed to keep breathing. Would the feelings of guilt never go away?

Walter moaned. "But Prof, we need that book. It helped us get Excalibur. Who knows what else it could tell us?"

"You are correct, Walter, but I did not say that no one could read it. I shall continue to observe any new text and act according to wisdom's counsel."

When they arrived on campus, Billy's mum parked near the Skaggs Building, and they hurried toward the door, dodging ploughed snow mounds and keeping their arms tucked close to their bodies while jogging headlong into a whipping wind. After they hustled through the entryway and crossed the mop-streaked terrazzo floor, they chose to tiptoe up the stairs to the third floor rather than take the elevator.

At the top of the stairs they stepped into a deserted hall, the unblemished vacuum cleaner imprints on the carpet proving that a janitor had recently prepared for the morning's new stampede. Billy prowled down the corridor, his eyes scanning the number plates on each door. The longer they kept their approach secret, the better, since they had no way of knowing who or what awaited them. He stopped and pointed, keeping his voice low. "Here it is. Right here. Room 340."

The others came up beside him, and Walter leaned over Billy's shoulder. "The door's open a crack."

Billy's danger monitor sent him a warning signal, not really strong, but enough to give him an eerie sense that something wasn't quite right. He shushed the others, then handed the flower box to the professor, whispering. "Mum left her gun in the plane, so you'd better take Excalibur. I can use my own weapon better anyway."

The professor took the box but kept his arms extended toward Billy. "William," he said in a near whisper, "the sword *is* your weapon now. It was bestowed to you as a gift from above. It was meant for you to wield in battle."

Billy slid his shoe across one of the vacuum marks. "Maybe, but it would be better if we both had something to fight with. I can't lend you my fire breathing."

The professor bowed his head. "Nor can I lend you my faith."

Billy bit his tongue. Had the professor noticed that the sword never glowed in his hands? Billy tried to shake off the thought and focus on the door. "Okay," he said, still keeping his voice low. "I'm going in."

"Be on your guard, William," the professor warned. "An open door indicates an occupied room. An ambush is not out of the question."

"Right," Walter agreed, whispering. "Get your fire stoked, Billy. Turn the dial past 'broil' and go straight to 'nuclear holocaust.'"

Billy glanced through the window to the left of the door. No one in sight. He pulled the door, and it creaked on its hinges until it swung about halfway open. The reception area lights shone brightly, allowing him to scan the anteroom for signs of danger. Licking his lips, he pushed his head inside and listened. Nothing. No sound, no movement, no sign of anyone in the office. He took two steps in and looked all around before gesturing for the others to follow.

A long, waist-high desk with a curved front faced the door. To the right of the desk, the anteroom opened into a sitting area, complete with a grey love seat, a small table for magazines, and three single chairs covered with gingham upholstery. A painting of a lunging grizzly bear hung above the love seat, making Billy wonder if he and his company might be someone's unsuspecting prey.

To the left and behind the reception desk, offices lined a hallway that led to the back end of the suite. Another hallway at the rear wall passed behind a set of partitions out of Billy's view. He heard faint sounds from the rear hall, clinking glass and running water.

"Someone's back there," Billy said, motioning with his head. "You guys wait here. It might just be a secretary or something."

While the others took off their coats, Billy tiptoed down the hall, following the corridor to the right as it led him across the rear of the suite near the back exit. As he closed in on the source of the noise, he slowed down, each stride a furtive, silent step, his sense of danger growing.

Nearing a partially open door, Billy stretched out and pushed it fully open, then retreated behind a partition several feet down the hall.

An elderly lady poked her head out, an empty coffee pot jiggling in her hand. "Is someone out there?"

Billy blew out a long sigh. All this fear over a harmless little old lady! He stepped out from behind the partition and gave her a polite nod. "I'm sorry I startled you, ma'am. I'm here to see Dr Conner. Is he available?"

The grey-haired lady, about a head shorter than Billy and wearing thick glasses, smiled. "Oh, no. He's not here right now." She walked back into the kitchen, still talking. "Let me get the coffee on, and I'll be right out."

When the lady disappeared, Billy called toward the front of the suite. "Come on around. There's just a lady back here. I think it's the receptionist."

Walter showed up first, hustling around the corner. "Does she look like trouble? You never know about those clerical types. Their letter openers can be sharp!"

Though he still felt his danger meter throbbing, Billy shook his head. "Don't be so paranoid. She seems friendly enough, kind of like an old librarian."

"Well, I knew a librarian who threw an eraser fifty feet and hit me right between the eyes."

"What made her mad? Were you burping at a hundred decibels?"

"Yeah. Maybe more."

Billy peeked into the kitchen. "I don't think she's hiding an assault eraser, but she said she'd be right out."

When his mother and the professor came around the corner, Billy turned to greet them, wiping his brow to show his relief. Suddenly he felt a sharp pain in his back, and the old lady's voice returned, this time gruff and sour.

"You're feeling the barrel of a three-fifty-seven magnum, Dragon Boy, and I know how to use it. Don't give me one spark of that fire from hell or it'll be pouring out your backside."

CHAPTER 12

THE VALLEY OF THE SHADOW OF DEATH

Ashley bent over a thick logbook, filling in the boxes with a sharp yellow pencil and whispering the data as she wrote. "Bonnie Silver – Age, fourteen years, one month. Height – five foot six. Weight—" *Hmmm. Never had a chance to weigh her. I'll just guess one twenty.* She scratched the digits in the box and continued. "Blood type – A positive with dragon simplex allele and phototropic receptor 1-A." She looked up from the book and listened. The lab had been dead quiet in the early morning hours, giving Ashley an opportunity to check her equipment. Now she could hear the faint morning bustle in the girls' hall.

Ashley sniffed the air and detected a hint of bacon. Karen's work. She'd planned to rise early and make breakfast, and Bonnie had volunteered to help, though she couldn't have slept much the night before, not with the greatest adventure of her life ahead. Ashley hadn't slept much herself, and she couldn't eat. No way. Her stomach had twisted into a double-knotted rope as doubts streamed into her mind. Would this work? The final step had never been accomplished. Pulling Bonnie's mum out of the candlestone and restoring her body was only possible in theory. And now to try it, Ashley would risk Bonnie's life. She would send her on a journey into a dark, mysterious oblivion that required her to trust a vastly complicated machine – a machine that a teenager had pieced together with her own hands.

Ashley let out a deep sigh, closed the book, and laid it on the console. Soon Bonnie would emerge from the girls' dorm, using the key Ashley had left for her. Mere moments separated Bonnie from either a grand reunion with her mother or perhaps death or eternal imprisonment, tormented forever by the enemy of all dragons. Devin would be sure to transform the crystal prism into a living hell if given a chance.

B illy had to think fast. Surely he could jump away and overpower a little old lady before she could pull the trigger, couldn't he? His belly felt like a world war raged within, an inferno ready to burst through. Just a quick turn, and this lady would be toast.

He leaped to the side and spun around, shooting a jet stream of yellow flames toward the woman's hands, enveloping them in a rushing rage of fire. With a shriek, she fell backwards into the kitchen, firing a bullet into the ceiling and then rolling on the floor, cursing like a sailor's parrot. The river of fire scorched the walls and carpet, and Billy fell back against the corridor's wall, wincing and holding his hands over his cheeks. He had never breathed such a huge burst of blazing heat before.

The professor, still carrying the flower box, dashed past the others into the kitchen. He threw the box on the floor and dove for the writhing woman's body, reaching for her thrashing hand. "William!" he shouted. "The gun is fused to her fingers. I can't remove it."

The woman spat at the professor and cursed. "Get off me you dragon lover! You friend of the devil! Let go of my hand so I can send you straight to hell!" With another loud cry, she fainted away. Walter rushed to the professor's side and wrapped his fingers around the gun barrel. He tried to dump the bullets from the revolver's wheel, but with the handle still attached to the woman's hand, he couldn't shake them out. While shifting his body around in the tiny room, Walter pushed the door closed with his feet.

Another door at the end of the hallway opened, and two men slunk into the corridor, one dressed completely in black.

"Billy!" his mother cried, running toward him. "Look out!"

The man in black jumped on Billy and wrapped a twisted piece of fibrous cloth around his mouth. The second man grabbed his arms and held them firmly behind his back. Brandishing a long serrated dagger, the first man shouted at Billy's mother. "Don't move, or the mongrel's dead!" She froze in place, her eyes riveted on Billy and his captors.

With one hand the man in black held the gag in place, and with the other he pressed the blade against Billy's throat. The cold sharp steel pricked his skin, drawing a trickle of blood that oozed toward his chest. The coarse gag smashed his lips against his teeth and ripped at his tender skin. He took a breath and tried to spew fire, but the flame rebounded as if hitting a thermal shield. The smell of his own blood caught in his nose. Intense heat parched his throat. He couldn't breathe fire; he could barely breathe at all.

185

A click and a slow creak made Ashley twist her head. Bonnie stood with her back to the lab, apparently relocking the door, her enormous wings shielding most of her body. Ashley couldn't help staring as Bonnie gracefully twirled toward the lab. In her white flowing robes, and with her peaceful radiant face, she looked like a storybook angel, her dragon wings set perfectly behind her shining, blonde-streaked hair. Her eyes danced, and if a smile could sing, Bonnie's song would have melted the most cynical heart.

Ashley felt ragged, almost dirty in Bonnie's presence, a blanket of shame falling on her like a smothering cloud of soot. Bonnie came closer and touched Ashley on the shoulder. "What's wrong? Is your grandfather still getting worse?"

Ashley turned back to the console, trying to hide the tears in her eyes. "Yes. Doc called for a nurse to come in, but we'll have to get him to a hospital soon if he doesn't get any better." She sniffed and gestured toward the boys' dorm. "But I can't worry about that right now. Your father will be leading Derrick out any minute."

Bonnie laid Ashley's keys on the control panel. "Leading him out?"

"Yes. There's something I didn't tell you about him. He's—"

Ashley was interrupted by the sound of the boys' hall door opening. Dr Conner emerged, leading a short, thin black youth by the hand.

Bonnie whispered. "Is that Derrick?"

Ashley nodded. "Yes. He doesn't look seventeen, does he?"

With unblinking eyes staring straight ahead, Derrick followed Dr Conner's lead.

"Is he blind?" Bonnie asked.

"Uh-huh. He got some kind of disease that killed his optic nerves. His parents died trying to get to Florida from Haiti on an overcrowded boat, but when it sank, he was rescued. The government worker on the case didn't have the heart to ship him back. Your father got word and sent for him."

Bonnie followed his progress, her mouth falling open. "Wow! How does he know what to do?"

"He's very intelligent and brave. Ever since we first transluminated him, he keeps begging to do it again." She turned to Bonnie, not caring any longer that her tears were evident. "When he's transformed into light energy, he says he can see."

"Come and meet him," Ashley said, holding out her hand. "He's very inspiring."

The two walked over to the anchor dome, and Dr Conner stepped toward the control panel, leaving Derrick with Ashley. "Derrick," Ashley said, "I'd like for you to meet Bonnie, the girl I told you about."

Derrick extended his hand and angled his head slightly away from Bonnie. "I'm very glad to meet you." His sweet voice sounded like a song, decorated with a hint of a French accent.

Bonnie grabbed his hand and shook it firmly, and Derrick adjusted his head to point in her direction. "Is it permissible to touch your wings?"

Bonnie guided his hand to her right wing. He caressed the outer rib with his fingers for a moment and then pulled away. "May I have your hand again?" he asked.

Bonnie put her hand gently back into his. He gripped it firmly. "I will hold your hand again," he said slowly, "and when I do, I will see your face." He pulled back and felt his way to the anchor dome platform.

Ashley extended her arm toward one of the other glass cylinders. "Are you ready, Bonnie?"

Bonnie retied the sash on her robe, smiling and bouncing lightly on her toes. "All dressed and ready to go!"

Ashley surveyed Bonnie from top to bottom, halting her scan when she saw Bonnie's ring. She reached for her arm. "I noticed your ring when we met. Is it an heirloom?"

Bonnie spread out her fingers in front of her face. "Not really, but a very good friend gave it to me. I never take it off."

"Well, if you don't want to lose it," Ashley said, "you'd better give it to me. It'll just fall to the floor when you get transluminated."

Bonnie curled her other hand around her fingers. "Then could you just pick it up for me? I want to wear it until the last second."

Ashley nodded with a slight shrug of her shoulders. "Sure. No problem."

Bonnie's smile returned, and she began bouncing again. "Great. Let's get going!"

Ashley glowered at Bonnie, hoping to communicate the gravity of the hour, the enormous risk that the next few moments would bring. Bonnie's bouncy, in-place dance slowed, and her smile faded. In a way it pleased Ashley to see it. Maybe this immovable rock of faith was finally having doubts.

As Bonnie neared the diver's position, she placed a hand on Ashley's arm. "Don't worry about me, Ashley. I won't be alone." With that, she stepped under the dome, and as the glass lowered, her serene face radiated perfect peace.

Billy bucked and twisted against his captors, but they clamped him down. His mother circled toward them, her knees flexed, obviously ready to spring to his aid at the first opportunity. Billy had no idea what the professor or Walter were doing behind that closed kitchen door. His captors might not even know they were inside. His mother held her position and kept her gaze fastened on him.

The second assailant bound Billy's wrists behind him with duct tape while the man in black kept the knife against his throat. He pressed the blade deeper into Billy's skin and barked at his partner. "Where's Gretchen?"

Billy stiffened. He recognized the voice. The man in black was the dark knight, Palin. The second man spoke up. "I think she's in the kitchen with the old man."

"I'll take the mongrel to Flathead," Palin said. "Gather the others, take them to the gorge, and dispose of them. Make it quiet. Then get back here and clean up the mess." Still holding the knife at Billy's throat, Palin dragged him toward the door, speaking gruffly into his ear. "It's early, so there shouldn't be anyone around to see us, but if you try to attract attention, I'll slice your throat like a ripe tomato. I'm pretty good with a blade. Remember, Dragon Boy?"

The second man drew a gun from his coat and pointed it at Billy's mum. "Stay there!" he ordered. He then pushed the kitchen door open with his foot.

Suddenly, the man disappeared into the room, and Walter hurtled headfirst into the hall, sprawling onto the carpet. The door slammed behind him. Something banged against the door and muffled grunts erupted. A gunshot sounded, then another. Billy tried to slow Palin's progress, dragging his heels against the carpet. *The professor! Did that guy kill him?*

As Palin hauled him out of the office suite, Billy's mother helped Walter to his feet, and a bright light flashed into the hallway from under the kitchen door. Billy craned his neck to see what would happen, but it was no use; the exit door swung shut. He heard his mother crying out his name. He wanted to answer, but the gag held firm. He wanted to break free and help the professor fight, but every second drew him farther and farther away from the scene of the battle, the painful knife preventing any sudden moves. Had the professor used the sword? Did he transluminate everyone in the kitchen, including himself?

Without warning, Billy fell to the ground, and his head struck the carpeted floor with a thud. Palin's body toppled over him, and the knife scraped his ear as it jerked away from his throat.

Billy struggled under Palin's weight, trying to turn his head to see what was going on. His mother sprawled on Palin's back, pounding him viciously, and Walter wrapped both arms around the dark knight's legs. Palin flailed against his attackers and threw Billy's mother to the side. He shook his legs, trying to dislodge Walter, but Walter hung on like a sticky mass of super glue.

Billy squirmed away and kicked Palin's head, but his blow was weak. With his hands bound he couldn't brace himself to really let him have it. His mother jumped up and took a step toward the jerking, squirming bodies, looking for a place to dive in. Palin, still clutching the jagged knife, raised his hand as if ready to strike. Billy tried to scream a warning to his rescuers, but the gag stifled his voice, turning his call into a loud grunt.

It was enough. Billy's mother lunged at the dagger. Clasping Palin's wrist with both hands, she pushed the blade away just before he could plunge it into Walter's back. "Walter!" she called. "Let go! He's got a knife!"

Walter scrambled to his feet and stomped at Palin's clenched fist, but the dark knight held fast to his blade. Walter jumped to the other side and yanked Palin's hair with one hand and gouged his eyes with the other. Billy swung his leg toward Palin's head, hoping to deliver a knockout blow, but his foot glanced off his shoulder.

Palin grabbed Billy's mother by the neck and threw her to the side again. He then slammed his arm into Walter's face and jumped to his feet. With quick hands, he jerked Billy up by his hair and pressed the dagger against his throat. Palin glared at them, sweat and blood trickling from his face and dripping to the floor. He gasped for air. "Don't . . . move . . . one muscle . . . or he's dead!"

Billy's two defenders froze while Palin caught his breath. "I don't know what you did in there to my partner, but I don't have the weapons to fight both of you right now." He took another deep breath and stumbled toward the elevator.

The blade pressed mercilessly into Billy's flesh, and he staggered along. His mother crept down the hall after him, her face a horrified mask. Walter slumped against the wall, his eyes swelling and a huge splotch of red growing on the left shoulder of his sweatshirt. Billy wanted to watch what would happen to his would-be rescuers, but the elevator doors slid closed like a curtain of despair.

When the elevator opened again, Billy shuffled through the empty hall, following Palin's lead to the building's exit. The dark knight towed him across the barren campus yard toward the parking lot and shoved him against a faded blue sedan. With the click of a button on his key fob, Palin popped open the trunk. He lowered the dagger from Billy's neck and heaved him inside, slamming the trunk shut.

Billy tumbled face first into icy darkness and bumped his head. Twisting his body out of its pretzel shape, he managed to roll to his back, but as he tried to catch his breath, he gagged on

191

the terrible smell. The taunting voice of the dark knight penetrated the stillness. "You'd better not try any fire-breathing, boy! I put four plastic jugs of gasoline in there to keep you company!"

Ashley took her place at the master control panel while Dr Conner positioned Derrick at the centre of the anchor dome. Derrick smiled as the glass shield lowered, and Ashley caught herself staring at him. His courage was amazing, definitely something to admire, but she had work to do.

Dr Conner stepped to the panel next to the anchor dome, one with fewer controls and displays than on the master board. He flipped a switch, rotated two dials to their maximum settings, and hurried toward the safe on the wall.

Ashley stretched a headset to fit over her ears and spoke into the microphone, a tiny transmitter on the end of a flexible stem. "Derrick, can you hear me?"

"Yes." Derrick's smile widened.

"Bonnie? You there?"

Bonnie nodded, her eyes partially closed and her head tilted toward the ceiling.

"Go ahead and answer, Bonnie. I want to make sure the sound works both ways."

"Yes," she replied softly. "I can hear you."

"Good. Okay, Derrick knows the drill, so I'm going to talk through this for your sake, Bonnie. I know I explained everything in detail last night, but it won't hurt to remind you as we go." She pushed a slider bar up a couple of notches, and a low hum emanated from under the domes. "The vibration you're now feeling is just the magneto that creates part of our power grid. The real action will start in a minute when Doc brings out the candlestone."

Ashley slowly turned a small dial on the upper left corner of the panel. "I'm dimming the lights now." Dr Conner soft-stepped across the floor, opening the box as she darkened the huge room. "Bonnie," Ashley continued, a grin breaking out on her face, "your father is bringing your mother to the pedestal. Are you ready to go in and see her?"

Bonnie's lips rounded into a faint smile, and she gave the thumbs-up signal.

Ashley drummed the panel with her fingers. Bonnie's confidence in the face of uncertainty was unnerving, enough to make Ashley worry. She had to make this work. Devin or no Devin, she wouldn't let Bonnie fall into a trap. She would bring her home one way or another.

Ashley raised the panel's covering to block out the display lights, but she could still see over its top edge to monitor the domes. When Dr Conner placed the candlestone in the centre of the room, Bonnie lifted the hood of her robe to cover her hair, and her lips began moving. Ashley strained to hear. The whisper-soft words came to her ears like a lilting voice singing in a faraway land.

"The Lord is my Shepherd; I shall not want."

Ashley turned up the volume and stared at the peaceful figure inside the dome.

"He maketh me to lie down in green pastures. He leadeth me beside the still waters."

Ashley didn't want to interrupt. The words sang to her heart like a sacred aria, a moving tribute of spirit, but she knew she had to get back to work. With her hands shaking and her voice trembling, she slid another bar up. "It . . . It's time, Bonnie. I'm turning on the transluminating beam."

"He restoreth my soul. He leadeth me in the paths of righteousness for his name's sake."

193

Ashley wiped away a tear. "Five . . . ahem . . . five seconds, Bonnie. You'll see a flash, and . . . and grab Derrick's hand when he comes through."

"Yea, though I walk through the valley of the shadow of death, I will fear no evil, for thou art with me; thy rod and thy staff they comfort me."

A blaze of sparkling light engulfed Bonnie's lower half. Her hood slipped down as the sparks advanced upward, consuming her body until her glowing face disappeared, swallowed in the blinding display.

Bonnie heard Derrick's gentle voice. "Take my hand, Bonnie." In a strange vision she saw bursts of light and felt a firm tug. Was that his hand? She felt it latch on, and somehow she was able to will herself to return a firm grasp. As though she were listening to a sound that came from beyond the stars, she heard another voice, sizzling and warped amid a host of eerie, humming sounds.

"Attachment successful. She's going in."

Bonnie felt herself being painlessly stretched, her body unravelling like a spool of thread tumbling down in a rushing river of light, hurtling into a deep, dark canyon. As she fell, the outside noises blurred, fading away in the distance. Although she couldn't feel the g-forces she had expected, she sensed speed and a rapid dimming of her strange new world.

She slammed into a thick, pliable barrier and passed through what seemed like a supple membrane, as though her body were travelling through a wall of black jelly. The river of light she was riding vanished, somehow blocked by the viscous wall and diverted somewhere she couldn't see. Finally, she stopped in a totally dark realm, not bumping into anything solid, just coming out of the membrane and into a floating existence of absolute gloom.

She could still feel a slight pull from above, her attachment to Derrick and the world outside, and she had a detached sense that she had to hold to it, though her hands no longer felt like hands at all. Every input seemed different – seeing, hearing, smelling, even her sense of being came to her through new impulses, more spiritual than earthly, as though she had passed from one life to another. But heaven could never feel like this. The whole place weighed down on her, a stifling, heavy burden of impending doom, like watching a best friend slowly die.

Trying to orient herself, she took in her dark surroundings. She could see her own form, a pulsing mass of disturbed light, but for some reason, her body, if you could call it that, had no effect on the black nebulous hole she had entered. She didn't light up the area at all. But that didn't matter. In this tiny house of glass there probably wasn't anything to see, anyway.

Looking up, she noticed a faint trail of light, thin and taut, stretching into an empty expanse – her lifeline to Derrick – but there was nothing else, no sounds and no other bright pulses besides her own. She knew her mother should appear somewhere as another mass of light, but was this a place she could explore? She forgot to ask Ashley about that. She had no map to guide her way, but since she only had a short time, she couldn't just sit and wait.

Trying to figure out how to move was a trick in itself. There was no ground, no walls, nothing she could use to propel her new body. In total blackness, there was no way to tell if she was moving even if she tried. With her "hand" still clutching Derrick's, she decided that if she pulled against the force he exerted, and if his pull increased, that would mean she was travelling somewhere.

Movement seemed an act of the will rather than physical flexing of muscles. Pushing her shimmering body was like resisting the darkness in front of her. The black space split apart and fled as she guided her mind into its void, searching through it like a beacon in a black fog.

After a few seconds, she sensed something, another light, just a glimmer, but it was definitely there. As she adjusted to her newly discovered locomotion, she figured out how to accelerate and turn, guiding herself toward the spark of energy. As she approached, the other light grew as it moved in her direction.

Was this her mother, at last? Bonnie could hardly wait. Just a few more seconds and they would be together. She could tell that her own body brightened, pulsating more rapidly. The other light grew, sparkling, radiant, vibrating with excitement. It took shape, a human form, without detail or sharp features, but definitely human. As it drew closer, the feminine shape of a woman became clear, sharpening with each step, a radiant torso, long gleaming arms and legs, and finally her mother's sweet gentle face. Bonnie felt it communicating – an excited voice in her mind, no, a stream of ecstatic thoughts, calling to her, "Bonnie! At last, you're here!"

An arm of light stretched out to Bonnie, and she tried to reach out her own to meet it, but, in a brilliant flash, their embrace was suddenly blocked. A huge wall of radiance, more dazzling than any earthly blaze, rushed between them and completely encircled Bonnie. It became a ring of magnificent, dancing fire, white and shimmering.

Bonnie retreated to the centre of the ring. For some reason she felt no fear, just surprise and amazement. The hedge of light seemed almost to laugh, not with sinister contempt, but with joy, like a proud father in the midst of a playful encounter with a child. Bonnie could only sit still and stare at the sight, awestruck wonder mixing with dazed disappointment.

What's going on? Why is this thing stopping me from meeting Mama?

Ashley pushed her microphone stem away from her lips and watched a digital timer on her panel. "Ninety seconds to go, Doc, and I see data for two human images on B frequency very clearly."

"Have they seen each other?"

"I think so. They seem to be in the same phase, but there's been no attachment yet." She reached for a dial on the upper right corner of the panel. "Let's check A to make sure Devin's still there."

Dr Conner swiped her hand away. "No. We'll see him come into B if he makes a move."

Ashley rolled her hand into a loose fist. *That was weird. Why so rough?* She followed the numbers and graph lines as they flashed across the screen. Suddenly, she gasped and pointed. "What's that?"

Dr Conner stared at the monitor. "It can't be!"

"It is! It's another presence in B!"

"Impossible!"

Ashley glared at him. "Impossible? Why is it impossible? It has to be Devin. You said we'd see him if he moved over!"

Dr Conner returned her combative stare. "I tell you, it's not possible!"

Ashley stamped her foot. "There's something going on! What are you keeping from me?"

197

Dr Conner broke away from her icy gaze. "Well, it's too late for you to stop us now." He pointed at the glimmering gem on the pedestal. "Bonnie's mother isn't in the candlestone. She never has been. Devin's been able to move to B all along, and he answers for Irene when we call to talk to her."

Ashley shot up from her seat. "What? You've been lying to me all this time? Why?"

"It was the only way," he shouted back. "You wouldn't have helped me if you knew the truth."

Ashley's eyes burned. In her fury, the mass of dials and displays seemed to mix into a soup of boiling upheaval. "But I can't—"

"No time to argue," he snapped, pushing her back into her seat. "Just listen. If Devin stays in the candlestone, your grandfather will die. If you want to save him and Bonnie, you'd better get back to work. I don't know what that third presence is, but let's hope it doesn't get in the way."

Ashley shook her head and drew in a deep breath, trying to concentrate on the data again. She managed a businesslike tone but clipped her words to punctuate her turmoil. "The third one's different. Its phase isn't human; its signal is much stronger. But there's been no attachment among the three."

"How's Derrick holding out?"

Ashley read another meter. "Oh, no! He's stretching thin, like something's pulling harder than usual." She turned a dial and jerked the microphone up to her lips. "Derrick, hang on!"

Dr Conner put his finger on the main display. "We're at minus twenty seconds. When does our restoration confidence go below fifty per cent?"

Ashley glanced his way. "At plus fifteen, but we can't go past zero. We're only at eighty per cent, even then."

"We'll go past if we have to. Plus fifteen is our new drop dead point."

"But Derrick can't make that. Maybe plus five. He's stretching to the breaking point. He'll have to let go or one of them will be dismembered."

"No choice. Ten seconds to zero now."

"He's down to less than a millimetre. He'll never make it! We have to reverse!"

"No! Look! Attachment is close! He can do it."

"He's under a hundred microns!" Ashley said, fear stripping her voice. "We can't even measure his attachment anymore! If he lets go, Bonnie will be trapped! We have to get her out now!"

Dr Conner shouted. "We're at zero!" He raised his arm like a starter at a race. "Prepare to reverse at my command! Twelve seconds to the drop dead point."

Ashley's fingers flew across a separate portion of the panel, setting the dials based on what her darting eyes read on the displays. "I'm putting the reverse power on ninety-five. It has to go quick!"

"Right. There's no choice. We're at plus eleven."

Ashley shouted, nearly jumping from her seat. "We have attachment!"

Dr Conner threw down his arm. "Hit it!"

CHAPTER 13

THE GATES OF HELL

Walter dashed down the stairs and raced toward the exit. With a mighty shove, he banged open the double doors and bolted into the nearly empty parking lot. Swivelling his head back and forth, he searched for Billy's kidnapper.

There he is! He just slammed that trunk closed!

Walter burst into a sprint. Keeping his eyes riveted on the kidnapper, he leaped over a snow mound and hurdled a tipped-over garbage can. Billy's captor slammed the car door just as Walter made a lunge for the handle. Walter grabbed hold, wrenching the door open a crack. As Palin yanked in the opposite direction, Walter slid his hands inside and clutched the door frame.

The car started and lurched forward. Walter hung on, his shoes dragging against the road as the car swerved back and forth. His scraped fingers slipped on the frame. *I can't let go! Gotta hang on!*

With a tight doughnut turn, the car spun him away, sending his body tumbling across the lot. Still turning, the car careened in his direction. Walter jerked his body up and lunged to the side, barely avoiding the squealing tyres as the car sped toward the exit.

Lying on his stomach, Walter peered through the grey plume of exhaust to read the Montana licence plate. The first digit on the sky blue background was a seven, followed by a dot and the characters "A1". The other three digits looked like either fives or sixes, but he wasn't sure. He rolled to his backside, spitting, coughing, and rubbing his aching eyes. After gathering his wits, he scrambled to his feet and hustled back toward the building.

When he jerked the outer door open, he nearly collided with Mrs Bannister. She held her head with both hands, and her eyes seemed wild with fear. "Did you see Billy? What happened?"

Breathless and weak, Walter bent over, propping himself on his knees. "I think that guy . . . threw him . . . in the trunk. Couldn't stop him. He got away. But I got part of the plate." He hooked his arm in hers and started toward the elevator. "Let's check on the professor and call the cops!"

When they reached the office, they hobbled straight to the kitchen where they found the professor sitting on the floor against the back wall. His eyes were open, and he held Excalibur on his lap, the blade glowing, covering his thighs with iridescent white.

"Prof!" Walter shouted, sliding on his knees to his teacher's side. "Are you okay?"

The professor, his face contorted and a tear streaming down one cheek, tried to shift his body and sit upright. "I have been better, Walter, but it seems that I have been shot in the heel of my left foot. I regret that I was not able to come to William's aid."

202

Walter grimaced at the wounded foot. The trouser leg had already been turned up, and a trickle of blood oozed through the exposed heel of the sock. The back third of his shoe had been ripped off, part of the leather still hanging on one side. Mrs Bannister scooted up and began carefully untying the laces.

Using his shoe, Walter nudged a handgun that lay on the kitchen floor. "What happened to the other guy and that old hag?"

"I am happy to report—" Professor Hamilton paused and winced as the front of the shoe slipped off. "I am happy to report that Excalibur works quite well. The two fiends are now scattered light. It was quite a display, actually. Yet, although it seems I had no choice in the matter, I am distressed with having to dispatch two human beings. After I pulled the man inside, I confronted him face to face, so my integrity is intact. Yet, death always seems a tragedy to me, no matter how vile the victims." He sighed, shaking his head and speaking more softly. "Wasted lives, wasted souls."

Walter glanced around toward the walls and ceiling, trying to find any trace of sparkling debris. "Shouldn't it have zapped you, too? Isn't that what happened to Merlin?"

"Yes, Walter. One moment, please."

The professor turned to Billy's mother, who was trying to fashion his sock into a bandage. "I think the bleeding has subsided, Marilyn. The wound is painful, but the bullet passed through, so I don't think it's dangerous."

He handed Walter the sword and lifted his arms. "If you wouldn't mind lending me assistance." Mrs Bannister and Walter obliged, each putting a shoulder under an arm.

"Walter," the professor said, now standing with his weight on his good foot, "in my efforts to dispose of the two aggressors,

203

I did not think about what the sword might do to me. I was, however, concerned about you. That's why I shoved you out of the room."

Walter smiled from under the professor's arm. "Yeah. I guessed that."

"As soon as I raised the sword, an extraordinary beam emanated from its end. Although it startled me, I believe it terrified the other chap even more. He stumbled and fired his weapon at me, missing with his first shot and striking my foot with the second. Then, in an amazing flash of light, the beam consumed him along with the – ahem – lady on the floor."

Walter dragged his shoe along the floor where the woman had fallen, letting his toe sort through the various items the bad guys had left behind – a watch, a bracelet, a set of keys, and a grey wig lying beside two guns and a brown jacket.

"I suspect," the professor continued, "that Excalibur's bearer has more control over its power than we expected. Bonnie was not affected when she used it, nor was I, and I was able to guide it toward my targets. It makes me wonder if Merlin intended to bring about his own disintegration."

"Merlin zapped himself on purpose?"

Mrs Bannister took a step forward and pushed the professor along. "We can make our guesses later. Right now we have to call the police and an ambulance. Walter got part of the licence plate. And you, Professor, have to go to the hospital."

The professor hobbled along with his two helpers toward the reception area. He grimaced at every step but managed to keep his voice calm. "I beg your pardon, Marilyn, but I think going to the hospital would not be wise. Our delay would be unpredictable, and my wound is not life threatening. I also think involving the police would hamper our efforts. We would not be able to answer all their questions, and based on Devin's record of keeping his affairs untraceable, my guess is that the licence plate would lead to a dead end even if we had the entire number. We have no real obligation to involve the authorities, since there are no bodies here."

When they reached the chairs, Mrs Bannister pulled the professor's arm from around her neck and slowly released him. She ran her hand through her tousled hair and took a deep breath. "But what about your foot? It needs treatment. And what about Billy? Who's going to find him?"

The professor lowered his tall frame down to the love seat, letting out a lengthy sigh. He gazed up at her with sad eyes. "Trust me, Marilyn. This crude villain cannot harm your son. I am sure of that. You may wish to pray about a later battle, but for now, William is safe. As for me, I suggest we purchase a bandage and crutches, perhaps a topical antibiotic as well. More thorough treatment can wait." The professor pointed toward Walter. "Walter, however, may need attention."

Mrs Bannister's eyes widened, and she reached for his shoulder. "Walter! You're bleeding!"

Walter wrinkled his nose and stepped back. "It's nothing. Just a scratch from that creep's knife."

She cupped his chin in her hand and tilted his face toward the light. "And your eyes, they're swollen half shut!"

"Mrs B," Walter said, pulling away from her hand, "I don't mean any disrespect, but Prof and I don't need a mother right now." He tightened his grip on Excalibur. "We need to go skewer a slayer."

She glanced at the professor and then at Walter. New determination flashed in her eyes. "Right!" She clenched her fist. "Where do we start?"

205

The professor's gaze seemed far away, as though he were staring straight through the wall. "Walter," he said slowly, "do you remember the assailant's words? We were listening from the kitchen. He said that he was going to take William somewhere."

"Yeah, I heard him. He said to Flathead."

His eyes narrowed to two slits. "Flathead? Are you sure?"

"Yeah. It was a weird name, so I picked up on it."

The professor lowered his gaze as if to study the grey carpet at his feet. "I perused our map of Montana during our flight. I'm sure there's a Flathead Lake, but I believe there is also Flathead County and Flathead Forest. I'm afraid with all those options, our search region is far too large." With a brighter expression he looked up at the others and tried to stand. "I don't think we can risk asking questions around the campus. We'll just drive into Flathead County and ask in that area if anyone knows Dr Conner. Perhaps someone will be able to provide inform—"

A loud ring interrupted the professor. He bent forward to reach for his phone but lost his balance, and Walter and Mrs Bannister caught him by the shoulder. The professor pointed toward his hip. "Walter, would you please answer my cell phone. It's on my belt."

Walter grabbed the phone and flipped it open. "Hello. . . . Yeah, Dad. What's up? . . . From Bonnie? Cool! What's it say?" Walter was quiet for almost half a minute, nodding as he listened. "The address? Sure. Hold on." He held a pretend pencil and wrote in the air. "Hey, Prof. You got anything to write with?"

The professor shook his head. "Have your father send his information to my email address. I can bring it up on my phone."

"Gotcha!" He turned back to the cell phone. "Hey, Dad. Send it to Prof's email. We'll get it. . . . Here? Oh, not much.

We've been reading prophetic poems in a diary written by Merlin, and we found a real fire-breathing dragon in a cave, and after we got waylaid by a couple of gun-toting goons and an ugly old witch, Billy got kidnapped at knifepoint and thrown into a trunk. The kidnapper sped off just before I could get to him, and he tried to squash my head with his tyres, but he missed. I'm okay, and it didn't hurt much when he stabbed me. Oh yeah, the professor's been shot. Other than that, it's been pretty quiet. See ya later." Walter pressed the disconnect button and snapped the phone back on the professor's belt.

"Walter!" Mrs Bannister cried. "Shouldn't you explain it to your father a little better than that?"

He squinted with one eye and waved his hand. "Nah. It would take too long. He probably thinks I was kidding, anyway."

The professor pointed toward their coats piled on the end of the sofa and wobbled to his feet. "What information is he sending, Walter?"

Walter picked up the professor's coat and handed it to him. "Looks like Bonnie knew something was up. She gave a lady at some convenience store a postcard to send, and the lady happened to be the owner of the place. Anyway, she got worried about Bonnie and sent it overnight express with a note explaining what she saw."

The professor wriggled into his parka and limped heavily toward the door. Mrs Bannister stayed close to his side and placed a hand on Walter's shoulder. "What did the card say?"

Walter zipped his coat, then held the door open. "It had the name of the store on it, and Bonnie wrote something like, 'My father's taking me to a place he said was about thirty minutes from here. He said it's a lab near Flathead Lake, and the lab must be a pretty big place, because people live there.

I hope you can find it. I don't trust him. Something's definitely wrong.' "

The professor stopped in the hallway and raised a finger. "Aha! Flathead Lake! Was there any other information?"

"Not from Bonnie," Walter continued. "The lady wrote that Bonnie was travelling with a man and another teenaged girl. They were riding in an SUV. She wasn't sure what kind, but it was sort of a maroon colour, and new."

The professor held out his arms. "I see now that my foot is too badly damaged for walking. If you will assist me to the car, I can retrieve my email there. After we procure a pair of crutches, our first stop will be this lady's store. Perhaps our eyewitness will be able to tell us a bit more. Walter, please fetch the box for the sword. We may have more transluminating to do."

208

The magneto engines whined, and Ashley's hands and fingers flew across the control panel. She half-sat and half-stood while she watched the display, rocking her body and peeking around the light-deflecting hood every couple of seconds to see what was going on in the diver's dome. With a gasp, she fell back to her seat and cried out. "Noooo!"

Dr Conner ran out to the triangle. Two of the glass cylinders remained empty, while the anchor dome filled with sparkling light. Ashley, her face hot and her fingers trembling, turned a knob fully anticlockwise.

Within seconds, the dancing light solidified, re-creating Derrick's slender body. He collapsed to his knees, his thin dark hands covering his weeping face. Ashley heard his mournful words through her headphones. "She let go! I tried to hold on, but she let go!"

Ashley threw off the headphones, flipped a switch to raise the glass, and ran to Derrick. Dr Conner took one hand while Ashley gently held the other, and they led him down to floor level.

"Ashley, get back and monitor the activity. I'll take care of Derrick." He picked up the trembling youth, cradling him in both arms, and carried him to the dorm while Ashley stood alone in the midst of her trinity of glass domes. She gazed at the diver's platform, the last place she had seen Bonnie's shining face. As she dragged her feet toward it, her shoulders slumped. A million thoughts zipped through her mind, clogging even her powerful brain. The thoughts hurt, each one like a pricking needle, reminding her of her vows. *I know you want your mother back. We need to get her out of that candlestone, and I'm not going to let you down.*

She sniffed, trying to keep the tears back, but they broke through. She wiped the first few, and then gave up, letting them flow. When she reached the diver's platform, she stooped and pressed the button on the base. With a low hum, the glass slowly ascended, and the sight of the exposed platform reminded her of Bonnie's request. She dropped to her knees, searching the floor of the platform carefully. A single tear splashed where Bonnie's feet had recently stood.

Her ring should be around here somewhere. But where? It couldn't have gone far.

A loud voice interrupted her search. "Ashley! Why aren't you at the panel?"

Ashley jumped and ran back to the controls, peering again into the displays through a glaze of tears. Dr Conner's footsteps pounded toward her. "What's going on?"

Ashley pressed her lips together and squeezed her eyes shut for a moment, trying to hold back an emerging sob. "Only—"

209

She gulped and took a breath, trying not to whine. "Only two presences. That third one is gone."

Dr Conner put one hand on his hip and shook a finger at the monitor. "You said there was an attachment. What happened?"

Ashley took another breath, finding strength in her anger. "There was," she said, flipping a switch near the bottom of the panel. "I'll run the data back on the screen. You can see for yourself." They both watched the stream of numbers while Ashley pointed. "Look, there's Bonnie. She's at six point two, and there's Devin. He's at seven point five. Then, here's the third presence, ranging from three point eight all the way to seven point two."

He squinted at the monitor, glancing now and then at the settings on the panel. "How can that be? We're not showing any shadow effect in the other two."

"Some kind of multiple presentation I guess, but it's clearly the same entity." She pressed her finger on the display. "Now here's the connection. Bonnie was moving up, and when she reached six point eight—"

Dr Conner frowned and shook his head, his scowl growing once again and his voice deepening to a growl as he continued to watch the data. "It wasn't Devin attaching to her; it was that other thing, whatever it was."

Ashley lowered her head and replied softly. "Yeah. I see that now."

Dr Conner glared at her. "Are you playing me for a fool?"

Ashley jerked her head up and met his angry eyes. "Me playing you? Look who's talking! You and your lies about Bonnie's mum! What really happened to her? And what was all that about my grandfather dying?"

Dr Conner stepped away from the control panel and stuffed his hands into his pockets, taking a few steps in a small circle before looking at Ashley again, the creases on his brow deepening. "You've been wondering why your grandfather's health has been levelling off," he said, sarcasm coating his words. "And now he's sick . . . very sick. It seems that our model patient is deteriorating. Your wonderful photoreceptors don't work. They never have."

He waved his arm at the glass domes glowing faintly in the dim room. "The receptors I've been putting into your restoration engine are real ones. And all this time I've been using the candlestone and dragon's blood to restore your precious 'Daddy.' Didn't you notice that he stopped improving at the same time Devin took the candlestone to West Virginia?"

The two glared at each other, but after a few seconds his scowl faded and he returned his hand to his pocket. "But now that the stone's back here, it doesn't work. I think it's because Devin's in there, somehow messing up the process. He's trying to force us to get him out. He knows I can't leave him there if I want our research to continue. That's why I needed Bonnie. No one else has been able to get him out."

211

Ashley gripped the sides of the control panel until her knuckles turned white. This creep had used his own daughter as a glorified guinea pig! He had put her in danger just so he could keep his precious research going! Not only that, he lied about why her grandfather was sick!

Her thoughts stretched back to months ago, before her grandfather's treatments had started. Day after day she had told Daddy how much she loved him, explaining her research and how it would help him recover. It didn't matter that he sometimes couldn't respond; she was willing to do whatever he needed. On his nurse's day off, she would change his soiled sheets, clean his feeding tube, and wash his body. And every day she begged God to heal him . . . but God never answered.

She pinched the bridge of her nose to hold back her tears. Letting Dr Conner see her pain was out of the question. She steadied her voice, but a tight squeak slipped out. "Why didn't you just tell me the truth?"

Dr Conner kicked a power cord out of his way and resumed a slow pace around the lab. "Oh, come now! Would you have helped me if you knew that I needed dragon's blood every time we treated your grandfather and every time we sent a diver into the stone?" He made a full circuit before continuing his rant. "Devin agreed not to hurt Bonnie if I got him out of the stone, but would you help set a monster like Devin free, knowing that his lust for Bonnie's blood would never die? Yes, Daddy's dying, but are you willing to risk someone else's life to save him?" He stopped and faced her, a strange expression moving from his eyes to his lips, as if a light had flashed on in his brain. "Maybe you were willing after all. You knew Devin was in the candlestone, and you were easy to convince that he was trapped in 'A' frequency. You noticed his frequency drift, but it didn't stop you from sending Bonnie in there, did it?"

Ashley hesitated. His questions stung like a thousand hornets. And they raised so many new questions, her brain felt overloaded again. She took a deep breath. "Where have you been getting dragon's blood?"

Dr Conner dug his hands back into his pockets. Finally, he sighed and nodded his head. "I guess you might as well know everything." He started walking toward the back of the lab and gestured with his head. "Come on. Follow me. It's time to open the Omega door."

Karen stepped out of the hall and motioned for the other girls. She whispered hoarsely, "Let's go! The coast is clear!"

All bundled in heavy coats, thick trousers, and high boots, the four girls stole through the lab. Karen paused to pick up Pebbles, and Stacey and Rebecca crowded beside her. They skirted the central lab area, travelling the long way around the perimeter of the cavern. When they reached the door to the Alpha exit tunnel, Karen turned the knob. "It's unlocked. Let's go." She tapped the other two girls with her free hand and pointed to a flashlight hanging on a hook. "Beck, you first, then Stacey. Pebbles and I'll bring up the rear. On tiptoes, now!"

Snagging the flashlight, Beck snapped it on, and she and Stacey crept down the narrow corridor. Karen peeked out the door then closed it behind her. She blew out a long sigh. *So far, so good.* She shifted Pebbles in her arms, balancing her against her hip. Karen felt weak, and her knees wobbled. *I have to do it! I just have to! There's a bunch of stairs, but I've done it before.* She set her jaw, pressing her lips together, and gave a firm nod. *Bonnie did her part. Now I've gotta do mine!*

A s quickly as it came, the shimmering hedge disappeared, and Bonnie felt her "hand" zipping back toward her like a retractable measuring tape. In a way, it was a relief to have her new body all in one place, but her returning hand brought with it a new mystery. It carried a sparkle of some kind, a dark red glow that seemed attached to her own white light.

My ring! Somehow it came through with me!

The other light, the one she thought was her mother, had fallen back, as though cowering in the distance. She knew who it was now. The glowing fence of light had touched her, and it seemed as though it had fed her information, a gentle stream of loving thoughts that flowed from mind to mind.

213

The first light was none other than Devin, the dragon slayer, the very one who had plunged his sword into her mother's belly and ripped her open, the same hateful maniac who would kill Bonnie if he had the chance. Somehow he had morphed his light energy to look like her mother's body, and now he was reshaping again, his light congealing into a radiant image of his human form.

Bonnie felt the slayer's words, his thoughts now buzzing into her mind like irritating static as he drew closer. "You're trapped in here with me, Demon Witch, at least for now. You're doomed to hell, where you belong."

Bonnie stayed quiet. She didn't know how to talk anyway, though changes in her thoughts seemed to alter the ripples in her light pulses. She wondered if he could read her mind by watching the variations in her light patterns. Although his light had drawn a human shape, hers was still disorganized, more like a flashing blob of Play-Doh than anything resembling a girl.

"I, on the other hand," Devin continued, "plan to escape very soon. The good doctor, you see, knows that all of his plans will crumble if he doesn't get me out of here. We got close this time. If not for that cursed phantom, I'd be out of here now."

The slayer moved even closer, but he stopped suddenly. He took another step only to rebound, as though Bonnie had some kind of shield around her. He stayed still for a moment and then sent another stream of thoughts her way. "I suppose you want to know where your mother is, don't you?" The slayer's light moved away. "Follow me, and I'll show you."

Bonnie's light pulsed like a frenzied strobe. She didn't trust that liar, not for one second. It was time to search for her mother, and she didn't need a low-life scoundrel like him pretending to help her.

She tried to sigh, tried to settle her throbbing light. If she could display a calm, trusting glow, maybe she'd be able to coax some information out of him, ask enough questions to get him to slip. Since she seemed to have a force field protecting her, it was worth a try.

Bonnie inched forward, careful to keep out of Devin's reach. It was much easier to move now without her link to the anchor. The slayer led her deeper into the crystal's mysterious depths, and he stopped abruptly at a place that seemed just a shade brighter. Bonnie kept her distance and waited for him to speak. His glowing arm extended downward, and part of it disappeared into the blackness. As he pulled his arm back into place, his scratchy static filled her head. "That, my dear, is a crack in the floor, a flaw in the candlestone's structure. That's where your mother went."

Bonnie sent out her reply, a thought stream of sorts. "Why should I believe you?"

"Oh, you can talk now. You're a fast learner." He laughed, sending a wave of skinny ripples through his body of light. "You should believe me, because it's in my best interests to help you. This is an exit, the only exit. I use it to send encoded light to speak to your father. Normally, this stone doesn't allow any encoded light to escape. You see, encoded light, like your body and mine, passes through that black membrane you probably felt when you came in. It gets lodged in this inner core. Fractured light, on the other hand, passes around that membrane and gets arrested and assembled before going through the exit channel that's right below this crack.

"The doctor's messages are encoded, so they come into this core to me. I can read that light and send it back through, encoded with my response, by sending it through this crack. It goes straight to the exit, bypassing the arresting stage."

"If that's a way out, why haven't you gone through it?"

"Because the channel would put me out of phase too much. I couldn't be restored. The good doctor's little genius, Ashley, hasn't figured out why yet, but it seems that the encoding of a female is not disturbed when she passes through this part of the structure. She sent both male and female animals in here, and I put them through the channel. Every female survived, and every male was disintegrated. That's why they always used girls as their divers. If Derrick were ever to lose a diver, she could just go through this crack to get out again. Your mother was in here, but when we learned about the escape route, we were able to send her back out when Dr Conner was ready with her cure."

Bonnie's light dimmed and then flashed like blinking neon. "I don't believe you. Ashley would have told me. I know she would have."

Devin's light rippled from the centre in tight halos, like rings from a tiny splash in a pond. "Ashley didn't know," he replied. "Brilliant or not, she's as easy to dupe as you are. Dr Conner and I have been using her for our purposes, and I've been speaking to them in your mother's place ever since she left. Dr Conner knew all along, but we had to keep Ashley in the dark. I don't think she would want to help us if she knew what we were really doing."

"No, she wouldn't. That much I do believe."

Devin's light flashed brightly, stripes of energy passing from his head to his toes. "Well, believe this, Witch. I'm telling you this because I need you to dive back in here and get me out. Once you're out there, I'll tell you where to find your mother. She's alive and restored."

Bonnie moved closer to the crack, but she kept her distance from the slayer. As she approached, she noticed a change in the blackness, a slight grey streak in what appeared to be a floor-like structure, a fault in one of the jewel's inner planes.

Devin continued, and Bonnie felt his voice come across in softer tones. "The candlestone is still on the pedestal outside, so if you decide to go in, you'll go straight to the restoration process." Devin drifted away. "I'll move out of sight. Take your time. Your mother didn't take long to decide, though. She hates dark places."

A few seconds later, Devin was gone, his light vanishing more quickly than Bonnie thought possible. Did this place have secret passages or walls he could hide behind?

Bonnie slowly approached the grey streak, skirting close enough to get a glimpse into the jagged fissure. It opened into a chasm, and way below, at the bottom of a glassy gorge, a stream of soft, white light poured through. It looked like a gentle river flowing in a peaceful valley, but she couldn't see where it went.

She felt a pull, like the candlestone's light-drawing power was somehow stronger in the lower area. If she went in, there would probably be no way to get back up. She replayed the slayer's explanation in her mind, piecing together the candlestone's flow channels, and imagining this stream of light as a passage to the outside.

With all her senses focused on the newly found chasm, Bonnie heard faint voices from far away. Though she didn't recognize the words, she could tell they were mournful, lamenting a sad existence, as though ghosts whispered eternal chants from haunted halls. If only she could understand. Were they calling her in? Was it a warning?

She pulled back and turned toward the blackness, resting her shining body and allowing her rapidly pulsating energy to settle down. As she gazed at her light, in stark contrast to the black

217

surroundings, she thought about how much easier it would be if everything would get brighter so she could see clearly.

Months ago, when she was moving from foster home to foster home, she remembered crying in her bed at night, worrying about what the next day would bring. Every night, darkness covered her with a blanket of sorrow, but morning always brought new hope with the rising sun. Light was sort of like truth. It always showed a liar for what he really was. And when someone gave a word of encouragement, it was like the sun rising, showing her that things weren't really as bad as they seemed.

She peeked again at the chasm and listened to the voices, soft and dreary, one or two counterpoint solos tangled in the melancholy chorus. As they droned on, she heard a familiar call, the call she had heard all the way back in West Virginia, her name floating into her mind the same way her mother used to call at the end of a summer day. She rushed to the edge of the crack and peered down. "Mama! Mama, is that you?"

There was no answer. The sad drone played on.

Bonnie floated away from the crack. Her light diminished as the blackness swallowed the edges of her body. This became her new way to cry, letting the dark oppression creep into her dimming soul and lay her energy to waste, as though allowing a black predator to consume her bit by bit.

"Mama!" she cried out. "Where are you?" With her waning soul quaking, her pulsing light failing with each beat, Bonnie wept, her words seeping out in tormented thoughts.

As the darkness gnawed away at her sanity, Bonnie shivered. If she gave in to sadness now, how could she help her mother? Putting her sorrowful thoughts away, she lifted her soul in song, streaming the words into the darkness with trembling quivers of light.

*Whither shall I go from thy spirit? Or whither shall I flee from
thy presence?*

*If I ascend up into heaven, thou art there: If I make my bed in
hell, behold, thou art there.*

*If I take the wings of the morning, and dwell in the uttermost
parts of the sea;*

*Even there shall thy hand lead me, and thy right hand shall
hold me.*

*If I say, Surely the darkness shall cover me; even the night shall be
light about me.*

*Yea, the darkness hideth not from thee; but the night shineth as
the day:*

The darkness and the light are both alike to thee.

With each uttered word, with each phrase of truth, Bonnie's
light increased, clearing her mind and refreshing her soul. When
she finished, the darkness crawled away like a wounded shadow,
and for the first time, she could see more clearly, as though her
own body illuminated the maze of dark walls that bordered the
gem's centre. Then, as though whispered into her ear by a close
friend, a stream of words flowed into her mind. *Everyone who
is of the truth hears my voice. No lie is of the truth.*

219

The voice was soft, pure, and whisper-quiet.

After a few seconds, the slayer's words came back to her, his
static-filled voice grinding into her mind like a power drill. *She
hates dark places.*

When everything fell silent again, Bonnie sat still and pondered the voices. *She hates dark places? But that can't be true.
Mama used to turn all the lights off just to tell me stories in the dark.*

She looked again into the crevice and saw a whole new world.
The river of light was still there, but she also saw a swirling mass

of ghostly phantoms at the river's edge, barely visible, yet she could see expressions of sadness, regret, remorse, the pain of lost opportunity, never to be found again. Were these human beings? Did each dim pulse in that forsaken chasm represent a soul trapped in a lost netherworld?

Bonnie hurried to the far side of her crystal prison. That's what the slayer really wanted, for her to cast herself into that hell. But is that really what happened to her mother? Was she fooled by Devin? Was she one of those poor, tormented souls?

And now there seemed to be no way out. Even if Karen could dive back into the candlestone, Ashley said she would probably be out of phase. It took someone with dragon blood to search the depths of this dungeon, and there was only one person she knew who could possibly do it.

It was time to pray. The light of truth had sparked new, robust energy, and she knew that her best friend needed to find the same power. It was time to pray for Billy.

CHAPTER 14

SEEING RED

Billy slammed against the side of the trunk as the car roared away, and at each careening turn his arms pinched against cold steel. He squirmed to his side and felt around with his fingers, searching for something sharp near his back, anything with a metal edge to cut the strangling tape on his wrists. But the tape contracted with every move, numbing his fingers. He knew he was in a mess, and he felt that familiar boiling rage in his belly. Billy flopped to his stomach and rested his cheek against the rough, gas-scented carpet.

Okay, get a grip and just relax. I don't want to be spewing sparks in here! There's got to be some good news. My throat's been slit, but I haven't bled to death yet. That's good news. This gag's about to cave my mouth in and scratch my lips off, but it feels like it might be starting to slip.

He pressed his lips against the rag as hard as he could, and it budged downward just a hair.

Okay, it moves. That's even better news. It'll take a while to get it off, but it does move.

While Billy worked on the gag, the car's engine settled into a high-pitched drone, and the road straightened out.

We must be on a main highway now. I wonder how far we have to go. If the exhaust doesn't knock me out, the gas fumes will. And it's freezing in here. My hands are so numb I can hardly feel them. But I have to keep working. If I don't get this rag off, I'll be dead meat when he comes back to get me.

Once more twisting to his side, Billy pulled his knees to his chest, lowered his head, and rubbed the scratchy cloth against his jeans. Each fibre felt like sharp nails digging into his bleeding lips, but he kept working the gag downward.

As long as he could stay conscious, he had to keep working on an escape plan. Palin was a slayer in his own right, so Billy had expected to get sliced into a spiral ham. What could be the reason for tossing him in this icebox trunk instead? This was no joyride. Was the slayer hauling him to where they kept Bonnie? That was some comfort, to be by her side even if it meant torture or death. Maybe by some twist of fate he could figure out a way to save her, to have just one second with his mouth free to send the slayers to a fiery hell . . . even if he died trying.

Oh, well. Dying bravely beats just letting that maniac do whatever he wants to Bonnie.

But would he really die for her? His loyalty was strong, but that strong?

It was a no-brainer. He would definitely die if he could save her. There was no one else like her, no one else he'd lay down his life for. Well, he would for Walter, but that was different.

222

He and Walter would fight together, battling enemies with everything they had until they either conquered their foes or fell in combat.

But Bonnie was different . . . special . . . like . . . well, she was just special.

In his mind he could see her staring up at him with her trusting eyes, could feel her gentle hand in his. On the mountain after their airplane crashed, she'd been braver than anyone he knew, stronger than he'd imagined possible, with her wings extended, more beautiful than—

Billy lay still. He didn't want to think about it any further. If he wanted to survive, he needed to work on that gag.

I'm cold," little Monique complained, her tiny voice muffled by the falling snow.

Karen lowered her coat's white hood so she could hear better, and a dusting of snowflakes quickly covered her head. She stooped and grabbed a pair of purple mittens, whispering as she put them back on Monique's hands. "Well, it's no wonder. Your hands are like ice." Karen stripped off her own gloves and set them on a five-foot-high boulder she had chosen to shelter the girls from the whistling wind and to screen them from view.

Monique's shrill voice cut through the wind. "When are we going inside, Red? This isn't fun anymore."

After shaking the snow out of her mop of red hair, Karen put her hood back up and tied it in place with the white drawstring. "We can't go back, Pebbles, not yet. We have to get to that house out near the highway. Remember? The old man with the friendly horse?"

Monique nodded, but shivered.

"We'd get lost if we tried to get there in this storm though. If the snow doesn't let up soon, we'll go back to the stairs. I promise." Karen knelt and tightened Monique's hood, brushing away a little snowcap from the top. "Don't worry; I won't let you freeze." Karen grabbed her own gloves and slowly put them back on, covering her stiffening fingers and sighing. *If I don't freeze first. We have a long way to go.*

A few minutes later, Karen heard a distant roar and lowered her hood again, tilting her head to keep the wind out of her ears. "It's a car!" she whispered urgently, pushing Monique's head lower. "Everyone duck and be quiet!"

With the three younger girls safely hidden, Karen stood on her tiptoes and peered cautiously over the boulder. A faded blue car, a late-model Grand Marquis, toiled up the snowy incline, sliding and spinning, but managing to navigate the final turn into the narrow driveway toward the stones that bordered the lab's entrance.

Karen watched it zip past their hiding place, less than a snowball's throw from the stairway door. It parked at least thirty feet behind Doc's SUV, and the driver jumped out and hurried to the rear of the car, brandishing a pistol in one hand.

Karen gasped and pushed the other girls' heads even lower. Would he see their footprints? The snow had fallen heavily since they had come outside, but she couldn't tell if it had covered their tracks completely. The man paced behind the car as if he didn't quite know what to do. Finally, he yelled right at the car's trunk.

"I've got a gun, kid. Do you think your breath's quicker than my trigger finger? Maybe that gag's still on, and maybe it's not, but I'll bet a bullet would discourage you real quick, either way."

The man lifted the car's remote locking device and pointed the gun at the trunk. His arm shook, and he shifted his weight from left to right, shivering in the bitter breeze. After what seemed like a full minute, he lowered the weapon and let out a string of obscenities, giving a hefty kick to the rear bumper.

"Don't make a sound. If you try to escape, I'll blow your brains out. I'm not the one who wants to keep you alive, you know."

The man stalked toward the stairway door and jerked it open. After glaring back at the car for a brief second, he disappeared into the mountain.

Billy managed to slip the gag down enough to open his mouth. He positioned his head to blast Palin at the first sign of light, to fry that creep quicker than he could aim and fire. He pictured the dark knight burning in agony, and the satisfaction of sweet revenge swelled his heart. In his imagination, Palin cooked down to a dirty pile of soot, and Billy kicked the remains and scattered them in the dust.

A hard lump grew in Billy's throat, but he swallowed it away. *It's okay. Palin deserves to die. He's a dragon slayer, and he wants to kill both Bonnie and me.*

Billy had heard Palin yelling about having a gun, but now there was no sound at all. Did he leave? Was he waiting for help? Did he go to get another weapon?

With the tape still strangling his wrists, Billy could do little to improve his situation. The trunk was too dark for him to hunt for a latch, and so far he hadn't found anything sharp. He could feel a couple of gasoline containers at his feet, and his nose told him that another one sat near his head.

He needed a plan. He couldn't yell. Palin might be standing right there. For all Billy knew, Palin could pop open the trunk from well beyond the range of Billy's fiery breath and shoot him just for having the gag off.

Billy didn't stand a chance.

225

Merlin's book was right. I shouldn't have turned that page. It's all my fault.

Although he had read the gloomy oracle only once, some of the words came back to him, defying the limits of normal memory.

Cruel yokes and whips designed for slaves
No, not for heirs nor sons by birth
They tear the backs of stiff-necked knaves
Who think their power comes from earth

Yet hope remains, dispelling fears
A faithful heart, entrapped, alone
Who prays for thee unceasing tears
And casts appeals before his throne

If hope really did remain, Billy didn't see it, and if anyone was praying for him, no one seemed to be listening.

"Who's in the trunk?"

A voice! It sounded like a young woman, trembling and kind of squeaky. *Should I answer? If she doesn't know who's in here, she must not be with Palin.*

"It's Billy Bannister!" he yelled. "Some goon stuffed me in here! Please, help me get out!"

"Hold on!"

Billy heard the faint sound of shuffling steps and a muffled click. The voice returned, this time sounding much younger. "The door's locked!"

Billy yelled back. "Did you try all the doors?"

"They're all locked."

Billy wrestled again with the tape. So close, yet so far! Some girl must have wandered by and heard him struggling. Now she was in danger too. "You'd better get out of sight. The guy who kidnapped me will probably be back soon."

"Not a chance. I saw where he went. It'll be a while."

"Can you call the police?"

"No. But I do have an idea."

Billy let out an exasperated sigh. "Okay. Let's hear it."

"This is a Grand Marquis. It oughta have a trunk release on the inside. It's a T-shaped handle that glows in the dark, and it should be dangling from a pull wire near the lock."

Billy glanced around the dark trunk. "No. There's nothing glowing. I would've seen that by now."

"Then he might have cut it off to hide it. If he did, the bare wire might still be sticking out near the latch. If you can get hold of it, the trunk should pop open easily."

"Easily . . . yeah, right. My hands are tied behind my back."

"How about your feet? Can you maybe get it between your feet and yank on it?"

"I don't think so. I'll try to arch my back up there. My fingers are kind of numb, but maybe I can find it."

Billy twisted his body and pushed his backside toward the trunk latch, bracing his feet against the floor. His fingers were like icicles, and he could barely feel anything he touched. As he worked, he heard the girl's voice again.

"By the way, my name's Karen."

Billy grunted. "Pleased . . . to meet you."

"If that guy comes back, I'll tap the trunk and—"

"I think I got it!" Billy squeezed the wire between his frozen fingers and pulled. He heard a click, and the lid flew open, filling the trunk with daylight and falling snow. Billy sat up on the frame with his back to Karen. "Can you get me loose?"

227

Karen stripped off her gloves and started tearing away the wide strips of duct tape around Billy's wrists, stuffing the pieces into her coat pocket. "It's all twisted up," she said, "but it's coming off." She glanced over her shoulder at the mountainside a couple of times but kept working. "He must have really worked you over. Your lips look like they lost a fight with an orbital sander."

"Yeah. The gag just about tore them off."

"And your neck! Did you cut yourself shaving with a buzz saw?"

"Never mind! Just get me loose before he comes back to finish me off!"

At last the final band of grey tape gave way. Billy yanked the gag down from his chin to his neck and climbed slowly out of the trunk. With his muscles cramping like knotted steel, he staggered and gripped his left calf. He glanced up at the perky redhead's beaming face. "Can you help me walk? We have to get out of sight before Palin comes back."

Karen closed the trunk and pushed her shoulder under his arm. "You bet." She led the way toward a boulder next to a clearing, following a line of footprints in the tyre tracks. When they reached the other side of the boulder, Billy was surprised to find three bundled girls, all younger than Karen, hiding there. He pulled off his coat and began rubbing his arms and legs.

The oldest of the three girls gave him a big smile, glancing over at Karen. "Who's your friend?"

Karen leaned over to pick up Billy's coat and grinned. "His name's Billy, uh, Bannister, I think he said."

Billy stopped rubbing his limbs and gave them all a nod of greeting, ending with Karen. "You got it right. I'm Billy Bannister. You said your name's Karen, right?"

Karen handed him back his coat. "Right, but you can call me Red if you want to." She pointed to the others in turn. "And that's Stacey, Rebecca, and Monique."

Billy lowered his head for a moment, still wincing, and tried to smile with his cracked lips. "The weather's pretty bad for playing outside. What are you doing out here?"

"Actually, we're just hiding right now. We're—" Karen jerked her head around. "He's back!"

Billy signalled for the girls to crouch behind the boulder, and he sneaked to the edge of their refuge to watch the returning kidnapper. Palin stepped from the passageway carrying a shield in his left arm and the pistol in his right hand.

Karen leaned over Billy's shoulder, her lips next to his ear, and whispered, "What do you think he'll do when he finds out you're gone?"

Billy kept his eyes focused straight ahead. He felt Karen's warm breath and grew uneasy about her closeness. With Palin in sight, that murderous demon who had nearly killed him once before, Billy knew what he wanted to do: fry the creep. Rage boiled inside, and he felt a good fire brewing in his belly, but with Karen literally breathing down his neck, he hesitated. Was he ashamed of what he wanted to do or just nervous about the girls seeing it? He shook the turmoil away. *Palin tried to kill me, and he'd kill Bonnie, too, if he had the chance!*

Like the warmth of Karen's breath, the professor's words blew across his mind. *"A knight opposes his enemy face to face. A stab in the back is the way of the coward. If you must fight, attack your enemy head-on. That is the way of valour."*

But he's a slayer! It's okay to fry a creep like him. It's not cowardly!

229

The professor's words responded like an echoing call. *Considering the words of this prophecy, we can assume that God has ordained that we carry out no surprise attacks. Do you understand?*

Billy understood . . . but he didn't care. Palin had sliced his throat, beat up his mum and Walter, and tossed him into a trunk like a bag of dirty laundry. Palin had tried to kill him and Bonnie once before; he was sure to try again. It was time to light this torch and let it blaze.

He waved his hand at Karen. "You might not want to watch. This won't be pretty." She stepped back but stayed close.

Palin extended his left hand with the remote control device between his thumb and forefinger, and the lid jumped open a crack. He swung the shield in front of him, reached with his foot, and kicked the lid up the rest of the way.

Billy didn't wait another second. Thrusting with his whole body, he launched a stream of fire. The river of flames roared from his mouth and landed in the trunk, engulfing the interior in a tidal wave of raging heat and consuming the plastic gasoline containers.

The fuel ignited, erupting in a tremendous ball of yellow and orange, and flames billowed into the sky. As the car's frame ripped apart, the flames blew over Palin like a wall of white-hot fury, knocking him flat. His shield kept his face and chest from taking the brunt of the onslaught, but the blaze covered his legs and gun arm, eating his limbs like a ravenous lion.

Within seconds, the fire died down, and Palin lay on his back with his shield still on his chest. Billy jumped out from hiding and ran to him, sliding to his knees. He grabbed the gun and then threw armfuls of snow onto the smouldering lower body.

Palin threw off the shield, ripping away his scorched sleeve. Billy jumped to his feet and aimed the gun at the wounded man's head, his own legs trembling in pain. His mouth, once again torched by an unusually hot stream, felt like a nest of scorpions.

Palin propped himself up on his elbows and glared at Billy. With his body devastated, Billy knew that the wounded man couldn't hope to fight.

The dark knight tried to speak, but his voice cracked, and the words rasped like sandpaper on rough wood. Keeping the gun trained on Palin, Billy leaned over to listen.

Palin's eyes pierced Billy's with cold malice, and his coarse voice spewed mocking venom. "You think you're a hero now, don't you, boy? You're no hero, oh no, not a hero. You're just like me, boy, just like me. Does a hero kill a man whose back is turned? Couldn't fight me face to face, could you? I tried to kill you when you were wounded back on the mountain, and now you cook me like a goose when my back's turned. Yes, boy, you're just like me. You kill to get what you want."

Palin coughed. He tried to continue, but his voice trailed away. He slumped back, and his body shuddered.

Billy drew closer, still wary of Palin's devices. The dying man clenched his fist and spat out his final pain-streaked words. "My master will live on. He's a true believer, not a hypocrite like you or me. He endured Arthur; he survived Napoleon and Hitler; he will outlive you, too." The creaking voice faded away, as did the life of Devin's evil minion.

Billy laid the dead man's hand gently on his wet, blackened chest. His enemy was gone, yet he felt no joy, no joy at all. His belly gurgled and sent burning fluid into his throat. *What have I done? The professor warned me, but I didn't listen!* His tears flowed, dripping down his nose and falling onto the snow-swept ground.

231

Billy chided himself, mentally buffeting his body. How could he weep over this brutal man, this hate-filled maniac? Was it the words he had spoken? Did his speech stab him like poisoned darts, accusing him of the same heinous crimes that dressed this foul creature in his cruel raiment of blood? It couldn't be! There hadn't been any other way, had there?

Billy slowly straightened his body and gazed for a moment at the blackened shell of a car. Leaning over, he dragged Palin's corpse toward the boulder but stopped short, not wanting the girls to see the grotesque, half-melted body. He shoved a pile of snow together to conceal Palin and then hurried around the hiding place.

The girls were gone! He spotted them far away, running across a field and into a line of skinny, naked trees. "Wait!" Billy's voice died in the blanket of falling snow. He ran after them, his cramped legs still complaining about their ordeal in the trunk. He knew he would eventually catch them. The youngest girl couldn't possibly outrun him in the snow, and even if Karen helped her, they couldn't stay ahead for very long.

After an exhausting chase, he finally came within a few feet of them. "Wait! Why are you running?"

"Stay away!" Karen screamed, running at the rear of the group with Monique in her arms. But as she yelled, she tripped and tumbled head first into a snowdrift. Monique flew from her arms and joined her in the powdery drift.

Billy dashed ahead and scooped Monique up in his arms. She gasped and stared straight into Billy's eyes. Rather than trying to escape, she kept staring, her large brown eyes reflecting Billy's war-torn face.

Karen pushed up on all fours. "Don't hurt Pebbles, you . . . you monster!" The other two girls had scurried behind a tree and peered out from either side.

Billy wanted to laugh at their antics, but his mental image of Palin's grotesque body kept his spirits low. He set Monique down gently. "I'm not a monster," he said, holding out his arms in peace. "If you'll give me a minute, I'll explain."

Karen stood up and brushed the snow from her coat and trousers. Monique ran to her side, lifting up her arms. Karen motioned for Monique to stay put, and the little girl latched onto her leg. The other two girls crept out from behind their tree and crowded behind Karen.

With snow cascading in thick torrents all around, she crossed her arms in front of her chest. "Okay, let's hear it," she said, her expression mixing fear with scepticism. "This oughta be good."

When Bonnie finished a long session of prayer and singing, she settled down to gaze into the darkness. With her improving vision she was able to see a collection of shadowy walls bending into myriad corridors and corners, like black halls in a blacker house. Every now and then, she thought she caught a faint glimmer of light, perhaps some other being watching, maybe hiding in a faraway recess.

She doubted it was Devin. He tended to come out boldly rather than hide around corners. Could it be that phantom, that strange picket fence of light that first kept her out of the slayer's clutches? Bonnie had told Ashley that she wouldn't be alone in the candlestone, so why couldn't God's spirit show up in a spectacular way like he did in the fiery furnace with Shadrach, Meshach, and Abed-nego?

But that glimmer of light could be something else. Maybe, just maybe, her mother really was in there somewhere. Whom should she believe?

Bonnie bit her bottom lip. *Ashley thought Mama was in the candlestone. Could she be held prisoner somehow, trapped by the slayer in one of those dark corridors? Could she have fallen into that crack, drifting now in that sad sea of souls?*

There's the glimmer again!

Bonnie moved toward it, and it disappeared, but this time she kept going, trying to follow a faint trail of luminescence. As she turned a corner, she noticed a bright gleam from around the next angle. She stopped and called out. "Who's there?"

A bright radiance flashed into Bonnie's hallway, but she couldn't see its source. A voice, a slow, sad voice replied. "It is a friend. Draw no closer, child."

Bonnie had no idea what to think about this new presence. Its voice was nothing like Devin's; it was soft, and smooth. "Are you who I think you are?" she asked. "Are you . . . Him?"

A gentle laugh echoed in the darkness. "Only one who knows your thoughts would be able to answer that question, so I must not be who you think I am. As I said, I am a friend. That is all you need know about me. But I know who you are, Bonnie Silver, and I have watched you for a long time. You have an enemy here, and he can harm you, yes, kill you, should you let down your shield."

"My shield?"

"Yes, lass. And a strong one it is. It nearly withered away, but you built it up again. Despair is the way of destruction. It will consume your light like a raging cancer and cast you into eternal shadows."

Bonnie caught a new glimpse of her own light. It had changed quite a bit. Her human shape was now forming, arms and legs, even a hint of fingers at the end of her flowing robe, and her glow did seem pretty bright, but she didn't want to dwell on that; she had to ask her most burning question. "Do you know my mother? Is she here?"

It seemed that she felt a sigh, an old, tired sigh, emanating from her mysterious friend. "Quite a number have entered this prison, but Irene has not passed by my eyes."

Bonnie's light dimmed, and the edges turned ragged. Her mother wasn't here after all? But the strange being did seem to know something. "You called her Irene. So you do know her?"

"I know her well, perhaps better than you do."

"But how is that possible? If you're in here, and she's never entered, how can you know her?"

"Although I knew Irene long before I entered this stone, I have seen her since that time. It took many years, but I have learned to see beyond these walls. We do not have vision, so to speak; our minds adapt to other input. If you stay long enough, you will learn. Your shape will naturally conform in appearance to that of your earthly body as your agitation at being transluminated diminishes. You can even learn to change your shape at will. Your enemy has learned. That is why he has an advantage over you."

"But why won't you let me see you? Why won't you tell me who you are?"

"Because viewing me will lower your shield. When faith is made sight, it is no longer faith. We may lower our shields when the danger has passed, but the danger is ever lurking. I perceive even now that your defences are lowering, so I must leave you."

Bonnie felt an evil presence, the eerie sense of a ghostly sentinel watching her, stalking her. As the light from the other hall faded, she heard its final words.

"Sing, child! Sing! For psalms and hymns are your leather and mail."

235

Bonnie shuddered and immediately lifted her voice.

If I say, Surely the darkness shall cover me; even the night shall be
*   light about me.*
Yea, the darkness hideth not from thee; but the night shineth as
*   the day:*
The darkness and the light are both alike to thee.

The eerie feeling, like tickling hairs on a cold neck, slowly faded away. The light of her friend also disappeared, slipping away into an imperceptible hall.

B illy finished his story and waited for Karen to react. She kept her arms crossed, and a hint of a grin peeked through her lips. "So, I'm supposed to believe that you're a dragon? Human and dragon in one body?"

Billy pushed his boot across the deepening snow. "Well, yeah. I was hoping you'd believe me."

"And what's next?" she continued, her smile bursting forth. "A girl with dragon wings?"

"Yeah, in fact—" Billy stopped and read Karen's grin. "Hey, do you know Bonnie?"

Karen ran to Billy's side and hooked her arm in his. "Like a sister," she said, beginning to lead him back to the stone archway. "Come on. Let's get you to the lab. Bonnie told us to escape and call for help. We were trying to get to a farmhouse I know, 'cause we couldn't really do anything to help her. But with that flame thrower you've got, you can do some serious damage."

The other girls followed while Karen and Billy hurried ahead. Billy, puffing with excitement, tried to talk while running through the drifting snow. "Where is she? Is she safe?"

"I can't say for sure. She went into the candlestone to get her mother out. That's the last I heard."

Billy stopped and clenched a fist. "Oh, no! That's what I was afraid of. Her mother's dead, and she doesn't know it."

Karen squinted at Billy and shook her head. "Dead? What are you talking about?"

"Bonnie's father told her that her mother's still alive, but we found out that isn't true. We found her death certificate in the hospital's records."

"Well," Karen replied, looking back at the girls who were just now catching up. "I don't know about any death certificate, but I saw Bonnie's mum down in the lab with Dr Conner. I heard she was in a coma and they were going to transluminate her to keep her from dying."

"Transluminate her? You know about all that stuff?"

"Yeah." Karen grinned and lowered her head for a second before gazing up at him again. "What else do you want to know?"

Billy couldn't help laughing at this spirited girl. Karen's hood had fallen back, and as the snow settled on her head, Billy thought her fiery hair would melt it away. He sighed and blew a long stream of white into the sky. "I just want to know what's going on. That rat, Devin, is probably in the candlestone, and I think Bonnie's father wants her to drag him out. It's gotta be a trap."

Karen hooked his arm again and pulled him along. "Then all the more reason for you to get into the lab. The door to the stairway is framed by those rocks over there. C'mon! Let's go!"

"No. Wait." Billy withdrew a pencil from the deep pocket on the side of his trouser leg, along with a small tablet of paper. He scratched down a number and began sketching a face. "How far is it to the farmhouse you're trying to find?"

"Pretty far." Karen pointed down the western slope. "I have to go to the end of this trail and then about a mile down the forest road. You probably passed right by it. We could get there in about thirty minutes if the storm lets up. But I don't want to get lost in this weather, especially with Pebbles."

"Yeah, I'll bet." After a few more seconds, he tore off the front page of the tablet. "Here. It's a drawing and a phone number."

Karen took the paper and studied the drawing while Billy pointed at the trail. "Just follow the car tracks. They should still be visible if you hurry, and they'll keep you on the path. Call that number and ask for the professor."

"The professor?" she asked, pointing at the sketch. "Is he this freaky dude with the big eyebrows?"

Billy laughed. "Yeah, the freaky dude. Now you'll be able to recognize him. Tell him everything that's going on, especially what you told me about Bonnie's mum. Just give him the address of the house. He'll find you. And tell him to get here on the double."

CHAPTER 15

DADDY'S DREAM

H ow could you do such a thing?" Ashley stormed back from the cave room, stomping across the lab. She sat heavily at the master control panel, making her chair spin half way around to avoid looking at Doc. She crossed her arms in front of her chest and heaved an angry sigh. "It's despicable! It's criminal!"

Dr Conner called from across the room as he approached. "And it was keeping your grandfather alive!"

Ashley didn't know what to say. The whole world was crashing down on her. All her brilliant plans were falling apart. And they were good plans, plans that would have helped a lot of sick and elderly people.

But now Ashley despised herself. She stood as an evil, mad scientist, holding children captive as lab rats, performing dangerous experiments on them, disintegrating an angelic girl to get a devil out of a crystal chamber, and now . . . and now, this!

And all for what? Nothing worked! Her photoreceptors had failed, Bonnie was trapped with that demon, and her grandfather was dying! Ashley broke down and sobbed.

Dr Conner's hand fell gently on her shoulder. She jumped to her feet and spun away, holding her hand up for him to stop. Her body stiffened and her face flushed. "Just . . . just stay away from me!" She walked backwards toward the girls' dorm. "I'm going to get Karen. We have to get Bonnie out of there!"

"Yes," Dr Conner said, nodding slowly. "Bonnie and Devin have to come out. It's the only way for your grandfather to survive, the only way to keep our research going. I'm glad you finally understand."

Ashley's blood boiled, and she exploded in rage. "No! Don't you get it? We can't keep using people to get what we want! I'm not doing this for my grandfather; it's for Bonnie!"

"Fine, fine." He waved her away with his hand. "Whatever. Go ahead and get Karen dressed; we'll use her one more time."

Ashley sprinted toward the dorm hall. She stretched her key coil and pushed the key into the lock, turning it absentmindedly. Something felt different. There was no resistance, no opening click. Hadn't Bonnie locked it?

She hurried down the hall toward Karen's room, still pondering Doc's words. *"We'll use her one more time."* She paused in front of Karen's sign, "Red and Pebbles." *Use her? No! That's not right!*

She swung the door open and stuck her head in. Quiet. *Could they both be in the bathroom?* She stepped back into the hall and listened to the eerie silence. Where were all the little-girl noises she'd grown accustomed to? She bolted into the room and threw open Karen's closet door. *Her coat's gone!* She dashed to Stacey's and Beck's room. *Empty!*

She flew down the hall, ready to shout the terrible news, but as she passed by her own open door, she suddenly stopped and glanced inside. The lamp on her desk was on and pointed toward her bed, the bright light shining on a three-ring binder that lay on the neatly made spread.

Bonnie's journal?

She stepped inside and sat on the bed, picking up the journal and setting it on her lap. A note taped to the front said, "The girls are okay. Trust me." The finger-worn binder flopped open to the first page, a hand-written title page decorated with squiggly doodles and a half-dozen or so smiley faces. In beautiful script, the title spelled out:

Silver Tokens
My Hopes, My Prayers, My Dreams

Ashley turned the pages, drinking in Bonnie's beautiful prose. Though a rush of thoughts shouted to sound an alarm, Bonnie's simple words held her back. *"Trust me."* Ashley's gifted mind raced through Bonnie's flowery sonnets, exciting stories, and tender dedications, each one garnished with a dash of spiritual insight.

When she reached the end, she found an entry with today's date, and she read it more slowly, savouring each word.

"Greater love hath no man than this, that a man lay down his life for his friends."

Ashley, I know you will understand this verse, and I pray that the heart of its message will fill yours. Daddy's dream may yet be fulfilled, though perhaps in a way you do not expect. You may think no one understands you, but God knows everything about you. He knows who you really are.

"Come now, and let us reason together, saith the LORD: though your sins be as scarlet, they shall be as white as snow; though they be red like crimson, they shall be as wool."

Red will be made white
Darkness shall become light
Faith will be made sight
Squire shall become knight

May God bless you as he speaks to your heart.

Bonnie was right; Ashley did understand, perhaps at a deeper level than Bonnie could possibly have intended. Not only did Ashley now understand the heart of Bonnie Silver, a heart of pure refined gold, she knew what it all meant to her own heart; she knew what she had to do.

There was no need to sound the alarm, no need to recapture the scarlet-haired symbol of her dark experiments; all remnants of her selfish desires had to be purged, even if it meant sacrificing herself to save Bonnie.

Ashley looked up, the eyes of her mind seeing through the ceiling and dozens of feet of earth, and a feeling of peace descended on her like a dove flittering down to alight. Her thoughts drifted, and for a moment she focused on the invisible world outside. *It must be snowing up there.*

Billy stepped cautiously down the dark stairway. Karen had told him to look for a flashlight on a hook just inside the door, but it wasn't anywhere around. He guessed that Palin took it when he went to get his shield and hadn't put it back.

It was good to get out of the bitter wind and snow, but tiptoeing down a pitch-black staircase into the unknown wasn't much better. Every few seconds he let out a puff of fire to light his way, quickly memorizing the fifteen or so steps in front of him during the brief seconds the flame endured. Though the stairway was straight, every now and then a stair would be slanted or broken, and he needed the warning to keep from stumbling on a misshapen board.

He finally reached the bottom of the stairs and followed the gently curving corridor. The narrow, level tunnel was easier on his legs, but darkness still ruled the stuffy cave. His puffs of fire revealed a rocky ceiling with sporadic crossbeams less than a foot above his head and close, wood-framed walls at each side.

A door at the end of a long straightaway appeared, and a faint light emanated from its borders. When he reached it, he stared at its dark panels and weighed the possibilities.

Would anyone be able to hear him if he opened it just a crack to peek in? His dragon senses whispered warnings of danger, feelings of stark dread that ran from his tingling toes to the hairs standing up on his neck. The fire in his belly heated up again, ready to spew something more substantial than a temporary flashlight. Taking a deep breath, he dropped his hand to the cold knob.

As he turned it and pushed, he listened, hoping the hinges would behave themselves and not whine to alert those inside. The door inched open in silence. From the other side a low hum drifted through the gap. Billy shoved the door open wider, enough for him to poke his head through.

The huge room inside was dim with only a few blinking lights in the middle, enough to show a hint of movement. Near the lights a man's shadow hunched over in silence – watching, studying. A glow cast a white light into his face, but the angle and distance kept his features indistinct.

Billy nudged the door open just far enough to squeeze his body through. Hoping his boots would stay quiet, he tiptoed forward. When he came within about ten feet of the man, he spotted a large metal box on the floor. He crouched behind it, peering over the rim. The man sat at some kind of control panel watching a display screen that ran streams of changing numbers above a series of wavy lines.

At regular intervals, the man looked up at something in front of the panel. Billy traced his line of sight to a pedestal in the middle of a bunch of equipment. A red laser beam shot directly into an object perched on top, a sparkling gem. *The candlestone!*

As the man stared at the crimson ray, Billy recognized his short red hair and strong jaw. Dr Conner slipped on a headset and adjusted a series of dials on the panel, then spoke into a microphone. "Devin? Conner here. Can you hear me?"

Devin? So he is in the candlestone! And Dr Conner can talk to him?

A static-filled reply sent shivers across Billy's skin. He closed his eyes and gritted his teeth until the horrible buzz died away and transformed into a voice, the voice Billy had grown to despise.

"My good doctor, it seems that you have failed again. Your daughter is trapped in here with me, and I am not able to approach her. There must be some kind of polarity factor that repels me."

"I know of no polarity issues in your energy matrices that would cause that," Dr Conner replied with an air of scientific precision. "According to these readings, you should be perfectly matched. But now we have to get both of you out if we're going to make the crystal pure again. The candlestone is worthless to me in this state."

The sinister voice returned. "We could get her to try the dive again. I could force her into the abyss where I dumped all the animals you left in here, and then your little genius, Ashley, can try to get her out that way. I have not yet exhausted my arsenal of ideas to make her go willingly."

"I'm not going to risk my daughter's life any further. I only let her dive in because that's been tested so many times, but that exit channel has never been tried. I notice you've never volunteered to go through it."

There was a short pause before Devin continued. "Do you have the mongrel?"

"The Bannister boy? Yes. Palin came down to get a shield from the weapons cache and went back topside to get him. They should both be here any minute."

"Good. You can lock him up in my old stockade in the cave."

"That's what I was thinking. The chains and locks are still in working order."

"Of course they are!" Devin bellowed. "At least one part of my fortress didn't fall prey to your precious lab project." He settled down again, his voice becoming slow and meditative. "With the mongrel out of the way, my colleagues and I can storm the mountain and find that cursed Clefspeare. He is the last one, the very last one."

"Yes," Dr Conner replied. He coughed, covering his mouth with his fist. "The last one."

"But first thing's first," Devin continued. "We need a diver."

"I thought I should try Karen again. She's the most experienced. Maybe she can pull both of you out."

"She translates badly, always has. She comes in so out of phase, I couldn't even see her until her last dive. Your adjustments aren't working. I'm growing impatient with your constant tweaking. It's time to try someone different. Send in the mongrel."

"But the male chimp came back as a blithering idiot." Dr Conner's voice gave away a hint of fear. "All the males lost more than half their brain function during restoration."

Devin shouted, loud static punctuating his words. "What do I care about his brain function? Just make sure he's in phase!" The static died away. "If I can attach, it won't matter if he's as dumb as a salamander. You pull him out, and I'll hang on. I know what causes male brain damage, and it can't happen to me."

"Just be sure to bring Bonnie, too."

"Yes, yes," Devin snapped back. "Don't worry. Just get moving."

"But we need a good anchor. Derrick is sick and exhausted. It would be too dangerous to let him—"

A new voice interrupted. "I'll do it!"

The female voice came from the other side of the room. Billy squinted into the darkness to find the source.

Dr Conner spun around. "Ashley? What did you say?"

"I said, 'I'll do it!' I'll be the anchor."

Walter opened the driver's door for Mrs Bannister and then got in the back. He leaned forward between Mrs Bannister and the professor, watching the BARBARA'S MARKET sign as they pulled out of the parking lot. "She wasn't much help, was she?"

The professor sighed. "Not much, Walter, but we do have a few clues. We know the lab is about thirty minutes away and that there were rumours of a secret construction project up near Camp Misery." He unfolded a map and set his finger next to the image of Flathead Lake. "We can drive up into these mountains and ask the locals about the rumours. It may not take long to narrow down the possibilities."

"Maybe, but it'll be like finding a needle in a haystack."

The professor raised his index finger. "Not exactly, Walter. You see, needles and hay have a similar appearance, making visual discernment very difficult, while a laboratory in the mountains would have a unique—"

"Prof!" Walter said, rolling his eyes. "It was just an expression!"

The professor slowly lowered his finger. "Sorry, Walter. My mind is in analytical mode. Even idioms are not spared." He turned to Mrs Bannister and pointed at a road to the right. "Marilyn. Proceed eastbound on highway eighty-three. We are looking for Echo Lake Road on the left. Obviously a secret lab will not be labelled, so we'll have to be on the lookout for a newly forged road, perhaps a crude path for construction vehicles or a foot trail with a security gate."

The professor's cell phone rang, and he grabbed it from his belt, snapping it up to his ear. "Charles Hamilton here. . . . Yes. I am the professor. . . . Yes, Karen. Go on." The professor snatched a pen from the dashboard and scribbled on the map. "Yes. We will find it. . . . No, I'm not sure how far we are. Can you put the owner on the phone? . . . Thank you."

As he paused, Walter and Mrs Bannister glanced at each other, then back at the professor. Goose bumps popped up on Walter's arms, and he leaned back, drumming the seat with his fingers. Finally, the professor continued. "Yes sir. We are on highway eighty-three. . . . Very good. I believe we can be there in about twenty minutes, if the snow doesn't delay us any more than that. . . . Yes, it might help if you plough the road. Thank you."

The professor put the phone back in place and smiled, his wild white eyebrows lifting in delight. "A young lady named Karen is at a farmhouse near Camp Misery. She said that William is free from his captor, and she will take us to him."

Walter pumped his fist. "All right!"

"Thank God!" Mrs Bannister placed a trembling hand over her heart and heaved a sigh. "Which way?"

The professor snapped his arm forward. "Straight ahead, Marilyn! And hurry! William is not out of the woods, yet."

Billy shrank deeper into the shadowy darkness while Ashley walked resolutely toward the panel, her hands behind her back. In her flowing gown, she swept across the floor like a grey ghost, holding something in her hidden hands.

Dr Conner pulled off his headset. "You can't be the anchor; you've never been trained. It took Derrick three times before he could hang on to anything."

"He trained with monkeys," Ashley countered as she stepped up to the control area. "They were scared and tried to pull away."

Dr Conner reached out and felt Ashley's gown. "You're in an organic robe! Didn't you bring Karen?"

Ashley hesitated and lowered her head. "No . . . No, I didn't."

Dr Conner glared at her dark silhouette. "What's going on?"

Ashley kept her hands behind her back. "Nothing," she replied, gazing at the display. "What's going on here?"

Dr Conner tilted his head and looked past her, and Billy followed his eyes to the back of the lab room where an open door led into a brightly lit hallway. Dr Conner grabbed Ashley's shoulder. "Where are they?"

Ashley stiffened in his grasp, but her voice was casual, almost indifferent. "I honestly don't know. Long gone, from what I can tell. Their hats and coats are missing."

Dr Conner glanced at his watch. "It can't be that long. It's been less than an hour since we went in the cave." He ran toward the door, passing right by Billy's hiding place, and grabbed a coat from a hook on the wall. "Devin can wait! Those girls will freeze in this weather."

He pushed his arms through the coat sleeves and threw open the door. After fishing his keys from his pocket, he flicked on a tiny light hooked to the ring. "Maybe Palin found them and that's what's taking him so long. If not, maybe I can track them in the snow." As the door began to swing shut, he added, "The laser's still running, and the mike's on. Just keep an eye on the data and report anything unusual."

When the door slammed, Billy jerked his head around toward Ashley, who stood staring into the darkness. Billy tried not to breathe. The stately girl's gaze swept the shadowy cavern like a lighthouse beacon in the fog.

It seemed as though she could make sense out of the shadows, as though she could recognize ghosts in the dancing darkness and discern secret voices amid the humming din. She placed her palm on her chest as though feeling for her own heartbeat or covering it to keep others from hearing it pound.

Ashley cleared her throat and spoke straight into the dim room, her voice haunting, yet sweet. "You can come out now."

Billy gulped. *Is she talking to me?* He tried to swallow again, but it felt like a grapefruit had suddenly lodged in his throat.

Her voice continued, this time louder and more fervent. "Billy Bannister, my name is Ashley. I'm a friend of Bonnie's. I know you're here. Come on out. You can trust me."

Trust her? Why should I trust her? It looked like she was working with that creep. Billy stayed low and peeked around the edge of the box. Ashley pulled her hands out from behind her back and held up a notebook.

"This is Bonnie's journal, Billy. She says that dragons can sense certain presences. They can sense when another dragon is near, and they can sense danger." She turned directly toward Billy's hiding place, and it seemed that she spoke right to him, her voice calling like an alluring echo in a faraway valley. "Do you sense danger, Billy Bannister? Am I a threat to you?"

Her questions reached across the black void, grasped his quaking heart, and shook out his fear. His sense of dread, his dragon alarm, had vanished when Dr Conner shut the door to the dark passageway, but his own fears had remained – his lack of confidence, his knowledge that without his fire he would probably be helpless, and his certainty that the candlestone would strip away his only weapon.

Yes, Ashley was right about the sense of danger. It was gone. How did she know so much? Did Bonnie really write stuff about dragons in her journal? Even if she did, it still didn't explain how Ashley knew he was there. Billy needed to find out more, and he saw there was only one way to do it. He stood up slowly, his gaze meeting hers through a curtain of shifting darkness.

She walked toward him, holding out the journal, her light brown eyes soft and warm. She placed the journal in Billy's hands. "We have work to do," her gentle tone matched her eyes, "but there's something here you have to read first."

Yielding to Ashley's serious, formal manner, Billy reined in his suspicion and bowed his head. "If Bonnie wrote it, then I'm sure it's worth reading."

She placed a hand on his shoulder, motioning upward with her head, her voice still quiet. "Did you see any girls up there, a redheaded teenager and three younger girls?"

Ashley's fingers kneaded his back. He understood her feelings – she was scared and trying not to show it, wanting to draw close and find comfort. He wanted to trust her – to have an ally to confide in, a source of comfort of his own. The blinking lights reflected in her dark wide pupils. He nodded. "Yeah, I saw them."

Ashley pressed closer, so close he could smell a hint of toothpaste on her breath. Her nearness brought a strange sensation, like she was drawing warmth from his body, the same way it felt whenever Bonnie touched him. It was almost like she was trying to read his mind by extracting his thoughts through his skin.

251

Her voice grew a notch louder. "Were they okay?"

Billy pulled back a little to keep his own breath from singeing her lips. "Yeah, they were heading to a farmhouse that Karen knows. They might be there by now. I don't know if Dr Conner will follow them or not when he sees what happened up there."

Ashley released his shoulder, allowing him to edge another step back. "What happened? How did you find your way down here?"

Billy shifted his weight from one foot to the other. "Well, that's a long story, but basically, I dispatched the guy who brought me here."

Ashley drew her head back and replied in a loud whisper. "You killed him?"

Billy studied the floor and nodded. When Ashley didn't say anything, he gazed into her face. Sadness clouded her expression, and the corners of her lips wilted. She opened the notebook in Billy's hands, flipped a few pages, and tapped her finger on the words. "It starts here. You'll know when it's finished." With tears now forming in her eyes, Ashley pulled aside Billy's coat and fingered the hem of his shirt. "Is it cotton?"

"Yeah, I think so."

"Good. I already saw your jeans. They should work fine, but I'll get a robe and a cotton belt for you anyway. If you have any metal fasteners, they'll be gone when you're restored." She turned her gaze to the middle of the room and gestured toward the pedestal. "You were listening in on Doc's conversation. Do you understand what's going on?"

Billy took a step closer to the centre, and a familiar surge of nausea flooded his stomach. He nodded and waved his finger toward the candlestone. "I think I figured it out. I'm supposed to go in there somehow and get Bonnie."

"That's right. I'll explain how in a little while." She pointed toward the girls' dorm. "There's a light in that hallway. Why don't you go there to read? I have to pay someone a visit. I'll be back in a few minutes."

Billy held up his hand, bidding her to come back. "How did Bonnie get in there? And how do I go in? Can Devin hurt her? And what was that about losing brain function?"

Ashley stepped back and put a gentle hand on the side of Billy's head. "Hold your questions and be patient. I'll tell you a little at a time. Too much information can make your brain choke."

Ashley smiled again before turning away. She took a step toward the glowing red candlestone and reached for the panel, turning off the laser and the microphone. She then walked to a door that was similar to the one she had pointed out for Billy, a closed door on the opposite side of the huge room. She used a key to unlock it and went inside, shutting it behind her.

With his finger lodged in the pages, Billy tucked the notebook under his arm and marched straight to the light. He placed the notebook on the floor, pulled off his coat, and sat on the tile floor just inside the hallway. He took a deep breath and settled down to read.

Ashley knocked on the first door on the left inside the boy's dorm. "Daddy? Are you there?"

She waited. There was no answer. She tapped again, this time with a bit more force.

"Daddy? It's Ashley."

Still no answer.

Ashley reached for the doorknob and turned it slowly. She swung the door open, and a push of warm, stuffy air fanned her face as she stuck her head into the dim room.

Next to a bed, a single lamp pitched a slender ray of light on a man's sleeping form, the dim yellow beam shining from a miserably inadequate bulb. A single fly buzzed around the lamp's black shade in lazy, elliptical orbits. Ashley stepped inside and watched it for a moment. How had a fly found its way deep into the heart of this mountain in the dead of winter? For that matter, why would anyone choose to live in a dark cave, far from life and love?

Her eyes followed the light back to the bed and her peaceful grandfather. An open book rode the tide of his rhythmic wheezing, its pages lying face down on the man's thick belly.

Ashley knelt at his bedside, tenderly pushing a strand of hair from his forehead and then stroking his thin, silvery mane.

"Daddy," she whispered. "It's Ashley. Can you hear me?"

His open pyjama top exposed a forest of white hair and a wide, red scar, evidence of his heart surgery years ago.

Ashley put her head on his once strengthening chest, now sunken and so much weaker than just a few days ago. She began crying, her heart ripping open in despair. "Oh, Daddy! I'm so sorry! I . . . I tried to make the receptors work . . . I really tried. But I failed you. I'm so sorry!"

She listened to his laboured heartbeats as she cried on and on, tears rolling down her cheeks and wetting his pyjama top. She leaned up and kissed him on the forehead. It was all right; she would take care of his shirt for him, just like she had a hundred times before.

Just a few months earlier she'd thought she would never have to be his nurse again. Now she didn't care if she had to wash him or change his clothes. She just wanted her Daddy. She pushed the book away, draping her arm over his waist, hugging him close as her gaze fell across his chest. She watched the complementary colours of injury and decay, the angry red scar and the white mat of hair, as they rose and fell in time with his laboured breaths.

Still on her knees, and with her head resting on her Daddy's chest, she tried to speak again, anguish filling her squeaking, faltering voice. "Re . . . red will be made whi . . . white . . . Red will be—" She squeezed her eyes shut, her mouth opening in a silent wail.

When she finally settled herself, something brushed against her hair. Was it that fly? She raised her hand to shoo it away, but her fingers swiped against flesh. A hand! She grabbed it eagerly and popped her head up. Her grandfather smiled and stroked her hand.

"Ashley," he said softly, "I'm sorry you have to see me like this."

Ashley caressed his hand and kissed it. "Oh, Daddy!" New tears flooded her eyes, and her voice cracked. "It's . . . it's all my fault. I couldn't get the photoreceptors to work, and now you're . . . you're—"

"Dying?"

Ashley kept her eyes focused on their clasping hands and nodded.

"I know you wanted me to live so we could be together, Ashley. I wanted it, too. But I guess God has other ideas." He tried to lift himself up on his pillow, and his voice deepened. "Don't worry about me. I'm ready to face my maker. Remember? Amazing grace, how sweet the sound, that saved a wretch like me."

She nodded again, her eyes still on their hands. "I remember."

He sighed and lifted her hand to his lips, kissing it softly. "Maybe someday you'll sing it with me . . . even if it's in heaven."

Ashley gazed into his face. His eyes and gentle smile melted away her anguish. She wanted to sing with him, to join his happy bass and cry out, "I once was lost, but now am found; was blind, but now I see." But she couldn't. . . . She couldn't.

A soft breeze whispered through her tangled, flyaway hair – a ceiling fan lazily paddling through the room's thick warmth. She wanted to stay like this forever, to squeeze out every possible moment in his presence. But she knew she didn't have much time left. Doc would be back soon, and she had to get some information, the story her grandfather had never been willing to tell before. She gazed into his pale grey eyes and pushed her fingers through his wispy hair. "Daddy, what really happened to my mum and dad? Something's come up, and I really need to know."

Her grandfather shifted on his bed and looked at the wall for a moment before fixing his eyes on hers again. "I guess I'd better tell you before I die. Are you sure you can take a surprise, I mean, a real shock?"

Ashley wiped her wet cheeks with her free hand. "After what I've seen, I think I'm ready for anything."

CHAPTER 16

To Summon a Dragon

Bonnie looked high above into the candlestone's upper walls – dark crystalline planes that created an angled, bending sky. A stream of white light poured into the gem's stratosphere like a perpetual shooting star, striking the inner core and streaming around its black skin. Then, like sparkling dew rolling off polished obsidian, it spilled into a channel that disappeared into a blazing horizon – a waterfall of dancing sparkles splashing into a distant river of light.

Through the dark hours, she had grown accustomed to her sunless, moonless prison, a domain where gloom held sway over the remnants of light that lived and moved within. The slayer lurked. She had seen his angry sparks, sometimes peering around hidden planes, sometimes slowly approaching and then backing away.

It didn't take long for Bonnie to figure out that her singing kept the slayer at bay. With each musical phrase her shimmering light created a faint dome of luminescence that built her confidence and made the protective glow persist. Adding to her unearthly light, her ring's dark red radiance pulsed like a beating heart, resonating in time with her song.

During a quiet moment, as excited particles from the laboratory lights continued to flow, Bonnie once again sensed the slayer's growing presence, an increase in staccato flashes and fleeing shadows. She released a stream of song, but this time he didn't retreat.

He crept across the glass floor, as though testing his barriers, and stopped at a safe distance. "I have been speaking to your father." His static-crusted voice wasn't as irritating as usual. "It seems that your half-breed boyfriend is in hand. My old friend, Palin, was able to capture him, as I expected."

Bonnie ended her song abruptly. "He has nothing to do with this. Why don't you just leave him alone?"

"How little you know! Or should I say, how much you pretend not to know?" Devin drew closer, bending Bonnie's shield until it halted his progress. "The boy will dive in here to get you, and we will attach to him and ride out to freedom."

"Not if I can help it," Bonnie said, backing away. "You can't even come close to me anymore. I'll go with him alone, and we'll leave you behind."

Devin let out a spiteful snort. "Oh, really? Do you know where a diver enters? I'll see him first. He knows nothing about creating shields, so I'll be able to attach to him, and we'll leave you here in this nice cozy prison."

Bonnie's light pulsated rapidly, and her ring glowed like a flashing red beacon. "He'll find a way! Even if you do go without me, he'll come back!"

"Not so fast, my dear. There's something else you don't know. There's another reason why they always send females in here. The male animals they tested couldn't be restored properly; they always lost brain function, making them simpletons, or worse." A flash of light erupted from one side of his electric body, like a long electrostatic finger, and he held it out in front of him. "I saved that part of the conversation for you. Listen."

The flash sparked and flowed into Bonnie's mind like an echo from the past. It was her father's voice.

"But the male chimp came back as a blithering idiot. All the males lost more than half their brain function during restoration."

The flash died away, and Devin's energy field throbbed, as if laughing with delight. "Your sweetheart will turn into a gentle vegetable. He won't care about diving back in to fetch you out; he'll be dribbling from sippy cups and soiling baby diapers for the rest of his life."

Bonnie's light flashed like a strobe and then dissipated as the vivid image of Billy that the slayer had painted penetrated her mind. The horrible vision lingered, and her protective dome faded. Devin slithered closer.

She wanted to sing but couldn't think of the words. She tried to battle; she tried to think through the turmoil of doubts and fears that waged war with her courage. *Could it be true? How could Devin conjure up a recording like that?*

Bonnie finally managed to hum, the familiar tune trickling out on trembling light waves. After a few seconds, the words flowed to her mind and then into the glowing stream. *If I make my bed in hell, behold, thou art there. If I take—*

"Don't sing that blasted song again!" Devin shouted. "No ancient Bible ditty will do you any good in this hellhole." His light-filled body floated back and forth in Bonnie's field of vision, like a man pacing in anger. "God isn't here. I should know. I've been in this forsaken place for weeks, and there's nothing but gloom and despair. There is no salvation within these walls."

Devin paused, and his voice softened, flowing into her mind like a gentle shower, smooth, yet dripping with malevolence. "But you can still save your boyfriend and yourself if you're willing to make a deal."

Bonnie's light flashed again and sparked. "I don't make deals with the devil!"

Devin took a step back, but his voice remained calm. "Fair enough. I know you don't trust me, but you heard your father's unguarded words for yourself. It might help if I explain why he's correct. Males don't translate well. Rather than adapt to their transluminated state, their bodies fight against it. It isn't an act of the will; it's just the way they're built. I can see it in their light patterns when they come in; they're all twisted and shaky. They don't have enough time in here to settle down. When the system tries to restore them, it can't translate the agitated state of their minds, and their brains aren't reconstructed properly. A few have even died."

"So what about you? Won't you lose brain function if you leave?"

"I've adapted. I felt my brain fighting it at first, but over time I've gotten it under control. It took a few weeks, but now my light patterns are smooth and even, so I'm not in an agitated state. Your mongrel friend, however, will be fully agitated. I wager that he'll come in here ready for a fight. His heart is full of rage."

He paused again, and his light began swirling like a pinwheel in a soft breeze. A thin stream of light oozed from Bonnie's glow as if pulled by Devin's bright whirlpool. His soft voice continued, rising slightly with the victorious tone of discovery. "And you know that, don't you? Perhaps better than I?"

Bonnie edged away. Devin knew. Somehow her thoughts had spilled into the open, and the truth was out. She redoubled the guard on her mind. "So what kind of deal were you thinking about?"

Devin returned to his human form and grinned, the expression of a riverboat gambler gathering his winnings. "I figured out that I can't get close to you because of all that infernal singing you do. I can't attach unless you let your defences down, so for your part, you'll have to stop singing. And for my part, I'll show Billy the secret to leaving with his brain intact."

He waited for a moment, his flashing lips stretching out into a thin line. "You're a smart girl," he added. "That's why I've never been able to defeat you. I'm sure you'll figure out that you have to trust me on this one."

Bonnie's light sparked and sputtered. *Trust him? Ha! Now that's a laugh!* She glared at him, watchful of his mind-reading trick. What was he up to? Obviously he wanted to get out, and the key was through attachment. But couldn't he just try to attach to Billy like he had said? Why did he want to attach to her? No, she didn't trust him, but she wanted to know his secret, the way to protect Billy's brain from damage. She couldn't just ask him to tell her. That would be silly. If he really had a secret, he wouldn't hand it over free of charge. He wouldn't have anything left to bargain with. So what could she do to discover it? Let him attach? The thought sent bursts of shivering light across her body. Here she was, a glittering pebble in a twisting black kaleidoscope, confused in a surreal existence and having to deal with a silky-tongued liar. Maybe there was another way. Maybe she could find that friendly light again and ask him. He had helped her before.

"I'll think about it." She turned and hurried away.

Billy leaned over the neat, flowing script, the shadow of his head dimming the page. He heaved a deep sigh, mentally preparing himself for the words in his lap. He knew Bonnie was a gifted writer, possessing a dragon-inspired talent far beyond that of a normal girl, but remembering Ashley's manner when she gave him the journal made him think this entry might be more than he could handle.

His gaze focused on the top line. It was a prayer, and though Billy didn't know much about praying, he guessed he should read it with reverence.

My Prayer for Billy

Dearest Heavenly Father, my heart longs for your presence, for you to sit by my side and whisper in my ear. Grant me counsel, the deep wisdom that listens to my heart and understands my pain in the midst of my groanings.

I have a friend who stands as close as a brother, a brave soul. Yet, you know him better than I. He is Billy Bannister, the son of Clefspeare, a dragon. I have seen in him the heart of a warrior, a knight's squire who follows the code, ready to die if need be to slay the forces of evil and rescue vulnerable maidens, broken-hearted widows, and grieving orphans. He is gallant, loyal, and true, sacrificing his esteem, forfeiting his comfort, even spilling his blood. But, what colour is his soul?

Tell me, Father, holy and true, I have borne in my heart this ache for so long! My dear friend has a desperate need, and I have seen it. How can I be his accuser, condemning the one who has gladly poured out his blood in my stead? But shall I deny my witness? There is a darkness, a gnawing void behind those eyes of steel. And even in those placid pools, I see turmoil, uncertainty, even pride. Oh, how can love and vexation so violently mix, a brew of man and beast stirred in a cauldron of scales and flesh?

Yes, there is violence, a rage that does not rest, for he battles in the fields of his mind, resolutely standing his ground, his faith in the old ways, the ways of the code, the ways of the dragon, the ways of his father. Yet, his father has left him an orphan, a squire without a knight, and the cruelty of his passing has never ceased to consume his standing as he guzzles from the old wineskins on which he relies.

It is not a slayer who haunts his thoughts and dreams. Dare I ask it? Shall I be so bold? Is it you, my father, the pursuer of men's hearts, who brings war to his battlefield? Are you the fire that will purge his pride, his reliance on things of this world, honourable deeds, yet filthy rags in your sight? Will you teach him what pleases you? Will you tell him about weapons from above, the sword of truth and the shield of faith? Will you give him new wineskins, pouring into his heart the wine from above, the blood of the sacred covenant? Will you make him a knight, dressed in holy raiment, fit to take a seat at your table?

I fear the battle, Lord, lest you slay him with penetrating light, driving your two-edged sword deep into his fragile bosom, and searching out the dark recesses of his heart. For who can stand when your word declares judgment? How will he survive unless someone takes him to wash in the river, the wellspring of eternal life?

Who am I? How can I take him to your fountain? You know him far better than I, yet I feel I know his heart as well as my own. From dragon to dragon, I feel when he is near, as though his heart pounds in my own breast. When he touches me, the heat of his passion and the fire of his breath spread warming flames all around this cold orphan's crying soul. Yet I am not his counsellor, nor his judge. I stand as one who bears a gift but knows not how to give it, for though I am emboldened in my closet, in his presence I melt like wax.

Dear Father, I confess. I confess that I love him. Yet how little I understand these words. We are bound by prophecy, destined for oneness, and this virgin's heart quakes at the thought. My heart longs for his, yet I know we cannot be one until the sun chases away his shadows, for light and darkness can have no fellowship.

Oh, Father! Whisper now in my ear. Shall I tell him of your saving grace? If I do, will he respond to you or to his passions? Would my feminine voice distract him from hearing yours? Would my face be his vision, or would he see the face of Christ? Oh, Father! Should such a maiden take this duty, to tell a heroic soldier that his scarlet soul needs to be made white?

And now, Heavenly Father, I ask you to take my entreaty and use it as you will. Whether in a whisper, a shout, or a song, let my voice be yours. Let my words be your balm. Use them to soften his heart, that you may inscribe your name there with indelible blood. Enlighten his mind, that truth may reside there forever. Cleanse his soul with fire and water, burning away the old and washing away the scarlet stain, that your spirit may indwell, empower, and preserve. Whatever must be done, whatever pain you must bring to make red into white, I pray that you will make the mortal squire into a holy knight.

Billy closed the notebook and hugged it close to his chest. His body trembled, ten thousand pounds of pressure building up inside and ready to burst out.

First one tear made its way to his eyes, then another. He looked up and sniffed, trying to blink away the tears and focus on the blank wall across the corridor – focus on anything but all his failures. Through the blur, a vision of Bonnie coalesced on the wall, her wings spread in full flight. She begged him to take something from her hands, but her gift was fuzzy, unfocused. He leaned closer until the object sharpened into a magnificent sword, the one and only Excalibur. The image was the portrait he had worked on in his studio, now complete and brought to life, and Excalibur's shining blade pierced his heart.

What were the professor's words that day? *"It was bestowed to you as a gift from above. It was meant for you to wield in battle."*

Billy had refused the sword. He had rejected a precious gift, a weapon of righteousness.

And now look at the mess everyone is in.

His inner rage was real, and Bonnie knew it well. Even Palin with his sneering accusation could see his private darkness. *"You're just like me, boy."* Billy had killed his accuser. He had scrapped his training, the professor's words of wisdom he was supposed to keep locked tightly in his heart. He refused to oppose his enemy face to face. Cries of "murderer" came from all around, like a lynch mob demanding his death, and Billy tried to swat them away. Oh, how he longed for freedom, for innocence, the purity he had always seen in Bonnie! But she couldn't bestow her integrity; she couldn't let him borrow her virtue, not even a slice of her righteousness that had always kept her in lasting peace.

The vision of Bonnie's eyes pierced Billy's own, and from her lips he heard what the professor had said not so long ago, *"Nor can I lend you my faith."*

Billy laid his head on Bonnie's journal and cried. Rage, hate, fear, loneliness, all dissolved into his tears and splashed onto the precious book. His body trembled, and lifting his head, he gasped for breath. "I . . . I don't know how! Help . . . help me believe in you!" As his tears subsided, he turned his eyes upward.

Above the ceiling lay countless tons of earth and rock, unseen, yet waiting to fall on him and crush his body. He'd always imagined God as that crushing rock. But Bonnie had painted God with majestic words of love, more like the sun and sky – beautiful, limitless, and forever giving light and warmth.

He took a deep breath and released it slowly, a few unbidden fiery sparks flying out. He tried to fashion a prayer in his mind, but all the thee's and thou's just wouldn't come together. Would God even listen to a dragon boy? Did he really care as much as Bonnie thought he did?

Billy lifted his head, looking straight up with unblinking eyes. "I don't have much faith," he said softly. "Maybe you can lend me a little of yours."

How will we know her?" Walter asked as the Jeep sped down the road through the heavily falling snowflakes.

The professor pulled his coat closed and zipped it up. "Karen told me she has red hair and that she would keep her hood down so we could see it. She also has three younger girls with her. They should be easy to spot."

Mrs Bannister pointed ahead. "That must be it." She slowed the Jeep, careful to avoid sliding on the thin sheet of white, and parked behind another SUV just beyond the farmhouse driveway. A ploughed drift blocked the entrance, preventing them from getting any closer to the house.

Walter jumped from the Jeep and hurdled the drift, while Mrs Bannister helped the professor through the snow on his crutches. When Walter came within fifty feet of the doorstep, he spotted Karen on the wooden porch passing by a big barrel stuffed with firewood. Three smaller girls crowded close to the redhead, and a man walked beside her, gripping her shoulder and herding the girls toward the snow-covered road. Except for a rumbling tractor pulling a snowplough toward a distant barn, the place seemed deserted.

"Wait!" Walter called, holding up his hand and sprinting toward them.

The man stopped, tilting his head and squinting. Walter skidded to a stop. *Bonnie's father!*

Dr Conner faced Walter, giving him an uneasy smile. "Well, if it isn't Walter Foley! It's a small world, isn't it?"

Walter glowered at him. "Too small, I think." He planted his hands on his hips and turned toward the redhead. "Are you Karen?"

Karen tightened her lips and nodded.

Dr Conner pulled the girl closer. "And how could you possibly know Karen?"

Walter folded his arms across his chest. "Like you said, Dr Conner. It's a small world."

Pounding his crutches through the snow, the professor drew within earshot, Mrs Bannister at his side. "Unhand that girl!" he shouted.

Dr Conner jerked his head toward the approaching adults, and his arm dropped from Karen's shoulders and grasped her forearm. Walter leaned over and whispered to Karen, "Do you want to get away from him?" Her frightened eyes sparkled with welling tears, and she nodded ever so slightly.

The professor hobbled up beside Walter and grabbed Dr Conner's wrist. "I shall tell you one more time, sir, before I become perturbed. Unhand this girl."

Dr Conner jerked his arm away. "Why should I? This is my daughter!" He waved toward the other three shivering girls. "They're all my daughters."

Mrs Bannister wiped snow off the shortest one's head and knelt to rebutton her coat. "And they're all freezing!"

Thick puffs of white billowed through the falling snow as the professor spoke. "Whether or not they are really your

267

daughters, Dr Conner, is immaterial to me. The eldest called me with an urgent message, and I believe you are the cause of her distress."

"Ridiculous!" He pulled Karen's hood up over her soaked hair. "They were out playing in the snow and went too far. I just found them, and I'm taking them home."

The professor lifted his brow, his eyelids drooping just a shade. "Indeed! And you told us we could visit Bonnie anytime we wished. Your card, however, carried the address of some rather unsavoury characters. They did not greet us well, so we decided to pay you a visit here to recommend that you correct your business cards, lest other visitors find the same rude greeting." He gestured toward their Jeep. "Shall we drive to your home and complete our visit? I'm certain Bonnie will be glad to see us."

Walter loved the professor's smooth sarcasm. It was biting, yet sprinkled with gentlemanly charm. He knew there was no way Dr Conner could refuse.

Dr Conner put his hands on his hips, and he nodded, letting out a long sigh. "Okay, okay."

Mrs Bannister hurried toward the Jeep. "I'll drive as close as I can and pick everyone up."

The professor smiled down at the trembling redhead. "Karen, I am at your service. You may speak freely." He gestured with his head toward Dr Conner. "You need not fear this man. I assure you that I will keep you from harm."

Karen cast a doubtful eye at the professor's crutches and smiled uneasily.

Dr Conner's voice shook with anger. "How dare you talk to my daughter that way? I'm her protector; not you, old man!" He grabbed Karen's hand. "Forget what I said. They're coming with me, and you can just—"

"Dr Conner!" The professor interrupted, his eyes blazing. "I suggest you reconsider." Mrs Bannister pulled the Jeep up close, and the professor turned to Walter. "Walter, please fetch the flower box."

Walter grinned. "Sure, Prof!" He hustled back to the Jeep.

The professor shifted on his crutches and faced Dr Conner. "A father certainly has protection rights, as you suggest. All rights, however, are forfeited if a child is abused."

"Abused?" Dr Conner replied, his voice rising again. "I've never abused her, and she knows it!"

Walter returned, carrying the flower box, and the professor handed one of his crutches to him. While leaning on the other crutch, the professor opened the box and withdrew Excalibur. At the moment he touched the hilt, the great sword began to glow. The professor dropped the other crutch and steadied himself on his good leg, holding Excalibur in ready stance with both hands. Dr Conner took a step backward, his eyes wide and mouth agape.

"Now," the professor said softly as the sword glowed brighter and brighter, "I will ask her myself." He lowered his gaze to meet Karen's and spoke tenderly. "Young lady, what is troubling you, and why did you call me? Do you wish to be free from this man?"

She jumped over to the professor's side and grabbed him around the waist, shivering and crying. Dr Conner stepped toward them, but the professor raised the sword higher. "I suggest you halt."

Dr Conner stopped. Excalibur's spectacular glow reflected in the scared doctor's eyes, and his legs shook like two autumn leaves.

The professor continued. "It seems that the maiden has spoken quite clearly, even in silence. So now, if you will acquiesce, sir, and do what I ask, I will put the sword away."

269

Dr Conner spun around and ran, slipping once and stopping his fall with his hands on the ground. With both legs churning, he dashed toward his SUV.

Mrs Bannister hopped from behind the wheel and ushered the three younger girls toward the Jeep. Walter grabbed the professor's crutch from the ground. "He's getting away!" He tossed both crutches into the rear of the Jeep and hustled back to help the professor. He and Karen supported him to the front seat and then squeezed in the back with the three girls.

Karen parked herself behind the driver. "I know the way. Just stay on this road for a few minutes. I'll let you know when to turn." After a couple of miles of slipping and sliding, Karen pointed to the right. "Up that path. We'd better hurry. Doc may have gone in the back way."

Mrs Bannister stepped on the gas, and the Jeep managed the first part of the slope with no problem. "I hope we can make it up these snowy slopes."

"No problem," Karen said confidently. "This Jeep has Quadra-Drive. I saw a Grand Marquis make it to the top, so I'm sure we can."

"What will happen if he gets there before we do?" Mrs Bannister asked.

Karen pulled her hood down and leaned forward, her teeth chattering. "Billy sneaked into the lab to try to find Bonnie. I don't know what Ashley would do, but if Doc catches him, there's sure to be trouble."

"Ashley?" Mrs Bannister repeated. "Who's Ashley?"

"Doc's lab assistant. Doc calls her that, anyway, but she really runs the place."

Walter shifted to the edge of his seat. "How did Billy escape from that creep, Palin?"

Karen sighed and leaned back. "You'll find out."

When they reached the mountaintop, she said, "Turn left here." She pointed to an arch of rocks. "That's the lab entrance, but it's a long way down a bunch of stairs and then through an even longer tunnel. I'll show you the way, but the other girls shouldn't go. They're real tired."

The professor touched Mrs Bannister's arm. "Marilyn, I assure you that Walter and I can handle this. We will find your son and restore him to you. Do you mind staying? The young ladies will be quite warm in here."

As she drove into the makeshift driveway, Mrs Bannister took a deep breath and nodded. "Okay, I'll—"

"What's that?" Walter cried out, pointing up ahead.

Karen shook her head sadly. "It's a burned-out Mercury Grand Marquis. Palin had Billy in the trunk with a bunch of gas cans. Billy set it on fire."

"And what happened to Palin?" the professor asked.

"He went up in flames. He's dead."

The professor's face turned white. He leaned over the seat, speaking earnestly. "Tell me, did you see it? Did William intentionally kill the man?"

Karen nodded. "Yeah. It was pretty scary. We girls all ran away."

The professor clutched the dashboard and his voice rose. "But was it in face to face combat?"

Karen shrank back against the upholstery. Her voice lowered to a whisper. "Not really. Billy had already escaped from the trunk, and we could've all sneaked into the woods. The guy's back was turned." Karen paused. "But the guy deserved it, right? Wouldn't he have killed Billy if he had the chance?"

"Oh, no doubt. That foul skunk would likely have killed all of you if he thought it would help him achieve his goals." His

271

voice calmed, and he took a deep breath before continuing. "Yes, he deserved to die, but the issue is not one of justification; it is a matter of valour, the code of a knight, of facing an enemy head-on rather than sneaking up on his unguarded flank. It's also a matter of obeying a command, of heeding prophecy."

The professor placed a trembling hand on Merlin's diary situated on a box between him and the driver's seat. As the Jeep came to a stop next to the blackened car, the professor pulled the book onto his lap. He kept his face forward while he spoke. "Marilyn, Walter, we must call for help."

"Call who?" Mrs Bannister asked. "The police? Walter's Dad?"

"No." He opened the diary to the prayer on the first page. "I have the translation here on a card. Please grant me silence as I read."

The little girls straightened in their seats, and Karen put her arm around Monique, snuggling her close. Walter propped his wrist against the headrest in front of him and held his breath. In a clear voice, the professor read the prayer, speaking the last four lines with a great flourish.

> *God, my lord, do send my plea*
> *To dragons' ears both far and nigh*
> *Send me help I ask on knee*
> *Transluminate me lest I die*

When the professor fell silent again, Walter pulled on the back of his teacher's seat. "What's wrong, Prof? Why did you call for a dragon?"

The professor ran his palm over the rough parchment. "It's part of what I could not reveal to you earlier, Walter. A con-

272

ditional prophecy has been fulfilled, and it seems that we will soon see a veritable eruption of crises, too many for us to handle alone."

"But can Clefspeare possibly get here in time to help?"

The professor sighed, a faraway look taking over his expression. "I don't know, Walter. I just don't know. I merely followed the prophecy's suggestion." He turned a couple of pages and placed a firm finger on the top line of text. "Here. I can read this one to you now. I have been given leave to reveal prophecies already set in motion." The professor cleared his throat.

The child of doubt, still chained, still torn
Must choose his fateful path;
To take revenge and valour scorn,
Or quell his heart of wrath?

And should he choose the wanton way,
Appeasing vengeance due,
He sets the course for Judgment Day
And brings the end in view.

Yet hope remains, a dragon's aid
May come to quench the fire.
A fervent summons rightly prayed
Will call them to the squire.

But make no haste to quote the prayer
For dragons here to fly,
For if the child acquits the slayer
The dragons called shall die.

"That one's not too hard to figure out," Walter said. "I think I liked it better when it was confusing."

273

"What is that book?" Karen asked, her bobbing head leaning forward. "It sounds scary, like something real bad's going to happen."

"It is a very special diary," the professor replied, "an old, prophetic book. Its author uses a simple rhyme and metre scheme, but his prophecies are deep and mysterious. And, yes, I would say that the coming of Judgment Day is something about which we might all be alarmed. I don't think he's speaking of a literal end-of-the-world scenario, but even with poetic licence, I'm sure it could be very bad, indeed."

Mrs Bannister took a deep breath and regripped the steering wheel. "Well, you'd better get going. There's no telling if Billy's in trouble or not."

Without another word, the professor, Walter, and Karen popped open the doors and exited the Jeep. Karen led the way toward the arch of stones, crunching through the deep snow-drifts. Walter held the box containing Excalibur under one arm and used the other to steady his teacher as he hobbled on crutches along the slippery trail.

As they neared the entrance, Walter tugged on the professor's coat. "Hey, Prof. Do you feel something?"

They halted at a clearing, snow falling all around. The ground swayed, then rocked. Walter widened his stance and bent his knees, keeping a firm grip on the professor's arm.

The professor spoke in a hushed tone. "It's a tremor, Walter. A slight one, to be sure, but it may be a harbinger of events to come."

"A tremor?" Karen asked. "You mean, like an earthquake?"

"Yes. It seems that our local Judgment Day may already be dawning."

CHAPTER 17

THROUGH A GLASS DARKLY

B illy approached the candlestone, tingling weakness spreading through his arms and legs. Even with stabbing pain shooting through his back and sickening gases churning his stomach, he allowed himself to be drawn to the gem's unearthly pull.

A thin swirl of barely visible light streamed into a dense grouping of the stone's minute facets. It looked like a tiny vacuum cleaner sucking in a trail of dancing pixies from all around the room. On the other side of the gem, a steady, dim beam poured out, like someone inside the stone had strangled the pixies, flattened their corpses with a mallet, and squeezed their bodies into a shaft of dead light.

The nausea worsened, and a throbbing headache pounded his brain. Even with dozens of odd gadgets surrounding him in the cold shadows, he could focus on only one thought. Bonnie was in that stone, and his passion to set her free helped him brave the pain. As sick as he felt while standing on the outside, there was no telling how much it would hurt to actually be inside that rock. Billy held his hand over his stomach and sighed. *I guess I might as well get used to it.*

"Billy!" Ashley's voice called out of the darkness on the other side of the room. A shaft of light from an open door provided a backdrop for her beckoning silhouette. "You need a robe! Come over here!"

Billy hurried toward Ashley. She stood at the cave's back wall near the doorway where she had exited earlier. As he approached, her dark form took shape, sharpening with each step. With the hood of her robe raised, and her face still in the shadows, she looked like a cowled monk. She held out another robe in her left hand, folded once and draped over her palm.

"Take this and pull it over your clothes. It should protect you from the candlestone's effects." She unfolded the robe and held it by its shoulders. "And you'll have to swap your belt. The robe has its own sash, but I wrapped an extra cotton belt in it for your jeans. You'll lose your metal buckle during the process, and we don't want your trousers falling off when you come back."

Billy replaced his belt and pulled the robe over his head, pushing his arms through the sleeves. The shoulders were comfortable, but with the hemline dropping to just above his knees, it wasn't a perfect fit.

Ashley smoothed out the wrinkles. "It'll have to do." She grabbed a cuff on one of Billy's sleeves and straightened it around his arm, then took his hand and held it closer to her face. "This ring looks a lot like Bonnie's, except bigger and older."

"Yeah. We have matching rings, sort of a dragon friendship thing."

She rubbed the gem's surface with her thumb. "It's for dragons? What kind of stone is it?"

"It's called a rubellite; it's a kind of tourmaline."

"A rubellite? Where do you find those?"

Billy curled his fingers and slowly pulled his hand away. "My dad brought it to me." He pointed toward the candlestone in the central lab area. "Shouldn't we get going?"

Ashley took a step toward the domes, but a sudden jolt threw her back. She took a long step to keep from falling and spread out her hands, balancing with her knees bent. "Oh, no!"

Billy slapped his hand against the wall to brace himself. The lights swayed, and vibrations drilled into his feet. "What's going on?"

Ashley grabbed Billy around the waist and pulled him toward the door frame. She sank to her knees, dragging him down with her. "It felt like an earthquake," she said as the two huddled under the frame. "It's happened once before."

Steady ripples ran through Billy's back as he leaned against the frame's side, and a gentle tapping of grit sounded from the drop ceiling. "Could this place collapse?"

Ashley didn't answer for a moment while the tremor settled down. "It's not out of the question," she finally replied. After a few seconds of calm, she took Billy's hand and stood up. "The tremor's over, but there's a chance another one will follow. We'll have to hurry."

With his hand still in Ashley's, he led the way toward the candlestone. "C'mon, then! Let's get transluminated!"

Bonnie cast a glance around a crystal wall, straining her sharpening eyes down one of the myriad dark halls. She hoped for a trace of light, a friendly shadow of luminescence. In this murky house, it seemed that light itself was a shadow, shades of mortal essence cast by wandering phantoms.

In the distance, a trail of light disappeared around the corner. She hurried down the dark corridor, hoping to find where

277

the spectre had gone, but there were dozens of corners, some leading to abrupt dead ends. A few halls were too dark to probe, and she passed them by. After an unsuccessful foray into a narrow cubbyhole, she spied the light again near the end of a wide hallway. It turned out of view, its sparkling trail vanishing in a corridor on the right.

"Wait! Please, wait!" Bonnie's thought stream raced after the glimmer.

The glowing trail halted, and Bonnie dashed ahead, her light flashing like a strobe. "May I talk to you again?"

"Come no closer, child."

Bonnie stopped just before reaching the turn, and the voice spoke again, this time joyfully, like a delighted grandfather. "What do you seek, my frightened little lamb?"

She waited a second, allowing her light pulses to slow down. "I seek advice. Devin wants to make a deal with me."

"I see." The voice was slow and deliberate, yet it still carried a hint of mirth. "Has that foul creature tried to twist your mind?"

Bonnie felt that her thoughts were being read again, but this time it didn't bother her. "Well, I do feel sort of confused. Devin wants me to let my shield down so we can both attach to my friend, Billy, when he comes in here. He says that Billy will lose brain function, maybe even die, when he gets restored. Devin says he has a way to keep that from happening, and he'll tell us how it works if we cooperate and all go together."

The voice laughed gently. "And you believed him?"

"Well, yeah. Sort of. He played this recording of my father, and it sounded real."

"It was real, but that is not the issue."

The white glow that seeped from around the corner morphed into a fiery red mist, rolling across the dark crystalline floor like bloody fog. A current of darkness flowed through Bonnie's

278

mind, as though a breeze had channelled down the hall, carrying the voice like an echo riding the wind. "Devin petitions your fears. He bids them to come out and wrestle with your faith. The battle is already met in fields of darkness, where fears are born and faith is proven."

Bonnie stepped back, feeling a strange uneasiness. "My fears? But if my father was telling the truth, aren't my fears valid?"

The fog congealed, separating and forming tiny red mounds of luminescent goop, like pliable bubbles plucked from a lava light. With invisible legs, they moved toward Bonnie, each one emitting sparks, electrically charged robots marching in rows, spitting and sizzling as they came. Bonnie backed away again, first a step, and then another as they approached. Finally, she stopped and let them surround her, standing still as they closed in. With a loud buzz, they all popped and disappeared, their static charges dispersing into the darkness.

The voice returned. "You stepped back, child. Were your fears valid?"

"I . . . I was surprised. I didn't know what those things were."

"But then you stood your ground. Why?"

"I'm not sure. I just . . ." Bonnie's voice trailed off. Her troubled thoughts burst into confused sparks that caught the hall's dark current and blew away. Her friend's light glowed brighter, reverting to white and casting its effervescent shadow farther into her hallway. The winds of darkness died away, and Bonnie felt her own glow strengthening.

"What is the nature of faith, child?" the voice continued. "Why did you stand fast? Your answer will guide you through the battle."

As he spoke, the entire hallway filled with light, and the laboratory appeared before her as if she were standing outside the candlestone. Ashley and Billy, each wearing a diver's robe,

279

huddled together as Ashley studied Billy's rubellite ring. Bonnie couldn't make out what they were saying, but she figured out what they were about to do.

Suddenly, darkness clouded the lab, and the scene dissolved into an expanding sea of blackness. Bonnie was again in the dark hallway, back in her gloomy prison, listening to the friendly voice.

"Learn the secret of seeing beyond the walls of your existence," it said. "When we were on the outside, we saw everything as though we were looking through a glass darkly. We were restricted, earthly, blinded by the limitations of our eyes. Now, we are no longer flesh and bone, and we are able to see with spiritual eyes."

Bonnie sensed that her friend was ready to leave, that he had given as much advice as he was willing to give. "Thank you for building that fence of light around me when I first came in here. If you hadn't protected me, Devin would have grabbed me. Who knows what he might have done?"

The voice laughed merrily and began to fade away. "But, dear child, it was not I who protected you."

The trail of light disappeared, and Bonnie knew he had spoken his last. His words were puzzling, yet enlightening, and he raised more questions than he answered.

What is faith? What did the marching red blobs mean? But one question brought hope, and the possibilities sparked a surge of brilliance in Bonnie's light. Who built that radiant wall of protection? Maybe she was right after all, and God had been there, just as she had sung over and over.

She retreated down the corridor to try to find the candlestone's entry point. Billy could show up at any time. The number of turns seemed endless, and darkness draped the passages, but she wound through the maze with a new kind of ability. Was she using the spiritual eyes her mysterious friend had mentioned?

As she approached an area that reminded her of the entry point, a new, unnerving sensation arose. The whole dark world pitched and yawed like a ghost ship on a midnight sea, her tiny cosmos shaking like someone was trying to split the candlestone with a jackhammer. Then, after several seconds, it stopped.

New fears crawled into her mind, like a horde of dark soldiers creeping onto a battlefield. It was time to sing. A Bible verse swirled up from Bonnie's memory, and she made up a tune to go with it.

For now we see through a glass, darkly; but then face to face: now I know in part; but then shall I know even as also I am known. And now abideth faith, hope, love, these three; but the greatest of these is love.

I put the flashlight here," Karen said, pointing at a hook. "but I told Billy about it, so he must have taken it."

The professor reached into his oversized inner coat pocket where he had packed Merlin's diary and withdrew a penlight. "Fear not," he said confidently. He clicked a button on the end and cast a tiny beam into the steep, black entryway. "It's my American Express flashlight. I never leave home without it." The professor struggled to the edge of the stairwell and propped his crutches against the wall. "I'll have to do without these."

Walter held the sword's box in both arms. "We can carry them . . . somehow."

The professor pointed the beam at the walls on each side of the steps. "There's no handrail, so I'll need one of you to support me on the way down. Walter, can you carry the sword and the crutches? Excalibur is very heavy in the hands of one who is not meant to use it."

"You're telling me! And it's getting heavier by the minute." Walter tucked the box under one arm and picked up the crutches with his free hand. "But these are light. I can do it."

"Very well. You and Karen can take turns if you should tire."

The professor draped an arm over Karen's shoulders, and Walter trailed them by a couple of steps. Their progress was slow, and the grey daylight shining through the open entrance faded like the setting of the sun. As darkness folded in, the professor's flashlight brightened, its laser-like beam illuminating each stair.

"Hey, Prof," Walter said, his whisper magnified in the cold stillness, "does this remind you of anything?"

"Not exactly, Walter. I am not accustomed to tromping down a dark, endless stairway with a bullet hole in my heel."

"Not that. I mean, we've been out hunting for Billy before. Last time we had a crossbow. This time we have a sword. Don't you get a feeling like déjà vu?"

"Indeed, the parallels are striking. I do expect, however, that there will be a drastic change. It is time for someone else's light to grow while mine diminishes."

"What? What do you mean by that?"

The professor just sighed and said no more. Walter clutched the sword box to his chest and hung back an extra step. Prof had always kept a few secrets, revealing what he thought necessary at appropriate times. Walter knew better than to press his teacher for more information. The earlier tremor had shaken him, and thoughts of disasters and end-of-the-world catastrophes tapped at his brain like a deadly ghost tiptoeing just a few steps behind. Darkness had a way of creating those stealthy phantoms, and Walter peeked over his shoulder to make sure they were alone.

After negotiating at least a hundred stairs, Walter whispered, "Karen, let me know when you think we're about two-thirds of the way."

"Okay," she whispered back. "Why?"

"From there on, we'll have to keep our mouths shut. We might need the element of surprise."

The professor kept his face forward while talking. "Walter is correct, Karen. Although Dr Conner doesn't seem to be either in front of us or behind us, you told us that there exists another entrance into the laboratory. Silence is advisable in case he is already there."

"Yeah, it exists, all right. It's a tunnel that comes out into the valley near Camp Misery. And it leads through a big cave near the lab."

"A tunnel?" Walter repeated. "Why don't you use that instead of this crazy stairway? Wouldn't it be easier?"

Karen looped her arm around the professor's waist and grunted, adding to the sound of boots clopping on creaking stair boards. She finally muttered, "You wouldn't believe me."

The professor stopped and pointed his beam at Karen's chin. "Karen, you need not fear ridicule. We have seen enough oddities and peculiar phenomena to keep us from doubting almost anything."

"Right." Walter propped the crutches against the wall and balanced the sword box on the step behind them. "Anything short of ten-foot bunnies dancing in purple top hats and carrying bazookas, and we'll probably believe you."

"No," Karen deadpanned, "they don't have bazookas; they carry missile launchers."

Walter laughed out loud, then clamped his free hand over his mouth. When he regained control, he whispered, "Girl, I like your style!"

Walter retrieved his load, and the three resumed their descent. "Truthfully," Karen continued, after another twenty steps, "Doc told us there's a monster in the cave, and I've heard it. It sounds like rumbling and growling, and sometimes like an old man with a terrible rattling wheeze, like someone dumped a bag of rocks down a garbage disposal."

Walter thought about the description. It sounded familiar somehow. He stayed quiet for a moment, hoping the professor would speak up. Apparently his teacher was lost in thought. "So, Prof," Walter said in a whisper, "now we might have to deal with a monster. Do you want me to take him, or can you handle it by yourself?"

Karen snapped back, her voice sarcastically sweet. "We're about two-thirds of the way, Walter, dear. I think it's time for you to shut up."

The professor stopped and turned around, forcing the other two to halt. He shone the thin beam, first in Walter's face, then in Karen's. "Walter, Karen," the professor began, his voice spiked with agitation, "although it is time for silence, I must make an entreaty." He took a deep breath before continuing more calmly. "Let us proceed as a team. We may be called upon to sacrifice a great deal for one another. A house divided against itself cannot stand."

Walter and Karen faced each other, neither saying a word for a few seconds until Walter stripped off his glove and extended his hand. "The prof's right. I shouldn't tease like that. I believe you heard a monster; I just like to joke around a lot. Still friends?"

Karen pulled off her glove and grasped his hand. "Don't worry, friend." She then took Excalibur's box from him and tucked it under her arm, patting it with her free hand. "If any ten-foot bunnies come hopping around, I've got your back."

After explaining the translumination procedure to Billy, Ashley pointed out a digital display on the control panel with large illuminated numerals. She spoke hurriedly. "The controls will be set on a timer to reverse automatically. Right now it's showing the time until we transluminate. Then it will reset and count down again. When that counter gets to zero, there's no choice, we have to come back, with or without Bonnie. I can't override it, because I'll be hanging on to you. Understand?"

Billy gave her a quick nod. "Got it."

"Now there's one more decision to make," Ashley said as she smoothed out Billy's sleeve again. "I assume you want to be the diver."

Billy drew his arm back and readjusted the cuff. "Well, yeah. Don't you think so? I mean, I've faced Devin before. I know his tricks."

Ashley walked across the lab to the diver's dome. "Yes, that's true. But there's a problem." Once at the dome, she sat on the platform, the glass enclosure hanging a few feet above her head. "We never properly restored any of the male chimps we tested, and we don't know why. It couldn't be a coincidence. The females all worked fine."

Billy stepped over to the platform and placed one foot on it. "I overheard Dr Conner talking about that." He sat down next to her, glad that the robe was keeping his nausea at bay. He tried to read Ashley's eyes, shadowy, yet penetrating. Would she understand? "I'm not a chimp. And I'm not worried about what happens to me, as long as I get Bonnie out. I'm not afraid."

Ashley stood up, holding her hand over her heart. "Well . . . maybe you should be." She waved toward the candlestone. "I read about your fire breathing, but I don't think you'll be able to use it in there."

Billy checked the cotton belt on his jeans and stepped up to the platform. "I won't need it."

Ashley pulled on the loose ends of his sash, tightening it further. "So I can't talk you out of it? I could be the diver. I know I could do it."

Billy slid his ring up and down on his finger, then balled his hand into a fist. The slayer was crafty, brutal. How could he let anyone else face that monster? This was his fight and his fight alone. He had to make up for his failure against Palin.

The last words of one of Merlin's prophecies drifted back into his mind.

The soul set free must face the beast
And break his chains to fears of earth
To free the faithful heart of love
And prove the seeds of royal birth

Billy clenched his fists. "I'm going."

Ashley smiled, gazing at him again with her piercing eyes. "You're just like Bonnie, aren't you?" She pressed a button on the base of the platform, lowering the glass dome. As the bottom edge passed below Billy's chest, she called, "Just remember; don't let go of my hand!"

Billy gave a thumbs-up signal, but his legs shook, and he knew if he hadn't been clenching his fingers into a tight ball, his hands would be as jittery as a chihuahua in a tiger's cage. Only Ashley's words could bring peace to his mind. *You're just like Bonnie.* He closed his eyes and smiled. *I'm not exactly like her. We're both dragons, and she's taught me a lot, but I know I'm the one who has to defeat Devin.*

Walter crept up behind the professor, who had stopped abruptly. "What's that light up ahead?" he whispered.

The professor shone his beam on the source of light and kept his voice low. "It appears to be a door."

"It's the door to the lab," Karen said. "The Alpha entrance."

The professor clicked off his light. "Then alpha marks the beginning of our next adventure. I suggest we listen for a few moments to ascertain the possible dangers we might face inside."

Walter placed the crutches and box next to the wall, then blew softly on his cupped hands. "Good. I need a breather."

Karen sighed. "We were supposed to take turns. You only let me carry it for two minutes."

"So I like flower boxes," Walter quipped. "Can't a guy show a little culture?"

Karen let out a low groan, and the professor stifled a laugh. "Very well, Walter. Our signal to enter will be your readiness to continue. I see no reason to burst in hastily."

Karen placed her ear on the door. "I hear something. It may be the equipment engines." She pulled on Walter's sleeve. "Rest up quick."

Walter slid down the wall and plopped on the floor. "I'm resting as fast as I can."

Ashley quickstepped toward the anchor dome. As she passed the pedestal, she noticed that the candlestone had moved slightly, shaken from its place by the recent tremor. She picked it up gently and held it in the palm of her hand, peering through its input facets. She marvelled at the mystery of a hidden world and at the power of a light-absorbing stone. *Why does it sap the power of a dragon? Why does it steal Billy's breath and rob Bonnie's strength to fly? And yet, it seems to choose its victims. Very strange!*

She put the gem back on its spot and jumped up on her dome pedestal, bending over to press the button to lower the glass. She checked the starting timer and signalled to Billy. "Thirty seconds to go."

Ashley shivered, though it wasn't that cold. Looking around the circle to her left, she watched Billy, his eyes closed, his face adorned with a peaceful smile. He was courageous, perhaps naively so. Yet, he seemed to exude confidence, the kind of peace that comes from a single-minded purpose. It was a good thing. In just a few seconds they would go on their greatest adventure, hand-in-hand, a thought that encouraged Ashley's trembling mind.

I think I'll need to borrow some of his courage.

A loud slam disrupted the chamber's peaceful hum. Ashley spun in her dome. Someone was entering the lab area from the Omega entrance. *Impossible! No one has the key to that door except—*

"Ashley!" Dr Conner shouted. "Are you in here?"

Ashley's throat twisted like a tourniquet. They were caught! Would he try to stop them? She couldn't even squeak a reply. Only twelve seconds to translumination!

Dr Conner turned on the lights and leaped onto the lab platform, his eyes wild. "Ashley! The cave's collapsed. I could barely crawl through. I can't find her anywhere. She's gone!"

Doc's clothes were dirty, and blood smudged his face. Ashley glanced at the timer and held up her hand with her fingers splayed. Five seconds!

Dr Conner spun in a quick circle as if taking in the scene for the first time. "What?" he yelled, almost shrieking. "You're doing a dive?"

Ashley nodded her head, and as the vibrations shot through her feet and legs, turmoil clenched her face into a knot. As Doc ran toward the control panel, everything in her vision buzzed and blurred, scattering into weird shapes and wild, chaotic shards of light. Even Dr Conner's words stirred into the confusing mix as they died away in her new world of dazzling light. She could barely hear him say, "I'll put a stop to this!"

CHAPTER 18

THE CHASM

Ashley had no choice. Even though Doc might try to stop her, she was already transluminated. She had to continue. But how? Everything felt weird – puzzling and confusing – yet so bright she could hardly take in all her surroundings.

She had to think, pause a second and just think. *I have to find the exit point. Where is it? The whole room's swirling. I've got to get a grip!*

She tried to move. Her brain's normal motion signals transformed into light pulses, a new kind of command her transluminated body struggled to understand. After a few tries, she had some success, and the flood of light in her strange world shifted as she inched along in her dome. Finally, she found the exit point and poured her flashing body into the flexible tube, grasping the anchoring spurs as she slid through the glass. *Watch out, Billy! Here I come!*

A flood of light poured into Billy's brain, snapping him to attention. Everything was different – altered and distorted. He remembered Ashley's instructions. The whole procedure was timed, including when he would be sucked into the stone, so he expected her to come through to his cylinder at any second. She had to get through to him and attach or else he'd be slurped down that photon straw without an anchor.

A burst of light erupted from the anchor tube. Ashley!

Somehow she extended her hand and grabbed his, and not too soon. One second later, he was falling, zipping down a gushing waterfall of light. An avalanche of flashing strobes zoomed all around his body. He rocketed downward, free-falling at a million miles per hour, and a tidal wave of agitated light stung his face like a swarm of angry gnats poking with hot needles.

After a few seconds, he slammed into a black, jelly-like membrane, and his body punched right through, leaving the flood of light, gnats and all, behind. The breakneck plunge slowed to a gentle, floating sensation.

Except for Ashley's pull from above, he floated freely. His body pulsated – a chaotic jumble of white flashes with a circle of red at one edge. He stared at the crimson glow.

My rubellite?

He came to a stop in a chasm of utter darkness, a land of charcoal drawings on a black canvas.

This must be the place. Time to find Bonnie.

Bonnie searched the dark crystal skies for Billy's entrance. She could see the entry stream, which had suddenly exploded into a raging river, but she couldn't tell where a diver might push through to the inner core. As she watched, a glimmer of light appeared in the sky and floated in her direction. *Could that be Billy? It has to be!*

A voice, soft and sweet, flowed from the light. It wasn't of the same quality she had been hearing from Devin or her mysterious friend; it sounded faraway and choppy.

"You can come out now," the voice said.

That sounds like Ashley's voice!

"I know you're here. Come on out."

It is! It is Ashley's voice! She came in instead of Billy!

The mass of light grew and floated into her presence, extending a ragged arm in her direction.

"Come on out. You can trust me."

Ashley's voice still sounded far off and strange, but there was no mistaking it. Of course, Ashley had never done a dive, so she hadn't learned to communicate very well in her new form. And since she had only been in the stone for a few seconds, she had not yet begun to take on her normal shape.

Bonnie put out her hand, and in her willingness to join her rescuer, her shield of light eroded. The two hands inched closer. Bonnie noticed her shield weakening and paused.

The voice spoke again. "Do you sense danger?" The words were still choppy, still faraway, but still Ashley's.

"No. No, it's just—"

"Hold your questions and be patient. . . . Too much information can make your brain choke."

That has to be Ashley! Bonnie wanted to leave her dark prison and find her mother more than anything, and her friend was there to make it happen. She thrust her hand forward. "C'mon!" Bonnie called, "let's get out of here!" When the lights touched, the two melded, and the joining burned like an electric shock.

"I've got you now, Witch!"

Bonnie screamed and jerked back, but Devin's grip clamped down like the jaws of a pit bull. "How . . . how did you?" She couldn't continue; the slayer's electric vice scorched all her senses, sending shock waves of intense pain throughout her body.

The indistinct form swirled, reshaping into Devin's persona, returning a sinister smile to his malevolent face. "It was child's play, my dear. Recording voices is quite simple once you've been in here long enough. Our friends outside were kind enough to leave the communication lines open, and I did a bit of eaves-dropping."

Bonnie struggled, twisting and pulling back with all her might. Sparks flew, but she couldn't shake loose his hold.

Devin dragged her away, his spiteful voice ripping its coarse static into her mind. "Time for you to join the monkeys and the fools, little angel." He stopped at the edge of the chasm, dangling her body over its narrow opening. "You were a fierce enemy. It's a shame you were on the wrong side."

Bonnie froze, not wanting to slip from his grasp. She peered below, and the swirling ghosts came together, like crocodiles swarming to meet a fallen victim. "Billy will come," she cried. "He'll take care of you."

"Oh, I know he'll come. And he'll be duped as easily as you were. You've given me a nice collection of sounds to work with." His raspy voice mutated into Bonnie's recent, excited call. "C'mon! Let's get out of here!"

The words were hers! The tone was hers! What would Billy do? This would all be new to him. Would he be fooled? She shook away her fears, and with all her might, she shouted, "You won't get away with it!"

"Oh, yes. Yes, I will. I've been getting away with it for over a thousand years. And I still have more dragon-kind to kill."

Bonnie tried to sing. "If I say, Surely the darkness shall cover—"

"Too late, Witch!" Devin released Bonnie, and she plummeted through the blackness of the gem's dungeon. She tried to grab with her hands of light, but nothing held; the walls were pure, crystalline glass, and something from beneath pulled with relentless force. She plunged farther and farther into the pit as the slayer's scornful laughter faded into a rush of dark wind.

Walter nudged the door open a crack and peeked out into the huge room. Near the centre he saw Dr Conner pounding on a panel of some kind. He ducked back inside the tunnel. "Prof! It's the lab, all right. And Dr Conner's in there. He's mad as a hornet."

The professor turned to Karen. "The sword, please."

Karen opened the box, and the professor grasped the hilt. Instantly the sword changed from a lifeless grey blade into a blazing white sabre. He took one crutch and pressed it under his armpit before turning back to Walter. "The time has come. Wisdom and caution must unite with action and speed. Let's go!"

Billy searched through the vast darkness. It was like floating in a windowless closet without a speck of light in the universe except his own, and even that bounced off the blanket of blackness without making a dent. A wind blew through his body, dark streams criss-crossing his shining form.

At last he spotted another light. *Bonnie?*

"Careful, Billy."

What? The warning voice seemed to come from inside his mind. *Who said that?*

"It's Ashley. We're connected, so I can talk to you. And I can hear some of your thoughts. Guard them well."

Hear my thoughts? How does that work?

"I don't know. It's sort of a mind meld, I guess. Don't worry; I haven't heard much, so I guess I can only hear your louder thoughts. Let's get going. I can't see what you see, but I'm going to stretch out as far as I can so you can go find out who that is."

You may not have to. It's coming this way.

The light closed in rapidly, the shapeless mass forming into a young female body. The face, though non-distinct, radiated, and Billy heard an excited voice coming from its direction. "C'mon! Let's get out of here!"

It was Bonnie! The light stretched out an appendage, and Billy reached toward it, his glowing red ring floating in the black surroundings. The approaching light drew closer and closer, filled with energy and flashing white . . . but no circle of red.

No ring!

A hard yank jerked Billy backwards. "I heard that Billy! I know Bonnie's ring went in there with her."

He flew away from the imposter, and its bright light flashed crimson, crisscrossed with pulsating yellow stripes.

Billy yelled to Ashley, his thoughts now loud streams of static words. "I know it's Devin, but I have to go back."

"No! You can't possibly fight him. He knows the ways of the candlestone better than you do. He's been in there for weeks!"

"I'm not looking for a fight," Billy said as he pulled against Ashley's pressure. "I'm looking for Bonnie! But if I have to fight him, I will . . . face to face."

Bonnie shivered, her glowing skin flickering in what felt like a chilling breeze. She had crashed to the floor of the cavern, her flashing body flattened against the crystalline surface. *I guess it doesn't hurt to splat against anything in this place.* She pushed herself off the floor. One good piece of news — the circling phantoms were nowhere in sight. Somehow the swirling forces had tossed her body to one side, though she couldn't tell how far.

It wasn't so dark here. The river of light flowed through this area, gushing toward the candlestone's exit point, and it lent a shimmering glow to the chasm's lower chamber.

Another light approached, its gentle radiance strengthening as it drew closer. A second light appeared, then a third! Within seconds six flashing phantoms, a group of men with hardened faces and bright, flowing hair, surrounded her. They pressed around her and stared, almost as if they were sniffing, like a pack of dogs trying to detect who or what she was.

"It is not Devin," one of them said.

"Another ape?" a second one asked.

"Probably. It has arms and legs. Its features are not yet distinct."

A third voice joined in. "Well, I didn't expect that he'd just slip and fall down here."

"Perhaps not. If he ever does, it will be his last mistake."

The lights began drifting away, apparently no longer concerned about Bonnie's arrival.

"Wait!" she called. "I'm not an ape. I'm human. My name is Bonnie Silver."

One of the lights turned back. "Have you a tale?" it asked.

"No. I don't have a tail. I'm human."

The light rejoined the others, and the group dispersed, floating away like clouds in the wind. They sang a moaning dirge, much like the one she had heard when she first peered down into the crack from up above.

Bonnie felt the constant pull that carried them away, a strange air current that tried to draw everything toward the exiting river. The phantoms floated in the current, resisting at the last moment before it would have plunged them into the river, and they curved back to where they started, only to begin another circuit.

Bonnie moved as far away from the river as she could, inching along the glass floor, pushing against the current. She found a pocket of angled planes carved into a lower part of the chasm's cliff. It was a cave of sorts, a narrow opening, depressed into the wall and lower than the surrounding floor, a good place to hide in case other ghosts came sniffing by.

Burying herself in the cleft, Bonnie peered out at the slow waltz of swirling spectres. She imagined men and apes, rats and rabbits, all meshed in a dizzying eternal torture. Would she be the next victim of the candlestone's version of hell, joining the everlasting lament in this turmoil of dark despair?

She tried to shake away the sorrow, the agony of hopelessness. She remembered a similar cycle of misery, being passed from foster home to foster home, unwanted, unloved, still aching over her mother's recent death. And now—

A sob rose in her throat, her light dimming and wasting away in a shudder of weakening flickers. She cried out in her mind, her sorrows pouring forth as her world turned darker and darker.

Where are you, Mama?

Anguish lashed at her, the threat of being locked in a forsaken tomb for an eternity. What could she do but cry? Although no liquid tears fell, Bonnie wept, and the cleansing flow of emotions helped her form a prayer in her mind – a prayer for her mother, for herself, and especially for Billy.

After a few minutes, a gentle breath, a glimmer of passing light, brightened her own. It carried a sense of hope, a tiny spark, yet as real as a candle in a dark room. Somehow Billy would make his way to her side . . . but how could he possibly find her in this hidden dungeon?

The professor limped into the lab, one hand gripping a crutch and the other carrying the glowing Excalibur. Walter and Karen crept close behind.

Dr Conner sat with his head in his hand, studying the control panel, barely moving a muscle.

The professor whispered to Karen. "Does anyone else live here?"

"Uh-huh. Ashley's grandfather and a boy named Derrick."

"Can you take Walter to them?"

She glanced across to the other side of the lab. "Yeah. The boys' dorm door is open, and—Wow! The Omega door, too!"

Walter shielded his eyes from the laboratory lights. "Where's the Omega door?"

The professor put a shushing finger to his lips. He handed his crutch to Walter, balancing his weight on his good foot. "Set this down. Go with Karen and close the door behind you. Find them and make sure they're safe. Lead them back, but don't come in unless I call."

"Gotcha, Prof."

"And go quickly. Don't worry about Dr Conner seeing you. I'll handle him."

Walter and Karen dashed across the chamber, their shoes clattering on the stone. Dr Conner jerked his head up and yelled. "Karen! What are you doing? Come back here!" In a flash of motion, he turned two dials on the panel and sprang from his chair.

The professor tightened his grip on the sword. "Halt!"

The doctor spun around. Terror filled his eyes. The professor held Excalibur up in both hands. The glowing blade shot a brilliant beam upward, ripping a hole in the ceiling, and the laser stream pierced the darkness above.

Walter and Karen disappeared into the hallway, and the door slammed with a loud clap. The professor eyed Dr Conner and allowed the sword's beam to diminish, though its fiery glow continued to drape the blade like a shining scabbard. "Dr Conner," the professor began, his tone crisp and matter-of-fact, "would you be so kind as to tell me the whereabouts of Billy Bannister and Bonnie Silver?"

Dr Conner stepped back against the control panel. A shroud of fear clouded his eyes and lined his smudged face. He pointed at the candlestone. "They're . . . they're in there." Wringing his hands, he continued. "Bonnie went . . . went into the candlestone, and . . . and she got trapped. Ashley and Billy went in, too, to . . . to try to get her out, I'm sure. I think they're all in there now. I . . . I tried to reverse it, but it's on automatic. Ashley changed the override password, so I can't bring them back." He swallowed hard and his voice strengthened. "We have to get them out, and fast!"

The professor lowered his sword. "Is there immediate danger?"

"Yes. I came in through the back tunnel. A major support wall caved in, so this mountain's entire structure has been compromised. Another tremor could bring this whole place down on top of us."

"What would happen if we were to simply remove the stone and leave?"

"We can't. Ashley's anchoring. She's halfway in and halfway out. If we moved the stone, we'd tear her body in two. And our equipment is the only way in the world to restore them. I could never rebuild it without Ashley."

Dr Conner's eyes suddenly widened. The ceiling panels rattled, and the lights flickered wildly. The floor of the cave began vibrating, the intensity building. Dr Conner leaped toward the candlestone's pedestal, shouting, "I have to hold the stone in place!"

Limping painfully toward the centre of the chamber, the professor called through a growing din, "Walter! Karen! Come out!"

They scrambled out of the hallway, Karen pulling Derrick by the hand and Walter propelling Ashley's grandfather in a wheelchair. The floor bucked and swayed, and they careened back and forth like sailors on the deck of a wind-tossed ship.

Pellets of sand sprinkled the floor, bouncing across the tile. Taps from above signalled pebbles dancing on the tops of the ceiling panels. The professor waved them forward. "You must evacuate immediately."

Walter hunched over to shield Ashley's grandfather. "You gotta be kidding me! I can't get this wheelchair up the stairs!"

A rush of rocks and sand ripped through a ceiling tile, burying a chair near a control panel. Dr Conner squatted next to the central pedestal, holding the candlestone in place.

"The Omega entrance," Dr Conner shouted. He nodded toward the door. "I cleared a path through the rubble. Try that."

"But what about the monster?" Karen shouted.

"There's no monster! Just go!"

Karen tugged on Walter's coat sleeve. "I know the way!" She and Derrick see-sawed their way over the teetering ground toward the Omega door.

The professor pointed toward the exit. "Walter! Go! Now!"

"But what about you?"

"Go!"

Ashley's pull on Billy's arm lessened. As he floated back toward the slayer, he shouted his thoughts. "What have you done with Bonnie?"

"So," Devin said, his scratchy voice buzzing like a dentist's drill, "you've learned how to speak in here. Not bad."

Devin sprang toward Billy, but Billy backed away just in time to avoid his touch. The slayer laughed. "A little quicker now, I see. Well, you're obviously not much smarter than when you lost your battle with me on the mountain. All it took was a lock of hair to bring you stumbling up the slopes like an idiot to rescue your stupid girlfriend. What a surprise! She wasn't there! And now here you are again, swaggering in to fight me on my home turf. Didn't your old man teach you any better? Oh, yes. I forgot. He's a dragon, a stupid beast, just like all the others I've conquered over the years."

Billy listened to Devin's sarcastic tirade, ignoring a dozen clever retorts that clamoured in his head. When the slayer paused, Billy said, "So is your sharp tongue your only sword now?"

Devin's light burst into radiant crimson. "You fool! You have no idea what I've learned in this cursed stone!" A sphere of energy grew in the centre of Devin's body like a swarming nest of supercharged fireflies. He raised the sphere like a weapon, a cannonball of electrostatic fury. "I could have scattered you into

300

a million lost electrons, mongrel. You're defenceless, without a weapon or even a song."

"A song?"

"Never mind." Devin's colour slowly faded to white. "If you want to survive, you'd better cooperate with me. I'll bet they didn't tell you what happens to males when they're restored, did they?"

"I heard, and I don't care." Billy's own light changed to off-white. He couldn't let the slayer prod him into a fit of anger . . . not now. He composed himself and continued, calmness oozing from his voice. "Just tell me where Bonnie is."

"You'd better deal with me, kid. I'll tell you where she is, and I'll tell you how to save your brain if you'll let me attach and ride out of here with you."

"Is she alive?"

"She's alive."

Billy tried to sort out what to do, but his brain felt frazzled. *There're too many options! And the system could go into reverse at any minute! There's no time!*

Ashley's voice popped into his head. "You're right, Billy. My guess is about seventy seconds to reversal."

Did you hear all of the conversation, Ashley? What should I do?

"I didn't hear much. You don't have time to explain what's going on. You're on your own, and you have to act fast."

Devin's glow flashed, a rippling mass of humanoid light set against pure blackness. His blurry facial features gave no hint of an expression, nothing to help Billy decide how to deal with this liar. But the surrounding emptiness reminded Billy of his father's story. Shouldn't there be others trapped in the candlestone, Devin's fellow conspirators? If so, where were they? If they

301

were partners in crime, why wasn't Devin with them now? *Hmmm. There's more going on here than meets the eye.*

"Okay," Billy finally said. "Show me where Bonnie is first. If I see you're telling the truth, you can go with me."

Devin drifted away, a finger of light gesturing as his glow delved into the darkness. "Follow me."

Give me some slack, Ashley. I have to go somewhere. Billy felt Ashley's release of tension, and he followed Devin's energy trail until he stopped. Billy drew closer but kept a safe distance. *Okay, Ashley. Be ready to yank me away if I call.*

"Just say the word."

"Do you see this little fault?" Devin said, his glowing finger pointing toward the floor.

"A fault? You mean, like a crack inside the stone?"

"Yes." He pushed his arm through, and it disappeared below the surface of the floor. "It leads to the candlestone's exit. Bonnie went down there to try to get out."

Ashley, did you catch that?

"All I heard was you saying something about a crack in the stone. I've mapped this entire matrix, and there is a crack leading from the inner core down into the exit channel. Doc told me that Devin said he couldn't use it to escape. But he might have been lying. We don't have much time, Billy. Less than forty seconds! Hurry!"

Got it. Billy addressed Devin again. "Why should I believe you?"

"You have no choice. I can't get out that way; only females can. There's a basic difference in how genders transluminate. Pull me out, and not only will I save your worthless brain, I'll tell you how to get her out through the exit channel. You made the deal, Bannister. I showed you where she is, now it's your turn."

Billy crept toward the fault. Their two masses of light stood at the edge of the narrow chasm, peering into the darkness. Down below, Billy saw the exiting river of light and radiant phantoms circling in a tight coil. "What are those?"

"Other souls like us who would like to get out. Bonnie is one of them, I'm sure."

Ashley's voice interrupted. "Billy! It has to be down to fifteen seconds by now! Are you ready?"

Billy kept his thoughts focused on Devin. "They look like sharks in a feeding tank, like they're angry or something."

"Perhaps they are. Some have been here for a very long time."

Aha! His cronies! My hunch was right! "Really? Longer than you?"

"Yes. Much longer."

Ashley, can you set up your system to restore from the exit channel?

"Yes. But why?"

No time to explain. Just get ready to do it. Billy let go of Ashley's hand, and the release made her snap back into the darkness.

"What!" Devin yelled. "What are you doing?"

"I'm keeping my word. I only agreed that you could come with me." Billy looked down into the chasm and then back at Devin. "You're welcome to come along." Billy took a long step and fell into the darkness.

303

CHAPTER **19**

CATCHING THE LIGHT

Ashley, still clutching the anchor tube in the lab, rode on a heart-stopping updraft as her invention sucked her out of the candlestone. Her arm and torso battled against a surging current of raging light that tried to drag her back into the stone. Her stretched-out body felt like a spaghetti noodle zipping up toward a hungry, slurping mouth. She released the anchor spurs, and her body congealed. Seconds later, she was floating in a bath of blazing light. As she tried to orient herself, a mosaic of flashing puzzle pieces came together to form the familiar laboratory.

Wrapping her arms around her restored body, she rubbed her chilled skin, bouncing impatiently while the glass cylinder rose exactly as programmed. Her vision quickly adjusted. She could see Doc holding the candlestone in place and a strange old man leaning on a crutch. *The man with the crutch is carrying a glowing sword. Who in the world could he be?*

But there's no time for questions!

Ashley jumped from the platform and lunged toward the pedestal. "I have to turn it!" She grabbed Doc's forearm with a quick twist, forcing him to release the stone. She squatted low and lined up the candlestone's exit beam with the tube leading to the diver's dome, but the gem didn't sit right. The way the bottom facet rested on the pedestal didn't allow the beam to go into the tube at the proper angle. She glanced up at Doc. "What were you doing to it?"

"Another tremor hit, and I was holding it in place." Doc dropped to one knee beside her. "What are you planning?"

"Shhh! I'm thinking." Ashley stood up, her hands on her hips. She surveyed her equipment, studying the connections before nodding her head. *We'll fix that easily enough.*

She lifted the candlestone from its pedestal and tiptoed to the diver's dome. After gently placing the flashing gem on the platform floor, she ran to the control panel. "Doc, they're coming out the exit channel. I'll have to shut off the anchor access tube and open the restore tube, but how am I going to get them through the restore tube so the computer can analyse them before the candlestone just sucks them back in?"

While Ashley's hands flew across the panel, flipping switches and turning knobs, Dr Conner hustled over to join her. "You can bring an anchor person over from the restoration dome," he said, using his hands to clarify the process, "and have him pull exiting people through the tube."

Ashley studied a display and whispered a calculation. "That's fifteen point seven from neutral." She flipped her hair back with a shake of her head. "Who could be the anchor? Karen's gone."

Dr Conner raised his chin. "I'll do it."

"You?"

"Yes." His voice cracked as if painful words lodged in his throat. "I've got to do something to fix the mess I've made."

Ashley hesitated. She would probably never trust Doc again, but at this point there was no other choice. She just had to get the job done. She let out a shallow sigh. "Okay. Then let's get going."

Ashley barked out instructions like a rapid-fire machine gun. "Since there's no Excalibur beam in the restoration dome, you'll have to get in the diver's dome with the candlestone. Remember to hang on to the tube, or you'll get sucked into the candlestone right after you get transluminated. Once you're a mass of light, I'll need you to go back and forth through the recovery tube a couple of times so I can read your light structure and quarantine your data in the computer. When you see something come out of the candlestone that's not normal light, try to grab it and escort it to the restoration dome.

"The photo analysers in the tube will be able to read the person while it passes through, and I'll make sure the computer blocks your data out. Leave the person in the restoration dome and then go back through the tube to the diver's dome while I restore whoever you brought over."

She took a deep breath and looked around at the dust and debris. "We'll have to work fast. Another tremor would give us serious problems, and we need to be ready when the first person comes out of the stone. I don't know how many are in there. I could only catch a few of Billy's thoughts, but I think we might get pretty busy."

Dr Conner peered over her shoulder. "We didn't plan for an army. How are the photoreceptors holding out?"

Ashley rubbed a thin layer of dust away from a meter on the panel. "Probably enough for several restorations, but I can't be sure."

"It'll have to do. Our source is gone." Dr Conner ran toward the boys' dorm. "I'll get a robe."

Gone? How is that possible? Ashley wanted to yell her question, but it was too late. She would have to find out later. Her hands flew across the board, tweaking dials and switches, each adjustment bringing new readings to the meters. She studied the data, a million calculations clicking in her souped-up brain.

"Miss, may I be of any assistance?" The gentle voice with a distinct English accent interrupted her concentration.

Ashley spun around. An older man with wild white hair and a pain-pierced grimace hobbled toward her, the man with the crutch she had seen earlier. A fine layer of chalky dust coated his face, and he carried a glowing sword in his right hand. "Let me guess," she said, resuming her work. "You're the professor, right?"

The professor bowed his head. "Charles Hamilton, at your service. I inspected the rear exit. It seems that my friend, Walter, and your relation, Karen, have safely guided a young man named Derrick and your grandfather through the first part of the passage."

Ashley breathed a heavy sigh. "Thank God!" As the professor joined her on the platform, she extended her hand. "I'm Ashley Stalworth. I read about you in Bonnie's journal, and yes, you can help." She flipped another series of switches and hustled toward the restoration dome. "Do you know about the candlestone?"

The professor followed her across the lab at half her speed. "I have heard of it. My students, Bonnie Silver and William Bannister, are inside if I am not mistaken."

"Billy, Bonnie, and quite a few others, I think. If everything goes right, we'll be restoring people in this enclosure." She touched the glass on the cylinder, dropped to a stoop, and pressed a button on the low platform, making the shield slowly rise. "This switch raises and lowers the glass. When someone appears, I'll give a signal when they're completely restored. Your job is to raise the glass, get the person out, and close the cylinder again as quickly as possible. I could do it from the panel, but once people are being restored, my hands may be too busy, and I can't help anyone get out of the dome from here anyway."

The professor leaned on his crutch and laid Excalibur on the floor next to the restoration platform. "I believe I will be able to handle that task." After testing the switch, he straightened his body. "I am ready."

As soon as Ashley returned to the control panel, Dr Conner dashed back into the lab, a white robe covering his dirty clothes. She pointed at the dome. "Go ahead, Doc. Get in position."

Dr Conner hurried to the centre of the lab and hopped up to the diver's platform, straddling the candlestone.

"Okay," Ashley called. "I'm going to lower your glass and douse the lights. Let's get those people out of there!"

The Omega door slammed against the chamber wall, and Walter burst from the corridor. "Dr Conner! Karen's been hurt! It's really bad!"

Billy pulled himself off the chasm floor. Here at the bottom of the pit the background brightened to a dull grey. The floating river of light emanated a halo that muted the darkness, its aura fading to black at the chasm's borders. The spiral of ghostly lights he had seen from above formed a tightening circle around him, and when they drew too close for comfort, he put up his hand. "Stop! Who are you?"

The radiant men slowed to a halt, coming to a point just out of Billy's reach. A buzz of chatter surrounded him, and he caught snatches, English-sounding phrases spoken with unfamiliar accents. Finally one of the spectres stepped forward, his voice strong and polite, transforming to a traditional British accent. "We are loyal knights of Arthur's court. My name is Barlow, Lord of Hickling Manor. And what type of beast might you be?"

Billy stood his ground. "I am William, son of Jared. If you are of the king's court, Sir Barlow, you should know Jared's name."

"Yes." Barlow's glowing fingers rubbed his chin. "I remember Jared. He was appointed the king's adviser just before the rebellion. But that was centuries ago. How can someone who speaks the modern American tongue be the son of Jared? And you are new to the stone. Your indistinct form gives away your recent entry. Please, tell us your tale."

Billy's light sputtered and faded. He had guessed that these were knights from the rebellion, but he wasn't sure yet of his second guess, that they were no longer Devin's allies. He decided to keep his knowledge to himself, at least for a while, and stay on this guy's good side. "Begging your pardon, Sir Barlow. I'm looking for a lost friend. Please allow me to find her, and then I will tell you my tale. And you can tell me how you know about American English and speak it so well."

The glowing sentry didn't move, yet his voice remained polite. "What is your hurry, William? We know of no way to safely leave this place. We have been here in Limbo for hundreds of years, and the only entertainment we have is to tell each other tales. We have long since exhausted both true stories and absurd fables, though a traveller occasionally passes through and tells us of life on the outside. That's how we learned your language and some of your customs. We know about your sport utility vehicles, your widescreen televisions, and," he added, rubbing his middle section, "deep-dish pepperoni pizza."

Billy laughed in spite of his worry, but his amusement faded quickly. He glanced around for a sign of Bonnie's light before turning back to Barlow. "You said there's a traveller?"

"Yes, a mysterious fellow. Though we have never found a way out of this pit, he seems to come and go as he pleases and refuses to explain how. He gives no name, just a story or two." He waved his arm with a friendly gesture. "Come now. Tell us your tale."

Billy decided he wasn't going to get anywhere until he talked with Barlow for a while. "Okay. Let me start with a question." He pointed toward the cliff high above, still illuminated by Devin's glow. "When I was up there, I saw you circling. Were you hoping Devin would fall in?"

Barlow's light dimmed and then flashed bright green. "Do you know Devin? Because if he is your friend—" Sir Barlow was interrupted by the loud buzzing of the other lights; they turned several shades of crimson as they grumbled.

Billy held up his hands. "No, no. Devin's no friend of mine. But weren't you in league with Devin to overthrow the king?"

"Alas, it is true!" Barlow moaned, his aura changing briefly to pale blue before shimmering back to white. "We have had centuries to unravel the plot in our minds. It seems that Devin and his foul scribe, Palin, hatched the scheme. They convinced us, fools that we were, to believe that an imposter had deposed our great king. They claimed that Merlin craved the throne and that he used black arts to transform a dragon into Arthur's twin. Most of the knights scoffed, but I heard a strange tale from a certain wayfarer. He fancied seeing Merlin transforming dragons into humans on Bald Top in the middle of the night. He even claimed to see a man there who looked exactly like the king! Most said the wayfarer was a madman."

311

The other lights flashed as if to confirm Barlow's explanation. He continued. "I told the wayfarer, 'No sane human would set foot on Bald Top, and King Arthur would never go there. Yes, Merlin is powerful, but changing dragons into humans? Ridiculous!'

"But this traveller insisted on taking me to the scene. There was something in his wild eyes that spoke truth, so I went with him, his insanity taking me over, I suppose. Bald Top was a curious sight, indeed. I saw dragon tracks interspersed with human prints, a pile of discarded clothing, and Merlin's own saddlebag. I would have sworn it was witch's work; the human prints had no source but from whence the dragons stood. Yet with the old prophet's saddlebag there, could it be true? In my superstitious terror, I convinced my friends that Devin's story was the only explanation."

"How did you finally figure out Devin was lying?"

Barlow put his glowing hand on the shoulder of one of the knights. "The six of us you see before you now are loyal." He then extended his fingers away from the circle toward the flowing currents of light, and Billy watched the ghosts riding the eerie waves. "In conversing with those others, the traitors among us," the knight continued, "we discovered their ruse. They could not hide their lies over all these years, and the traveller explained how the candlestone drew us all in, even as it hung around the neck of that fiend, Devin. I only wish he had fallen down here instead of you. We would have cast him into the river, and he would have ridden out of this cursed stone and into oblivion."

Billy pointed toward the river's exit point. "So it *is* possible to get out this way?"

"Yes," Barlow replied. "I captured one of the conspirators, and I threw him into the river. We were able to see his body fly apart once he got out in the open. He is now a twinkle in the twilight and will never deceive anyone again."

"That's weird. I wonder why the candlestone didn't just suck him back in again."

"A good question. We wondered about that, too." Barlow gave a heavy sigh, and his voice changed to a quiet melancholy. "So, to answer your question, William, yes, it is possible to leave, but it is better to be in here and still have hope than to die in eternal darkness, scattered into the heavens and yet separated from God forever."

Walter gasped in time with his throbbing heart. "A boulder . . . fell . . . just before we got out of the cave! Karen . . . pushed Derrick . . . out of the way, and he . . . he and the old guy are okay, but the rock knocked her down. Her leg . . . her leg's broken!"

Dr Conner jumped off the diver's platform and clutched Walter's shoulders. "Is she bleeding? Was the bone sticking out?"

Tears formed in Walter's eyes, and sweat dripped down his face. He brushed at the tears with the sleeve of his jacket, leaving a sooty stain on the material. He hacked and coughed to clear the dust from his lungs, but his voice still cracked. "Yeah . . . it's real bad!"

Dr Conner stripped the robe off and stuffed it into Walter's arms. "Ashley will tell you what to do." He ran over to a cabinet near the cavern wall, withdrew a large medical bag with a red cross emblazoned on its side, and sprinted out the Omega door.

Clutching the wad of clothing, Walter stared into the dark lab. The silhouette of a girl hovered near the panel. He coughed again. "Ashley?"

313

"Yes. Put the robe on, whoever you are. I guess you'll have to go in."

Walter rested a hand on his knee and took in quick, deep breaths. "Go in? Where?"

"Over here, Walter." The professor waved his hand at Ashley. "May I suggest, Miss Stalworth, that I be transluminated? I heard your instructions, and I assume I shall not be crippled in there. I'm sure Walter can handle my duties."

Ashley let out a frustrated sigh. "That's fine. But we have to hurry!"

The professor pulled the robe on over his head. "Walter, look at the base of this platform, and you'll find a switch. Press once to raise the glass and again to lower it. When someone shows up in this restoration cylinder, Miss Stalworth will signal. Raise the glass, pull the person from the platform, and lower the glass again immediately. Got it?"

Walter nodded. "Got it."

"Be sure to wait for my signal!" Ashley added with a shout. "If you do it too early, it could kill whoever's in there."

The professor limped over to the diver's dome, placed his healthy foot on the platform, and stepped up, careful to avoid the candlestone.

"I'll lower your glass from here," Ashley called. "Go back and forth through the tube twice," she continued. "I want to be sure to map your matrix accurately. It won't take you long to figure out how to move. And don't forget to grab hold of the tube right at the start, or you'll get sucked in!"

She pressed a button, and the diver's cylinder slowly descended. When the dome's edge clicked shut, she turned a knob clockwise to its maximum setting. "Here we go!"

Billy counted the six shining faces in the circle around him. "Listen, Sir Barlow, I'd love to sit and chat with you for a couple of centuries, but I'm looking for a friend of mine. Her name is Bonnie Silver. Have you seen her?"

"Bonnie Silver," Barlow repeated. "The name . . . how do you say it? Ah, yes! The name 'rings a bell'. I enjoy your American idioms, so I hope you don't mind if I practise."

One of the other knights moved forward, his voice deep, with a hint of Irish brogue. "It's the talking she-ape we found. Silver is the name she used."

"Yes, yes," Barlow said. "Of course I remember. I just wanted to test the idiom."

Billy's light blazed. "So she *is* in here? You saw her?"

"Only briefly," Barlow replied. "She said she had no tale, so we weren't interested."

"I wanted to talk to her," the other knight said. "The old traveller told us about your trained zoo apes, but he never said they could talk."

"Obviously, my dear Newman," Barlow said, his light flickering from top to bottom, "it was a lass, not an ape." He turned to Billy. "You see, William, they sent a number of apes and other animals in here, and now it seems that they're sending humans. What a pity! I judged her too quickly, and I apologize for ignoring your friend."

Billy put his hand on Barlow's shoulder. "It's okay, really, but do you have any idea where she is now?"

"No, William, but my men and I will help you search. She could not have gone far; there is really no place to go." Barlow faced the other knights, and as he raised his hand, they lined up in a not-so-straight row. He issued a loud proclamation.

315

"Attention, fellow soldiers of the cross – Newman, Edward, Fiske, Standish, Woodrow. It seems that we finally have a fair damsel to rescue." He paused and whispered to Billy, "She is fair, isn't she?"

Billy suppressed a laugh. Even in his hurry he enjoyed the knights' comical display. "Yes. Very fair, indeed, Sir Barlow."

"And this fair damsel," Barlow continued, "is lost in our eternal chasm. We must find her at all costs."

Billy copied the knight's oratory style. "And after we find her, we will leave this place once and for all."

A loud, frightened buzz in their native language erupted from the spectres, and a number of them backed away, their lights flashing to grey, then yellow.

"No!" Barlow held up his hands to his troops. "Not like what happened to Lester. Our friend, William, is saying we will leave this place in one piece!" He turned to Billy again. "You did mean that, didn't you?"

"Yes. Everyone will be restored to their physical bodies."

"Let us begin the search, then," Barlow commanded. "Fan out. If you find the damsel, bring her back here and call for the others."

Billy held up his glowing rubellite. "She should be wearing a reddish ring. If you find someone who doesn't have it and claims to be Bonnie, let me know. I'll be able to tell."

The knights dispersed, each one searching a different section of the chasm's dark shadows. Billy followed Sir Barlow as he hunted in a particularly dark area. There were so many corners that carried hidden coves and short corridors, and they all needed to be explored. A fading glow could easily be overlooked in this land of flickering lights and wandering shadows.

One of the knights hustled toward Barlow. "A report, sir!"

316

"Proceed, Newman."

"We found another entity cowering in a crevice. I shouted questions at it, but to no avail."

"One of the dumb animals," Sir Barlow reported to Billy. "Most likely a chimp."

"Yes sir," Newman continued. "That makes three chimps, an overly excited dog, and a terrified rabbit. I wish to keep them corralled, sir, so that we are not wasting our time finding them repeatedly."

"I agree," Barlow said. "See to it."

Newman gave Barlow a slight bow. "May I have your assistance, sir? The rabbit is in my possession, and the chimps are currently teasing the dog, but I fear it will not last long."

Barlow turned to Billy. "By your leave, William?"

Billy nodded. "Sure. I think I know my way around now." When Barlow left, Billy continued his search, trying to feel his way with all his senses. Ever since he entered the pit, he had felt Bonnie's presence, though the perception seemed cold and weak. He used his awareness of her as a divining rod, trying to gauge his nearness to her hiding place. At times he felt warmer, but he still couldn't find a strong signal that would take him to her.

He had to hurry. Ashley might be ready to restore them at any minute. But in this dark, confusing place, he couldn't afford to pass by even the smallest alcoves. There was no way he would ever leave without making sure Bonnie was safe.

Bonnie peered out of her crystalline cleft and watched the passing ghosts of light. They were searching; their stretching appendages of flashing energy poked around corners and sniffed under ledges. *I wonder if they're looking for me. What would they do if they found me?* From across the expanse, Bonnie heard strange voices with odd accents. Their words echoed in the chasm, bouncing from plane to plane. "Boonnniiieee Siillvveerr!" The voices created an eerie, haunting harmony.

Why are they calling me? I told them my name, but they thought I was an ape.

Bonnie scooted farther into her cove. With her body pressed against the back of the crevice, she watched one of the phantoms float up to her hiding place. As it slowed to sniff near the opening, it buzzed in a strange language. It paused, and flickers of its radiance spilled into her refuge. Bonnie froze in place, trying to contain any hint of a glimmer. After a few seconds, the phantom left, and she exhaled a stream of light. *Whew! It almost found me.*

How much of this could she take? Would this go on for years? Centuries? Time itself in this twisted stone seemed skewed, and she couldn't be certain how long she'd been there. Had it been weeks or even years? Had her friends given her up for lost?

Does anyone even care anymore?

As her faith sagged, her light dimmed, but she dared not sing. The weird predators had already come too close for comfort. She would meditate instead – on the past, her friends, and how they had never failed her before. The professor was smart and brave and would try to figure out how to restore her if Ashley failed . . . if he ever discovered her plight. But neither he nor Walter even knew about her dragon secrets. Though they were wonderful friends, how could they help?

Her only hope rested on Billy, but how could he outwit Devin? The evil slayer was crafty beyond belief. His trap had fooled her, even though she knew how evil he was and that he would try any trick to destroy her.

No! I have to have faith! Keep my mind on what's good!

An image of Billy's gentle eyes drifted into her thoughts, his words of comfort from not so long ago. "You can believe this," he had said, his ringed hand extended, "you can always trust me. This hand will never lead you astray." She had answered that she would never forget those words, and now, in the hour of her greatest loneliness, she took them again into her heart and caressed each syllable with tender passion. "I do trust you," she had said on that day, and with her heart filling with faith, she spoke them again. "I do trust you, Billy Bannister. I do trust you." Her own words increased her faith, and with it, her shimmering light.

Another spectre approached, pausing to investigate. Bonnie slid against the back wall and worked to still the pulsing of her newly energized glow. An appendage of light slipped into the narrow crevice, searching, probing. It stretched toward her until it nearly touched her light with a white finger circled in red.

A red glow! A ring!

With a loud cry, Bonnie lunged for the hand and grasped it with her own. The other hand entwined around hers, and a gush of warmth surged through her body. The two rings met and created a fiery halo, and Bonnie allowed Billy to pull her out of hiding. The radiant red corona spread out to encircle them as she emerged and stood at his side.

The halo slowly vanished, but other searching lights drew nearer. "Billy!" she said, squeezing his hand. "What are those? What's going on? How did you find me?"

"Shhh! No time! Ashley's probably waiting by now. We have to try to get out of here."

"But how?"

He pointed toward the chasm's light source. "Through the river. We know it leaves the candlestone, so if we just go with the flow, we should be able to get out, too."

Six other bodies of light had now gathered and were listening intently, so Billy introduced Bonnie to them and quickly explained their story, including Clefspeare's and Barlow's tales about Devin's treachery against King Arthur and how he had deceived these loyal knights.

Billy took a deep breath when he finished the tale. "My guess is that everything should be ready by now. The river's not flowing so heavily, so she must have turned off the lights. That's a good enough signal for me. The only problem is that if Ashley can't restore us, we'll probably disintegrate right after we leave."

"Have no fear, William," Barlow said, stepping closer. "I volunteer to go first. If you see me disintegrate, then you will know it is unsafe for you. If I am restored, I will signal my safe arrival in your world."

Before Billy could protest, Barlow released himself into the ever-swirling current that drew all light toward the river. Bonnie followed Billy and the knights as they hurried toward the exiting stream to watch Barlow's progress. The knight plunged into the river, a silent entry that raised a splash of static. Though he melded with the river's light, his shimmering form remained clear, like bubbling seltzer in a stagnant pool. He rushed forward in the flow, and his body hurtled toward the exit. With a flashing spew of sparks, the candlestone flung him out into the open air.

CHAPTER 20

RESTORATION

Walter placed his hand over the accordion-like hose that stretched between the domes, letting his fingers hover over the flexible glass. The professor had melted into a mass of sparkling light, and now he was spreading out through the semi-transparent tube toward the restoration dome. He moved his body back and forth through the tube, then extended a limb back into the diver's cylinder where the candlestone lay. Drying sweat cooled Walter's skin and tightened his face as he concentrated on his teacher's photo-gymnastics. "Prof's in the tube, and he's reaching back toward the candlestone."

"Good. I'm monitoring the activity in the exit chamber." Ashley blew a fresh coating of dust away from a screen. "I think something just came out. Do you see it?"

"Yeah," Walter shouted. "I saw a fizz of light! Prof's got it!"

Ashley kept each hand on a dial and nudged a slider bar with an elbow. She then flipped a switch on the side of the panel with her knee.

Pushing Excalibur to the side, Walter knelt beside the button at the base of the restoration dome. *I don't like it. She sent Prof in there like some electric rescue dog, like he's Lightning Lassie or something. And it looks like she's dancing with that machine. Does she really know what she's doing? Can she really bring him back to normal?*

Ashley ran her finger across the display. "It's working. I've got the new form isolated in the computer, and the professor is about to take it into the restoration dome." She looked up and pointed at the glass cylinder. "Walter, get ready."

Walter put his finger on the switch. Within seconds a stream of luminescence flowed from the connecting tube, filling the glass cylinder. The flashing light gathered into a translucent human form, a hefty, broad-shouldered male.

Ashley gasped. "It's already in human form! It's still light energy, but it's perfectly shaped!"

"Yeah." Walter rubbed his sweaty palm on his jeans. "And it's sure nobody I know."

Ashley turned a knob on the panel. "The professor's out. I'm beginning the restoration."

The glow dispersed as the human form solidified into a mustachioed man. Dressed in black breeches and a flowing, long-sleeved shirt, he stared wide-eyed into the dimly lit room.

"Now, Walter!" Ashley called. "The professor's out."

Walter pressed the switch, and the glass slowly lifted. The man waited until the shield rose above his eyes, then stepped down to floor level, his head erect and his back straight. Walter hit the switch again to lower the glass and stood to face the new arrival.

The man nodded formally. "I am Sir Winston Barlow, Lord of Hickling Manor, and I am a faithful servant of King Arthur."

322

Walter nodded in return. "Uh . . . I'm Walter Foley."

"Master Foley, in the interest of avoiding catastrophe, I shall waive any further formalities." He glanced around the room. "Do you have light switches?"

Walter shrugged. "Ashley, where are the light switches?"

Ashley gestured with her arm. "Over here."

The knight marched toward the panel and stopped, gazing at the display of meters and blinking lights. Ashley put her finger on a dial. "I can control the lights from here by turning this knob."

Sir Barlow bowed and placed his hand on Ashley's. "I must signal the remaining prisoners, my lady, including young Bannister. May I?"

Ashley slipped her hand from underneath Barlow's. "My name is Ashley Stalworth. Certainly you may."

Sir Barlow smiled broadly and turned the dial. As the lights brightened, he laughed out loud. "Ha! When Newman sees this, he will have to pay double! Torches in the ceiling, just as the old traveller said! Who would have believed it?"

With a few more quick twists, the lights flashed off and then on two more times before he finally restored the room to darkness. "That should do it. The others will be coming out momentarily."

"The others?" Ashley repeated. "How many?"

Barlow counted on his brawny fingers, moving his lips through a series of names. "Depending on how many attempt the escape, it could be twelve. Some may be rancorous, even violent."

"Twelve?" Ashley whispered. She read a meter and knitted her brow. "There's no way the receptors can hold out for that many."

"There may be a thirteenth," Barlow added, "if the scoundrel follows us."

323

"The scoundrel?" Ashley glanced at Walter. "You mean Devin, I presume?"

"Yes." He stood upright and fixed his gaze on her. "Are you in league with him?"

Ashley scowled. "Most definitely not!"

"In that case," Barlow said, bowing his head and closing his eyes, "I am at your service."

Ashley pointed toward the recovery dome. "Good. Go and help Walter. There's a sword over there. If some of our escapees get out of line, we can send them right back where they came from."

Barlow smiled, a set of yellow crooked teeth showing his delight. "Miss Stalworth, that would be my pleasure!" He hustled over to Walter. "Where is the sword, lad?"

Walter nudged the sword with his foot. "Right here on the floor."

Barlow leaned over and picked it up. A glow of faint light spread across the blade, illuminating Barlow's wide eyes. "Excalibur!" His tone was solemn, almost reverent. "The king's sword!" He returned it to the floor and backed away. "I am not worthy!"

"It's either you or me, Sir Barlow. If we've got some mean ones coming, I'd rather you do the slicing and dicing. And if you're a knight, you're probably more worthy than I am."

Barlow retrieved the sword and raised its glowing blade, a proud smile spreading across his face. "Very well, Walter, my lad. The conspirators will not be armed, so I shall use the sword only if necessary. If anyone gives us trouble, however, he will learn the meaning of slice and dice!"

Billy trained his gaze on the exiting stream of light. "That's got to be Barlow's signal. That's the third time the river's gushed like crazy and then calmed down." He led Bonnie toward the river's edge, fighting the current's pull as they drew closer. "Are you ready?"

She grasped his hand more tightly. "We're going together, right?"

Billy paused and gazed at her. Her features were becoming more and more clear, her blue eyes, her creamy smooth skin, and her dainty nose and lips forming in shades of shifting light. "Uh . . . no. I think I should make sure everyone gets out."

"Even all the animals?"

He nodded. "Yeah, I guess so. They probably don't want to be in here either."

She let go of his hand and retreated from the stream of light. "Then I'll help you gather them up. I don't want to leave without you."

Billy reached out and grabbed her wrist. "No, the knights and I will get them." He guided her back to the edge of the receding river. "I want you out of here now."

She resisted his pull, and her light flashed bright white. "Billy Bannister, I know you too well. What do you really have in mind?"

Billy dragged his glowing foot along the crystalline floor. "I'm not lying. I'll get the animals, but . . ."

"But what?"

He folded his arms across his chest and squeezed his biceps. "I have to face him."

"Him? You mean Devin?"

"Yeah. I can't keep running away. I can't keep ignoring the prophecies."

Bonnie's eyes lit up like two sapphires. "There are prophecies that say you have to face him?"

"Yeah, remember that old book the professor had? It's Merlin's diary, and prophecies appear in it." Billy pressed his

325

palms against his temples. "The words kept repeating in my head, almost like a bad song you can't get rid of. It was something about having to face the beast to break some chains. Don't you think it means I have to face him, once and for all?"

Bonnie lowered her gaze for several seconds, not making a sound. Finally, she lifted her head again, her light shimmering like the sun on a wind-blown pond. "I think you're right. You have to face him." Her flashing eyes suddenly dimmed, becoming grey and weak. "That means I have to leave without you."

He pulled her toward the river again. "And we have to hustle. They're probably waiting."

"Okay, okay. I'll go." She touched him gently on the shoulder. "I don't know how to say this, but . . . try to be . . . well . . ."

"You want me to stay cool, right?"

Bonnie smiled and nodded. "And don't wait too long if Devin decides not to show his face. Okay?"

"Don't worry." Billy's form shivered out a stream of sparkles. "This place gives me the creeps."

Bonnie stepped close enough to dip her toe in the river's shallows. Just before the current swept her in, she held up her hand, showing her glowing ring to Billy. Billy copied her gesture. Their palms faced each other, and the red glow from each ring bridged the gap between them, joining in a pulsating web of scarlet. The river then enveloped Bonnie and carried her away.

Billy watched helplessly as her body flew out of the candlestone. He could barely see her flashing light dangling in the air on the outside, her particles already beginning to separate. Her ring highlighted her groping hand as her fingers stretched for something to grasp. Over and over again she clutched at empty air.

C'mon, Bonnie! Hang in there!

Bonnie's light suddenly vanished.

What? Did she disperse? Was she sucked back into the candlestone?

Billy's legs dwindled into two spindly sparks, more like trembling, electric toothpicks than legs. He closed his eyes and balled his hands into flashing fists. *I gotta have faith!*

"Sir William," Newman said. "Will you go next?"

Billy shook his head slowly. He could barely think. Bonnie's last seconds haunted him, her radiant smile, her trusting eyes. Was she okay? He let out a sigh. "No, the rest of the knights should go next, but can you stay long enough to help me collect the animals and toss them into the river?"

"Certainly. The poor beasts cannot find their own way out. To leave them to their own devices would not be chivalrous. I know the places they usually congregate, so it won't take long to find them. We will all stay to help."

Newman lifted a small glowing animal at his feet. "This dog should go first. He refuses to leave my side, and I keep tripping on him."

Billy laughed. "Sir Newman, how can you trip over a body of light?" He took the dog from the knight and set him down. "Let's throw in the animals you've trapped, then we'll use the dog to hunt for the others together, okay?"

"My pleasure, William." Newman shouted into the cavern. "Men! Get ready for some chimp tossing!"

327

Walter waited at the recovery dome, his hand poised over the platform button. Another body congealed under the glass. Its shape wasn't as distinct as Barlow's, but it was obviously human, with glittering arms and legs and strands of luminescence flowing from its head.

"Starting restoration," Ashley called. "Get ready!"

The light solidified into a feminine shape, the strands falling on her shoulders as blondish-brown tresses. A mass on her back morphed into folded wings, and within seconds, Bonnie's body materialized, her white robe shining bright. She blinked her eyes and took in a long, deep breath.

Ashley's voice boomed across the lab. "Walter! Now!"

Walter slapped the switch and jumped to his feet, bouncing on his toes while waiting for the glass to rise. "You can lower your sword, Sir Barlow. It's a friend." The knight relaxed his arm, resting Excalibur at his side.

Bonnie glanced around with glazed eyes, her arms and legs motionless. Walter leaped onto the platform and took her hand, gently guiding her to floor level.

"Walter?" she said dreamily. She clutched his forearm as her legs wobbled on the stone surface. "What are you doing here?"

"Walter!" Ashley called from the control panel. "She's disoriented. Her light waves were frazzled when she came out. We almost lost her."

Still holding her hand, Walter tapped the switch with the toe of his shoe, sending the glass shield down again. "We're all here," he explained. "I mean, the professor and me and Billy's mum." He pointed toward the glass cylinders. "The professor's the one who pulled you into that dome."

Bonnie glanced over her shoulder at the restoration process. When she did, she spied her uncovered wings and gasped.

Walter's gaze followed hers. With a wave of his hand, he said, "Don't worry. I've known about your wings for a long time."

"You've known?" Bonnie's wings trembled. "But how?"

Ashley interrupted. "We'll have time for explanations later. Right now Walter has a job to do."

"Is that Ashley?"

"Right here, Bonnie!" Ashley called, waving. "It's good to see you again! Sorry I can't come over there; I'm sort of busy."

"Ahem," Sir Barlow said, kneeling. "Fair maiden, forgive me. I did not realize you were an angel. It is you who should bear the great sword." He extended Excalibur, hilt first.

Bonnie reached for the sword and grasped its ornate handle with both hands. Its glow brightened to a fiery white blaze.

Barlow gasped and fell backward, sliding away on his elbows. "By all that is holy!"

"Oh, get up!" Walter said, laughing and reaching his hand to help the frightened knight. "Bonnie's not an angel! She's a dragon!"

"A dragon?" Barlow repeated as Walter hoisted him to his feet.

Ashley's voice boomed again out of the darkness. "Explain it later, Walter! Another one's coming!"

As a new mass of light filtered into the dome, Walter jumped to his post. Barlow whispered to Bonnie. "Whatever you are, lass, be ready to strike. It may be one of the scoundrels."

Bonnie leaned over to offer him the hilt. "I'd feel better if you were the one holding it."

Barlow wrapped his fingers around the grip and bowed his head. "If you so command, my lady. It will be my honour to bear it."

Walter dropped to his knees near the cylinder switch. "Whatever just came out of the stone is taking shape!"

The light in the dome coalesced into a short, stooped form.

"An ape!" Barlow cried.

Ashley squinted at the hairy face. "That's Betsy! She was one of our first chimps to go in." Betsy pressed her nose and lips against the glass. "She's ready, Walter. Get her out of there."

Walter hit the button, and Betsy scrambled down on all fours.

329

Ashley clapped her hands. "C'mere, Betsy!" The chimp dashed across the floor and jumped into her mistress's arms, and Ashley let out a sigh. "If they send out all the animals, we're in for a long night."

Billy wrestled a young chimp off his back and released him into the river. "You think that's the last one, Sir Newman?"

"By my count Master William, yes."

"Then let's start sending your men. Who do you think should go first?"

Newman looked his fellow knights over, each one now standing at attention. "Since our leader is already out there, he can assemble the men when they arrive. I volunteer to go last. The next to go should be—"

Ploof!

Billy jerked his head around. "What was that?" The remnants of an electric splash rose from the river, leaving an effervescent fizz. Two seconds later, another splash plumed in a surge of spritzing static, then another.

"The conspirators!" Newman shouted.

"Get your men in there now!" Billy yelled. "We can't have them outnumbering our people out in the lab!"

Newman waved his glowing arms toward the river. "Edward! Fly to the exit! Fiske! You follow him! Standish! Woodrow! Go! Now!"

The four phantoms dashed into the current, allowing it to hurtle their bodies into the river. Their splashes combined with those of the remaining conspirators as they all flushed through the candlestone's wash.

Newman faced Billy and bowed. "You next, lad."

"No," Billy replied, shaking his head. "You go. I . . . I have something to do."

Newman straightened and folded his hands behind his back. "I am at your service, William. With that fiend lurking in the shadows, I stand as your ready guard."

"Thank you Newman, but they need you out there." He gripped Newman's shoulder. "Trust me. This is something I have to do alone."

Newman bowed. "William, you are a brave knight indeed. I will look forward to seeing you on the other side."

Without another word, Newman stepped toward the river, his body elongating as the current pulled him into its flow. His noble smile stretched with his thinning face, and he vanished into a vapour of streaming light.

Now alone in the chasm, Billy scanned the upper rim. *Where is he? He fooled me last time, so I guess my danger sensing doesn't work in here.* He turned to continue his search. *I guess I—*

"Going somewhere, mongrel?" A flashing storm of light blocked his path. An electric hand throttled his neck, jolting him like a thousand stinging wasps. "This party is just getting started."

331

G et Bobo away from that machine!" Ashley yelled. "If she turns it on, this show's over for good!"

"I'm trying to catch the rabbit!" Walter called back. "It's chewing the cables!"

Ashley groaned. "The chimp first, then the rabbit!"

Bonnie flew across the lab, swooping low and snatching Bobo into her arms. She carried the chimp through the air toward the girls' dorm. With a sweep of her arm, she slid Bobo inside and closed the door.

"Bonnie!" Ashley shouted. "Get Betsy, too! She's trying to fiddle with the lights. We need them to stay dim." She slapped the imp's hairy hand away from the dial.

Airborne again, Bonnie zipped to the control panel and grabbed Betsy, holding the struggling ape away from the controls.

Ashley let out a loud relieved sigh, but immediately tensed. "Oh no! There're four, no, five in the diver's dome! There's no way the professor can grab them all before the candlestone reabsorbs them!"

Ashley's brow bent toward her nose. "The candlestone's not affecting them at all! Could it be because their light isn't agitated anymore?" She began shouting again. "Now there are six! Seven! What are we going to do? The receptors will never last!"

"Bonnie!" Walter yelled. "I've got the rabbit, but now one of the chimps is trying to mess with the shield's switch!"

"I'm on my way!" Bonnie took Ashley's hand and softly patted her knuckles. "If anyone can figure out what to do, you can!"

"But how? There're eight! No, nine!"

Bonnie zoomed toward the recovery dome with Betsy in one arm and scooped Walter's miscreant chimp into her other. As she flew by, she saw Sir Barlow wrestling for the sword with a larger chimp while an overzealous Scottish terrier nipped at his stockings. She sighed. "Those two will just have to wait."

Waves of pain shot through Billy's body, rippling through his energy field like lightning bolts. The stinging current drove into his brain, like hot needles zapping him over and over again. The slayer's grip tightened around Billy's throat until he felt woozy, every light dimming and spinning. The slayer lifted him until his feet floated above the chasm floor.

"You have no idea who you're dealing with, Dragon Boy," the slayer growled. "I am the Minister of The New Table. I am Arthur's Bane. I am the Wandering Spirit who cannot die."

Billy could barely think. The slayer's words were surreal, a wave of strange ideas. *The New Table? Arthur's bane? What's he talking about?*

Devin's arm drew back. He threw a raging punch at Billy's face, like a blacksmith's mighty hammer crushing molten steel. Billy flew against one of the chasm's walls, splattering his body against the crystal and creating a splash of sizzling electrons.

The slayer stalked toward him again, his arms reaching forward as if he were a demonic mantis. His evil voice sounded like an echo from the pit of hell. "It's time to end this for good, you whelp of a jackal!"

A blinding flash of light surged through the gap between the demon and his prey. In a split second the light gathered into the tall stately form of a man, robed, with flowing silver hair. His arms spread wide, and light beams shot out from his hands to form a glowing shield, an oblong bubble that enveloped Billy and his defender.

The slayer burst into enraged flames, and his fiery red finger shook with dripping sparks. "Begone, you old sorcerer. Your black magic won't keep me from slaying this foul son of the devil!"

Billy's ghostly friend replied in a soft but firm tone. "It is not young William who springs from Satan's loins, Devin. It is the liar who finds his home in the devil's house of worship. Darkness breeds there, and you are its offspring, the minister of the darkest of lies."

"Oh, so eloquent!" Devin sneered. "Is that what you've been doing for a thousand years, making up oral gems like that one? It makes me feel better knowing that you were in here conjuring up your trite little sayings while I was taking care of your dragon friends. Would you like an accounting of how many now remain in your draconic collection?"

The defender's voice remained calm. "I am aware of your deeds, but the prophecy is still intact."

"And so is mine," Devin replied, flame still rippling across his fierce body. "Is your little lamb aware of the prophecies about me? I'll bet you haven't told him, have you?"

"No. It is not necessary to drink poison in order to understand its harm. He has seen enough of evil to know its character. A stinking pool need not be waded to learn that it is foul."

"Well, perhaps the mongrel would like to know more about my power in his world. Has he ever asked why I was able to become a school principal, how I could manipulate the Castlewood police, how I was able to stow away in his father's guarded airplane? Have you told him the truth about me?"

Billy pulled himself up to his knees. Devin's questions were his questions – ones he had asked himself a hundred times.

"He will learn the truth," the defender replied. "But it will not come through your twisted words. I will not allow it." The silver-haired man lifted Billy to his feet, keeping a flashing hand on his back.

Billy stared into the face of the radiant defender. "Professor?" he whispered. "How did you get in here?"

"It is time for you to go, brave lad."

"But it's not over. I have to face Devin."

"Not here and not now. You have to face him, but you have not yet taken hold of your greatest weapons."

The defender lifted Billy into the air and threw him into the dark currents. Billy sailed toward the stream of light, pulled through the swirling blackness without the strength to fight it. A flash surrounded him as he plunged into the electrostatic river. Millions of tiny sparks pecked away at his body, and the pulsing lights dimmed to black.

Edward!" Sir Barlow cried as the glass rose. "You made it!"

The knight, dressed only in loose-fitting silk breeches and shirt, stepped down to the floor. "Yes," he replied breathlessly, "but our enemies may soon follow. I am the first, it seems, but the others are floating back in that glass case. I cannot tell who will be taken next."

Bonnie peered into the diver's dome. "What about Billy? Is he floating in there?"

Edward bowed. "The lad is still in the stone, as far as I know. He is a valiant one, to be sure. My guess is that he wanted to oversee everyone's escape."

Ashley called from the control panel. "The receptors are dying! If the professor brings anyone else over, I won't be able to restore them! I might have to—"

A shout filled the lab. "She's gone!"

Ashley spun her head toward the sound. "Who's gone?"

Dr Conner appeared in the dim light, leading Derrick and pushing Ashley's grandfather in his wheelchair.

"Daddy!" Ashley cried, rushing toward them. Her grandfather's head lolled to one side, and he shivered violently, his eyes tightly shut and his hands clenched into fists. Bonnie followed close behind Ashley and took Derrick's hand from Doc.

Dirty tears streamed down Dr Conner's earth-caked cheeks, and he put a trembling hand on Ashley's shoulder. "Karen's gone!"

335

CHAPTER 21

COLLAPSE

Ashley enfolded her grandfather's stiff, wrinkled hands and held them against her cheeks. "He's freezing!" She searched all around his wheelchair. "Where's his blanket?"

"It was gone when I got there!" Dr Conner pointed toward the Omega door. "There's deep snow where the cave comes out into the valley, but I couldn't see any human tracks, just depressions and scratches in the snow. I saw blood next to the boulder that must have hit Karen, but there wasn't any trail." He dropped his medical bag and raised his hands. "It's like she just vanished into thin air. And the cave collapsed behind me on my way back in. There's no escaping that way now."

Ashley stroked Derrick's forearm. "Derrick. Did you hear anything? Can you even guess what happened?"

Derrick, his ebony skin streaked with tear tracks through grey dust, spoke slowly. "I heard weird noises, like wind . . . wind whipping a blanket on a clothes line." He wiped his face with his sleeve. "And there was a smell, a smell like ploughed soil, and I felt a warm breeze for just a second or two."

Bonnie took Derrick in her arms and held his quivering face against her shoulder. Ashley grabbed the coat the professor had shed and laid it over her grandfather's shaking body, tucking it around his sides. "I . . . I can't do much more for Daddy now, Doc. And I can't go looking for Karen." She waved her arm toward the diver's dome. "There are a bunch of people floating over there, and the professor left one in the restoration dome. I can't restore any of them until I get more photoreceptors. If we don't hurry, the people will disperse and die."

"But where can we get receptors?" Dr Conner asked. He fumbled through his pocket and drew out his ring of keys. "You know our source is gone."

Bonnie extended her arms, exposing their scarred undersides. "Don't I have photoreceptors? Can't we use mine?"

"Yes, Bonnie," Ashley replied, "you have them, but after getting transluminated and restored, your receptors could be weak or useless. Instead of letting the machine restore you, the receptors tried to do the work and drained themselves. And, besides, since you'll have a low receptor density right now, it would take a lot of blood. We need you to stay strong to help search for Karen from the air."

Walter stepped in close to the wheelchair. "Search, smearch! If Bonnie's got photo-whatitz, then let's try to use them. Weak ones are better than none at all. Billy and Prof are going to die if we don't! And we'll find Karen one way or another."

Dr Conner popped open his medical bag and produced a syringe. "I promised myself I'd never draw another drop of Bonnie's blood, but I don't think we have any choice."

Ashley let out a deep sigh, rolled up a sleeve on her robe, and extended her arm toward Doc. "Take them from me."

Dr Conner stared at Ashley's bare forearm. "Take what from you? What are you talking about?"

She nodded toward her arm. "I have photoreceptors in my blood. We can use them in the engine."

Bonnie placed her hand on Ashley's exposed skin. "You have them? How?"

She jerked her arm back and raised her voice. "I can't explain now! We've wasted too much time already. Doc, just get the needle and do it!"

Dr Conner rummaged through the medical bag and pulled out a plastic tube. "We'll have to attach you directly to the equipment to be sure we get enough."

Ashley marched toward a machine near the lab's edge. "Can you run the board, Doc? It's programmed to isolate the professor's coding and analyse only who he brings with him. The code loop has already worked several times, so just keep the system tuned where I have it, experimental project eleven B. If everything keeps working, we could have a big search party in just a few minutes." She wheeled up a chair and held out her arm.

"I can run the board. Just be ready to answer any questions I have." Dr Conner stooped and pushed one end of the plastic tube into an adapter on the machine. With a quick twist, he fastened a sharp needle on the other end of the tube and pressed the point into the crook of Ashley's arm. A dark stream of red seeped through the plastic and ran toward a collection tank on the machine. Doc jumped up and hustled to the control panel.

"Everyone back to your posts!" Ashley barked. "Doc, signal Walter when each restoration is complete. Barlow, have the sword ready. Bonnie, see if you can keep my grandfather warm."

"You were right!" Dr Conner called. "The system is showing functional receptors!" He turned a dial clockwise. "Here we go!"

339

Leading Derrick by the hand, Bonnie pushed the wheelchair closer to the dome near Walter and Sir Barlow. Barlow leaned over and whispered to Walter. "I can already identify who is in there. It is one of the conspirators, Addison by name. He is not very bright." Barlow lifted Excalibur to an attack position.

The form in the recovery dome congealed, creating a thin, shaking little man dressed only in a grey, girded loincloth.

Walter dropped to his knees. "Is he ready?"

Dr Conner waved his hand. "Yes, go ahead."

Walter hit the switch, and as soon as the glass rose to his chest, Addison fell to his knees, his eyes wide. He pointed at Bonnie and squeaked. "An angel! Am I in heaven?"

Sir Barlow lunged toward the conspirator with Excalibur. "Death to all who dare enter heaven naked!" Addison shrieked and dashed into the darkness. With a hearty laugh, Barlow returned to his post. "The fool never did learn to wear proper garments under his mail. Serves him right."

A sudden jolt knocked Walter to his seat. "What was that?"

The ground trembled, then shook. "Another tremor!" Ashley yelled.

The tile floor buckled and cracked, swallowing a loop of cables into a shallow depression. Dr Conner gripped the sides of the control panel. "Will the equipment hold out?"

Ashley pressed her hand on the needle in her arm to keep it steady. "Your guess is as good as mine." She twisted her head toward the wheelchair. "Bonnie! Does your professor know Morse code?"

"Probably."

"Go to the wall switches. We need to send him an SOS."

Three ceiling panels gave way under a small landslide. Rocks and dirt crashed into the anchor dome, shattering the glass and sending fragments crunching to the floor. Bonnie hopped over the shards and dashed to the wall near the Alpha door. "Okay! Ready!"

"Find the switch on the far left and flip it on," Ashley called.

"Got it!"

"Now you've got control of the lights. Use the middle switch and flip it three times – quick, short bursts. Follow that with three longer ones." Ashley counted the flashes above her head. "Now repeat the short ones."

She held the tube against her arm and stood up. "Doc, turn on both generators. Local power is bound to go out."

Dr Conner opened a small plastic flap over a red switch. "I already fired up the first one." He flicked the switch and closed the flap. "Second one's up!"

Ashley leaned over the machine and yelled at Barlow. "I need Edward to go with Bonnie! When she's done with her signal, she'll fly him over the ceiling to shore it up." She spun around. "Bonnie, can you do that?"

"I think so. He's no bigger than Billy, and I've carried him—"

"Good. Leave the lights on. Everyone should be out of the stone by now." She turned to Dr Conner. "Doc, move slider C14 to max. That should speed up the restorations. We'll have to risk a power sag."

"To max? It'll drain the receptors!" Another hard shake jolted the lab. Black dirt poured onto the control panel, and Dr Conner threw his body over it.

"I'm mainlining the supply, Doc! They'll last!"

He straightened, letting a pile of debris slide down his back. He pushed the buffer control to the top. "But will you last?"

Excited shrieks rose within the dorm halls. "It's the chimps," Ashley yelled amidst the growing clamour. "Local power must be out, or else the dorms are caving in!"

"The professor's moving faster," Doc shouted back. "He must have gotten the signal. We have a new body in the dome. The professor's clear. Restoring now!"

"It's Standish!" Barlow yelled. "A very good knight. A bit eccentric, however."

"Get him out, Walter!" Doc called. "The professor's already waiting."

Walter slapped the switch and reached under the glass, dragging Standish off the platform. As soon as the knight was clear, Walter hit the switch again.

Dr Conner brushed dirt from one of the panel's meters. "Good job, Walter." He rotated a dial with one hand and wiped his forehead with the other. "Get ready. We'll have another one in a few seconds."

Loose dirt pelted the ceiling, and Dr Conner glanced up. "Bonnie, the panel above the dome is sagging!"

The shadow of enormous wings passed across the lab floor, and Bonnie scooped Edward up from behind.

"Aaaah!" The knight's feet flailed in the air as he glided across the lab.

Bonnie zoomed to the outer wall and shot up into the upper reaches of the cavern. She flew Edward over the ceiling, and they landed on top of one of the horizontal beams that held the ceiling panels' support wires. Tiny stones and dirt pelted both maiden and knight as Bonnie strained to examine the ceiling below while bracing herself against a vertical beam. Shafts of light illuminated the area, pouring through gaps in the drop ceiling.

Bonnie pointed to a spot several feet away. "That's the one. I think that pile of stuff is right over the diver's dome. Let's try to move the bigger stones away."

"Do you feel that?" Edward asked, holding out his hand.

Bonnie looked up. "Snow!" She held out her own hand and an icy flake settled on her palm. *How could snow get in here?*

Bonnie pulled on Edward's sleeve. "Hang on. I'll be right back." She leaped into the dimness, dodging a protruding rock formation, and found a gaping hole in the ceiling. Shooting through the gap, she cleared the rim of a volcano-like cone and flew into cold, snow-filled sky. After surveying the area, she made a sharp U-turn, zipped back through the gap, and landed softly next to Edward, who was busily clearing debris from the sagging panel.

"We'd better hurry. The mountain looks like its splitting open."

"Almost done, Miss." Edward lifted a cannonball-sized stone, slid across the snow-slicked beam, and heaved it toward the far side of the cavern. "That should do it."

"Are you ready to fly back down?"

"Not to insult your skills, m'lady, but if you don't mind, I will take a more direct route." Edward leaped toward a hole in the ceiling, caught the frame, and swung down to the floor, landing with a graceful bend of his knees. Bonnie flew across the tops of the panels, then back down the side of the cavern, landing in a run at the edge of the lab.

Ashley sat quietly beside the blood receptacle, gaunt and pale. Barlow stood next to five other men who were similarly clad in dark breeches and loose cotton shirts. Walter squatted at his post waiting for the next signal.

Bonnie felt her throat catch. *Where's Billy? He must not be out yet. But there's no time to worry about that; I have to warn everyone about the mountain!* She cleared her throat. "We have a major problem! The mountain is opening up. There's a . . . a gap, like it's splitting apart."

343

Ashley jumped to her feet and yanked the needle from her arm. Applying pressure to her wound and walking like a determined drunkard, she staggered toward the panel, her voice small and feeble. "That must be Billy coming in now. We should have enough receptors. Restore him and then the professor, and let's get out of here!"

Dr Conner gave way and let Ashley step up to control the panel. She pulled on her headphones, adjusted the microphone, and flipped a switch. Her voice boomed through hidden speakers. "Barlow, get your men and carry my grandfather up the stairs in the Alpha exit. Bonnie will show you the way. Walter, as soon as Billy appears, help him out quickly. He might not recognize you or even understand what's going on."

"But the other males are fine," Bonnie said, wiping a smudge from her forehead. "Won't Billy be okay?"

Ashley took a deep breath. Her pale skin regained a hint of colour. "I can't be sure, but I have a theory. I think the longer a male's been in the candlestone, the better for his brain. Men are natural warriors, and they go in more agitated. Remember what I told you about ripples and a reflection in a pond?" Her eyes refocused on the recovery cylinder. "But there's no time to explain any further. Just pray that he's all right."

A male body materialized in the dome, but he sat crumpled, his head between his knees and his arms draped over his legs.

Walter punched the switch. "It's Billy!" He gripped the lower rim of the glass to make it rise faster.

Bonnie jumped toward the dome, but Barlow pushed the wheelchair into her path and put his hand on her elbow. "Show me the way out, lass. The conspirators have fled to the shadows, and we will allow the cowards to perish in God's wrath, but we must save the old man and the blind youth."

Bonnie looked at his kind, serious face and the solemn expressions of his men who stood close by. She spun back around to see Walter pulling Billy's limp body out of the dome and onto the floor while small stones and dirt rained all around.

Dr Conner dashed over and grabbed the wheelchair handles. "I'll take them, Bonnie! Go to Billy!"

Bonnie flapped her wings and half walked, half flew to Billy's side. Walter hit the switch again and shouted. "Now we just need to get the prof!"

Ashley's voice boomed through the speakers again. "The professor's already grabbed someone else, and they're passing through the tube!"

"But there isn't anyone else," Walter countered, "except—"

"Devin?" Bonnie knelt on the floor. She cradled Billy's head in her arms and shielded his body from the debris that rained on his translumination robe.

Ashley murmured. "No, it's not Devin, but it's real strange. The pre-analyser says it has the same data coding as the professor. Since I have the professor's coding blocked, the computer assumes it *is* the professor and won't complete the restoration. I'll have to turn off the block and let it analyse them together." She began typing madly on a keyboard, reprogramming the computer with her flying fingers. "I don't know if this will work, but here goes!"

Dr Conner burst back into the room. "The Alpha exit's caved in, too! The whole side of the mountain is giving way!" Barlow and his men re-entered, carrying Ashley's grandfather, wheelchair and all, and leading Derrick by the hand. Doc waved his arm. "Everyone to the centre of the lab!"

While Barlow and his knights rushed toward the central pedestal with Derrick and the wheelchair, Bonnie dragged Billy's limp body forward. He felt like a thousand-pound sack of sand. Lifting Edward and all those rocks had sapped her strength.

Barlow ran to her side and deftly lifted Billy over his shoulder. "I'll take him, Miss."

The crowd clustered around the pedestal while larger rocks crashed to the floor, piling in front of the Alpha exit and raising a thick wall of dust. Ceiling panels, along with their twisted frames and support beams, tumbled all around. Barlow deflected two panels with one of his massive arms, while Fiske, Standish, and Woodrow arched their bodies over Ashley's grandfather and Derrick. Edward and Newman stood like shade trees over Bonnie while she sat cross-legged on the floor. Barlow placed Billy in her arms. She laid her cheek against his and silently prayed.

Walter stayed at his post and kept his eyes trained on the restoration dome.

Ashley's voice crackled through the speakers. "They're both in there." Lights flickered and loud pops sounded all around. Ashley threw off the headphones and pushed three sliders fully to the right. "Power's going down on generator number one. Going max on restoration while the second generator lasts. Get ready, Walter! As soon as you can recognize him, count to three and pull him out!" Ashley left the panel to join the huddled group.

Walter placed his hand over the switch. Bulbs exploded, and every light went black, but the dome still buzzed with activity. One second later, the professor's familiar form appeared, standing erect on the platform. "No time to wait for that glass to rise," Walter muttered. He grabbed Excalibur from the floor, counted to three, and with a mighty swing, smashed the glass cylinder with the glowing sword. Glass flew everywhere, pelting the professor and scattering across the floor.

The professor brushed the glass from his robe and stepped down to floor level. With sharp, piercing eyes, he turned slowly and took in the battered lab – the ceiling debris on the cracked tiles, the mound of rocks blocking the Alpha door, and the huddled group in the centre of the cavern. A mangled frame and a few panels remained in the ceiling above. The sword in Walter's hands and a row of LED's still flickering on the control panel provided only scant light in the dim room. The professor's body shone against the blackness as if somehow he had retained some of his transluminated form.

All was still. He reached out his hand, and his voice echoed in the darkness. "The sword, please, Walter."

Walter flipped the sword around and extended the hilt. The professor grasped it and limped toward the central pedestal. He knelt at Bonnie's side and placed the sword in Billy's hands, wrapping his own fingers on top and elevating the blade. Billy opened his eyes and tightened his grasp on the hilt.

"William," the professor said, softly, "what now is your weapon?"

Bonnie could see Billy's eyes reflecting the professor's shining face, enhanced by Excalibur's glow. She held her breath, waiting for Billy's reply.

"Truth," he whispered, his voice rasping. He cleared his throat. "Truth is my sword."

The professor nodded, his eyes now flashing, and his voice erupted in deep, echoing tones as if Billy's answer strengthened him. "And what now is your defence?"

Colour returned to Billy's face, and his jaw tightened. His voice surged with emotion. "Faith . . . faith is my shield."

Excalibur flashed. Its glow exploded in dazzling brilliance, sending out a sparkling corona and bathing the lab in a spectacular

347

halo. A dozen shafts of light shot out from the sword's tip, angling in all directions and then bouncing back, combining into one huge bolt of lightning that plunged into Billy's chest.

His body lurched at the impact, and his skin shimmered like the sun on a perfectly polished suit of armour, his entire frame flashing like a human strobe light. He let out a long, loud yell, a warrior's battle cry that echoed across the littered cavern floor.

As the professor released his grip, the bright light faded, and Billy sat up, clutching the glowing sword. He took Bonnie's hand in his and stared at the union, soft fingers interlocked and two rings touching, creating a glow of their own.

He smiled at her, then whispered, "I have work to do."

Bonnie squeezed his hand and withdrew her fingers from their clutch, smiling. "Then you'd better get to it."

A strange noise buzzed across the chamber. The cap of the broken restoration dome, now dangling from a bent frame by a mangled wire, sent a feeble beam toward the platform below. A new phantom appeared in the ray, taking shape like a radiant ghost, his yellow-green eyes glowing like copper laser beams shooting through a night sky.

The professor reached for Billy's hand and pulled him to his feet. "Your work is beginning, William. The captives await their final liberation."

Billy raised the flashing sword high as though it weighed no more than a child's toy. "First thing's first. Where's the candlestone?"

Ashley pointed. "In the diver's dome!"

Billy shouted, "No more prisoners!"

He rushed to the diver's dome and smashed the glass cylinder with one blow of the sword. He swung again, this time driving the blade directly into the stone, slicing through it cleanly. A tiny explosion of sparks erupted, and the two halves fell dark.

Billy spun around to face the slayer, shuddering at the apparition on the recovery platform. Devin's body, not yet fully restored, pulsated between light and darkness, between man and glowing beast as the restoration ray continued to bathe his phantom form.

Billy raced to the control panel and ripped the metal surface with Excalibur's blade, sending a wave of sparks flying high into the air. The constant hum died, and every blinking light faded to black, leaving Excalibur's glow and the slayer's throbbing body the only lights in the room.

Devin remained on the platform, a glowing mass of electric plasma that seemed to float in place. "Addison!" he growled. "I know you're out there somewhere. Assemble our men!"

The nearly naked Addison ran to Devin's side, trembling like a chilled pup, and four fierce men followed him. Devin turned to the huddled group near the pedestal. "Conner, open the weapons cache for my soldiers. It's time to get rid of the mongrel blight."

Dr Conner rose to his feet. "Mongrel blight?" He glanced at Bonnie, gave her a weak smile, then spun back toward Devin, his chest puffing out. "You blind fool!" He waved his hand at the group sitting around his feet. "Look at them! You call them mongrels, but their love for each other, their willingness to sacrifice their lives for their friends, shows they have more heart than you'll ever have – more heart, more faith, and more courage."

Bonnie stood up and grasped her father's hand. He squeezed hers in return. As he kept his defiant glare trained on Devin, a tear streamed down his cheek. "Someone told me not too long ago that my plans could fail because love might turn on me and set all the captives free. She was right, and I'm one of those freed captives." He took a step forward, still clutching Bonnie's hand. "Get lost, *Sir* Devin. I'm not afraid of you anymore."

Devin flashed, and sparks flew from his hands and hair. "A bit late for that, you fool!" He jumped from the platform and glided toward a closet door, his own light illuminating his path. He put his hands on the doorknob, and a stream of fire engulfed the surface. With a Herculean pull, he jerked the door open, tearing it loose from its melting hinges. "Men," he said, motioning toward the inside, "arm yourselves."

Addison and the other four hustled toward the closet. Barlow leaped to his feet and raced to head them off. Edward surged ahead and tackled Addison, knocking him into two of the other conspirators. Barlow's remaining knights charged, each lifting a guttural battle cry. Devin thrashed Newman and Standish with his fiery arms, sending them flying, their clothes singed.

Billy pulled the protective robe over his head and tossed it to the side. He checked the cotton belt on his jeans, then dashed toward the fray, Excalibur sparkling in his hands.

"Mind the beam, William!" the professor shouted. "It will disintegrate your friends as well as your enemies!"

Walter grabbed a broken piece of metal and followed close behind. Dr Conner pried off a nail-studded two-by-four and sprinted toward the crowd, brandishing his weapon. With her strength renewed, Bonnie snatched up a fallen board and exploded into the air. She swooped down in front of Addison's right-hand man and bashed him across the back, then zoomed upward before he could retaliate.

Ashley took a step to join them, but the professor held her back. "You are too weak, child. See to your grandfather. Cover him."

Using her back as a shield, Ashley threw her arms around her grandfather. The professor dropped down to protect Derrick, resting one hand against the ground, his palm flat.

"Another tremor," he said softly, closing his eyes. "As you may have guessed, Ashley Stalworth, this is no normal earthquake." As the battle continued in front of the weapons room, his voice melted into a lilting song.

Tremors, O tremors of the earth
Come now with mercy
To those of royal birth

Answer, O answer to our cry
Open now the chasm
To bring fire from the sky

As he lifted his hand, a strong jolt shook the lab. The twisted ceiling frame crashed to the floor, followed by a hail of rocks and dirt. Knights and conspirators tumbled to the ground. As Billy knocked a sword from Addison's hand, the jolt threw him down to the gritty floor, scraping his back and jarring Excalibur from his hand. Addison sprang toward him, but Billy planted his feet in the conspirator's chest and thrust him into the air, tossing him toward a pile of rocks.

A falling panel struck Bonnie on her back and drove her to the floor, sending her weapon flying into the tangled heap of rubble. She smacked her palms and knees on the dirty, debris-strewn tiles and slid to a painful stop. The door to the dorm hall flew open, and a frightened chimp dashed out, along with the Scottish terrier and a scampering rabbit.

Devin, his bright, sizzling body radiating sparks, charged Billy, reaching for him with fiery hands. With his focus on the villain's eyes, Billy groped for Excalibur at his side.

Too late! Devin leaped toward him. Billy launched a stream of flames into the slayer's face. The force blew the glowing phantom backwards and slammed him into a back wall on the far side of the cavern. He disappeared in the midst of falling dirt and rock. His glow continued, penetrating the flying, swirling dust. He stalked out of the gloom, dazed, but larger and brighter than before.

Billy grabbed Excalibur and jumped to his feet, trying to keep a battle stance on the trembling ground, waiting to see what the dragon slayer would do.

Barlow bowled over one of the conspirators and burst into the weapons room. His arms bulging with swords and shields, he scrambled back to Dr Conner, Walter, and the knights, each one pulling out a blade and shield as Barlow passed by. The conspirators regrouped and drew back into the shadows.

Brushing a hand across her eyes, Bonnie shook the fog from her head. Her fingers came away cold and wet. She took wing once again, soaring upward to look around, then floated down toward Ashley. "The top of the mountain and the ceiling are completely gone! We're in the open!"

Ashley grabbed the wheelchair handles. "Then let's get Daddy and Derrick out of here, even if we have to climb over the rubble to get to the valley."

The professor put a hand on Ashley's shoulder. "That won't be necessary," he said, pointing to the skies. "The summoned one has arrived."

CHAPTER 22

SCORCHED EARTH

Shielded by a blanket of dense clouds, the moon's white glow painted ghostly images throughout the sky. The thick falling snow framed a tiny silhouette, a winged shadow approaching the toppled mountain. Bonnie brushed flecks of snow from her hair. *It's a dragon! Billy's dad? Did he fly all this way?* She stared into the dark chasm that had once been the lab. *Should I tell the others?*

A cry rang out. The conspirators charged, their swords swinging. Addison's sword pierced Walter's shield, the point stopping within inches of his face. He jerked the shield back, wrenching the sword from his attacker's grip. Barlow stepped in and landed a bruising elbow on Addison's cheek, sending his smaller opponent crashing to the ground. Woodrow and Fiske stood side by side, crossing swords with two conspirators, beating them back toward a wall. Edward and Newman battled the two remaining traitors, raising their shields next to Dr Conner and keeping him tucked between them. Pushing the terrier out of the way with his foot, Newman parried a sword thrust, spun gracefully on his toe, and plunged his blade into his enemy's midsection. Edward faced the biggest of the evil knights. He ducked under a sweeping sword, twirled on his knees, and swiped across the conspirator's ankles. The burly man toppled to the ground like a felled redwood. Standish stayed back, guarding Derrick and the others with a raised sword and shield.

With Excalibur blazing in his grip, Billy faced Devin. The slayer brought his palms close together and fashioned a ball of flames from his own light energy. The fireball shot out from his hands and hurtled toward Billy like a crawling nest of electric scorpions. With a quick swing, Billy smacked the ball with his blade, sending it rocketing into the night. The fireball lit up the cloud-covered sky, illuminating a silhouette with bat-like wings.

"A dragon!" Devin roared across the crater. "The time has come! My prophecy is now fulfilled!"

The dragon swooped, then pulled up, its massive body blocking the veiled moon. With its wings extended, it glided in a wide circle as if surveying the battle scene. The two remaining conspirators scampered into a dark pocket.

Angling its wings, the dragon swooped again, this time straight toward Devin. As the dragon opened its mouth to shoot a barrage of flames, Billy threw up his hands. "Dad! No!"

It was too late. A huge jet of yellow surged through the cloud of snow and plunged into Devin's chest. An explosion of fire erupted, sending a blazing plume all around, Devin's arms flapping wildly in the midst of the inferno. The wall of fire expanded, and Devin's body grew with it, seeming to absorb the energy until his form swelled into a massive, glowing monster of light. Now three times his normal size, Devin's evil face reappeared, his eyes radiating like demonic beacons in a human lighthouse.

The re-energized slayer created another fireball and flung it at Barlow. The spherical lightning rolled through the battlefield, knocking Barlow to the side and bowling over Edward and Newman. The two conspirators sprang from their hiding places and pounced toward the fallen knights, but Fiske and Walter held them at bay. Dr Conner ripped off his shirt and smothered the flames on Newman's clothes.

Bonnie grabbed two heavy stones, leaped into the air, and hurled them at the conspirators. The first stone crashed into the larger man's head while the second glanced off the smaller knight's hip. They ducked and retreated again to the shadows.

Away from the battle scene, Ashley caressed her grandfather's face. Even as the battle raged, the whole world seemed eerily quiet. Fear squelched her vision. Snow muffled every sound. Ashley felt alone in the world, just Daddy and her.

Ashley rubbed heat into her Daddy's frigid hands, but the warmth quickly died away. She couldn't coax any blood into his fingers. She pressed her hand on his neck, feeling for a pulse. A weak, chaotic beat thrummed against her fingers, then stopped. Ashley gulped, but the unsteady rhythm started again, weaker than before.

"Ashley," a voice whispered.

Ashley jerked her head around. She had forgotten the professor was sitting there.

The kindly faced gentleman scooted to her side. "Ashley, your grandfather is slipping away. You know that, don't you?"

Ashley nodded, squeezing her lips together to keep from crying.

He placed a tender hand on the side of her head. "He has made his peace with God. It's time for you to make your peace with your grandfather." The professor limped quietly away.

Ashley lowered her lips next to her grandfather's ear, her voice quaking. "Da . . . Daddy. I . . . I love you so much." She pushed her fingers through his wet hair and braced his head with her hand. "You're the best . . . the best daddy a girl could ever want." She sniffed and placed a hand over his heart. "I know now that you were right . . . about everything. I . . . I promise I'll believe . . . I mean, I'll try to believe. Bonnie'll be here to help me. . . . I'll try to make you proud of me again."

The dragon spread his wings and swooped again, but Devin sidestepped, as agile in his new form as a leaping gazelle. The huge wings angled, and Clefspeare made a wide turn around a distant mound of stones.

Billy couldn't let Devin feed off dragon fire and get stronger again. A quick kill was his only chance. He raised Excalibur and charged.

With the slayer keeping his eye on the dragon, Billy sneaked up close. He lunged and sliced into his opponent's side. The blow felt strange, like he had cut into a squishy mix of jelly and rocks. He sensed a buzzing tingle as the blade sliced through Devin's electric belly, and embers gushed out like a thousand silver sparklers on the Fourth of July.

Devin roared and smacked Billy away with the back of his hand, like a giant swatting at an annoying horsefly. Billy flew a dozen feet and bulldozed into what remained of the back wall of the lab, dropping Excalibur as his arm smashed against the ground.

Clefspeare approached again, and the dragon's mouth opened once more to fire. This time the flames shot near Devin's feet, making a scorched ring around his body, melting the surface to form a circle of bubbling, red rocks. The slayer froze. Clefspeare slammed into his huge electric body, flattening him against the melting ground before zooming back into the sky.

Billy jumped up, pain shooting down his spine. He snatched up Excalibur and sprinted toward the fallen giant, hoping to whack off his legs while he had the chance. Devin was too quick. He leaped to his feet, hurdled the ring of lava, and charged Walter, who was once again battling the determined pair of conspirators. Billy screamed, "Walter, look out!"

Walter ducked just as the slayer swung a flaming arm. He plunged his sword into Devin's thigh and pulled it out, jumping to the side. A fountain of sparks spewed from Devin's wound, but the loss of energy didn't seem to slow him down. The slayer roared and shot a bolt of lightning from his right hand, zapping Walter on the shoulder and sending his sword clanking to the ground. Walter grabbed at his wound and dropped to his knees, his face twisting in pain.

Devin repeated his attack, shooting two bolts in Walter's direction. Walter rolled. One bolt ripped the ground at his side; the second exploded at his ear.

Billy leaped in front of his friend, holding Excalibur high and bracing his legs. Devin launched another bolt, and Billy parried with the sword, deflecting the bolt into the air. His heart pounded, and he set his feet again. He couldn't hold off a barrage of lightning for long.

A loud roar pierced the darkness. Clefspeare circled through the blanket of falling snow, and a second dark figure swooped in from behind. Billy dropped to his knees. "Two dragons!"

Devin grabbed Walter's sword, a mere toy in his huge, glowing hands. As Clefspeare hurtled downward, the slayer thrust

357

the sword into the air. With a great beat of his wings, Clefspeare dodged the slayer's lunge and surged back into the sky.

"Hartanna!" the dragon yelled. "The slayer is armed. Use the flank, as we did at Chalice Hill." The dragons thrashed the air with their massive wings and disappeared high into the darkness.

Bonnie tugged on Edward's sleeve, her head tilted upward to search the sky. She gasped for breath. "Did he . . . did he say, 'Hartanna'?"

Edward pulled his bloodstained sword out of his fallen opponent and leaned on it to rest. His laboured breaths came in short gasps. "I can't be sure, Miss, but it did sound like Hartanna. The name is familiar to me, but I can't place it." He walked over to the fallen Addison and set the point of his sword near the man's bare chest. "These fools are beaten. Only Devin remains. If I had my horn, I would sound the victory call."

Bonnie unfurled her wings and lifted a few feet into the air. With a joyous smile, and with new tears sparkling in her brightening eyes, she clasped her hands together and shouted. "Hartanna was my mother's name!"

Devin's sizzling head turned in all directions as he scanned the skies. "Where are you, you cursed demons? Come out and fight in the open!"

Billy leaned over and gripped Walter's wrist. Walter returned the grip, and Billy pulled him to his feet. Walter grimaced and rotated his shoulder. "Wow! That overgrown Roman candle really packs a wallop!"

"C'mon," Billy whispered. "Let's find another sword for you. Maybe we can strike low while the dragons strike high."

Billy found Edward, and they scrounged for a sword and shield for Walter. The three allies, now armed but winded, charged the flaming giant.

Devin, still holding the sword high as he watched the skies, jerked around. Edward vaulted into the air. As Devin side-stepped, Edward cut a deep gash in the slayer's arm, sending a rain of sparkling blood to the floor. Devin smacked him away with the back of his hand, launching him toward a wall. Edward landed on his feet but toppled over, banging his head on a fallen boulder. He moved no more.

Billy clutched Walter's collar and held him back. "Let's see if we can wait for the dragons. We're no match for him until he's distracted."

Walter shook his head. "No. There's no use risking the drag-ons' lives. You have to attack now. I'll get Edward out of the way so you can turn that sword up to 'deep fat fry' and send that critter to join the Northern Lights."

Billy tightened his grip on the glowing sword. Could he do it? Could he use Excalibur as a transluminating torch? He took a deep breath. "Okay." He nodded toward a heap of stones. "Make a wide path around that pile, and drag Edward to Dr Conner. I'll see what I can do."

With head low and knees bent, Walter sneaked away. Billy raised the sword. The blade gleamed in the night with a steady, unchanged brightness. *The professor didn't mention any magic words, and, besides, a holy sword wouldn't use magic. Maybe the beam will just come out when I attack.*

The slayer spat a stream of electricity into the sky. "Death to Satan and his angels!" Two dragons hurtled toward him from opposite directions, one diving from a sharp angle, the other swooping low.

Clefspeare dodged the swinging sword, while Hartanna slammed into Devin's legs, sending him tumbling over her back. With a swipe of her tail, she smacked him like a neon tennis ball

359

against the mountainside, and a curtain of rocks cascaded over his body in a rumbling landslide. A bright flash blew a thousand sparks into the air like the glowing ashes of a bonfire's blaze.

Billy sprinted to the pile of rocks heaped over Devin's body. Nothing moved. He hoisted Excalibur over his shoulder and retreated a few steps toward his companions.

The two dragons landed near the professor and Ashley, and Bonnie flew over to join them. Her feet settled softly in front of the great female dragon. She inched closer and gazed at the scaly, winged creature, her tight brow rising and her lips quivering.

"Mama?"

Hartanna's coarse voice lowered to a dragon whisper. "Yes, I have been your mother. I am now Hartanna once again." The dragon sounded tired, yet sympathetic.

Bonnie extended her arms, but hesitated in the shadow of the strange beast. The dragon stretched out her forelegs and let out a soothing rumble. "Come, dearest one. I have called your name for these many weeks, and at last you have arrived. My claws are sharp and my scales are cold from lack of light, but my love for you burns warm and tender."

Bonnie threw herself into her mother's embrace and cried, wrapping her arms around her as far as she could. Bonnie's entire body shook, trembling in rhythmic sobs. "Mama!" she cried. "I missed you so much!"

Hartanna rubbed Bonnie's shoulders with her forelegs, hot dragon tears splashing and sizzling on the deepening snow.

"But how, Mama? How did you become a dragon again? I thought you were dead."

"I was near death, a dragon's blink from eternity. But your father kept me alive, in a hospital for a while, at least that's what he told me. When he needed my blood for his experiments, he transported me to his lab. Some weeks after we arrived, he said I took a turn for the worse, and he thought I was dead. Then, my body began a slow transformation. I grew in size, and dragon features replaced my human ones.

"While I was still small enough, he dragged me to the cave and chained me up, fearing that I would become a powerful dragon again. Being kept in the dark and having my blood drained, I could not escape. I was given only the barest of lights, candles and fireflies, just enough to keep me breathing. I could barely speak; groanings became my prayers as I called for my daughter to come and find me."

The professor edged up behind Bonnie. "And she was restored because of your faith, Miss Silver. The dragon shorn has new life."

When the professor spoke, Hartanna's eyes opened wide. She released Bonnie, and took a step back. "Master Merlin!" She bowed low. "Your servant, Hartanna, awaits your bidding."

Clefspeare snorted a stream of hot gases. "I made the same mistake, Hartanna. This is Professor Charles Hamilton. He does resemble Merlin, to be sure."

The professor pulled Bonnie into a warm embrace and looked up at the male dragon. "And the mistake is yours again, Clefspeare, for Merlin has returned. The professor and Merlin are melded in this body. It is very strange and unexpected, yet God's purpose will not be thwarted, as witnessed by your response to the summons."

"I did not wait for a summons. I left my cave soon after Billy did. It is a long journey from West Virginia, and I have only just now arrived."

361

"I am the one who responded," Hartanna explained. "The quake shook loose my chains, and I received a sudden surge of strength."

Billy shivered. *Wow! God answered that prayer, too!* He kicked one of the stones that had spilled away from Devin's burial pile. The stones on top began to glow, turning red, like hot oaken embers. The mound shook, sending vibrations across the ground. Billy stumbled backwards, then scrambled away on all fours.

An explosion rocked the mountain, sending flaming, red boulders in all directions. The slayer emerged from the pile of rubble, huge and menacing, his glow pulsating. In a blind rage, he charged, lightning bolts shooting from his hands. One hit Ashley's arm, setting fire to her sleeve. Another slammed into the ground at Billy's foot, the electricity going in through his toes and out the back, burning his heel. A third bolt struck Hartanna's flank. She spun her body around and roared. "It pierces scales! Clefspeare, take flight! We must mount another attack!"

The professor yelled, "No! Take cover! He has mastered the lightning. If you take to the skies now he will shoot you down. There is only one who can save us now!"

Billy limped toward the slayer, his scorched shoe sticking to the stone floor like old chewing gum. *I hope he doesn't mean me. I don't think I can even save myself!*

Dr Conner sprinted to Ashley's side and snuffed the flames on her robe. Another bolt shot out from the slayer's hand, ripping into Dr Conner's back and covering him with dancing arcs of electricity. He stiffened, then slumped to the ground.

Bonnie ran in front of Ashley and her grandfather, her wings spread to guard them. With her feet firmly set, she faced the approaching slayer. From his hiding place behind the wheelchair, Derrick broke into a song, but he kept his head low.

Devin halted, his two laser eyes focused on Bonnie. With one hand, he grabbed her around the waist and lifted her high in the air, crumpling her wings in his fingers as he would a wad of tissue paper. Billy hobbled forward and swung his sword against the slayer's leg with all his might. It cut halfway through, but the jolt of electricity shot Billy backwards, sending him skidding through the snow, the sword buzzing in his grip.

A sinister smile grew on Devin's electrified face. "My prophecy says that the mountains will glow with red when the host has ensnared the virgin bride, and darkness will envelop the skies." As he spoke, the overcast thickened. Snow fell like furious clouds of freezing cotton. Lightning flashed red across the ink-black sky, and thunder boomed like a battalion of cannons.

Bonnie wiggled her arms free, then pounded her fists against the slayer's vice-like grip. Flashing sparks shot across her skin, lighting up her face like an X-ray image. She slumped over his fingers, her chest heaving and her eyes wild.

The two dragons rose on their haunches, ready to attack, but with his other hand Devin sent a surge of lightning over their heads. "She's dead if you move! It only takes one squeeze, and your little princess bride will be no more."

Billy groped along the snow-covered ground to find his sword. Fumbling with the hilt, he struggled to his feet and pushed the point against the stone floor to keep his balance. He stumbled toward the slayer, approaching him from behind. Excalibur, now dim and wet, felt cold and heavy in his grip. When he came within a few feet of striking distance, he stood still in the slayer's wash of light. Bonnie's arms fell limp across Devin's hand, but the shining rubellite glowed bright red on her finger.

Billy lifted his own hand. His ring pulsed sporadically, dimming with each beat like a failing heart. He re-gripped the sword, took a deep breath, and shouted. "Turn and face me, Devin! It's time to break the chains."

The slayer's head slowly rotated, and his yellow-green eyes blazed. "You have no weapons against me, you stupid child! Arthur and Merlin were powerless against me. Your father cowers now in my presence. God Himself has blessed my might. Can't you see that a thousand years could not bring death to my door? Do you think your little blade can stop me now?" He waved his arms in the deepening gloom. "Look at the skies, fool! Darkness will overcome."

Billy raised his sword, gripping it so tightly he could feel his heart beating in his fingers. Snow covered his hair, and cold wetness chilled his skin. His strength faltering, and the sword seeming like an anchor, he clenched his teeth and glanced up at Bonnie. Seeing her helpless body trapped in the slayer's fist brought echoes of her prayer to his mind. He spoke with a clear, loud voice. "Light and darkness can have no fellowship."

He then glared at the slayer. "God is light," he said, his voice booming as he raised the sword to strike, "and so am I!" Excalibur's blade burst into glorious light, and a blinding beam shot from its point into the clouds, rending them like a torch burning through thin plastic. The moon shone through the hole, illuminating the entire mountain and casting a drape of white light across the gaping cavern.

Strength surged through Billy's arms. He pulled Excalibur back, and swung its beam through Devin's huge, electroplasmic head. The blade of light tore into his sparkling skull, slicing it from ear to ear. Devin's fingers flew open, and Bonnie's limp body plummeted into the snow.

Excalibur's wave of light enveloped the slayer's collapsing body and transformed him into a glowing red mass of sparks.

The particles spun into a cyclonic whirlpool and zipped away into the darkness like a shimmering scarlet tornado.

The sword's beam died away. Billy dropped his weapon and shuffled to Bonnie. He scooped her into his arms and carried her to a mound of rocks where the professor and Ashley knelt beside Dr Conner. Bonnie moaned as Billy gently laid her down, resting her head on his chest.

Clefspeare blew rivers of fire across the ground to melt the snow. Hartanna flailed her wings and scooted toward Bonnie. Her head drooped and her wings faltered as she skidded to her daughter's side. "Bonnie," Hartanna said weakly. "Are you all right?"

Bonnie opened her eyes and grimaced. "I think so. I might have a broken wing. I'm not sure." The dragon then spoke to Dr Conner. "Matthew, are you hurt?"

There was no answer.

"He's dead?" Hartanna asked.

Ashley nodded, sniffling, her contorted face fighting back the sobs. "He . . . he said, 'Tell Irene that . . . that I'm sorry. I was a fool, just like she said so . . . so many times.' "

Hartanna closed her eyes and lowered her head. "Perhaps I was too harsh." She let out a long, deep sigh. "It is a sin to withhold forgiveness from a contrite soul. He who held me captive in darkness, clasped in cold cruel chains, taking my life's blood and with it all of my strength, I forgive with all of my heart."

Bonnie gazed at the sad dragon and then at her dead father. Her mouth slowly opened. Her bottom lip quivered. Squeezing her eyes shut, she broke into tears and reached for Billy. He placed a hand behind her head and held her close.

Walter shuffled into the circle, his good shoulder under Edward's arm, helping him walk through the melting snow. "I checked on the others. Our knights are all alive, but Addison is the only survivor of the conspirators. He'll freeze soon, though, if we don't get him something to—"

"Ahem," Sir Barlow interrupted, limping to join them. He held Excalibur over one of his broad shoulders. "I have supplied the scoundrel with a purple cape from one of the dead conspirators. No need to worry about him." He bowed and handed the sword to Billy. "I found this on the ground, Master William."

The professor stood and spread out his arms, his own tears glistening in the bright moonlight. His voice sounded old, almost feeble, as his trembling hands wiped the moisture from his eyes. "We have witnessed a great tragedy, yet a great miracle. A man has died, a father, a husband – a traitor reborn to become a defender of the innocent. His sacrifice will not soon be forgotten. Yet, we must move on. The schemes of the evil one have been thwarted, and there are now more dragons in our midst. There is reason to weep and reason to rejoice, but there is much unfinished business."

"Yeah," Walter interjected. "Like, where's Karen?"

"And my mother," Billy added, shivering. "And where are the other girls?"

Hartanna put her nose near Bonnie's face and blew a stream of warm air across her and Billy. "Your mother and the girls are all together. Karen was unconscious, so I wrapped her in a blanket and carried her to your mother's vehicle. She told me who she was, so I left Karen in her care. I flew to Kalispell to find a hospital and then came back and led the way. I do not know her condition."

Bonnie's face brightened, and she pulled away from Billy. "We have to go see her."

"Not until we see to your wing," Hartanna said. "We dragons have to tend our wings carefully."

The professor raised his hand to quiet the group. "The word of God has come to me, and I have already revealed His will to Ashley. She has accepted it, and I tell it now to the rest of you." Closing his eyes and lifting his hands to the heavens, the professor spoke in bright sing-song.

Robust and strong, a body's dream
Can never last in earthly stream
In heaven's gates the faithful sing
With youth forever in their wings

The professor's eyes seemed older and wiser than ever before. "Billy Bannister. Come to me."

Billy limped forward, dragging his injured foot, Excalibur again at his side. *It's 'Billy' now? Not 'William'?*

The professor continued, but his familiar accent vanished. "The hour has come, Billy. It is time for me to go. Raise the beam once again, and strike me with it."

367

CHAPTER 23

HEAVEN'S GATES

B illy let Excalibur droop at his side. Had he heard the professor correctly? Strike him with it? "What are you talking about, Prof?"

The professor's face tightened into a stern frown, and his voice reverted to his usual, younger-sounding British accent. "Listen to him, William! This is the word of truth! Do not refuse a direct command!" He pointed at the sword. "Excalibur is not your source of strength; it is merely an extension of a greater power. Will you trust that power to do good and not evil in your hands?"

Billy gulped, his whole body trembling. His mentor had never steered him wrong before, but a mistake now could cost the professor his life. Billy lifted the sword again. "If . . . if you say so, Professor." He tightened his grip, and the beam burst forth through the tip in a rich shaft of ivory radiance, reaching beyond the few remaining clouds. The professor took a deep breath and closed his eyes, folding his hands at his waist. Bonnie threw her hands over her face. Walter clenched his teeth. The cavern became deathly still.

Billy flexed his arms and swung Excalibur's beam straight at his target. The white laser passed through the professor's tall frame, and a fountain of glittering light coated his body. Sparks jumped up and swirled in the sky, hovering in a circling cloud of luminescence.

Excalibur's beam died away, and the professor wiped his brow, his lively voice returning again. "Whew! Now that was quite an experience! I must say I never want to share my body with another mind, especially one as powerful as Merlin's. It's very confusing."

Bonnie pointed at the hovering haze of sparks. "Is that Merlin up there?"

The professor's wild hair blew around in time with the electrical swirl. "I do believe it is. He's waiting for the next step."

"The next step," Walter repeated. "What's that?"

The professor placed a hand on the wheelchair and turned toward Ashley. "It's time, Miss Stalworth. I don't know if your grandfather will be able to hear you, but do you have anything else you wish to say to him?"

Ashley gave a weak smile and shook her head. "I think we're both ready."

The professor took her grandfather's pale, limp hand and slid it under the coat that covered his upper body. As he set the hand in place, the teacher's eyebrows arched up. He reached farther under the coat and pulled a book from its inner pocket – Merlin's diary.

The hovering cloud of energy swirled downward and enveloped the old book. In a burst of light, the book dissolved and melded with Merlin's glittering whirlpool. The cloud then descended on Ashley's grandfather, catching his body upward and transforming it into its own shimmering swirl of light. The wheelchair sat empty on the ground with only the professor's coat hanging on the edge of the seat.

The new swirl settled around Ashley's head, bathing her face in dazzling glitter. She closed her eyes and smiled, as if listening to a secret message. The swirl then followed Merlin's, and they made a quick circuit around the chamber before shooting into the sky like a pair of Roman candle bursts. When the glow faded in the distance, darkness descended once again on the cavern, leaving only Excalibur's corona lighting the area.

Billy set Excalibur's point on the ground. His foot ached, and stabbing pain ran up and down his spine. He arched his back, feeling it pop several times. "What just happened, Prof?"

"Merlin took Ashley's grandfather home." The professor retrieved his coat from the wheelchair and slipped it on. He sighed, his breath pouring out in a heavy stream of white. "This is the natural order of things. Life and death decisions are best left in God's hands."

Ashley stepped up to the professor and hooked her arm around his. "My grandfather spoke to me from that swirl of light. He said, 'I got my new body, Ashley. I can hardly wait to hear how well it can sing.'"

The professor pulled Ashley's arm up and patted the back of her hand. He opened his mouth as if to speak, but he shook his head and patted her hand again instead.

"Ashley?" Derrick's weak voice called.

Ashley spun her head toward the sound. Derrick was sitting against a cracked wall at the cavern's edge, his head angled toward the sky. Ashley strode quickly toward him. "Yes, Derrick? Are you all right?"

Derrick smiled, his voice growing with excitement. "Ashley, I saw him."

"Saw him? Saw who?"

"Your grandfather. I saw a light, just for a second, and then I saw his face. Somehow I knew it was him."

Ashley knelt at his side and passed her hand in front of his face. "Can you see anything now?"

"No. It only lasted a second, but it reminded me that I'll see him again someday." He reached up and tugged on the sleeve of her robe. "And now I know how the translumination works." He caressed the sleeve with his slender fingers. "Would you like me to tell you?"

Ashley placed her hand over his and smiled. "Sure, Derrick. Tell me how it works."

Derrick's grin stretched across his face. "It's the light, Ashley. It's the light that makes us see."

Ashley's smile collapsed, and her jaw fell slack. For a moment she seemed in a trance; every muscle in her face relaxed, motionless. Finally, she grasped Derrick's hand and hoisted him to his feet. "I'm going to have to think about that one." She led him toward the wall where the professor was huddling with Bonnie and the dragons. "C'mon. We have to figure out a way to get you out of here."

Billy shuffled over to the others. Bonnie sat cross-legged on the ground, her ragged, dirty robe stretched out to cover her legs. Billy lowered his body slowly, feeling every muscle ache as he sat. "I have to rest. This transluminating business really wears me out."

"How badly are you hurt?" Bonnie asked.

He raised his hand to his neck. "The cut isn't so bad. It's mostly my foot that hurts right now."

Ashley crouched at Billy's feet and began untying his mangled shoe. "Do you want me to have a look at it?"

Billy shook his head. "There's plenty of people here worse off than I am."

Walter plopped down on a stone next to Billy. "Yeah, my shoulder got zapped by that overgrown thunderstorm. I think everyone gave at least a little blood today."

Bonnie slid Ashley's sleeve up her arm. "Okay, sister, speaking of blood, what's the story with the photoreceptors?"

Ashley stretched out her arm and pulled Bonnie's alongside it. "I guess 'sister' is right." She ran a finger across Bonnie's scars and then her own needle mark. "My grandfather told me that his daughter-in-law, my mother, was a dragon. I'll tell you the whole story later, but it seems that Devin killed my parents, and my grandfather altered my birth records to show that I was born to his son by a different woman. He decided the best place to hide me was right under Devin's nose, where he would least expect to find me, working with him and your dad."

When Ashley mentioned Dr Conner, Bonnie's face turned downward. Ashley pulled her into a warm embrace. "I'm so sorry about your father, Bonnie. I know how much pain he caused you, but at least he tried to defend us in the end."

Walter jumped to his feet and pointed at Ashley. "So you're a dragon, too? That's so cool! I have three dragons for friends!"

Ashley stood to join him. "Anthrozils is what Doc called us. Fully human and fully dragon."

"Anthrozils?" Walter shook his head. "No way! *Dragons* sounds cooler."

A small shadow moved among the rocks by the old Alpha entrance. It scampered over a ridge that bordered the entire

373

cavern like the rim of a coffee cup. Billy pointed toward another fleeing shadow. "Is that one of the chimps?"

Ashley scanned the ruined lab. "Could be. This is their home, so they'll come back when everything settles down. Maybe in the morning."

Billy pushed his sore heel back into his shoe and looked around the moon-bathed cavern. He spotted the professor near the old entrance to the boys' dorm examining a narrow gap in the cavern's wall. Billy stood up and brushed away a trace of mud from his trouser leg. "I'm sure we'll find the animals. I'll stay here and wait for the return of the chimps."

"Sounds like a horror movie," Walter quipped. "The sequel to *The Invasion of the Spider Monkeys*."

Sir Barlow stepped forward. "I offer my services. My men require care, but I am relatively unharmed."

Clefspeare blew a fiery snort at an alcove in a stone wall. "I will keep this area warm for whoever wishes to stay, but I cannot provide food or medical care."

Ashley placed her hand on one of the sheer walls. "It's gonna be tough to scale these hunks of granite. How're we going to get out of here?"

The professor edged his way into the gap in the wall. "We seem to have a new exit over here, but I have not decided on a Greek letter for its name."

Walter rubbed his belly. "How about *pi*? I could sure use some about now."

"Then *pi* it is." He leaned out the gap, his head disappearing from view. "It's a steep grade," he shouted, "but it seems that we can skirt the mountain and find where the Alpha entrance begins." He drew his head back in. "I can't be sure in this light."

Clefspeare unfurled his wings. "Whoever is not afraid to ride my back can take a shortcut to the top."

A new voice echoed across the cavern. "Hello down there!"

Billy swung his head upward. "That's my mum!"

Billy's mother stood at the upper edge of the canyon, her hands on her hips. She scanned the scene, nodding once with each count of a loved one. "You guys really know how to throw a party, don't you?"

"Yeah," Walter replied. "We gave Devin a going-away party. It was a real blast!"

The dragons ferried Billy, Bonnie, Walter, the professor, Derrick, and the wounded knights to the top of the cliff where Billy's mother had parked the Jeep. Ashley and Barlow helped Betsy and Bobo climb out the Pi entrance and up the steep slope. Rebecca emerged from the Jeep and played "monkey see, monkey do" with Betsy, until the chimp tired of the game. When they all had gathered, Billy spread his arms and gave his mum a strong hug.

The professor limped forward and braced himself on the Jeep's hood. "Marilyn, how is Karen?"

Marilyn nodded. "She's going to make it. The doctor seemed pessimistic at first, but that girl's got a fighting spirit in her. She lost a lot of blood, but she came through surgery fine." She pulled Rebecca close to her side and rubbed her shoulder. "I left Stacey and Pebbles with a security guard at the hospital, so I need to get back there soon."

"Yeah," Rebecca added. "We're going out to get the latest copy of *Car and Driver* so Karen'll have it when she wakes up."

Billy whispered into his mother's ear, pointing toward the knights who were sprawled across the clearing. She winked and cupped her hands around her mouth. "Which one of you is Sir Barlow?"

Sir Barlow strode forward, bowing low. "I am at your service, Madam."

She jerked her thumb toward the SUV. "I understand you've never ridden in a Jeep."

Sir Barlow stared at the vehicle, his eyes wide. "No. No, Madam. Indeed, none of us has."

"And have your men ever had a large pepperoni pizza?"

Barlow's smile grew so wide, his moustache lifted into his nose. He shouted at his knights. "Did you hear that, men? Pepperoni pizza!"

She motioned with her thumb again. "I can't fit in all your men, but if you'll come with me we'll bring back enough pizza for everyone."

Barlow climbed into the backseat while Billy quickly filled his mother in on the night's harrowing activities, finishing with, "And Dr Conner's body is still down in the cavern."

His mother shook her head sadly as she looked at each bloody, dirty face and the torn shirts and jackets. She reached down to Bonnie and pulled her to her feet, hugging her close and stroking her dampened hair. "When I first saw Hartanna, she told me what she thought was happening, so I bought some first aid stuff on the way back. It's in the Jeep."

"Aw, we won't need it," Walter said, waving his hand. "What's a little blood?"

Billy's mother pushed Bonnie out to arm's length to get a look at her injuries. "Bonnie will need it. She can't get treated at the hospital."

Hartanna doused Bonnie with another surge of warm breath. "I know how to treat her, but I will need human help."

Ashley ran her fingers tenderly across Bonnie's wounded wing. "I'm your girl. Just tell me what to do."

Billy's mum dug for the keys in her coat pocket. "That's fine. I can't fit everyone in the Jeep anyway. I'll bring back food for those who are staying." She looked up at her son. "Billy? Are you coming?"

Billy scraped the toe of his shoe through the snow. "No, I think I'll stay here. There are quite a few dead bodies to take care of, including Palin's. And maybe Dad and I will get a chance to talk." He angled his head toward a boulder near the newly formed cliff. "He's over there keeping Derrick warm."

She nodded. "Then I think I can squeeze in one more. Professor?"

"Yes," the professor replied. "Pizza sounds good. But could we have one with mushrooms instead of pepperoni?"

377

CHAPTER 24

SONG OF THE BARD

Billy knelt in front of the fireplace in the crowded den and blew a stream of fire at the stack of kindling. Within seconds, the thin boards burst into flames. He plopped onto a green beanbag chair between two identical beanbags that held Bonnie and Walter.

His mum set down two snack trays next to several empty bottles on the glass-covered coffee table. "Anyone hungry?"

Walter's dad and the professor each filled a small plate with raw vegetables, crackers, cubes of cheddar cheese, and slices of lean ham. Walter lifted an entire tray, but a sharp look from his dad brought it back to the table. Walter settled for a heaping pile of ham, cheese, and potato chips and slid back into his beanbag.

A loud clatter sounded at Walter's feet, and Billy jumped up. "Walter, you kicked Excalibur."

Walter pulled his feet back. "Oops! Sorry."

Billy retrieved the sword and leaned it against the sofa's end table. With his fingers on the hilt, Excalibur brightened the den, its silver blade reflecting every light in the room. Billy paused to straighten the other items on the table, a clear plastic folder that held Bonnie's adoption papers, signed and sealed, and an ornate pen at its side. Next to the folder, Bonnie's journal lay open to the last chapter, her description of their latest adventures. Dirt smudged a few pages, literal evidence that it had been unearthed from the very mountain quake it described.

Billy kicked Walter's socked feet. "Where's your mum?"

Walter kicked back, landing a blow on Billy's shin. "She's in the kitchen getting more food." Walter smirked. "Barlow and his knights act like they haven't eaten in over a thousand years."

"Yeah, well look whose plate's stacked higher than his nose." Billy kicked at Walter again, but Walter dodged. "What video did they decide on, *Planet of the Apes* or *Braveheart*"?

"You missed out on a good scrap while you were fetching the wood. Newman argued for the apes, but Barlow finally convinced the others to vote for *Braveheart*. Dad sent them down to the basement TV when Barlow got too loud with his colour commentary."

Billy grabbed a poker and stirred up the logs. "Yeah, I'll bet he knows quite a bit about warfare." The flames licked the firewood and blazed brightly.

Mr Foley ploughed a potato chip into a large bowl of salsa. "Well, with you around, I guess I won't need to buy starter logs for a while."

"Yes," the professor added, taking a sip from a steaming cup. "I believe there could be many practical uses for young William's talents."

Walter grabbed a big handful of chips and winked at Billy. "And some not so practical."

"What?" Billy's mother glared at him with a pretend scowl.

"What are you up to, Mister?"

Billy raised his eyebrows innocently as he slid into a bean-bag next to Walter. "Uh, fireworks, Mum. We were going to set off some fireworks. Right, Walter?"

"Yeah," Walter said, his mouthful of potato chips crumbling into his hand, "for the next celebration, when Ashley and Karen and the others come to stay."

Mrs Foley walked in with a tray of chicken wings and set them down on the snack table. She took two wings, snuggled into her husband's lap, and handed one to him. After a taste, she licked her fingers. "Carl, tell them what Fred said when you asked if Ashley could have a job."

The professor put down his cup. "Yes, Carl. Did he make her an offer?"

Carl snickered. "Are you kidding? He offered her twice what I make. He took one look at Ashley's computer schematic, and he acted like a goof! He actually danced a jig on top of his desk! And he sang a song that went something like, 'Watch out big boys, here comes Fred, the techno-mouse that's gonna roar!' "

Mrs Foley stuffed another chicken wing in her husband's mouth, and everyone laughed, even Mr Foley, his face turning fire-alarm red.

The professor sat back, smiling, and took another sip of tea. "So Miss Stalworth will build the next generation supercomputer."

Mr Foley took a bite from his chicken wing. "Ashley *is* the next generation supercomputer. But, yeah, she's already got it all in her head. She could have made even more money in a bigger city, but," he turned and nodded toward Bonnie, "she has certain people she wants to be close to."

Bonnie smiled. A thin new chain hung around her neck, a broken crystal dangling at the bottom – a fractured half of the

381

candlestone. With the blinds closed, she had shed her backpack, but her wings stayed folded close to her body, a homemade bandage wrapping one of the outer mainstays. "Did Ashley say when she's coming?"

Mr Foley nibbled away a last bit of chicken and dropped the stripped wing on a plate at his side. "As soon as Karen's cleared to travel, probably next week. Fred was going to send her plane tickets, but Ashley wants to drive."

The professor stood up and limped to the centre of the room. "Very good." He set his cup down on the coffee table and cleared his throat. "All is going well, my friends, and now that many secrets have been revealed, I must bring a few more items into the light."

"Like what, Prof? Is Billy going to transluminate someone else?"

Billy kicked Walter again. "Just listen!" Walter drew a halo over his head, and Billy stifled a laugh, but not very well.

The professor glared at the two boys and cleared his throat again. "As did Devin, I came to Castlewood in search of someone – he for a dragon, I for an heir. It is clear that we fulfilled our quest in the same person, William Bannister, for he and Bonnie are the keys to all the prophecies concerning the future of the dragon race."

Billy sneaked a look at Bonnie. Her eyes were focused on the floor, and her face glowed red. He swivelled his head back before she could notice his glance.

"You may have guessed by now that my appearance is remarkably similar to Merlin's. That's because I am his direct descendant. Also, because of my resemblance to an ancient sketch that the people of my order possess, I have actually been dubbed Merlin by the Steward of The Circle of Knights."

Walter wrinkled his nose. "The Circle of Knights?"

The professor placed his palm on his chest. "We are a protectorate, six men of knightly ancestry who continue to meet without their king. One man, Sir Patrick, has been named steward until he passes away or is found unworthy, or until Arthur returns to take his place as the head of the Circle."

Walter's face brightened. "The return of the king to replace a steward? Sounds like *Lord of the Rings,* doesn't it? Like Aragorn returning to replace Denethor?"

"Not exactly, Walter, though there are similarities. Although Aragorn is cast in the image of Arthur, our Sir Patrick is not the fool, Denethor, of Mr Tolkien's wondrous epic. In any case, the return of Arthur has been awaited since long before Mr Tolkien took up a pen, and the Circle will welcome the great event."

"What does this 'Circle' do?" Bonnie asked.

The professor shook his head slowly. "I cannot say while all of you are present, although I will tell William the details later." He grasped the back of a chair, and his knuckles turned white. "I can tell you that a different order is our enemy, a group of seven called 'The New Table'."

Walter punched Billy's leg. "Why can you tell Billy and not the rest of us?"

"Because," the professor said, reaching for Billy's hand, "he is the heir I have sought. We have believed that Arthur would return at our time of greatest need, and our peril is truly great, a ticking time bomb that threatens not only England, but every man, woman, and child in the world." The professor pulled Billy to his feet and then dropped to one knee before him, bowing his head. "I salute you, William, Guardian of the True Light. May your service be long and prosperous."

383

Billy couldn't believe what he was hearing. "You think I'm Arthur?" He put his hand under the professor's arm to try to lift him up. "I'm no king!"

The professor rose to his feet again. "Arthur's rule and his return are symbolic of a deliverer, typifying the Christ. You will soon learn of your mission, and you must learn quickly. The date of destruction is set in stone, and it is fast approaching. Our enemies have not rested."

"Enemies?" Billy lifted a necklace of his own. The other half of the candlestone dangled at the bottom. "Didn't we get rid of Devin? The candlestone's powerless. What can they do?"

"Merlin told me of another vulnerability in dragons, and I can only assume from observing your behavior that you and Bonnie have both inherited it. Apparently, Devin knew of this weakness – although I only call it a weakness for lack of a better word – and he has used it to kill many dragons in the past. I will tell you about it in private when the time is right."

Billy tucked the gem beneath his shirt. What was behind the professor's mysterious manner? "But if Devin's gone, maybe the secret will die with him."

"Perhaps Devin is gone, but do you have his body? And what of Palin?"

Billy balled one hand into a fist. "Yeah, no one found Palin. There was too much rubble where I dragged him."

"And there are more like him. Although Devin was not one of the seven in The New Table, he was their assassin, the cruel mind who commanded their violent activities. The claws and tail contain the poison of this beast, and there is yet another enemy who influences their minds, more cruel and sinister than Devin, a creature whose name I will not utter here."

Billy took a deep breath and exhaled heavily. "So what do I have to do?"

The professor withdrew an airline ticket from his trouser pocket and handed it to Billy. "I request that you come with me to England to meet Patrick and take on your mission."

"England!" Walter exclaimed. "Cool!"

Billy studied the ticket, reading his name there in computer print. He folded the ticket in half and slowly raised his head again. "How about Walter and Bonnie? Can they come, too?"

"We must first go alone and meet the Circle. After I explain your mission, it is essential that Bonnie come to help you. Her place in the prophecy is vital. Regarding Walter, I will have to ask Patrick if he will be allowed to join you."

"What about Barlow and his knights? Are they part of this mission? They can't live in the Foleys' basement forever." Billy smirked. "That *Braveheart* video won't last a thousand years."

The professor smiled and placed a hand on Billy's back. "William, with your addition, the Circle will possess seven members; there are no other seats available. But our order will require the services of brave soldiers. Again, these assignments will be up to you, but Barlow and company are courageous and loyal men, true, authentic knights. As Merlin, your trusted adviser, I will likely make application for them, and they will be tested to prove their worth."

"And what about the dragons?" Billy asked. "Clefspeare and Hartanna."

The professor withdrew his hand and stepped back. "I can tell you this, William; if not for dragons, you would never succeed in your mission. Their role may make all the difference."

The professor's eyes mellowed into two ageing oracles, as if they had seen hundreds of battles, scores of earthquakes, and

385

even the changing of the guard in heaven. "Merlin has left me with many of his thoughts, William, as though I have retained his memories and learned his prophecies. In the light of his remaining flame, I see villains, ambushes, and tortures. Great danger is in your path."

The aged teacher pulled a handkerchief from his pocket and wiped his brow. "There is also another prophecy I can share with you now. It was in the diary, and Merlin has somehow burned it indelibly in my memory. I will sing it, but do not bother to ask its meaning. As yet, I have no idea. I assume, however, that its message will become clear, and helpful, as we journey into our new adventure."

He cleared his throat and closed his eyes, his voice transforming into a rich, sweet tenor. He sang as a prophetic bard of old, his song mysterious and captivating.

> *With sword and stone, the holy knight,*
> *Darkness as his bane,*
> *Will gather warriors in the light*
> *Cast in heaven's flame.*
>
> *He comes to save a remnant band,*
> *Searching with his maid,*
> *But in a sea of sadness finds*
> *His warriors lying splayed.*
>
> *A valley deep, a valley long*
> *Lay angels dry and dead*
> *Now who can wake their cold, stone hearts*
> *Their bones on table spread?*
>
> *Like wine that flows in skins made new*
> *The spirit pours out fresh*

Can hymns of love bring forth the dead
And give them hearts of flesh?

O will you learn from words of faith
That sing in psalms from heaven
To valley floors where terrors lurk
In circles numbering seven?

Billy placed his hands on the sides of his head. This was just too much to take in all at once. He had already been through a bloody battle! The professor just piped this weird new song that made no sense at all. And now . . . he was supposed to be a deliverer? "What next?"

"Only to say whether or not you will go with me. I guarantee nothing save that your trials are not complete."

Billy unfolded the plane ticket and stared at it. The professor really meant for him to fly to England. *He's never been so serious before, so solemn. Is he afraid? And that song! Scary stuff!* He glanced at his mother. *Poor Mum. What's she thinking? Sure, she's proud of me, but should I go off halfway around the world chasing after the professor's dream? Still, I really can't ask her. It wouldn't be fair.*

Walter's ever-present smile faded. With a tight jaw and clenched fist, he gave Billy a firm nod. Bonnie, on the other hand, beamed like the glory of the rising sun. Having faced her greatest fears, she came out of the darkness to find the one she had sought through pain and tears. Billy also found a beacon in the darkness – the light that radiated in Bonnie's spirit – and she had shown him the way to its source. Now that light burned within Billy's heart more fervently than any dragon's fire. What could he do but pour it forth, shining his light down whatever path he might be called?

Billy folded the ticket and put it in his pocket. "I'll do it."

Bonnie and Walter jumped to their feet. Bonnie gave him a warm embrace. "Trust in the Lord with all your heart," she whispered as she drew away.

Walter slapped him on the back. "You'd better learn to speak their language before you go. You won't even be able to find a bathroom if you don't learn to say 'water closet'."

Billy's mother reached over and gave her son a hug. "I'm sure the professor will help him with the culture, Walter. If the professor is any indication, Billy will be among the finest of gentlemen."

A door slammed open, and a line of men tromped into the room from the basement stairwell. With a bag of potato chips in his right hand and the cat, Gandalf, cradled in his left arm, Sir Barlow led the way. Newman followed, his face buried in a *National Geographic* magazine, and Edward marched behind him, playing a high note on a trumpet. The three others brought up the rear, each wearing seventies era leisure suits, Fiske in ice-lolly orange, Standish in avocado green, and Woodrow in electric grape.

"Yes," Mr Foley said, his head shaking. "Real gentlemen."

"We found a fascinating little room," Barlow explained, "packed with boxes marked 'Goodwill'. If these boxes are filled with goodwill, I thought, it should be no harm to investigate their contents. I was surprised to see this assortment of oddities." He bowed again and handed Gandalf to Billy. "Your cat, sir, has taken quite a liking to me. Perhaps he thinks I am his pyjamas."

Billy took the purring cat. "You mean Gandalf thinks you're the cat's pyjamas?"

Barlow wiggled his moustache, a crimson blush creeping up from his neck into his cheeks. "That's what I said, isn't it?"

Excerpt from volume three

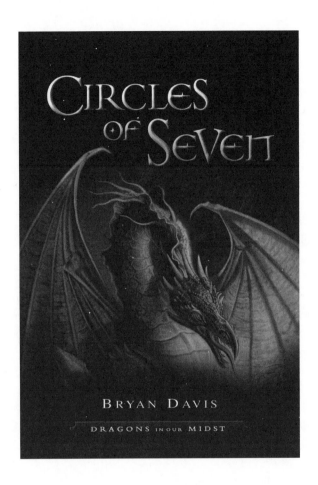

CIRCLES
OF SEVEN

BRYAN DAVIS

DRAGONS IN OUR MIDST

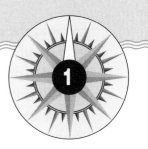

THE MONOGRAM

D anger!

Billy 's internal alarm blared. Something evil approached, creeping up slowly through one of the hallways of the huge English mansion. Sitting back in an easy chair, he closed his book and flicked off the floor lamp at his side. He waited, allowing his eyes to adjust to the dimness of the unfamiliar bedroom. Only a ray of moonlight seeped in from the window on the opposite wall, its yellowish-white glow casting odd shadows across the oak floor.

He slowly rose to his feet, cringing at the sound of the creaking boards under his heels. He tiptoed to the door and pushed it silently closed, carefully releasing the knob and begging the latch not to click.

Icy dread crawled along his skin. The sense of danger grew in intensity with each creak from the bowels of the centuries-old house. Not able to sleep, he had decided to read a book of King Arthur lore borrowed from his teacher, Professor Hamilton. As he sat in the corner, he had thought the post-midnight noises were simply trees brushing the windows or maybe his host getting up to potter around on the first floor. Now, as the clock on the wall ticked past 3 a.m., he knew better.

He stretched his legs into long, stealthy strides across the room. He snatched Excalibur's scabbard from a belt hanging around the bedpost. Grasping the hilt, he slowly drew out the blade. The sound of metal sliding on metal drilled courage into his heart, and the sword's illuminating glow chased the shadows from the room.

Holding the sword with his arms extended, he planted his feet and kept his body perfectly still . . . waiting . . . listening. The clock marked the seconds – tick . . . tick . . . tick. Cold sweat seeped through his pores, dampening his oversized T-shirt and raising goose bumps on his arms. The air in the oversized bedroom felt heavy . . . suffocating, creating a sense of desperation, like being stuck in an underground cavern with a dying flashlight.

A slow creak groaned from the hallway. Was it a floorboard bending under a skulking footstep? The door hinges grating, ready to fly open at any second?

Billy's eyes riveted on the door. The creaking stopped, but a spine-tingling alarm kept blaring in his mind. What could be lurking out there? Professor Hamilton was supposed to be sleeping in the next room. Had the approaching menace already paid him a deadly visit? With a dozen bedrooms lining the hall on this second-storey wing, maybe it – whatever it was – had passed the professor by.

Billy licked his lips. *Should I call Prof? Should I go check on him?*

The door creaked again. He regripped Excalibur's hilt and

tensed his arms. In the dimness, he could see no movement, only shifting light as the sword vibrated in his trembling hands. He didn't feel scared – not much, anyway – mostly just cold in the spacious, draughty bedroom. His sweatpants and damp T-shirt weren't enough to ward off the chill.

As he watched for a hint of movement, an unusual scent drifted past his nose, a sweet blossom of some kind, not pungent like perfume, more like the soft fragrance of gardenias or jasmine. It was pleasant, soothing, even peaceful.

Billy yawned. His eyelids drooped. His brain felt light . . . tired . . . sleepy. He backed up a few steps, bumping into his bed-frame. It was the middle of the night, so why not just go to bed? That noise wasn't really anything. This spooky old mansion just creaked like that all the time.

A vague sense of danger still lurked in the back of his mind, but he shooed it away, yawning again. It was nothing; there was no danger. He sat down on the bed and breathed in the wonderful aroma, sweet flowers . . . so peaceful . . . so relaxing. He imagined lying in a bed of soft rose petals on a sunny day, a cool breeze caressing him to sleep. Was he really lying down now?

Yes, I must be. It's so soft, so comfortable.

Consciousness began slipping away.

There's that creaking noise again. But it's nothing . . . just the wind blowing through this old house.

His sense of danger faded, vanishing in a whirlpool of images – his friends, Bonnie and Walter; the dragon, Clefspeare; his mother – all mixing into a confused dream.

More creaking? Footsteps? Mum, is that you?

He felt a cool hand softly touch his neck. He smiled. *Okay, Mum. I'll get up. I just have to—*

393

A wild shout pierced his senses. "William!"

Billy shot upward, but a strong grip shoved him back to the bed, iron fingers squeezing his throat. He couldn't breathe. His eyes bulged. A hooded form, a shadow in the dimness, pressed close to his face, almost eye to eye, as he straddled Billy's body, choking his life away.

The dark figure suddenly lurched backward, releasing its strangling grip. Wearing a long, black robe, his attacker looked like a spectre flying away from his bed. Loud bumps erupted from the floor, and the professor's voice shouted,

"William! . . . I require . . . your assistance . . . immediately!"

Billy sat up, caressing his throat and blinking away the mind fog. The professor and the dark intruder rolled on the floor, their arms and legs intertwined, the professor's white hair tossing wildly. Billy's senses came roaring back, and he threw himself into the mix, punching the assailant with both fists, then gouging his hooded face with his fingers. It was no use. He seemed impenetrable.

The man pulled the professor into a bear hug, and his muscular arms squeezed the elderly teacher's chest. The professor grunted, "The sword. . . . Use . . . the sword!"

Billy jumped up and searched for Excalibur. Where had he put it? He threw back the covers on the bed. *Ah! There it is!*

He grabbed the hilt and summoned Excalibur's transluminating beam, a laser-like shaft of radiance shooting out of the tip. Although he had practised using it countless times, he wasn't sure he could strike the intruder with the disintegrating ray without hurting the professor. One touch would send this dark burglar into oblivion, making him nothing but a holiday sparkler, but he didn't want the professor to become part of the fireworks.

With a savage thrust, Billy kicked the hooded man in the ribs.

"Arrgh!" The man arched his back and released the professor, who rolled away like a log on a steep hill. Rising to his knees the teacher called out, "Now, William! Now!"

Billy swung the sword's beam, slamming it against the intruder's torso. The shaft of light sizzled across his body, sparks popping like water droplets on a hot frying pan. The man's black robe absorbed the fiery light, framing his shadowy form with a flashing halo.

The intruder sprang to his feet and kicked the professor in the head with a heavy boot, sending him sprawling to the ground. The black hood slowly turned. Two eye slots rotated to the front with hate-filled eyes blazing through.

Billy stepped back, stunned. Blood oozed from the side of the professor's head as he lay crumpled on the floor. Was he breathing? A hard lump grew in Billy's throat. He couldn't swallow it away.

395

The hooded man snorted. "Not so brave when your ultimate weapon fails, are you, Dragon Boy?" He blew on his hand with a mocking puff and laughed. "How about your fire breathing? Doesn't it work? Why don't you give it a try?"

Billy felt a good blast of fire growing in his belly. But should he use it? Excalibur's beam didn't work on this creep, and his challenge probably meant that fire wouldn't faze him either. But what could it hurt?

He took a deep breath and hurled a stream of fire from his mouth. The orange tongue of flame splattered against the intruder, but he just spread his arms as though he were basking in sunshine, allowing the blaze to caress his black suit, making it glow like a heated stove-top coil. As the colour faded to a dull orange, he crossed his arms and laughed. "I guess the mongrel's bark is worse than his bite."

Billy raised Excalibur to an attack position and bared his teeth. "I have not yet begun to bite."

"Oh, that's a good one," the intruder scoffed. He pulled a sword from under his cloak. "Let's see if your blade is as sharp as your wit."

Billy pulled his sword back and charged. With a hard, two-handed sweep he lunged at the intruder's neck. The man parried, blocking the swipe with his own silver blade. With a turn on his heel, Billy threw his body into a three-sixty spin, ducked low, and hacked at his opponent's ankles. The man hopped deftly over the blade and chopped downward at Billy's neck.

Billy lurched to the side and rolled away. The attacking blade sliced into the wood floor, wedging tightly.

As the intruder tugged on the hilt, Billy jumped to his feet and swung Excalibur like a baseball bat, aiming for the man's waist. Still hanging onto his sword, the man slid his feet forward, facing upward and ducking under the deadly swing. After Excalibur swiped harmlessly above his face, the intruder sprang back to his feet with the help of his recoiling sword. He finally yanked the blade out of the floor and straightened his body, his feet set and arms flexed.

With sweat dripping from his hair, Billy stepped back and stared at his opponent's fierce eyes, his chest heaving and his arms trembling. He gripped Excalibur tightly with both hands. Even if the beam wouldn't disintegrate the intruder, he knew Excalibur had to give him an advantage. It was more than just a sword; it was a holy sabre, generating its magnificent light energy only for certain people. It must have been guided by a greater power, an intelligence above and beyond his own. Billy glanced at the professor. Blood dripped from his head to the floor, making a pool next to his motionless hand.

The hooded man charged, his sword swinging. Billy blocked it with Excalibur, and when the two blades met, Excalibur's glow burst into a glorious blaze, so bright he had to squint.

The intruder held out his hand to block the brilliant light. Fear and agony flooded his eyes. With a wild, one-handed swipe, he swung his sword high. Billy ducked just in time, feeling the blade swish above his head. The intruder dropped to his knees and swung again, this time aiming low. Billy jumped, and the razor edge passed under his bare feet like a chilling wind. The intruder slumped, his cloaked head drooping. He seemed drained, exhausted.

Billy leaped at the chance. He swung Excalibur at the man's head, smashing the flat side against his skull. A burst of electrostatic energy covered the intruder's hood and ran across his black suit like a swarm of lightning bugs, buzzing and flashing in chaotic twinkles. His arms stiffened, and he toppled to the side, his head smacking the floor with a sickening thud. The black mass of body, cloak, and hood lay motionless at Billy's feet.

The twinkling died away. Billy, his eyes wide, lowered Excalibur, letting its point rest on the floor. The sword's light diminished, yet still retained enough radiance to illuminate much of the room.

He dashed to the professor's side and dropped to his knees. He placed a cool hand on the old man's wrinkled face and across his lips. The teacher's shallow breaths warmed his cold, trembling fingers. *He's alive!*

Billy set Excalibur on the floor and gently patted the professor's cheek, hoping the coolness of his touch would revive him. "Professor!" he called in a loud whisper. "Wake up!"

"Nonsense!" the professor replied, his eyes still closed. "There

397

are no gardenias in these gardens. Roses and daffodils, yes, but no gardenias."

Billy shook his teacher's shoulder. "Professor. It's me, Billy. You're dreaming. Wake up."

The professor's eyelids fluttered open. "William!" His eyes darted around the room. "The assailant. Where is he?"

Billy gestured with his head. "On the floor over by the door. I think I knocked him out cold."

The professor struggled to his feet and refastened the sash on his grey terrycloth bathrobe. When he lifted his head, he seemed to be in a daze, and his body swayed.

Billy grabbed the professor's forearm and steadied him. "That guy really gave you a hard lick with his boot." He stepped into the bathroom, snatched a hand towel off the rod, and gave it to his teacher. "But it looks like the bleeding's slowed down."

The professor dabbed the wound gingerly and examined the splotch of red on the otherwise white towel. "Yes, William. I don't believe I will require stitches."

A bump sounded from somewhere in the house, then padded footsteps and whispered commands. The professor waved his arm at a dresser next to the door. "Block the entry! Hurry!"

Billy dashed to the door and pushed it closed. Then, with a quiet grunt, he shoved the waist-high chest of drawers under the knob and pressed his ear against the door panel. "I hear noises, like people running on tiptoes."

The professor knelt next to the intruder's sprawled body and slid his hood off, revealing a young man with a wispy brown moustache and goatee. He pressed two fingers against the man's neck, then looked up, his brow wrinkling. "He appears to be dead, William."

"Dead? But I only hit him with the flat side! I didn't even draw blood!"

The professor felt the intruder's wrist and pressed his ear against his draped chest. He raised up again. "Flat side or no, he is certainly dead."

Billy picked up Excalibur and rushed to the professor's side. "Have you ever seen him before?"

"No." The professor lifted one of the intruder's arms. "We must hurry. Help me get this cloak off."

The professor rolled the burglar to one side while Billy tugged at a cloak sleeve with his free hand, pulling it off the assailant's arm. Repeating the motions, they slipped off the other sleeve and carefully slid the cloak out from under the man's body.

When the professor rolled the intruder to his back, he paused and stared at the man's exposed forearm. He reached for Billy's wrist and pulled his hand, sword and all, toward the intruder. The sword's light cast an iridescent glow across the man's skin, changing its colour to pale blue. The professor put his finger on a strange monogram, dark blue lines in the shape of the letter *M*.

"William! He bears the mark!"

"The mark? It just looks like an *M* to me."

"Exactly!" The professor pushed Billy's wrist, manoeuvring the sword's glow. As the light passed over the monogram, the outline of the *M* brightened into a phosphorescent purple brand. The professor kept his voice low. "It's the mark of a New Table knight, your opposition. It can only be seen within a certain range of light frequencies, such as gamma rays or X-rays. Excalibur emits such a frequency."

The professor rose abruptly and began pulling off his robe. "Get dressed! Hurry!"

Billy leaped toward the drawers and popped open a suitcase that sat on top. "How are we going to get out of here?"

The professor, now dressed only in long, thermal underwear, pushed an arm into the sleeve of the intruder's cloak. "By stealth, William."

Billy dug into his suitcase and tossed out a pair of calf-length socks, his off-white cargo trousers, and a brown, long-sleeved shirt. While he threw on his clothes, the professor peered into the suitcase. "May I borrow a pair of socks?"

Billy balanced on one foot, reaching down to tie a shoe. "Sure, Prof."

The professor fished out a wadded pair of socks, then picked something else out of the suitcase and slipped it into his pocket.

Billy grabbed his jacket. "What did you take from my—?"

"Aaaiieee!" A scream rifled through the room, freezing him in place.

The professor's eyes blazed. "The master of the house!" He threw the black hood over his head and pushed the drawers out of the way. "We must go! Now!"

Billy thrust Excalibur into its scabbard and fastened the belt to his waist. "That cloak may get you out of here, Prof, but I'll stick out like a mouse at a cat party."

The professor snatched up the intruder's fallen sword, then raised a finger to his lips. "Wait here while I fetch my keys." He slipped out the door and disappeared into the hallway shadows.

Billy waited in darkness, the ticking clock the only sound in the room. A dead body lay near his feet. Was he an advance scout of some kind? How many more of them were searching through the house?

A door slammed. Footsteps pounded in the hallway, louder

and louder.

Billy shivered. They were getting closer. Would they catch the professor? He slid Excalibur from its scabbard. The sword trembled in his hand. Should he try to make a run for it? Should he obey the professor and wait? He took a deep breath and cracked open the door.

A new voice sounded from the hallway, barely audible. "Did you find him?"

Billy froze. *Is he talking to me?* He positioned his ear next to the opening.

"Yes," another voice replied, whispering. "All is in hand."

"Is Foraker dead?" the first voice asked. "Do they have his cloak?"

"Yes and yes."

"Good. Exactly as planned." The first man's voice lowered to an even quieter whisper. "Let them out of the room, then chase them to the front door. We'll kill the old man and dump the kid at Patrick's doorstep. Remember, just scare them out. Morgan wants the Bannister boy deposited unharmed with the cloak."

The conversation ended. Billy moved away from the door and waited. Seconds later, the door swung open, and a black-cloaked figure stepped inside and jerked his hood off, revealing the professor's familiar face. His skin had turned ashen, and his wild white hair stood almost on end.

The professor closed the door and pressed his back against it, holding his hand on his chest and breathing heavily. "I fooled him . . . for now . . . but we must escape . . . by a way other than the front door."

"Yeah. I heard." Billy returned the sword to its sheath. "How long till we're supposed to meet Bonnie and the dragons?"

The professor took a deep breath and exhaled slowly. "About two hours. Five-thirty to be precise. We have plenty of time."

"Maybe, but if my dad's still like he was before he turned back into a dragon, he'll be early." Billy pointed at the window on the opposite side of the room. "Feel up to walking on the roof?"

The professor lifted his foot, displaying a mid-top hiking boot. "I managed to get my trousers and shoes on, and I collected my gloves, so I suppose I'm properly equipped." He squatted and began tying the laces. "But I have a splitting headache, which may indicate concussion. I'm not sure what will happen if I exert myself."

Billy opened the window and leaned out into the misty darkness, turning his head from side to side. He left the window up and hustled back to the professor, a cool breeze following in his wake. "Looks like it's all clear in the backyard."

The professor stood up, holding his hand on his head. "Then perhaps we'll make it if I can move slowly enough."

Billy zipped up his jacket and stuffed his gloves into one of the pockets. "It's a cinch. I've done it at my house a hundred times." He bounded to the window and vaulted onto the sill. "Come on," he said, waving his arm. "The roof's flat enough." He crawled onto the shingles and helped the professor squeeze through the window.

"Now to find a drainpipe or a trellis." Billy bent over and skulked to the edge of the roof, careful to keep Excalibur from dragging. He dropped to his knees and planted his palms on the gritty surface, then leaned over the side. The professor scooted on his knees, nearing the edge while Billy scanned the ground level. Directly underneath, two black-hooded figures stood next to a car, one with his hand on the hood.

Billy whispered. "Two more goons."

"Two that we can see," the professor whispered back. "There may be more."

"Is that your rental car?"

"Yes. Don't you remember it?"

"No." Billy lowered his voice even further. "I slept all the way from the airport."

The professor's voice matched Billy's. "It's a Vauxhall Vectra Elite, a fine British motor car."

"Well, it might as well be a unicycle without pedals. It's down there, and we're up here." Billy reached back and grabbed Excalibur's hilt. "Getting to it would be easy if I could just transluminate them. I wonder what went wrong."

The professor rubbed his fingers across his black cloak. "Very strange. It feels like a network of wires on the surface, as fine as silk thread, a metallic mesh of some fashion. And it's warm to the touch."

Billy passed his hand across one of the long sleeves. "Maybe that's what protected him from Excalibur's beam. When I blasted him with fire it just made those wires light up like some kind of heating grid."

The professor stroked the mesh again. "Remarkable. It seems to carry a faint residue." He rubbed his finger and thumb together and brought them close to his eyes. After sniffing the fine powder, he brushed it away with his other hand. "I believe it could be rust."

"Rust? You mean like from iron?"

"Yes. Hydrated ferrous oxide of some sort."

Billy straightened his back, keeping his knees firmly on the shingles. "So if I can't zap these guys, what're we going to do? If we try to climb down, they'll see us for sure."

The professor sat up on his haunches with his hand on his chin. "We will conquer them with a tried and true, surreptitious approach."

"Sir Who?"

The professor rose to his full height and helped Billy to his feet. "I'll take the one on the left," he said. "Are you ready?"

"Ready? Ready for what?"

"Jump!" The professor leaped off the roof, pulling Billy with him, and they plummeted toward the two men in black.